VALOR'S FLIGHT

THE NEW PROTECTORATE: BOOK FIVE

ABIGAIL KELLY

AUTHOR'S NOTE

Valor's Flight is a standalone novel within the wider *New Protectorate Series* and can be read as such. However, it does contain some spoilers for other books in the series, so I recommend reading *Consort's Glory, Burden's Bonds,* and *Devotion's Covenant* if you'd like to avoid them. A full character directory can be found at abigailkkelly.com. Content warnings can also be found there, as well as in the backmatter of this book, alongside a glossary.

~Abigail

Full Series List

The United Territories and Allies

ESTABLISHED 1917

The United Territories and Allies
Current borders (2044) established
in the 1917 Peace Charter.

Member territories share a common
currency and many laws, but
maintain individual sovereignty. Each
territory holds representation in the
UTA Congress and Court, found in
the United Neutral Zone.

CHAPTER ONE

July 2048 - Birchdale, The Shifter Alliance

Alashiya was torn from sleep by a catastrophe a century in the making.

The shockwave of all her wards being breached at once shook the crumbling foundations of her house, knocking photos off walls and bolts of fabric onto the floor. The scent of magic clung to the back of her throat like congealing blood as she surfaced from the easy nothingness of sleep with a gasp. For the span of several frantic heartbeats, the air was dense with residual energy, making it almost impossible to breathe. It covered her skin in a sticky residue that evaporated almost as quickly as she perceived it.

When the magic faded, it left her cold and trembling. The lush heat of the summer night was just a memory as she threw off her thin blankets. It'd been a long time since she'd dealt with a threat. Though her body remembered what to do, her limbs struggled to keep up as she stumbled around in the dark.

Her breath sawed in and out of her lungs as she strained to hear in the awful quiet. Even the normal night noises, always so cacophonous in the summer, had gone silent.

Every instinct screamed at her to run. She had no weapons, no offensive abilities. It was a nymph's natural inclination to put distance between themselves and a threat. They were fantastic runners and could hide themselves in the wilderness with ease.

But running came with its own risks, as she knew well. Sometimes running saved your life, but it just as often led to a death further up the road.

The sound of a crash from the direction of the barn nearly made her scream. Alashiya clapped a hand over her mouth and pressed herself against the nearest wall. Her windows were heavily obscured with thick, handmade curtains and moss to regulate the temperature, but if she dared to peer through the tiny gap between the fabric and the wall, she could make out the dark shape of the dilapidated barn across the sloping yard.

At first, she couldn't spot anything unusual. The moon was hidden behind a dense layer of clouds, which were no doubt biding their time until they could unleash the full torrent of a summer storm on the land. Even with her exemplary night vision, it was hard to see anything at all.

The noise *had* come from the barn, she thought, but it hadn't sounded like someone breaking in. It sounded more like someone had driven a truck through it. The idea wasn't *impossible*. Every year, some drunk hunter or hiker did something stupid like that in town. The result was typically a rescue from the local rangers and a very high bill.

But after her last unpleasant encounter with a group of hikers, she'd reinforced the wards that obscured the entrance to her property. Any vehicle, if that was indeed what had hit her barn, would've had to first find the gate and then come down the overgrown main road to do so.

I would've felt that, she decided, gut churning. *I would've felt the moment they crossed over the property line. So either they appeared out of thin air, or...*

Her gaze traveled up toward the roof of the barn. The high peak, meant to allow snow to slide easily off, had begun to slump a little as the building aged and fell into disrepair. She'd watched it happen over the course of a century and knew the shape of it like she knew her own face.

Even far across the yard, swathed in near-complete darkness, she could tell that it had changed.

A little bit of her fear eased as confusion set in. Her heart rate began to slow. Had something fallen from the *sky?* The vivid memories she had of her land being trespassed all involved men melting out of the trees or sauntering down the road. Some beings could fly, of course, but she'd never met one, nor even seen one pass through town. Winged people tended to avoid flat land, she'd heard, and Birchdale was nothing if not flat.

Maybe it's not an intruder at all. Another knot of unease unraveled in her belly.

She stood perfectly still against the wall for some time, her gaze glued to the shape of the barn. The heady rush of adrenaline eased back. She stood there for so long, her bones began to ache from the tension of pressing herself against the wall.

Night sounds resumed. There was no movement in the dark. No crunch of summer-wild vegetation underfoot. The door to the barn didn't swing open, though she could allow that she might not have been able to see it even if it did.

The longer she stood there, the more it seemed like she had imagined the whole thing. She might've believed it, too, if she didn't feel the residual *zing* of her wards settling back into their proper arrangement, or taste blood on the back of her tongue.

Going back to sleep was out of the question. Calling for help wasn't an option, since she hadn't had a working phone for years, and running to her nearest neighbors wasn't either, seeing as they were elderly. She could slip from the house and risk making for the woods on her own, reliving memories best left buried, or she could confront whoever or *whatever* crashed into her barn.

Her choices were all terrible, but doing nothing was untenable.

In the end, it came down to a fundamental question: If it really was an intruder, did she want to die like her grove?

Alashiya swallowed a sour mouthful of bile. *No,* she thought, *if there's someone out there, I'm not going to be hunted down and slaughtered in the dark.*

It went against every instinct, but she unpeeled herself from the wall. It was lucky that she'd moved nearly everything into one room when her grandfather passed. It saved on wood for the stove during the winter and it meant that her steel fabric scissors were close by.

Hastily throwing on her boots and a thin cover-up, she shoved a flashlight into her pocket and gripped the scissors in her right hand. She kept her mass of curly hair tied back at night, but tendrils escaped to tickle her clammy cheeks as she forced her legs to carry her across the creaky wood floor.

Her left hand shook as she unfastened the antique lock. *Maybe it's a meteor,* she tried to convince herself. Wasn't that more likely than someone flying through the roof of her barn?

Despite her heavy boots, Alashiya's footsteps were light on the mulch that blanketed the paths through her garden. During the growing season, the area was so lush with life that it was nearly impossible to walk through — a chaotic jumble of symbiotic plant life she depended on to survive. The plants, who normally hummed with pleasure and demands at her nearness, were disconcertingly quiet as she passed them.

Her home sat on a slight hill above the barn, where some enterprising farmers had once kept cattle but which her grove had begun to convert into communal housing. There was little wind that night, but the air was thick with moisture. Born and raised on the land, she knew in her bones that a storm was on its way.

She didn't use her flashlight as she silently picked her way around her labyrinth of a garden, fearing that it would alert any potential intruders to her approach. With every step she warred with herself. Why was she doing this? Was it a product of trauma or misplaced pride? What could she do against an intruder, armed with little more than a pair of sewing shears?

But everytime she nearly convinced herself to run, Alashiya

remembered the screams. She remembered her parents pushing her into the woods, urging her to run. She remembered what it was like to be found, days later, and to come home to a grove of ghosts.

She wasn't helpless, and this was *her* land. If someone wanted to take it from her, they'd just have to kill her.

So she walked, keeping to the darkest, wildest parts of the property. Gradually the barn resolved itself into more than just a sad shape in the dark. Her breath caught as she stumbled to a stop near the tree line. Behind her, birch trees stood like solemn spectators dressed in bone white, the patterns of black eyes on their trunks ever-watchful. A stately owl she'd known from a scrawny fledgling stood on the roof like a sentinel against the dark sky and its stormy clouds. The owl watched her, too.

Details were hard to come by, but she could see just enough to balk at. The roof had been nearly completely caved in. For a wild, wonderful moment, she nearly laughed at herself.

The roof had been falling apart for years. She didn't have the funds to fix it, and even if she did, perhaps she wouldn't have had the heart. What would she do with a large barn, anyway? There was no one and nothing to inhabit it, save the bats who dangled from the rafters and the mice who made their homes in the ephemera of lives long extinguished.

It felt like a fitting tribute to allow Blight to reclaim it, as he would do to all things eventually. Even her.

Perhaps that was all the noise was. One too many boards had rotted and it simply gave way. It didn't explain the wards, but neither did a meteor. Only a sapient intruder would've triggered those, but how likely was that? A far more reasonable answer was that something had gone awry when the roof collapsed. Perhaps an old ward laid down into the structure by one of the grove had activated, or maybe she'd simply done something wrong when she layered them again just before the start of recreation season.

Maybe it's Blight, she thought wryly, recalling all the stories her parents used to tell her. When she was little, she believed the god of forests, decay, and darkness would appear when she least expected it. He was in every shadow and rustling of leaves. She'd been told he'd show up when she needed him most.

Faced with the unlikely prospect, Alashiya wasn't sure what she'd say to a god except, perhaps, that he was a century too late to help her.

Whatever had happened, there appeared to be no sign of life in the barn — threatening, friendly, or divine. The large barn door was still closed. There were no voices, no footsteps. If there was a shifter about, an owl certainly wouldn't have perched contentedly on what remained of the peak of the roof, its golden eyes calmly surveying her. Animals usually became restless and wary when a bigger predator was about, so his relaxed posture eased her worries.

It's nothing. Thank the gods.

Alashiya's sweaty grip slackened on the scissors. She pressed the heel of her hand into her eye, fighting back the sting of tears. She could've collapsed into the undergrowth and wept with relief, but she wanted to get back to her bed far more.

She'd just begun to turn around when the horrendous clatter of something moving in the barn made her heart lurch. The owl let out a low, authoritative hoot, as if to say, *You should probably check on that.*

Her breath escaped her in a long, reedy exhale as she stared unblinkingly at the white trees. The warmth of the night had turned to cold needles, thousands of them pricking her from within and without.

It's just the debris settling. That's all.

The fantasy was shattered not a moment later by a terrifying animal rumble. Cold sweat dotted her forehead as she forced herself to turn back around. The owl remained where he was, but his head had cocked to peer down at the barn below his talons. He didn't appear alarmed in the slightest, but why would he? He could fly away at a moment's notice. What a relief it would be to have a pair of wings.

It's an animal, she thought, fighting the sharpest edge of hysteria. *It has to be.*

Animals tended to like nymphs. Even the most aggressive moose or wolves wouldn't attack her, so long as they weren't ill or injured. But a moose wouldn't have dropped out of the sky, so that left only a handful of terrifying options — almost all of which involved her being shredded by claws and potentially eaten.

Whatever it was, it sounded *big*. Bigger than big.

Alashiya's fingers had begun to numb from her grip on the scissors, but she didn't feel any discomfort as she stared at the old, rotted wood of the barn door. The air stung her eyes and forced her to blink. *This was stupid,* she decided. Running in the opposite direction of the intruder was obviously the right choice. It was all very clear to her now. Why hadn't she done that? Why didn't she ever actually listen to what her instincts tried to tell her?

A charged, syrupy summer breeze, a prelude to the coming storm, had picked up and was no doubt blowing her scent through the gaps between the wood of the barn. If the creature was alert at all, it probably already knew she was there.

The instincts of millennia, of every one of her line who'd come before her, were a live wire inside her, urging her feet to move. Her pulse jumped in her neck and wrists with a frenzied beat.

A plaintive whistling note pierced the air. Alashiya's right foot, which had moved backward without her conscious permission, froze. More noises came from the barn. A lower, sadder sound was followed by one she knew well — the involuntary, breathy moan of a creature in distress.

A lump lodged in her throat. Whoever or *whatever* had crashed into her barn was possibly injured. That changed things. It both lowered and escalated the risk of confronting it considerably. An injured intruder was less able to harm her, certainly, but the likelihood of attack from a large, wounded animal increased.

The smart thing would have been to make the trek through the woods to her closest neighbor's home. The Thompsons had a telephone she could use to call the rangers station. A wild-eyed troop of young, eager shifters with tranq guns could be there in twenty minutes.

It was funny how most of the time twenty minutes didn't seem very long. Twenty minutes of sleep was nothing. Twenty minutes of facing down an injured animal all by herself was very much *not*.

But doing the smart thing meant possibly leaving an injured creature — sapient or not — to die alone.

Alashiya couldn't make herself walk away, not when those terrifying but pitiful sounds continued to reach her. She tried to. She really tried.

But could she face herself if she turned her back on a dying creature?

No, she decided, at once resolute and annoyed with herself. *I may be the last, but that's not how we were made. If I die, it'll be because I chose to help. Even my ghosts couldn't blame me for that.*

Still gripping her scissors, she shuffled stiffly away from the treeline. One shaking hand rested on the handle of the door. She had to say something, make some noise to alert the animal to a friendly presence.

Her throat was almost too tight to make any sound, but she forced herself to speak. "Hello?"

It came out as barely a whisper, the syllables of the word nearly swept away by the breeze curling through the bony, watchful trees, but the creature must've heard her. There was a pause, followed by a low, menacing rumble. It sounded like some great engine roaring to life just beyond the door. Like every souped-up, nut-dangling, chrome-finished truck she'd ever had the misfortune of laying eyes on had melted together to have a monstrous metal baby in her barn.

It couldn't have been an animal. It just couldn't. It was unlike anything she'd ever heard before, and so *loud*—

Alashiya nearly stumbled back a step, but her fingers remained reflexively hooked around the handle, stopping her retreat. She couldn't pry her fingers away. Her arm was locked there, like it was drawn to the door by some invisible force.

The strangest feeling hooked its claws into her. It was a pull behind her breastbone, the faintest tug as all her blood rushed away from her head at once. It was that same force that held her arm captive, and now it sought to pull the rest of her toward the door. Her senses tingled with staticky awareness.

Whatever was beyond that door knotted a thread around her beating heart and *yanked*.

The boards that made up the door were in fairly good shape, considering their neglect, but time and the seasons had warped them enough that there were gaps between several. She peered into the largest one, but despite the hole in the roof, there was even less light inside the barn than outside. While she stared, desperate to discover what she was dealing with, the terrible warning growl grew louder and louder.

Figuring she was already in for a pound, Alashiya stuttered, "Ca—can you speak? Are you injured?"

The growl died away. For several seconds, the world went quiet. Shaking from head to toe, she dared to lean closer to the door, her head angled to look through the widest gap.

She saw nothing but darkness. It was an all-encompassing blackness that appeared, after a moment of inspection, strange. The fine hair had just lifted off the back of her neck when a violet eye the size of a dinner plate appeared an inch from the door. It was an almost unnatural color, so vibrant that it seemed to appear from some other world. It was the most purple thing she'd ever seen. It glowed beneath a pitch black lid, and its sinister expanse was broken by an almond-shaped pupil narrowed to a quivering, hair-thin line.

CHAPTER TWO

ALASHIYA DIDN'T SCREAM. SHE DIDN'T HAVE THE breath for it. Air escaped her in a nearly silent, high-pitched rush as she stumbled away from the door. Her foot slid in the dusty earth, sending her crashing to the ground. The pitiful amount of protection offered by her scissors vanished when her cramped fingers lost their grip. They sailed out of her hand and into the overgrown grass.

She swore she could feel the breath of the beast as it puffed through the gaps in the door. There was an almighty crash as it burst open, its rusty hinges protesting vehemently. Alashiya scrambled backward on her hands, the grit and scraggly vegetation biting cruelly into the skin of her palms, as the beast thrust its head and upper body through the doorway.

Disbelief held her in place. Even with its coloring, she didn't need her flashlight to see what she was dealing with. The beast came with its own light — the lick of blue flame behind its razor-sharp teeth.

The glow illuminated the massive shape of its head, crowned with four towering horns, as it advanced on her. The flicker danced over monstrous features unlike anything she'd ever seen in person.

Survival instincts finally kicked in. Alashiya twisted until she could scramble on her hands and knees. Behind her, timber crashed to the floor of the barn. That deep, thrumming growl picked up again. It was so much worse up close.

She swore she could feel its steps shaking the ground around her as she frantically searched the grass for her scissors. It was a miracle that her clumsy fingers closed around them just as a massive talon landed beside her. If she was going to die a stupid death, then she was determined to go down with her stupid weapon in hand.

She nearly made it onto her knees, but slipped again and landed hard on a stone. Pain lanced up her leg. She was forced to ignore it. A bruise wouldn't matter if she died, and it *really* wouldn't if she somehow managed to survive.

The beast's breath puffed against her back, each gust of air shockingly warm. It was close. So close. There would be no standing, let alone running away, with it hovering over her.

Alashiya's mind shut down to everything except the blind need to survive. She twisted back around, using the momentum of her movement to her advantage as her arm swung in a wide arc toward the beast's head.

There was a silver flash as the blades skimmed the flesh just above one glowing violet eye. A strange sound erupted from its throat when her scissors glanced off its leathery hide.

It reared back, its terrible mouth opened wide in offense. Alashiya took her chance. Surging to her feet, she stumbled once before she shot off toward the treeline. That tug in her chest was stronger, pulling harder in the direction of the beast, but nothing could override the will to live.

The pain in her left leg was intense, but she couldn't afford to limp. She didn't have a direction in mind. There was no use. She certainly couldn't direct the beast toward the Thompsons' farm, and there'd be no help in town even if she could get that far.

So she simply ran, the scissors somehow still in her hand, and prayed to any gods listening that the beast would be too big to make it through the narrow gaps between trees.

It was an optimistic thought. *Too* optimistic.

She barely made it to the trees before she was knocked down again. The massive head struck her from the side. It sent her careening into a dense patch of wild grasses, one that disguised an old water trough she kept full in the summer for her animal visitors.

Alashiya landed hard against it. Her head glanced off the ground and the air squeezed out of her chest. Stars exploded in front of her eyes. Her lungs refused to inflate. For a moment, she was certain she would suffocate there in the grass, head split open and useless scissors in hand.

An eye swung into view again. Anger at herself, at the beast who'd invaded her sanctuary, at the gods for letting something like this happen to her *again,* saw her swinging blindly once more.

Whatever advantage surprise had given her before was lost now. The beast didn't even bother moving its head away from her slashes, but merely tilted it so the blades skimmed uselessly over its flesh. Furious tears blurred her vision, but she continued her assault until its jaws, nearly large enough to swallow her whole, lowered enough that she could see clearly into its gaping maw. Pale blue fire boiled in its gullet and danced across its huge pink tongue.

"Dragon, stop," she gasped reflexively, jerking backward against the trough.

She'd known what the beast was, as she knew many things she'd never personally experienced, but it hadn't really hit her until that moment. She'd never seen one in person, and it was so dark. The driving need to live hadn't allowed any room for petty things like rational thought, likely maybe trying to stab a dragon wasn't a good idea. Not until it was too late.

I tried to fight a dragon with scissors.

Alashiya's bones turned to liquid. She slumped against the

trough and stared, wide-eyed, into the gullet of the dragon. Waiting.

She didn't know why a dragon might want to hurt her. Perhaps it didn't have a reason. Not every monster required an evil motivation to act, and not every evil act required a monster.

Of course, over the years she'd given a lot of thought to how she might go. Injury and disease were most likely, but she'd never ruled out bludgeoning, poison, and murder in the general sense. Nymphs were notoriously easy pickings, but it seemed cosmically unfair that her demise would be entirely worse than the expected: burned alive by dragonfire.

Alashiya's life didn't flash before her eyes. Stitches did. Every unfinished line of silk thread and glittering chip of gold bullion appeared to her as she stared into the maw of the dragon, past teeth the length of her hand, and into the burning heart of the beast.

I didn't finish Adon's robe, she thought, pierced by the unfairness of it all.

She'd labored over her latest commission for weeks. Her fingertips were nearly permanently bruised from forcing her needle and thread through stiff velvet every day. She dreamed of what the man who'd commissioned it would say when he peeled back the tissue paper to see it for the first time.

She always poured her heart into his projects and she was never, ever late. Because it was for Adon. *Her* Adon, the mysterious figure onto which all her fantasies clung.

When the date of delivery passed without a word, would he wonder what had happened to her? Would he spare her a thought when she was just an ashen smear against an old, rusty animal trough? Aside from her neighbors, he was probably the only person in the world who would think of her when she was gone. At least, she hoped he would.

Something hot splashed her cheek.

Alashiya reflexively touched her skin, but it wasn't a tear that dribbled down her cheek to fall from her chin. It was viscous. Hot.

Dragging her gaze away from the dragon's mouth, she was startled to see something dark and shiny streaming from its snout.

The dragon was bleeding. Not from anything she'd done, she thought, though she'd certainly tried her best. Fresh blood reflected the flickering light of the dragon's flame. The more she looked, the more she found: slashes along its long, scaly throat, a gouge across the width of its chest, and many more smaller wounds she could only just make out against the backdrop of its dark skin.

As she was looking, the dragon's lips peeled back from its pearly white teeth. There was a great movement of air all around her as it mantled its wings over them both, the appendages trembling violently with effort. The blue glow reflected off the underside of its wings, showing off their massive width and wickedly clawed tips.

Dragons were people just like everyone else. She knew that. They could understand speech and comprehend the world even in their four-legged forms. If they wanted to, her intruder could have communicated with her in some other way, but there was no compassion in their eyes, no clear desire to speak to her. There was only something animal, something base and possessive in them that made her blood curdle.

The dragon looked at her like he wanted to swallow her whole.

Alashiya's temper flared. She was weak and small, armed with sewing tools and a little good sense, but she was a wild thing, too. She bared her teeth right back at it.

Raising her scissor's high, she rasped, *"Go!* This is *my* home, dragon. Leave!"

A hot gust of air from the dragon's bloody nostrils was her only response. Before she could decide what that meant, it snapped its jaws at the hand clutching her scissors. A short scream erupted from her throat as she drew her arm in close, dropping the pitiful weapon.

Her mind blanked again as the prospect that she might actually be *eaten,* rather than burned alive, made itself comfortable in her. It'd happened to nymphs in her line before, but *gods,* she really thought she'd earned a better ending than that.

The dragon let loose another ground-shaking rumble before it lunged for her. There were no more screams in her. She didn't make a sound when its teeth closed around the front of her cover-up. They slid through the fabric with ease, and she immediately understood how very mundane it would be for the dragon to rip her open. One bite and she'd be little more than viscera in the grass.

But that bite never came. Neither did the fire.

Instead, she had the breath knocked out of her one more time as the dragon jerked her forward and began to drag her toward the barn, its head lowered and eyes roving wildly all around. Alashiya was pulled off balance. She was acutely aware of the fact that she was prey being dragged back to a den and that it was useless to try and kick or punch their snout, but she did it anyway.

If the dragon noticed her struggles, her blows, her howling outrage, or her frantic twisting to wriggle out of her clothing, they didn't acknowledge any of it. Wings folded in a threatening stance and violet eyes flickering around the wild yard and forebay, the dragon hunched low when their hind quarters reached the entrance of the barn.

Their wings snapped closed and twitched strangely against their back. With one final burst of speed, the dragon hauled them inside the musty, half-destroyed barn. She watched with horror as a long, spiked tail swung out from behind them to draw the barn door closed.

Darkness, nearly complete save for the tiny amount of ambient light let in through a portion of collapsed ceiling, settled over them both.

The adrenaline that buoyed her strength had fled. Her limbs

went heavy and numb, her mind fuzzy. The familiar scent of the converted barn — dust, hay, meals cooked over a communal fire many decades ago — filled her head as she fought to see anything beyond the dragon's eyes.

They dropped her onto the cracked concrete floor with a massive huff. Alashiya didn't dare move. She fought to catch her breath as she watched those eyes glow in the darkness. Even if she hadn't been able to see them, she could feel how close the dragon was as they huffed and puffed and breathed all over her. More blood splattered her face, her neck, as they snuffled at her hair.

It was an unspeakable relief when the dragon drew back. Perhaps the flames would come, but she didn't think she was in immediate danger of being eaten if it was moving like that. The fact that she had a preference for flame over becoming dinner was something that would have to be examined later.

She couldn't see the rest of the dragon's massive body, but she could feel the air shift as they moved. Old furniture, farm equipment, and debris clattered to the ground as the dragon made itself comfortable in the darkest part of the barn, away from the hole in the roof. All the while, Alashiya watched, unblinking and still, from her place on the floor. Outside, the owl let out another low, unbothered hoot.

Just when she'd begun to wonder if the dragon had somehow forgotten about its prey, they lowered their head again.

"Don't," she whispered, soft as a breath. She was too proud to beg for her life, but the word slipped out, yanked out by that hook in her chest.

There was no way of knowing if the dragon listened to her or not, but they didn't eat her. They gingerly pinched her ruined cover-up between their teeth once more and dragged her slowly across the filthy floor. Talons, massive and deadly, closed around her as they tucked her against their wounded breast. They caged her there, allowing virtually no wiggle-room as they settled down onto their haunches.

Something slithered across the floor, drawing itself in a circle behind her. *Their tail,* she suspected.

There was another great movement of air, a fluttering noise, and then the peculiar sensation of being enclosed came over her. What little light there was in the barn disappeared in an instant. The sound of its thundering heart was a drumbeat against her ear. For a split second, she thought it was her own panicked heartbeat, but it was far, far too loud.

The dragon, apparently satisfied with their arrangement, dropped its bloodied head onto the floor and closed its eyes, leaving Alashiya to stare into the darkness, trapped in its claws.

CHAPTER THREE

MAGIC SATURATED THE AIR IN HIS LUNGS, WIND howled through the gaps between old wooden boards, and Taevas was pretty sure that something was wrong with him.

His body hurt in too many places to count. The air was warm and moist in his nostrils, and a great many scents assailed him from all sides. Breathing was a problem, though he couldn't rightly explain why.

Thoughts were fleeting and disconnected. Everytime he thought he had a handle on a thread, it snapped and the pieces fluttered away into the ether.

Frequently, a warm wind carrying droplets of water would whip through his hiding spot and vibrate the sensitive membranes of his wings. He didn't mind. Dragons could take weather in all its extremes, and the warmth was better than the bitter cold of high altitude when he ached as much as he did.

But he couldn't allow the rain within the circle of his mantled wings. That was imperative. It was an urgent, throbbing directive — not a thought, per se, but as natural an urge as breathing. Within his wings, it must not be wet or uncomfortable. It must be safe. He mustn't squeeze too hard and be mindful of his tail, because something fragile lay there. His to guard, his to treasure.

The thought tickled something in the back of his mind. It was important, he was fairly certain.

Taevas tucked his snout closer to the fragrant thing in his arms. Thinking was exhausting. *He* was exhausted. He couldn't remember *not* being tired. He'd been ground down to dust, and now his body hurt too much to move, and all he wanted to do was sleep with the familiar, luscious scent of cypress and woman in his nose.

Woman? He flexed his wings, drawing them in just a little closer. *I don't bring women back to my roost.*

It was the first clear thought he'd had in... a long time. It *felt* like a long time. It was impossible to say concretely, though, because everytime he tried to focus on exactly what had happened, where he was, or how long he'd been there, the thread snapped and fell away like all the rest.

But even when he decided to stop grasping broken threads, the scent kept drawing his thoughts in a more linear direction. He explored them tentatively and was immensely relieved to find something he could hold onto. *Really* hold onto.

Soft, he thought, rubbing the end of his bloody nose against the fragile thing in his talons. *Soft like silk. Smells like home.*

But he wasn't home, and something about that was very, very wrong. His homes didn't smell of green things and decay. There was perfect environmental conditioning that filtered out too much humidity and the extremes of weather. There was no wood dust left by generations of termites or hard, unclean concrete floors. His homes were ultra modern, sparkling clean, and high up in towers. He had two of them, one in New York and one on Drummond Island, and even when he was away from them, he only slept in the best hotels in the world.

He'd spent too many years living in hovels to stomach anything less than the best. It was one of the rare luxuries he allowed himself as Isand of the Draakonriik, and one he took seriously. A dragon's pride was his roost and his heart was his nest. So why was he sleeping in the dirt?

More importantly, why was *she?*

Taevas lifted his head. He got the vague sense that it was early in the morning. The strangest impression came to him then, half-formed and fleeting: that it'd been a long time since he saw the sun.

Light, cool and bright, glowed through the thin membrane of his wings. It gave everything within their span a soft lavender glow — including the woman clutched possessively in his talons.

He didn't recognize her. Even in his foggy state — *drugs,* he thought with a slow blink — he would've recognized the proud nose, the thick, dark curls, and those sad eyes. But at the same time, he *knew* her. He knew the scent of her flesh, her hair. He knew it mingled with the scent of himself from the deepest, softest parts of his nest. Something ancient and needy slithered in the back of his mind, a great beast awakening from slumber.

Peering at her, trying to force his brain to work through what-ever had poisoned it, he was startled to at last notice she was looking back. Dark eyes watched him from beneath heavy, angular brows.

He was so used to the scent of congealed blood that he hadn't noticed it until he gave her a proper look. She was covered in it. It was smeared in her curls, along the front of her thin nightgown, down the curve of one supple cheek. There were bruises on her golden brown skin. The front of her thin housecoat wasn't just bloody. It was badly torn, too, revealing a lush shape covered in flimsy cotton.

Rage bubbled up his throat in boiling blue flame. Someone had hurt her. When? *Who?*

He tried to ask her, but all that came out was a furious growl. It was then that he realized he wasn't in his bipedal form. *Of course I'm not,* he thought uneasily. *But when did I last shift?* He couldn't remember that either. His memory was too slippery. There were too many of those damn broken threads.

The clearest recollection he possessed was the flash of silver in the dark, and the panic that overtook him when the little woman ran from him — directly into the claws of the enemy, out of the shelter of his wings.

There was danger everywhere. There were enemies everywhere. She couldn't run into the night without him. He wouldn't allow it.

He only wanted to protect her, to hide her, so why did she look at him like that? Her face was ashen. Her eyes were so wide he could see the white all around the reddish-brown irises. Combined with the blood and the bruises, she looked like every victim he'd ever pulled out of bombed buildings.

Except she didn't look at him like her savior. She looked at him like he was the bomb.

More alarmed than ever, Taevas clawed at clarity, desperate to explain what was going on. Without thinking, he deposited her on the floor and stood, wings snapping back into place as he struggled for balance. Blood rushed to his head and he swayed, his vision blotting. Pain ricocheted out from his wings in a blast. Unshielded by them, warm, wet air swept in to disorient him further.

The woman scrambled to her feet. Her legs gave out, but it didn't stop her from crawling away from him as quickly as possible. A loose braid, so thick it rivaled the width of his forearm — in his bipedal shape, at least — swung around to drag in the dirt.

Taevas tried to lunge for her, driven by jumbled instinct, but his limbs failed him. One foreleg gave out. If she hadn't crawled away, he would've crushed her under his great bulk.

He fell on his side, too dizzy to hold himself up. The force of it shook the building and all the detritus around him, sending boxes and rotten boards tumbling. He let out what would have been a curse if he'd been able to speak properly, and watched with horror as the woman managed to get back on her feet just out of his reach.

She looked wild. Windswept, bloodied, and dirty, she dodged debris and ran for the closed door to what he dimly suspected was a very old barn. The woman was his only point of focus as his vision swam.

Don't leave me, he silently begged. *It's not safe!*

It was all he could do to let out a long, beseeching whistle. Even in his state, he knew she wouldn't understand it like a dragon would. She was clearly not one of his kind, but it was all he had.

He didn't honestly expect her to stop.

The woman stood with her hand on the latch, her shoulders hunched and her legs trembling. She stuffed one hand into the pocket of her robe and retrieved what appeared to be a heavy-duty flashlight. Her knuckles bleached white with the strength of her grip.

"Can you understand me?"

Taevas jolted at the sound of her voice. It was slightly roughened and not at all friendly, but it was still pretty. Lilting, even, like she was on the edge of a song.

Realizing that she was waiting for a response, he let out an urgent chuff. *Come here. Come back.*

It was his job to protect people. He made them feel safe. He *needed* that, because if he didn't have that, he had nothing. Even when his mind refused to hold anything else, he understood that with perfect clarity.

He could barely lift his head up from the dirty floor, but he made the effort when she slowly turned around. It looked like it was the last thing in the world she wanted to do, which he found a little insulting. Memory was a slippery, elusive thing, but he knew people loved him. People wanted to be near him all the time. No one had looked at him with as much suspicion and fear as she did in... at least a century. Not since the war.

People gazed at him in awe, with reverence and pride. Occasionally he got an annoyed look, but admiring glances and blushing were much more common. People certainly didn't raise flashlights up like they needed a baton to keep him away.

"Shift so we can talk." Her voice shook, but the tilt of her chin was firm.

He didn't know why he found that charming. Perhaps because he was so used to giving orders, or possibly because she stood at all of five feet and five inches — a generous estimate — and thought she could command the Lord of the Dragon Clans under threat of an improvised club.

Unfortunately, no matter how amusing he found her, it didn't change the fact that he couldn't shift. Survival instinct wouldn't allow it. He was far too weak. Healing would happen faster if he stayed in one form, and even if it didn't, he was far less vulnerable in his tough dragonhide. It took a bold soul to attempt to hurt a transformed dragon, injured or not.

His mind was fuzzy. Details were slow to come, if they came at all, but he *knew* a threat loomed. He knew he'd been hunted. Ambushed. Shifting into a far weaker form would only give his enemies an advantage he couldn't afford.

Taevas huffed, sending flurries of dust into the air. Going by the way her plush mouth pressed into a hard line, he suspected she got his message.

Her throat bobbed with a hard swallow, but she kept her flashlight raised when she informed him, "You're an intruder on my land. You attacked me last night and held me here against my will. If you won't shift and explain yourself, then— then I'm going to call the authorities!"

An alarm blared in his mind. Taevas managed to shake his head vigorously. He hadn't attacked her. He was fairly certain he hadn't, anyway. Why would he? Even if she'd attacked *him*, she was only a little mouthful. Hurting her would mean he'd killed her. Instantly.

But the sight of the blood and bruises decorating her skin made him second guess that certainty. Bits of the previous night, blurry and warped by drugs, came to him in a disjointed parade. He recalled his desperation to find a safe haven. The crunch of old wood under his talons. The feeling of being watched. The scent of home. There was a flurry of activity — dust, blood, silver flashes, pain, reaching for her when she would've run heedless into danger. Then exhaustion came, and everything went dim.

None of those memories explained how she'd gotten in the terrible state she was, but his speculation came second in urgency to her threat. He wasn't sure *why* it was so vital, but he knew without a shadow of a doubt that she couldn't, under any circumstances, report his presence to the authorities. Or anyone.

Taevas tried to sit up, but he found it nearly impossible. It was all he could do to stare imploringly at her and offer a low, plaintive whistle. As a man, he could have ordered her. As a dragon, all he could do was beg.

"You're really not going to do it?" She looked to be on the edge of tears. And yet her chin remained in that stubborn angle, the flashlight held high. She was clearly determined to remain strong despite the fear that shook her from head to toe. The sight gutted him.

"I don't want any trouble. I really don't. I can call—"

He shook his head again, more firmly this time. The woman pressed her free hand against her eyes and took a deep breath. She looked terribly distressed, which only agitated him further.

If you'd come here, he silently told her, *I'd help. My wings can keep you warm and safe. Everything will be fine. Come, little thing, and do as your Isand commands.*

The hole in the roof had turned the barn into something of a wind tunnel. The beginnings of a storm whipped around her. His tough skin could take it, but her soft flesh couldn't. She didn't even have proper clothing on.

The more he looked at her, the more confused he became. He had no idea where he was, let alone how she'd ended up there with him dressed in little more than her pajamas. His heartbeat accelerated. That beast stirred with a great, furious growl in the back of his mind.

Dizziness made his vision swim. Growing increasingly

agitated, Taevas silently commanded her, *Come to me now. I order you to return to me!*

Oblivious, she said, "Look, you need medical attention. Even if you aren't here to hurt me, I *need* to call someone. You've got cuts everywhere, and you *look* sick."

Sick? Spots peppered his view of her. Taevas shuddered. *I don't get sick. It's only the drugs. I'll shake it off. I have to.*

The edges of his already blurry mind had begun to fade. Taevas fought it hard, some part of him screaming in the dark to hold on, to stay alert, that this was the most important thing he'd ever done and he couldn't miss a moment, but it was fruitless.

He was fairly certain he hadn't been ill in decades, but he strongly suspected that the woman was right. A feverish heat crept over him and both sets of his eyelids grew heavy.

The last of his strength evaporated from his limbs. Taevas's neck slumped and his wings folded haphazardly against his back. Resting his chin on the floor, he strained to keep his gaze fixed on the woman. She looked rather more alarmed than she had before.

Lowering her makeshift weapon, she took several halting steps toward him. "Hey," she called, voice gone an octave higher. "Hey, don't go to sleep!"

He tried to listen to her. He really did. It was little use. Taevas made a clicking sound deep in his throat — an apology and a stern order to stay near.

His eyes slid shut, but he was still conscious enough to be startled when a shaking hand patted his leathery cheek. Her voice came from a distance. "Is there some reason you don't want me to call for help?"

Taevas managed the smallest nod. The woman's sharp inhalation was loud in the lull between gusts of wind.

There was another tentative touch. Just fingertips glancing over the curve of his snout before they disappeared as quickly as they'd come. In a more hushed voice, she asked, "Are you in danger?"

Yes, he thought, unable to manage even a nod. Perhaps he

made some sound of affirmation, but he couldn't be sure. Darkness eased over him, tender and merciful in its escape, as those gentle hands returned to stroke his cheek.

CHAPTER FOUR

TAEVAS WOKE TO THE SOUND OF A DOOR SWINGING open on rusty hinges. He didn't recall having fallen asleep, and it felt as though he awoke with a terrible jolt, but in fact he didn't move at all. He lay partially on his side in the dust, his normally powerful limbs useless. All he could do was crack his eyes open in time to see a woman silhouetted against blinding light.

It took him a moment to recognize her, and not just because his mind was addled. She'd washed and changed since he closed his eyes what felt like a moment ago. Though she was still bruised and had a cut on her brow, her skin was scrubbed clean of blood and filth.

She wore a fine linen dress belted at the waist and neat little boots that had gone out of style a century past. One knee was badly bruised and swollen beneath the hem of her olive-green dress. Dark splatters decorated her shoulders and the slopes of her heavy bosom.

Rain, he thought, scenting the air. Droplets clung to the stray curls around her brow, too. Her dark hair was secured behind her head with a length of ribbon that appeared to snake in and out of her fascinating curls.

She was disarmingly lovely — even staring at him with that

grim expression. Nothing but soft curves and even softer brown skin, she looked like something otherworldly against the backdrop of squalor and decay of the barn.

That thought roused him a bit more. *Where am I?*

The woman didn't appear to notice he'd awoken. She was busy shutting the huge barn door with one hand, her other occupied with a comically oversized basket. When the door closed, he was startled to realize she'd built a large fire in the center of the floor. It was carefully ringed with stones and the smoke escaped through the collapsed portion of the ceiling.

She built me *a fire?*

It was a humbling thing for a powerful dragon, especially when he realized he needed it. Taevas was wracked with shivers. To him, it felt as though the temperature had dropped fifty degrees between one blink in the next.

The fire filled the building with flickering light and just a little bit of dry heat. He noticed she'd positioned it slightly closer to him rather than the true center of the room. A pang of feeling struck him — gratitude, certainly, but also mourning for a time when his parents stoked the fire to keep him warm at night.

It'd been a very long time since he thought of that old life. It seemed odd to him that those memories, best left in the past, would resurface when he couldn't even recall what had happened the day before.

The woman still didn't notice him. She hurried across the floor with her basket, her brow furrowed and her gaze down. It was a marked contrast from how she acted before, he thought. The memory was fuzzy, but he knew she'd been afraid of him.

Ridiculous. I'd never hurt you, he sternly informed her. *I'm your Isand, and I don't break pretty things. Don't you recognize me?*

Now she appeared not to care about him at all as she fearlessly scurried around the fire. He watched her avidly, fascinated by the dusky flush of her full cheeks and quick, efficient movements. She knelt beside him, close enough that he could feel the very slight heat of her body, and set her basket down.

She rummaged around in it for a moment before she extracted a series of glass containers and first aid supplies. That done, she pulled out a wicked-looking needle and a spool of thread, which she carefully set in one of the containers. Donning a pair of sterile gloves from her kit, she took up the sewing tools.

He watched all of this with rapt attention, his drowsy mind fascinated by her graceful movements and the way she bit the cushion of her lip, but the moment she leaned over his neck with the threaded needle, he found himself rearing back in alarm. Panic, searing and unreasonable, sent his heart rate skyrocketing.

She jumped, startled by his sudden movement, and sat back on her heels to stare at him with wide eyes.

"Oh! I'm sorry. I didn't realize you're awake." She swallowed hard and, with a somewhat awkward movement, lowered her needle. "Um, you've been asleep for several hours. I already cleaned and dressed most of your cuts as best I could, but this one is really deep. It needs stitches — or better yet, a healer."

It took him a long moment to understand what she was talking about. *I've been injured. Right. I was attacked, wasn't I?*

He blinked owlishly. His mind was a bit clearer than it'd been before, but only just. He got the sense that he'd been out of it for far longer than a couple days. There'd been the bite of a needle several times, each one followed by his mind going slushy and strange. Spots of clarity had been few and far between, but there'd been one in particular—

I escaped. I escaped and was nearly dragged back.

It'd been dark. The wind was like icy knives against his wings, which screamed in agony. He was disoriented, his higher functions nearly snuffed out altogether, and another dark, winged shape had appeared against the velvet black of the sky above the clouds. They'd tangled in the air, claws raking at soft underbellies and throats, wings snapping as they fought to stay afloat.

He thought he'd injured his opponent. There'd been a great push as he disengaged and plummeted toward the Earth. Then it all got fuzzy again. There were snatches of memory, of the view from high above the world, and then closer, closer—

"If you don't want me to do this, I can call the rangers. They'd come get you in a heartbeat," the woman gently offered, her soft voice breaking through his rising panic. A high note finished off the question. It was the unmistakable tone of someone who very much wanted whatever it was that she'd suggested.

He focused on her again. She was so very small. Even in his bipedal shape, he'd tower over her. An unnamed radiance seemed to shine from her, like the very essence of life itself lay just beneath her skin. Magic hummed in the air all around and saturated the very concrete on which he lay, but it seemed to emanate directly from her — like the glow cast by a brilliant little flame.

Despite that vitality, something about her seemed incredibly fragile. Yet she sat there with a needle in her hand, prepared to risk a dragon's ire in an attempt to help despite the fact that she clearly wanted him to leave.

Taevas respected her gumption, if not her lack of caution. The ancient beast in him hissed a warning. That would have to be addressed later.

He'd been under threat for a very long time. No one could be trusted. Even so, he laid his head down again, one eye fixed on her, and forced himself to relax. He wasn't entirely sure why, but he was certain it was the right choice.

She looked at him in silence for what felt like a long time. "You must really be in trouble."

He chuffed. *You have no idea.*

Leaning in again, more cautiously this time, she pressed her needle against the edge of a deep slash. He barely felt it. Taevas watched her dubiously, wondering if he could somehow warn her that dragon skin was a lot tougher than most people thought. A flimsy sewing needle wouldn't stand a chance of puncturing his flesh.

It was a bit of a shock, then, to feel the momentary bite of pain that accompanied it sliding in. The woman grunted with the force it took, but she'd done it. Maybe sensing his scrutiny, or perhaps merely uncomfortable with the silence, she explained, "This is an embroidery needle I use for leather. I thought it might work better than my smaller ones. And don't worry, the thread is nylon. I keep it in my first aid kit, so it's all sanitized. You'll have to have the stitches removed, but if we keep it clean, it shouldn't get infected."

You sound like you've done this before, he silently replied, ignoring the bite and sting of her work.

As if she could hear him, she said, "Living out here, it's good to have this stuff handy, you know? I've stitched people, animals, even myself a couple times when— well, when it's more convenient. We don't have any healers close, and the nearest medical center is forty-five minutes away by car."

Feeling more like himself with every painful stitch, he thought, *Forty-five minutes? Where am I — Siberia?* He looked around with growing disgust. It didn't appear that there were any electric lights, no modern amenities at all. In fact, he was fairly certain he was in some sort of converted barn, one built a century ago, if not more. The gods knew he'd seen enough of them in his youth.

He was once again reminded of an old life, an old pain, and he didn't like it at all.

This is worse than Siberia. I've gone back in fucking time.

"Mind you, I'm no healer. You really should get to one as soon as possible. I can walk to the Thompsons' farm and call the ranger station. They could send out an emergency unit for you." She didn't look at him as she said it, but kept her eyes lowered to her task. That's why it surprised her when he lifted his head just enough to blow a large, annoyed breath over her.

As if I'd let you walk anywhere in this weather, he thought, appalled by the very idea. Wherever they were, it was storming. Even if he trusted that he hadn't been tracked down by his attackers, he'd let her do that over his dead fucking body.

Casting him an exasperated look, she replied, "Fine! I get the message. No rangers. Stop moving, please."

He did as he was told, but it didn't stop him from giving her a stern look. Taevas knew rebellion when he saw it. There was a certain angle to the jaw, a flicker in the eyes that spoke of disobedience. Sometimes that could be fun, especially when it meant he got to squash a bully, but in this case, he didn't find it amusing. The thought of such a small, breakable creature wandering into danger was utterly untenable. And, perhaps, he simply didn't want to be alone.

You're not allowed to leave me, he told her. *I forbid it.*

As she settled into the rhythm of her work, he observed her with an unblinking stare. The scents of the fire and barn dust were strong, but with her so close, it couldn't quite tamp out her natural scent. She smelled like cypress. Like fresh water. Like warm, soft woman, salt, and home.

It was a familiar scent. Very familiar.

Is that why I was drawn here?

Taevas wracked his mind, but the answer was elusive. It made sense, though. If he'd been addled by drugs and blood loss, he might have mistaken the scent for that of home. Dragons had an incredibly acute sense of smell. When their internal navigation and their eyesight failed, they could use their noses to guide them to safety.

Even a whiff of her could've drawn him down, and when his strength gave way, he wouldn't have had a choice but to land. He wished he could ask her what had happened. He also wished she'd tell him her name.

Who are you? Taevas's nostrils flared as he took in one deep breath after another, analyzing her scent. *I'd remember if we met.*

He'd met thousands of people in his life. Citizens of the 'Riik, dignitaries, members of the United Territories Congress, admirers, enemies, soldiers. They tended to become a blur after a while. But *her*...

He'd remember. Even with drugs still coursing through his

system, he was absolutely certain he'd never seen her face. He'd know the glow of her skin, the beguiling shape of her sad eyes, the mind-boggling geometry of her curves. But he *knew* her. He'd smelled her in his sanctuary. On his skin. In his nest.

Home. Home. Home.

His thoughts picked up speed and his heart began to race, though the answer remained just out of reach, a flash of silver in the darkness of his mind.

"I really don't know how this will work with shifting and all. I suppose you'll have to stay in this form until your stitches come out," she muttered, sounding even more troubled. "That's going to make communication difficult." With one final grunt, she pulled the needle through his skin and began to tie off the thread.

It was essential he stay in his quadrupedal form, but that didn't mean he was happy with it. Figuring out what had happened to him, where he was, and how he could return to his people would be far more difficult if he couldn't speak.

And she still hasn't told me her name. Perhaps it wasn't the most urgent of matters, but it bothered him. Everything about her tickled all those loose and broken threads in the back of his mind.

"Okay," she announced, setting her bloody needle into a container by her knee. "I'm going to bandage you up now. We'll have to check it every day to make sure you don't have an infection brewing, but hopefully it should be fine."

While she twisted to retrieve the first aid supplies, Taevas spared a glance for the wound at the base of his throat. It wasn't too bad, all things considered. He'd certainly had closer calls, though it was never a fun experience when someone attempted to rip out one's throat.

And that's why elves wear those silly collars. They might be onto something for once, he mused.

His attacker had come dangerously close to an artery, but the swipe was shallow, merely slicing through thick hide and the first layer of fat. It was a wound that would heal in a few days and be forgotten.

And yet Taevas couldn't look away from it. His pupils widened as he fixed his gaze on the neat but oddly artistic row of stitches holding the gash together. They were perfectly even and done with an expert hand. He wasn't sure how she'd managed it, but she'd made a beautiful pattern with little more than white nylon thread and his flesh. More than aesthetically pleasing, it was familiar. Impossibly so.

Home, he thought numbly. *Why does that remind me of home?*

The woman, unaware that he was holding his breath, leaned over to slather some botanical-scented ointment on the wound. Using the better part of an entire roll of gauze, she bandaged it with the same methodical care as she did everything else, hiding the stitches from view.

"You're lucky I embroider for a living," she joked half-heartedly, "but you'd probably be luckier if I were a healer, huh?"

Rocking back on her haunches, she patted her lush thighs and sucked in a deep breath, unaware that he was frantically clawing at the shroud that obscured his memory. All those broken threads began to swirl into a hideous knot, defying his desperate attempts to untangle them.

She embroiders for a living. That's important. It's so important. Why? Gods, brain, fucking work!

Attention drawn to the act of peeling off her gloves, she rambled, "So, uh, listen. You seem pretty easy-going now, but I just want to— I just want to make it clear that I'm *letting* you stay here, okay? You say you're in danger and you clearly need to rest. I'm going to trust you for now because I don't have the heart to throw you out into the rain, but if you try to hurt me, I don't care what you think you know about nymphs — I *will* hurt you back. Got it?"

A nymph. Taevas watched her, wide-eyed, as she got to her feet. Awe wasn't something he experienced often, but he did then.

Even in his altered state, he knew he'd never met a nymph before. They existed, certainly, and a few tiny communities even thrived in the Draakonriik, but they were intensely private and preferred to live in seclusion. He'd only seen a nymph once, when they sent a representative to the United Congress for a vote on the allocation of funds to wild preservation areas, and that was from across a massive atrium. Even from a distance, he'd been fascinated by the way they seemed to alter the very air around them, making it brighter, more *alive*.

People sang ballads about their beauty, their wildness. Painters agonized over scenes of them dancing through glades or bathing in frothy water, their wet bodies draped in the fine cloth woven by their own skilled hands.

Nymphs were fragile creatures. Their skin was thin, their defenses almost non-existent. He'd once heard a song that compared their flesh to petals and their blood to water. Their lives, the song bemoaned, were just as easily snuffed out as a flower's.

A single thread unwound itself from the tangle. It came to him, tattered but shimmery gold, ready to be followed. *Cypress and freshwater. Warmth and honey.*

Tell me your name, he silently demanded as she stooped to pick up her basket. *I order you to stay. You* must *stay! Tell me!*

Turning to leave, she announced, "I'll let you rest. In a couple hours, I'll add some more logs to the fire, but I think you should be okay for now." With a hard push, she cracked open the barn door. Even the dim light that filtered through the layer of clouds seemed blinding when it reflected off puddles and into the barn.

He squinted against the glare, desperate to keep her in his view. Giving him a nervous smile over her shoulder, she added, "Oh, I never told you my name, did I? I'm Alashiya. Most people just call me Shiya, though. If you need anything, um, I guess you can just roar or something."

Alashiya. He raked weakly at the filthy concrete. If he'd had the strength, he would've crawled on his belly toward her. *Alashiya. No, I forbid you to go. Stay!*

She paused. Wild hope sprung to life in his chest. Taevas could practically see the scales of her mind weighing her next words. "And just so you know, this place is safe. Really safe. I've warded it to keep out just about everyone. That's part of the reason I was so— It was a shock that you landed here. Most people wouldn't be able to find my land even if I gave them a map. So... I hope that sets your mind at ease. Rest well."

And then she slid through the gap, out into the rain, and beyond his reach — defying him once again.

CHAPTER FIVE

THERE WAS A DRAGON IN HER BARN. A HUGE, ROYAL purple, injured dragon.

In her barn.

It didn't matter how many times she repeated it. Alashiya couldn't wrap her head around the fact that they were there, just down the hill from her home, let alone the notion that she hadn't turned tail and run to the authorities the moment it became clear they couldn't pursue her.

She'd had ample opportunities, and she'd nearly done it at least a dozen times as she made the trek back and forth to the barn, her arms laden with bloodied rags, medical supplies, and warm, soapy water. During the long, miserable night she'd spent trapped within their grasp, she'd done nothing except plot her escape, movement by movement. Her only other option had been to scream everytime they twitched in their sleep, fearing that they'd finally decided it was time for a midnight snack.

And yet she made another trip. She brought clean rags. She soaked and then gently rubbed off the copious dried blood from their thick hide. She built them a fire and checked that they were breathing.

Alashiya was fairly certain she was a coward of some fatal

degree, but that hook in her chest simply wouldn't let her abandon a person in need — even if that person could turn around and eat her with a single snap of its jaws. Maybe it was habit. Hundreds of wounded and dying animals had come into her care over the years, each one bringing her joy and heartbreak in turn, so she reckoned that the dragon had inadvertently plucked a well-used heartstring.

She could no more turn her back on them than she could an injured bird. Which was, of course, ridiculous.

They're the size of a bus, she groused, *and they attacked me. They could turn on me at any second. I'm well within my rights to call the rangers.*

But... they hadn't been quite so frightening in the light of day. And despite their rough handling the previous night, they'd been very polite since. As polite as one could be, she imagined, when communication was limited to weak head movements and growls.

The look in their eyes had been much more alert than the previous night. Even exhausted and in pain, there was an unmissable spark of intelligence in their gaze that hadn't been there before. It made her question whether they knew what they were doing at all when they crashed through her barn and snatched her.

It didn't excuse their behavior, of course. She still had a headache from slamming her head into the trough, and she sported a lovely patchwork of scrapes and bruises from their tussle. Her knee was swollen, and each limping step she took to the barn reminded her of the risks she was taking. Even if they hadn't attacked her, the responsible thing to do for *their* sake was to call the authorities, who could get them proper care.

But she couldn't shake off the look in their eyes whenever she broached the idea. There'd been a flare of wild panic, a desperation she knew well. They were afraid.

Alashiya knew what it was like to feel a fear so deep, it sank its teeth into the marrow of every bone. It shook her to realize someone as big and powerful as a dragon could feel it. Somewhere in the back of her mind, she'd always assumed that predators were immune to that sort of thing.

So she didn't walk in the opposite direction of the barn, toward the Thompsons' farm. She didn't make the long trek to town. Alashiya trudged up and down the slight hill several times that day to check on her unwanted guest, her mind whirring as she tried to summon up what scant knowledge she and her grove possessed about dragons.

They seemed comfortable enough by the fire she'd built after chills began to shake their powerful frame. A whisper of a memory teased her with the suggestion that dragons were nearly immune to most weather, so she tried not to worry about them overheating in her attempt to ward off humidity and the infections it could spawn beneath their dressings. Whether that was a true fact she'd heard decades ago or merely a figment of her imagination, she couldn't say.

All she knew for certain was that dragons were mighty beings who lived in tall towers. They could shift between two shapes, one beastly and another humanoid. And of course, she knew they breathed fire. The rest, like most of the world, was a mystery to her.

Learning about them had never been essential to her day to day survival, and seeing as she assumed she'd never encounter one, Alashiya was forced to base her decisions on what she could observe.

She was secretly delighted to discover the dragon changed color at sunrise and sunset. Royal purple gradually darkened into a black so deep it seemed to absorb the light of the fire. Only when the glow hit it *just* right did she discover it wasn't true black, but held a remarkable crimson undertone.

Alashiya tried not to get too close if she could help it, so she found herself observing the dragon. They were usually asleep when she slipped into the barn, their great, triangular head resting on their forelegs and their wings folded limply against their back. Their tail, which was the length of their body, lay in a lazy circle around the fire. She dodged it carefully and was always nearly silent when she visited, but they never failed to awaken as soon as she delicately crossed the boundary of their tail.

It was an awe-inspiring thing in the truest, oldest definition of the word to watch a sleeping dragon wake. No matter how many times it happened, Alashiya found herself freezing, a wave of goosebumps breaking out across her body as those massive eyes sprung open to fix her with an avid look.

There was no way of knowing what they saw when they looked at her. The most likely scenario was that she looked like a plump roast swaddled in linen, just ready for the oven.

Despite that, they never lunged for her. In fact, they held perfectly still as she fed logs to the fire and quickly inspected their bandages, ignoring how some part of her fought to linger there, skin to skin with them, drawn by that powerful force lodged behind her breastbone. A few of their bandages needed changing, but most were nearly clean of blood, which buoyed her optimism that the dragon would be able to see themself off in a few days.

Since she figured she would be stuck with them until then, Alashiya had several questions for the dragon, though she dreaded attempting to get any answers.

Hovering by the fire, she rubbed her toe into the dust and ash on the floor. The sun had hidden behind the dense clouds, obscuring what was probably a fiery summer sunset. She'd never liked being in the barn at night.

The spirits of her grove followed her, their whispers like the rustle of thousands of leaves in her ear. She got the sense that they grew mournful when they saw how cold and desolate their old home became after sunset. It was better to take them into her house, to feel them admiring her work as she embroidered by the light of her hearth, than to linger where so many of their mortal lives ended.

But having a dragon in the barn made it feel different. The air was alive again. The scent of smoke conjured memories of dancing and hot meals. She wouldn't go so far as to say they were good company, but the dragon's presence was big enough to fill the sad, empty space left by her grove, and that made it possible for her to stand there at all.

Alashiya took a deep breath. "You're probably going to be here for a few days, so..."

The dragon's head lifted, with some effort. They offered her a slow blink. It seemed to say, *Go on. I'm listening.*

"We should get some things out of the way," she explained, gesturing to the dragon with a nervous flick of her wrist. "How about you nod once for yes, shake your head for no, and nod twice for neither."

After another blink, the dragon nodded once.

Licking her lips, Alashiya forged ahead. "Let's start with whether you're male, female, or neither. Female?"

The dragon gave her a long look. At length, they shook their head.

Alashiya nodded. "Male?"

A nod.

"Are you an adult?"

The look in his eyes turned to one of unmistakable disbelief, like he couldn't understand why she was asking him something so basic. There was a huff, followed by a firm nod.

"Do you live near here?"

The dragon paused for a long time. His eyes went in and out of focus the way she'd seen several times, and his lower jaw worked from side to side. There was a struggle going on within that fearsome skull, but she couldn't discern what it was about — or what side was winning. Alashiya got the sense that whatever was happening, the dragon wasn't all *there*. He appeared dazed, and his eyes roved in a strange, skittering way she'd seen a handful of times in her life.

Eventually, he nodded twice. She frowned. "In this context, does that mean you don't know?"

Another nod. Low, almost bird-like chirps bubbled up from that long, reptilian throat. When she only stared uncomprehendingly at him, oblivious to their meaning, the dragon's lip curled with clear frustration, revealing those terrifying teeth.

"I'm sorry. I know this is hard for you." She looked away as she rubbed at the sore spot on her forehead. "I wish I could talk to you like I talk to plants."

The dragon's head eased into her view. One of those huge violet eyes blinked, but not in the normal way. A clear eyelid slid over from one side. The intensity of his expression wasn't dulled by its presence at all.

Feeling a bit like he was trying to urge her on, she offered him a wan smile and asked, "Do you need blankets? I know it's warm, but a storm is coming and if you get wet, you might get sick."

The dragon scrutinized her for a beat before his head slowly turned one way, then the other. He appeared to be judging the state of the barn, though she had no idea what conclusion he came to when he turned his gaze back onto her. The dragon shook his head slowly.

Relieved that she wouldn't have to spare any of her precious, hand-made bedding, Alashiya moved on to her next concern. "What about food? You haven't had any water or meals since you crashed here. You won't heal if you don't eat, and I'm pretty sure you'll die if you don't drink something."

During the warm months, nymphs needed to eat and drink nearly constantly, but that was because they traditionally subsisted on food gathered from their land. Berries, wild mushrooms, greens, and root vegetables were her grove's staples, but they'd learned to tend gardens and buy from shops when access to those things dwindled, both by design and by the god Craft's ever-flipping coin of famine and fortune.

Alashiya's larder was almost always bursting with canned, dried, and salted vegetables and tubers. Once upon a time, it was a tenet of her people to welcome all guests with food and water, no matter how scarce their resources were. Though she was long out of practice, she experienced an acute discomfort at the idea of the dragon going hungry on her watch.

She was happy to offer the dragon some of her food, but she wasn't sure he would be interested in her preserved eggplant — or that he might not eat her out of house and home in one meal.

"I don't have any meat," she confessed, brow crinkling with growing worry. Alashiya was almost certain dragons were carnivores. Nothing with teeth like his lived off plants alone. "I have lots of preserves and pickles and things, but I don't eat flesh. I know a man who sells game, though. I could go into town and get some, if you need it."

She tried not to wince at her own offer. There were several reasons she didn't enjoy the idea of buying meat for the dragon. The first was that she felt queasy at the thought of handling animal flesh. The second was that she had very little money to spare, and an unexpected expense like having to feed a creature the size of a truck for an indefinite period of time would no doubt deplete her meager savings almost instantly.

However, it was the third reason that made her hesitate the most: *Monty*.

Old enough to be her father and mean as the day was long, Monty Howard was a man she did her best to never find herself alone with. He'd had his eye on her land — and other things — for years. He never missed an opportunity to harass her, and if she went to him with a request, she had no doubt he'd find some way to leverage it to his advantage.

Alashiya nearly wilted with relief when the dragon, watching her face with an unblinking stare, firmly shook his head from side to side.

"You don't need to *eat?*"

He shook his head again.

Fascinated, but also not entirely certain that could possibly be correct, she pressed, "What about water?"

Another shake of his head.

"How long can you go without?"

It wasn't a yes or no question, which made things rather more difficult for him. The dragon let out a series of chirps and lifted his chin. Alashiya frowned and decided to work backward from an impossible starting point. "A year?"

The dragon shook his head.

"Six months?"

Another shake.

"Three months?"

The dragon didn't answer right away but appeared to think through her question before slowly shaking his head.

"Three months is closer," she surmised, strangely fascinated by his answers. "What about two?"

The dragon's face wasn't very expressive. Not in any way she could decipher, anyway. But he somehow managed to look haughty when he nodded.

"*Two months* without food or water?" Alashiya rocked back on her heels. She could only imagine what it must've been like to be such a powerful, resilient creature. Wryly, she noted, "Nymphs need to eat all the time — unless we're hibernating. It must be nice to not have to worry about that."

The dragon's long neck moved sinuously as he leaned toward the fire. A *shwush* drew her attention to his tail, which had slithered across the floor to make a slightly tighter ring around them.

Those great, violet eyes stared at her as his nostrils flared. She got the sense that he was speaking to her, but she couldn't for the life of her figure out what he was trying to say. The best she could do was decide he looked very intense — a bit like a dog who knows better than to outright beg his owner, so instead waits with bated breath for a food scrap to fall.

Alashiya cleared her throat and looked away, uncomfortable with the scrutiny. "Well, um, I could still make you a pot of broth, if you'd like." She eyed him speculatively. *Would he just stick his snout in it?* That wouldn't be a dignified sight, which somehow felt deeply wrong, but dignity didn't have a place at the table when survival was on the line. "A big one. You might not need it, but it wouldn't hurt, right? A good broth can fix anything."

The dragon shook his head more quickly this time as he drew

back. The thick, scaly skin above his eyes lowered in what she could only assume was a deep frown.

Compelled by manners she thought were long forgotten, she assured him, "It really wouldn't be any trouble. I have a huge stock pot and I keep all my scraps. I could bring it over and—"

It seemed impossible for something as big as the dragon to move as quickly as he did, but one moment he was across the fire and the next his snout was a few inches from her face. A growl rumbled from deep within his monstrous chest. With deliberate slowness, he shook his head.

No, he seemed to say. *And quit asking!*

Heart jammed in her throat, Alashiya squeaked, "Do you hate broth?"

The huff he released was nearly strong enough to knock her off her feet. His massive snout pressed against her middle. She stumbled back a step as he gave her a firm nudge. Whether he was trying to push her *out* or down to the ground, she couldn't say. Either way it was a clear sign that he was done listening to her.

I'm annoying him, she realized. Her cheeks warmed. *The nerve!*

Alashiya forcefully smoothed out the wrinkles in her dress and announced, "Fine, I get it. I'll leave you alone. I need to get work done anyway. Goodnight."

CHAPTER SIX

EMBARRASSMENT WAS SEARING. IT'D BEEN A LONG TIME since she felt it so acutely, and Alashiya didn't enjoy it at all. Flushed to the roots of her hair, she fled the barn as fast as she could without sprinting. The dragon made noises behind her, great chuffing sounds and growls from deep within his chest, but she didn't pay them any attention.

An unwanted guest was bad enough. She couldn't let go of the feeling of exposure, the sense that at any moment he might turn his massive jaws on her, but what she *really* couldn't stand was the pang of hurt she experienced when he turned down her hospitality.

For one shining moment, she'd almost enjoyed herself in his company. It didn't matter to her that he couldn't speak. It was probably better that he couldn't. It allowed her to feel somewhat in control of the interaction, despite their obvious power disparity. If he hadn't been so rude about the damn broth, she might have asked a dozen more questions. Which was, she realized with another jolt, probably why he'd shooed her off in the first place.

It wasn't every day that she met someone new. In fact, it wasn't every *decade.* She'd almost forgotten how much she liked to talk.

But he'd spoiled it. Perhaps he had good reason to — maybe dragons *couldn't* eat in their beastly form, or perhaps he just hated broth. Whatever the reason, it didn't matter to Alashiya as she limped back to the house.

It was fitting that the sky chose that moment to unleash the full fury of another summer storm.

She gnashed her teeth as she was soaked to the bone. At least a little bit of water was an easy problem to solve. Her dress would dry quickly, and rain did wonders for her garden. The dragon was a far bigger issue.

He'd be gone very soon. That was all she needed to think about. She'd done the kind thing — given him shelter and patched up his wounds. She didn't need to do any more for him at all. It was for the best, really, since she didn't want him to get too comfortable and think he could stick around.

Nymphs had their generous hospitality taken advantage of many, many times throughout history, and Alashiya knew the dangers of that better than most. Her grove had welcomed hungry strangers one too many times. Now they were dead.

Inside her home, Alashiya shoved that thought away as she yanked off her boots and placed them on the rack by the kitchen's door. She never came through the proper entryway, as she preferred the more direct route to the living room through the spacious kitchen.

The house was a sprawling warren of add-ons and attachments, meant to house the many families her grove once believed they'd have, but all she used were the living room, the kitchen, and one of the bathrooms. Everything else had been carefully sealed off — left to return to the earth in the same way the barn was.

She might've maintained it, but the expense of keeping up with repairs and the amount of wood it would've taken to heat the whole thing made it impossible. Her grandfather's room was the last one to be closed off. After his passing, she'd moved every-

thing she needed into the living room and never entered that side
of the house again.

The great metal belly of the cast iron stove in the center of
the living room was cold and dark. The house was as old as the
barn and if it wasn't for the layers of quilts she'd hung up on the
walls, the fire wouldn't have stood a chance against the cold in
the winter. They served a purpose in the summer, too, alongside
the thick layers of moss and vines that had grown over the walls.
Both helped insulate the house, keeping the temperature
comfortable in all seasons. If the dragon needed blankets, she'd
planned to take them down for him, so she was immensely glad
he didn't.

Grabbing a towel from a shelf, Alashiya sank into the dense
cushions of her couch with a heavy sigh and began to dry herself
off. She supposed that on the scale of unwanted guests, the
dragon could've been a lot worse. Perhaps he was a little rude, but
he didn't appear intent on clearing out her larder or causing her
harm. She reminded herself that he was in pain, seemed confused
at the best of times, and unable to communicate. In his place,
she'd be cranky, too.

She *was.* Her temper was frayed by more than just having her
home invaded. Her wounds, far less serious than his own, still
smarted. And he hadn't done her a damn favor by keeping her
pressed to his chest all night, unable to move or ease the cramping
that came with being in one position for several hours.

The sting of her embarrassment died down, leaving her deeply
exhausted. She'd spent the entire day, from sun-up to sundown,
looking after the dragon. After the sleepless, uncomfortable night
spent in his claws, her body protested doing anything other than
collapsing into her bed. It took a lot of effort to shove some bread
and cheese into her mouth, change into a robe and nightgown,
and take up her needle and thread.

But that reluctance to work was short-lived. As soon as her
needle passed through the lush, wine-red velvet, all was well again.
Her mind went quiet to all but the hum of her grove's spirits,

their quiet satisfaction and pride as she made something beautiful for a man she would never meet.

Work meant spending time with Adon, and that soothed even the worst of her discomfort. She imagined him there as she bent over the embroidery hoop clamped to the edge of her desk, a small smile curling her lips.

Hello, darling. It's been a long day. I've missed you. How was work?

This commission wasn't magical in nature. Most of his most sophisticated, luxury pieces weren't. The order slip she received from Stalton's Atelier always specified exactly what had been requested, but over the years, this particular client — labeled only as ITA — had nearly ceased asking for things altogether. He ordered so much that she supposed he'd probably run out of ideas. For the most part, she was asked to do whatever suited her fancy, with a suggestion here or there, and given free rein to fulfill her creative whims.

It was the highlight of her days. No expense was spared for his clothing, so she got to work with the finest silks, the richest velvets, and at least every six months, she was sent another goldwork commission.

The finest pieces didn't require any magic. That cost extra, and she noticed ITA tended to ask for it on simpler foundation garments — trousers, crisp shirts, the occasional coat or vest. Those garments had slits for wings, and the spellwork he asked for was all about making the clothing functionally indestructible.

She wasn't entirely certain what he was, but she tended to picture him as a gargoyle or a harpy, depending on the day. Clearly he was someone who was very active and needed to protect his clothing on a day to day basis. Both beings were known for their athleticism, and so it made sense to her that he'd need his clothing infused with spellwork, lest he go through them at an unsustainable rate.

Her speculation was, of course, fueled by her aunt's collection of romance novels and her own rampant imagination. During her life, Imilce was fond of the fantasy of an adoring sept of gargoyles, as well as being swept off her feet by a fearsome harpy. After seeing the width of the shoulders on the ITA's shirts, Alashiya thought she understood the appeal.

Over the years, she'd quietly added more and more sophisticated spellwork to his clothing. Stalton never appeared to notice that she'd included unpaid for additions to the garments, and since the orders kept coming, she saw no harm in adding sigils for protection, warding, and just about anything else she could manage.

Wild magic, sourced from the very essence of life all around her, whispered its song to her as she stitched. She mouthed the words to a language long forgotten as the gold-wrapped thread heated under her fingers, pulling the energy from her, from her line, into the coils.

Be safe, she willed. *Be healthy. Be happy.*

Spellwork had its limits, but intention, blessings, the meager protection her blood could offer — those she could give in abundance to a man she would never meet, but who was nonetheless someone she'd come to care for deeply.

My Adon.

After spending hundreds upon hundreds of hours working on his clothing, she thought she could be forgiven for creating a rich fantasy around the man she'd never meet.

It started with the name, as most things do.

ITA was silly, impractical. Adon was a name for a man who wore the grand clothing she stitched. Over ten years, the name had led to other imaginings: what he looked like when he wore the clothes, what his job was, where he lived. She knew nothing beyond the scant details on every order slip, and when she'd dared to ask for some details in her correspondence with the atelier, she'd been soundly reminded that it wasn't her place.

"He's an extremely important client," the letter crisply informed her. *"His private details are on a need to know basis only."*

She hadn't been asking for his home address or anything, but she supposed it really wasn't for her to know more than what was requested of her, no matter how curious she was. And of course, in the absence of knowledge, imagination took root.

In many ways, Adon was her sole companion. She'd had long conversations with him as she worked, and often went to sleep imagining soft, domestic scenes in which he starred. At some point, she'd jokingly referred to him as her husband — only ever in her mind, of course — and since then, the title had simply... stuck.

Adon, the husband of her lonely heart. A fantasy that kept her sane as the years crawled by, leaving her behind.

She was aware that it wasn't healthy. Adon was a real person out there in the world, most likely with a partner and a family and a life that had no intersection with her own, save for when he wore her work. But she was also aware that there was no harm in it. Not really.

He would never know. She would never have her fantasy burst. If she started to include extras, like more spellwork that wasn't paid for or tiny gifts of pressed flowers and embroidery, then it could be easily explained away by good customer service. No one would know that she wove in ancient spells reserved for loved ones, for spouses in particular, or that the hungry needles she used were always first given a drop of her blood, in the oldest tradition of her people.

It'd taken a long time to get to that point, but in the end, she couldn't resist the temptation. There was virtually no chance she'd ever do the same work for a real husband or children, so it felt like her only shot. And if she sometimes felt guilty for it when the occasional intrusive thought of a partner snuck through her armor of fantasy, then she soothed herself with the reminder that he was simply extra protected and nothing more.

Any *meaning*, any emotional connection to that special work, was all on her end.

The world fell away as she sewed in the light of her old lamp.

She didn't notice the roar of the rain on the roof, nor the first bump against the kitchen door. She didn't hear the second, either.

The third, however, caught her attention. It would've been impossible not to notice it, seeing as the door was ripped off its hinges.

Alashiya jolted. Her fingers slipped, resulting in a nasty prick with the end of her needle. Cursing, she quickly pulled her hand away from her embroidery stand. She didn't worry about the single drop of blood drawn by the needle staining the fabric. As soon as it escaped her, it was sucked up by the hungry gold with a low, sizzling sort of hiss. The tiny wound sealed as quickly as it appeared.

She pushed away from the cluttered work table and hurried across the room. There hadn't been enough time to consider the danger, nor the possibilities of what might've caused the crash. Perhaps in the back of her mind, she assumed it was the howling wind that had blown it open.

Even after everything, Alashiya wouldn't have guessed the cause to be a dragon.

She skidded to a stop in the center of the large kitchen and gaped at the massive, reptilian head that had invaded her home. The dragon was far too large to make it through her kitchen door — or any door, really — but he'd managed to fit his head and neck through.

She watched him survey her kitchen with a slow swivel of his head, shocked into utter stillness. Those massive eyes scanned the racks of dried herbs, garlic, onion, and corn hanging from the ceiling. They blinked at the ancient, wrought iron stove and the rows and rows of jars on the counters before settling back on her.

Neither of them made a sound. The dragon's gaze was intense but completely inscrutable. Alashiya had not the slightest idea what to do. She could hardly process the fact that the dragon was there at all. Surely he didn't think he could fit inside the house. *Surely.*

After several silent seconds, the dragon's nostrils expanded with a deep breath. His neck extended, allowing him to peer over her shoulder and through the doorway that led to her living space.

She briefly wondered what he could see from that angle. Her bedding on the floor by the fire? Her workstation strewn with fabric, thread, and hoops? A feeling of hideous exposure overcame her.

Alashiya felt no shame for how she lived, but she disliked being gawked at by an intruder.

Shaking off her surprise, she reached for the first thing she could find — a sturdy wooden spoon. Waving it at the dragon's head, she demanded, "What on Burden's Earth do you think you're *doing?* You won't fit in my house! Get out!"

The dragon let out a deep scoff. Not a huff, not a sigh, not a sound that could be interpreted as anything other than pure derision. One great eye flicked in her direction. This time, Alashiya had no trouble figuring out what he was trying to say to her.

You live here?

She had no idea what was wrong with what he saw. Her home was warm and well lit. Her kitchen was stocked and so was the larder. Her bed was plush with enough blankets and pillows to dress several beds. Her hearth was hot. It wasn't the palaces her ancestors had once lived in, no, but it was more than many people had, and she was grateful for every single inch of it.

She was utterly mystified as to what he could find fault with, besides the fact that he couldn't fit inside. Waving her spoon in front of his nose, she bit out, "I don't know what your problem is and I don't care. Leave."

The dragon gave her a long look. For just a moment, she thought he intended to listen to her, but she was quickly disabused of that notion when, to her utter disbelief, the dragon began to wedge himself into the doorway.

"What are you *doing?*"

She backed up slowly until her hip hit the kitchen counter. Dozens of jars and glass bottles rattled, and the racks over their heads began to sway as the dragon thrust one foreleg through the narrow doorway, followed by a shoulder, then, impossibly, a quivering wing.

It didn't look comfortable by any stretch of the imagination, particularly when spots of blood appeared on several of the dragon's rain-soaked bandages, but he met her gaze with a steely look and forged ahead.

Alashiya stared at the spectacle in horror. She'd once heard that a cat could fit through any hole the width of its head. Watching the dragon force its massive body through her kitchen doorway was a bit like that, except a thousand times more astonishing.

The walls creaked with alarm, and pieces of the doorway's frame sheared off as the dragon pushed his great bulk through, one limb at a time. Alashiya gripped the edge of the counter and leaned as far back as she could, making an infinitesimal amount of space for the beast.

"Please don't break my house," she begged, almost certainly too late.

The dragon clicked at her absently. His focus was on fitting his other wing inside. He seemed to struggle with it the most. A visible jolt of pain ran through him when he flexed it forward, then back, and a terrifying hiss escaped his long throat.

Worry pinched her, but only for a second, seeing as he'd pushed through the rest of the way. His hips were quite narrow, which made everything much easier. The dragon, looking exhausted but pleased with himself, had wriggled his way into the kitchen. He made his way to the center of the floor, dripping water and mud onto the tile, and panted with exertion.

"What..." Alashiya trailed off, speechless at the sight of her kitchen nearly swallowed up by a dragon.

He'd knocked her table out of the way, allowing him just enough room to collapse onto the floor. His tail slithered inside after him much more slowly. It looped around his great bulk to rest over his snout, which he'd dropped onto his forelegs in apparent exhaustion.

If it weren't for his heavy breathing and bloody bandages, she would've said he looked entirely content.

Alashiya was, for the third time in twenty-four hours, entirely at a loss. She watched as his eyelids drooped.

No one will ever believe me, she thought numbly as she set the spoon aside and, for want of anything better to do, squeezed around the dragon to shove the door back into place.

CHAPTER SEVEN

IT WAS THE WARM BACKGROUND HUM OF WARDS, strange and yet painfully familiar, that woke him. Magic soaked the very air he breathed. It tasted sweet on his tongue and woke him from his deep slumber like fingers of sunlight on his face — so soft, so loving, just ticklish enough to draw him to the land of the living once more.

It was a stark contrast to the chills that wracked his frame from the inside out.

His head was much clearer, though it took him some time to realize it. This was partially due to the pain that made his entire body into one great, throbbing wound, but most of the blame could be laid on his surroundings. Taevas had no idea where the fuck he was.

He knocked his tail off his snout and worked hard to lift his head. A splitting headache rang his skull like a bell, forcing him to squint his eyes against the harsh glare of sunlight streaming in through a partially obscured window. Something dark covered most of the old, bubbly glass from the outside. Only a few spots of light could come through the gaps, but it was more than enough to assault his sensitive eyes.

His tongue felt rough, his eyes gritty. Pain was a low but

constant roar in his mind. The chills were endless, and the churning of his guts reminded him of the handful of times he'd gotten the stomach flu. His body had turned on him. It had focused all its energy on hunting down some poison in his system, seeking to purge it, and he was left helpless as the war was waged.

And yet, despite everything, his muscles were loose. He'd slept hard and long, well into the late morning. His dreams had been blessedly blank. He was... comfortable.

A huff escaped him as he squinted at the old but well-kept tile of a kitchen floor. It gleamed in the light, freshly cleaned.

Ridiculous, he fumed. *My first good night's sleep in a century and it's on the floor of a hovel.* It was better than the barn, he supposed, but only just.

Why was I in a barn?

Memories came to him in a steady trickle. Much was patchy, but he could at least reason out why that was so.

Taevas's lips pulled back from his teeth. A terrible growl built in his chest as flame licked upward to flicker between incisors the length of a man's hand.

Ambushed. Drugged. Beaten. Captured.

He'd been leaving a meeting in New York and since it was a short flight, he and his Wing had decided to forgo the jet. It was all painfully mundane and safe. After all, they'd land on Drummond Island just before sunrise, which was more important that day than usual, since it was the summer solstice.

It was a holiday and a short routine flight in the darkness. There was no reason to think anything would go wrong. His last clear memory was of standing on the edge of the platform, ready to launch into the air, half his Wing ahead of him and the other half to follow.

What happened to my Wing?

Dread, cold and sickly, slithered through his veins. The dragons who made up his personal guard would've fought to the death to protect him. Taevas couldn't recall a fight, only a blinding flash, then nothing at all. His next memories were filled with the burn of drugs being injected into his thigh. He'd fought, he was certain, but beyond the impression of rage and pain and disorientation, there was vanishingly little to find in the recesses of his mind.

Taevas shook his head in an attempt to clear it and immediately regretted it. Agony bloomed behind his eyes. *Did they take out my implant?*

His stomach turned. The pain in his head suggested they might've removed the subdermal communication device he and his Wing used. It did nothing to dwell on possibilities without evidence, but he shuddered at the thought. If they could do that, what else had they done to him?

I need a phone. I have to find out what happened. Who's alive. Who needs killing.

But when he tried to climb to his feet, he found his limbs uncooperative. They could barely hold his weight, and the attempt saw him crashing into things on either side of the kitchen. A chair was sent flying, and pans came clattering down from hooks on the wall, making a terrible clatter.

Helpless anger sent his tail lashing against the far wall. He couldn't understand how he'd ended up in a damn kitchen in the first place, and the knowledge that he couldn't even shift to make the experience more comfortable was more fuel on the fire.

He needed to be *gone* from the hovel. He needed to know his people were safe. He needed to find some control again, to get back on his feet, and rain unholy retribution on those who'd thought to bring him down.

Fire snaked up his throat; a cruel, hungry serpent ready to strike.

A pair of bare feet stepped into view. They were attached to finely wrought ankles and shapely legs. Taevas blinked.

A woman stood before him, one hand on the door jamb. Her skin was a perfect, deep gold and her curly hair was the darkest shade of mahogany. Her generous hips and chest were swathed in a simple wrap dress. She wore no makeup, no ornament, and stood there silently, her full lips unsmiling. For just a moment, the great Isand felt all of two inches tall.

"If you're going to burn my house down, I'd appreciate a bit of warning."

How could I forget? Taevas's rage died in the space between heartbeats. *Alashiya. A nymph. Yes. Yes, I remember her. She's helping me. I need her.*

He stared at her, dumbfounded. Cypress and her unique personal fragrance filled the room. It mixed with the scent of hanging herbs, green things, the impressions of thousands of meals and cooking oil and cleaning solvents.

It was the scent of home.

He could say nothing even if he had the means. The almighty Isand was struck speechless as the nymph gave him a withering glare. Her feet made hardly any noise when she padded meaningfully around him, using the tiny amount of space he didn't occupy to reach the cooking area. She cast withering looks at the chair and the pans.

The narrow shafts of sunlight struck her as she filled a dented copper kettle in the deep basin of the sink. For just a moment, she appeared ethereal, her skin made of shining bronze, her curls of pure gold. His breath stuck in his throat.

Never in all his long life had Taevas seen a creature as lovely as Alashiya.

With a graceful flick of her wrist, she sealed the kettle's lid and placed it on the stove. He watched with confusion as she reached for a lighter on the spice rack. A few strikes saw a little flame spring to life, which she used to light the burner beneath the kettle. His sense of disorientation grew.

What on Earth... I haven't seen a stove like that in seventy years.

She didn't spare him another glance as she moved about. Even when she had to step over him, or nudge him aside to open a drawer, she kept her gaze firmly away from him.

Something deep and fundamental in him balked at that, but

Taevas could only watch her, his higher mental processes ground to a halt.

That scent. That face.

The events of the previous day came to him all at once. He'd crashed into this nymph's barn and she'd taken care of him. Then something went wrong. She left him there, defying orders she couldn't hear, and drove him into a panic so sharp it'd cut him deeper than any of his wounds.

It was an unbeatable compulsion, the urge he'd felt to follow her. It'd nearly killed him to do it. His progress was slow and painful. The sight of her narrow doorway had nearly driven him to tear the whole house apart in order to get to her, but he'd used what little sense he still possessed and managed to squeeze inside.

He'd been deeply vexed by her. She wasn't allowed to storm off, not when there was a threat around, and certainly not when he didn't know where she'd gone off to. Didn't she know who he *was?* He'd commanded her to stay.

He was Isand. His orders were followed without question. Taevas never had to ask twice, let alone *follow* someone.

But he'd followed her. He didn't have a choice.

He'd dragged himself through the rain, his belly and tail slipping through the mud, as thoughtless and desperate as a beast. There was no pride. There was no Isand. There wasn't even *Taevas*.

Just her.

He experienced the oddest sensation of vertigo. It was the result of realizing that, for only the second time in his life, he'd been driven by nothing other than instinct. It had possessed him, body and mind, until even the pain of his wounds hadn't been enough to deter him from seeing its will done.

Just as it'd been the first time, it was, in a word, revolting.

"I'd offer you a cup of coffee, but you said you don't drink in that form, so I won't."

Alashiya poured the hot water through an old-fashioned enamel pot. The scent of fresh coffee bloomed all around her as she slowly spun to face him. There was something flinty in her large doe eyes. Bruises decorated one side of her face, giving the look far more weight than it otherwise would've had.

He tensed, claws curling into the tile and tail rattling with furious intent. *Who did that to you?*

His knee-jerk reaction to the sight was just strong enough to out-muscle his instinctive revulsion to being so... not himself. Out of control. *Wrong.*

"I don't know who you are," she began, her tone painfully measured, "and at this point, I really don't care. You've scared me. Battered me. Held me against my will. And then, against all good sense, when I helped you anyway, *you broke into my house* and got mud *everywhere.*"

Taevas balked. *I did that to her?*

He had vague impressions of her saying something like that to him before, but his head was clearer now. Hurting her intentionally was still beyond outrageous, but if he'd been careless—

How could I be careless? I'm never, ever careless. I don't lose control like that.

Except for last night, he silently reminded himself. *Except for when you dragged yourself on your belly through the filth like an animal to follow her. Do you really think you're not capable of causing her harm after* that, *mighty Isand?*

Acid churned in his stomach. Every instinct screamed that he couldn't have hurt her, that he'd *never* hurt her, but he'd been drugged, injured, and hunted. If she stumbled on him at the wrong moment...

No wonder she'd defied him. He was lucky she hadn't run screaming to the nearest person with a bolt gun.

Taevas was famously good with words. He was charming, even rakish. Normally he could be as audacious as he wanted to be, knowing that there was very little he couldn't get away with. His reputation as Isand went far. His looks and wit carried him the rest of the way.

But absolutely none of that mattered now.

Charm and wit meant nothing when he couldn't speak or write. His looks were even less helpful. All he had to recommend him was his behavior and his reputation, and he'd been so drugged out of his mind that he'd already blown that.

I'm so sorry, but I need your help, he wanted to explain to her. *I can't shift until the worst of my injuries have healed. I wish this wasn't the case, but I need you.*

As much as he wanted to leave her hovel behind, he was grieved to realize that he couldn't. With the extent of his injuries, going to ground for a few days was his only option. The fact that he'd managed to land in what felt like a wild fortress of protective wards was a miracle — and perhaps the only thing that had saved him from being pursued by his captors.

It was a miracle he was thankful for, but he couldn't help but wonder why in the world she needed all that protection in the first place. Not that he could ask, of course.

Alashiya continued to stare at him from beneath her dark brows, unable to hear a word of his spinning thoughts. He was at a loss. There was no way to tell her what he needed. All he could do was plant himself there, praying she wouldn't do the smart thing and contact authorities to have him removed.

He'd been ambushed and kidnapped, then held only the gods knew where, drugged, and beaten. Protocol refined over decades dictated that he get a direct line to his Wing before contacting anyone else, eliminating the chances of interception by enemies. No one except his Wing could be trusted, and Taevas had no idea what territory he'd landed in, making it even less safe to seek the help of any authorities.

When he tried to use his innate internal navigation to figure out where he was relative to his roost, it spun in a confusingly tight circle around the kitchen. His instinct told him he *was* in his roost, in the very heart of it, but that was so laughably wrong that he could only blame the drugs still in his system. Or perhaps a head injury.

Either way, he had no damn idea where he was, which was historically a very, very bad thing for a dragon.

He *hoped* he was in the 'Riik, but there was every chance he was in the middle of the Orclind, even as far as the Elvish Protectorate. They were allies of the Draakonriik, but if his attackers were smart, they'd be watching, waiting for any sign that he might've been found, knowing he couldn't fly far when his wings were damaged.

It would be big news if Taevas Aždaja turned up in some small town. One stray word, one unencrypted message, and he'd be pounced on.

His mind raced as panic edged in. He *needed* to stay there, and he *needed* her to keep her mouth shut about it, and he *needed* her to stay close or he'd have to follow her again and—

Taevas shook his head. *Stop. Stop it.*

Chapter Eight

The nymph watched him for several moments longer before she let out a long sigh and turned to fix her cup of coffee. She said nothing more as she scooped sugar into an earthenware mug, and maintained that silence as she cut a thick slice of bread from a loaf. He watched her spread jam on its craggy face with quick strokes of a knife. He felt no hunger in his larger form, but that didn't mean he couldn't appreciate how good she *and* her breakfast looked.

The jam was raspberry, he thought, catching the tart scent on the tip of his tongue. It hardly felt like the time or place, but that didn't stop a part of him from wondering how good she'd taste with a little bit of raspberry on her lips.

"As much as I want to kick you out, I'm not going to. You're still injured, and you said you're in danger. I'm not heartless. Just annoyed that I've had to wash all my towels *twice* in twenty-four hours. I'd just gotten the blood out, you know."

Her back was to him. One of her elegant hands perched on the edge of the counter, and she appeared most comfortable balanced on one foot, with the top of the suspended one pressed against the back of the opposite calf. A hint of silver on bronze skin caught his eye — the light catching what appeared to be faint scars that slipped out from beneath her skirt and wrapped around her calf like the branches of roots.

He'd seen scars similar to it before, but only on those rare victims of lightning bolts. They were more jagged, though, compared to the fine, root-like lines that were barely visible on her warm skin.

Taevas eyed them, his claws curling at the thought of tracing their branches with his fingertips. Every inch of her was made specifically to distract him from what he needed to be thinking about, and she seemed entirely oblivious to that fact.

She took a bite of her bread and stared out the partially obscured kitchen window. It was a perfectly casual sort of pose. Effortlessly beautiful. For a moment, she was just a stunning woman standing barefoot in her kitchen, enjoying a simple breakfast before setting about the rest of her day.

A peculiar tightening took root in his chest — a grainy, hot-to-the-touch sort of nostalgia for something he'd never possessed. The sight of her made him ache, not only because she was beautiful, but because the picture was somehow incomplete.

It would be the most natural thing in the world to come up behind her, to wrap his arms around her waist and dip his head to steal a bite of her breakfast. A buzz passed over his skin in a head-to-toe wave. His senses sharpened to an almost painful degree as his heartbeat throbbed in his ears.

The picture would be complete, he realized, when she didn't stand alone.

Is she alone?

The thought startled him. The fact that he hadn't thought to check was even worse.

Taevas lifted his head and took several quick breaths. He forced himself to ignore the luscious cypress and woman, the unique syrupy-sweet magic in the air, then the scents of a long-occupied home. He sifted through everything from old fires to laundry soap to beeswax. Deep below it all were the faintest traces of other people, but they were so old they were barely discernible.

No mate, he thought, letting out a satisfied rumble. *Or at least, no mate here.*

He wanted to think it mattered because he couldn't afford the risk of being seen by another stranger, but Taevas wasn't entirely delusional. He'd stumbled across an unattached woman of unmatched beauty.

It was the natural, deeply dragonish inclination to snatch treasure when it was dropped into his claws. But he wasn't like every other dragon, and he didn't have the freedom to have his head turned by curvy nymphs in soft linen dresses. Not normally, and certainly not *now.*

And yet that buzz only grew stronger, almost uncomfortably electric. It was a lot like lust, but deeper. More dangerous. *More.*

Alashiya finished her breakfast and cleared the counter. Taking up her mug, she turned to him with a shrewd look. "I'm going to check to make sure the barn didn't burn down in the middle of the night and then work in my garden. After that, I'm going to fix your bandages and get on with the work I desperately need to finish for my— for Adon."

Taevas's hackles rose instantly. He didn't like how she said that name. He didn't like it at all.

Who the fuck is Adon?

Tilting her mug menacingly in his direction, she continued, "You are going to *stay here.* You aren't going to destroy anything or attempt to squeeze back out the door. I only have the one house, dragon, and I can't have you knocking it down. I'm giving you one last chance, okay? If you mess it up, I'm calling the rangers."

Taevas had a lot of questions and even more objections to her plan. Firstly, he didn't like being ordered to stay like a dog. Second, he thought it was deeply uncharitable to assume he'd destroy her dwelling by going in and out, considering he'd managed just fine the first time. And third... in what universe did she think she was allowed to leave him behind? *Again.*

His impulse was to follow her without hesitation or, failing that, stop her from leaving his sight by any means necessary.

Snatch her and hold her if you have to, something ancient and desperate in him hissed. *Don't let her go.*

It was the same need that had dragged him up the slight hill in the pouring rain, and it was the one that made his skin crawl. Never, in all his life, had Taevas been ruled by instinct. He'd watched from a distance as his fellow dragons lived their lives governed by it, their minds and their bodies forged into tools for its use. Compulsion was the domain of others, and it was his immunity to it that made him so very different.

What's wrong with me?

Uneasy, Taevas drew his gaze away from the object of his fixation and offered a quick nod. He settled weakly down on the floor, his mind churning as sickeningly as his stomach, as she puttered around him. The sounds of a wicker basket being picked up were followed by a low feminine grunt, then the door being opened.

Birdsong and the restless rushing sound of grasses blown about in the summer breeze reached him. A furtive peek over his shoulder revealed she'd left the door open, no doubt because it was, in fact, off its hinges and had to be rested against the side of the house.

Don't watch her, he sternly urged himself. *Don't do it.*

His normally steely will crumbled into nothing. After only a few minutes, he couldn't resist draping his long neck across the floor so he could peer outside.

The sky was a vivid blue speckled with small fluffy clouds, and the world beyond the kitchen door was a cacophony of green. It was unlike any garden he'd ever seen. There appeared to be no order to it, no neat lines or planter boxes or geometric fencing. Trees, their limbs heavy with fruit, hung over vegetables. Beans crawled up the stalks of corn. Tomatoes bubbled up from a carpet of arugula. There was no rhyme or reason to any of it.

And yet it was the liveliest garden he'd ever seen. Not one inch of it appeared to be barren or struggling. He could make out no irrigation system or spigot from where he lay. It was as if the gods had commanded that one patch of earth to grow as it would, with the only order being that all things must be edible.

Alashiya fluttered in and out of view. She criss-crossed the garden, coffee in one hand and shears in another. She often paused to take sips from her mug before popping some bit of greenery into her mouth. He watched with rapt attention as she slowly devoured a juicy pear.

She appeared perfectly at home. Her bare feet were light and nearly soundless as she padded between the plants, slowly filling up her basket. Something about it was uncanny, like the first time he watched spellwork being done. The air around her seemed almost too clear, the colors too bright, and when she stooped to brush her fingers over a broad leaf, he swore it stroked her back.

He fell into something like a trance as he watched her. The pain and discomfort of his body was muffled when she was within view. Everything seemed just a bit more real. More right.

Time passed, but he barely noticed it. Taevas blinked owlishly when her form darkened the doorway. Setting her full basket and empty mug down, she made quick work of rinsing her feet in a small basin of water by the door. Every movement was effortless, utterly lacking in artifice or performance. It was a beautiful sight, but something in him itched at the easiness of it, the implication that this was how she spent her days.

He knew how much work it was to grow one's own food, to live off the grid. To do it alone was even harder. There were no breaks or shortcuts. There was just endless, grinding work. Fulfilling work, to be sure, but work.

Did she get to relax? Did she have anyone to depend on? What happened if she hurt herself? It wasn't his business, but he couldn't help the thoughts from flashing through his mind as he watched her.

She acted as though he wasn't there, which irked him immensely, but he was too fascinated by her to do anything about it. He couldn't help but wonder what kind of woman took something like having the Isand of the Draakonriik as her guest in stride.

The thought tickled something in the back of his mind. *She... does know I'm the Isand, right?*

After washing her haul in the deep enamel sink, she set the vegetables on the counter and wiped her hands on a towel embroidered with tiny yellow sunflowers. "Thank you for putting out the fire in the barn before you followed me," she said, setting the towel back on its hook.

Taevas barely recalled doing that, but he inclined his head anyway. He'd take all the goodwill he could get.

That she might not know was a ridiculous thought, of course. *She must know. Surely she must.*

It wasn't always easy for other beings to tell dragons apart from one another in their shifted forms, but he was famous. More than famous. He was *Isand*. His picture, in both his forms, had been plastered across the news since the news *began*. Surely...

Brushing a curl behind her ear, Alashiya stepped over his foreleg to move into the short hallway beyond the kitchen. He watched her go with increasing agitation.

Stop leaving me, he ordered. *If you keep working like this, I'll be forced to do what's necessary, Alashiya. Do as I say and sit.*

She returned with a handful of medical supplies and said nothing more as she knelt to fix his bandages.

Adjusting his position to allow her to tend to the wound at his throat, Taevas took a furtive sniff of her hair. *Cypress.*

Fresh and botanical with just a little bite, it was one of his favorite smells in all the world. Compelled by the scent of comfort and soft things he loved — and seeing the perfect opportunity to get her to stop moving — he laid his head on the plush cushion of her thighs. He expected her to push him away, but she only hesitated for a long, taut moment before she hesitantly continued with her soft touches.

A barely audible sigh reached his ears. "Well, you don't make it easy to stay mad at you, do you? You're like a great big tomcat. One minute you're swiping at me, the next you want to lay in my lap and purr."

Tomcat? I'll take it. Taevas savored the warmth of her under his chin. *You'll come to like me just like everyone else. They all come around eventually.*

Gentle fingers skimmed his throat. It was an exploratory touch — and one that set his blood on fire. A shudder of need rippled through his aching body when she whispered, "I've never even seen a dragon before. Are you all like this?"

Taevas wanted to flash her a smile and answer, *"No, I'm one of a kind."* But he couldn't do that, so instead he turned his snout just a little toward her soft stomach, until he was breathing in nothing but the heady scent of her.

Home.

He was unclear how long they sat like that, but it was far longer than necessary for her to check his bandages. She didn't continue with her touches, but she didn't pull away from him, either, until a shrill birdsong pierced the air, startling her.

Clearing her throat, Alashiya made to stand up. Taevas opened his eyes. He hadn't realized he'd closed them. *No, don't go. Come back.*

The sight of her turning her back on him made his tail rattle against the tile. When she stepped away from him, it was like she took something essential with her. Something he needed but couldn't even remember. An uneasy feeling washed over him, that cavernous sensation of forgetfulness that came with untrustworthy memories.

Cypress. Home. Alashiya. What am I missing?

Taevas watched her set the medical supplies on the counter before she washed her hands again, her gaze averted from him.

"I've got to get to work now." She examined her short nails with a grimace. Reaching for the soap one more time, she muttered, "I can't get *your* blood on the fabric."

From deep within a distorted memory, he heard her joke, *"You're lucky I embroider for a living."*

Alashiya. Cypress. Home.

She said something to him then, but he couldn't hear her over the rush of blood in his ears. Taevas could only watch her as she dried her hands and turned to leave the kitchen. The electric buzzing, that feeling of more than lust, more than *need*, returned with a vengeance.

His gaze followed her path across the hall and into another room. Her scent was strongest there. He chased it mindlessly, until he'd stretched his neck far enough to place his head in the hall.

The tip of his snout just barely reached the doorway into a baffling room. It was one part bedroom, one part living room, and one part workspace. Bolts of fabric and headless dress forms lined the walls. In a corner sat two old arm chairs framed by what looked like a loom and spinning wheel — both a century old at least. A surprisingly fine-looking nest of blankets and pillows lay on the floor near an ancient iron hearth. A work table covered in thread, pincushions, wooden hoops, and a large, frame-like contraption took up most of one wall. It was there that Alashiya settled.

Her wooden chair creaked as she scooted to the edge of the seat and bent over the frame. She reached for a needle with her right hand while her left skimmed the wine-red velvet stretched within the confines of the frame, the tips of her fingers dancing over gold stitches and glittering bullion.

If she noticed him watching her, she didn't show it. Alashiya appeared completely absorbed in her work as she pushed a waxed thread through the eye of her needle. Her lips moved, but she didn't make a sound. Her mouth was very faintly curved in a secret smile.

A great many improbable things had happened to Taevas. He'd survived a century of war and famine. He'd united the dragon clans at the tender age of seventeen. He'd avenged his family and killed a foolish, cowardly tyrant. He signed the Peace Charter and he forged alliances and he built skyscrapers and he fought off assassins. He'd even once flown into the heart of an m-storm and came out no worse for wear, a new member of his clan in tow.

And yet it was this moment that became the single most improbable event of his life.

Because he recognized the robe stretched in the frame. He'd picked it out from the half dozen the stylist, who specialized in couture garments infused with magic, sent him. He'd even filled out the customization order himself, his only request being that it be done in real gold.

She'll do something incredible, no matter what. It'll be a birthday present for myself, he'd thought at the time. *A new formal robe, and a fresh hit of that scent. Maybe this will be the one that does it. That makes her look. That makes her answer. Maybe, maybe—*

It appeared, through some tectonic movement of chance, that he'd fallen from the sky and directly into the lap of the woman he'd been hunting for a decade.

CHAPTER NINE

HE THOUGHT IT WAS LIKELY THAT HE WAS STILL drugged. It was the only explanation that made sense to him. How else could he have ended up in Alashiya's kitchen?

Taevas felt like he'd stepped back in time, or flown through a portal into an alternate universe, one where he was no one, nothing, and yet had everything he'd longed for.

He vividly recalled the first time he'd opened a package and beheld Alashiya's work. All dragons had a keen eye for luxury, particularly when it came to textiles. They had tough but exquisitely sensitive skin, particularly on the undersides of their wings, so they were predisposed to being extraordinarily picky when it came to their clothing and bedding.

Taevas was pickier than most. He'd earned it. He'd kept so little of and for himself when he became Isand. Never having to feel the discomfort of filthy, homespun clothing or using rags for nesting seemed like a harmless but necessary indulgence.

Over the years, he'd touched the finest fabrics and spent hundreds of thousands of dollars on his textiles — everything from tapestries to bath towels to custom suits. He knew luxury and craftsmanship at a glance.

So when he laid his eyes on the embroidered sash in a display case in a New York atelier specializing in magically-enhanced garments, he knew immediately that he'd stumbled upon a treasure.

That's all it was at first: an honest appreciation of skill. He'd bought all the atelier had, to the delight of the sales associate, and proudly wore his pieces until he had an opportunity to request something custom. That was when things changed.

The pieces he bought from the atelier had been there for some time. They smelled of aged fabric, the indefinable but unmistakable city scent, and the owner's overpowering cologne. Nothing offensive, but nothing particularly desirable, either. But his commissioned piece — a silk shirt he'd sent to be customized with sigilwork and a flame motif — had returned to him smelling like the artisan herself.

Cypress. Woman. Home.

It'd startled him the first time. The scent perfumed the air around the open box. It saturated the tissue paper that carefully guarded the shirt. It clung to the fibers of the card included with the package. A delicate pressed flower, a white thing he had no hope of identifying, fell into the palm of his hand as he extracted the note.

Thank you for your order! I hope you like the design. I loved every stitch. -A

The handwriting was delicate and loopy, exactly the kind he'd expect from an artist. And the scent of the card...

Taevas wasn't a man moved by much. He'd experienced too much too quickly — ascended to the very summit of feeling so young that everything that had come since seemed to him a precipitous fall. Privately, he suspected that something vital had been broken in him. That mechanism that allowed his kin to chase their instincts, the wildest swings of their emotions, had a crack down its center.

It made him a good Isand. He wasn't prone to fits or getting drunk on his own ego. He could see things objectively and didn't run into trouble chasing his own high. His swagger was based entirely on objective fact, along with a keen understanding of exactly what he could get away with. Mating instincts didn't cloud his judgment. Lust was blessedly clinical, and he harbored no secret desire to share his life with someone he could lose.

It wasn't happiness, exactly, but it wasn't misery, either. Taevas existed at a pleasant equilibrium, and he took joy in his clan every chance he got. There was nothing missing from his life. If other dragons looked askance at him the longer he went without seeking out a mate, then they knew better than to mention it.

And then a flower fell into his palm, its nearly translucent petals turned lavender by the color of his skin, and he scented her for the first time.

The only thing he could equate it to was having a fuse pop in his brain. In an instant, he'd gone painfully hard, his mind blank. A soft, pleasant buzz filled his ears as he pressed his nose into the silk shirt. He'd shoved his hand down his slacks before he'd even thought the action through. It was utterly mindless, the animal urge that saw him pawing at his cock like he'd just discovered what to do with it.

There was no reason. Just the scent of her, so soft and earthy and warm, was enough to get him off. It was pure luck that his assistant hadn't stuck around after delivering the box. There was no one to see him squeeze the swollen head of his cock or hear the wet sounds of his fingers moving up and down the slick shaft as pre-come slid from it. There were no witnesses to the way his balls drew up tight against his body, his hips lifted from his seat, or the way his lips peeled back from his teeth in a snarl that was all pleasure-pain.

He swore he could feel her soft skin. He could taste her on his tongue — sweet and earthy and perfect. It wasn't just lust that compelled him, but the roaring need to claim, to mark. He needed his seed splashed across all that beautiful, warm skin. He needed to feel her cunt dripping against his hungry tongue. He needed her to tell him who she belonged to, and see the dark, flushed purple shaft of his cock disappear into the hot well of her body. He needed, needed, *needed...*

Her.

The image of her in his mind was a shifting thing, but it didn't seem to matter. He thrust into his fist with jagged rolls of his hips, his mind full of her. Her sighs and soft, fluttering touches were as real as his own hand.

She'd sound as sweet as she tasted. He knew it instinctively. She'd be supple and pliant and giving. It was in her scent, the very essence of her that fogged his mind.

He could see her in the nest, on her hands and knees with her fingers twisted into the blankets, her ass up and ready for him. He'd coil his tail around the crease of her thigh, right where the wetness gleamed, and he'd drape his wings over them both as he came down over her, caging her in. She'd never escape him. She'd never want to.

He could feel the satisfaction of thrusting inside her, knowing that she was *his*. No one could have her. No one could even *look* at her. She was his treasure and he'd fill her up again and again and again until—

Taevas didn't regain some tiny shred of reason until he came with a pathetic groan into his fist, his spend sliding over his violet knuckles until it dripped onto his slacks. The drops landed right beside the pressed flower, which had fluttered onto his thigh, making the scene appear like some artistic homage to perversion.

It was an earth-shattering experience, having his control stolen from him for the first time.

Taevas Aždaja didn't lose his mind. He certainly didn't jerk his cock to the scent of *clothing,* for pity's sake.

He'd run from his sitting room and directly into the shower, like he could rinse off the slimy, revolting feeling of losing control as easily as he could wash his seed down the drain.

The obvious result was that he shoved the shirt in a drawer and didn't look at it for months. He nearly threw it away but hadn't been able to stomach putting something so beautiful in the trash. The artisan had worked literal and figurative magic with her needle and thread, creating an art nouveau motif around the cuffs and collar. She'd no doubt spent hours and hours doing it. Though she would never know he'd thrown out her hard work, *he* would.

In the end, despite his revulsion at his lack of control, he couldn't force his claws to unlock their grip.

The shirt stayed, unseen but quietly obsessed over, until the memory of her scent weakened him enough to dig it out again. Even months later, the faint trace of her lingered in its fibers. It was made all the more potent, he grimly discovered, by the addition of his own. When their scents combined, it didn't just smell like the best sex of his life. It smelled like home.

He put in another order the next day.

Taevas wasn't entirely sure how it happened, except that it must have been in increments and through constant renegotiation with himself. It became something of an internal hostage negotiation — one of constant compromise with an ever-increasingly demanding aggressor.

He put rules on his obsession, hoping to manage it, but they were never enough.

Taevas couldn't seek her out, though something in him frothed with the need. It was precisely that need which solidified his resolve.

Control, renegotiation, control.

If he wanted to indulge his whims, he could only do so with the stipulation that he could never, ever hunt her down. Rules were control of the seemingly uncontrollable. It put him back on top of a beast that threatened to eat him whole.

One order turned into two, then two dozen. He renegotiated with himself again and again, making allowances, fighting for control over himself and the growing monster of his need.

No one was allowed to touch the garments except the artisan, he demanded. Not even the owner of the atelier. That concession to the needy beast came with the rule that Taevas couldn't order anything that might hint at his obsession, let alone his desire, and he couldn't, under any circumstance, communicate directly with the artisan herself.

It was a series of checks and balances, the rules that he needlessly and painfully enforced on himself. And it was precisely those rigid guidelines that had the exact opposite result of their intended purpose. Rather than keep a lid on the strange obsession he had with her, it dripped fuel on the fire, one syrupy droplet at a time.

He saved every notecard and flower she sent with the orders. One day it became more than just sexual desire, but the driving need to place her scent everywhere — in his nest, his living room, his office, his jet. *Another allowance. Another negotiation.*

He carried something of hers always, or else he couldn't focus properly. Over time, he began to notice a hum in the clothing itself, as if he became a flesh and blood lightning rod for her unique tenor of magic. He had no magic himself, so he couldn't properly say whether it was his growing sensitivity to it or a real change, but Taevas could've sworn that she put more and more of herself into the stitches over the years.

Every new garment he received practically glowed with it. When he delicately shrugged his arms and wings into a new shirt, he could feel the warmth of her magic as it settled into his very pores. He never felt as safe as he did when he wore something she'd touched. He never felt as close to another being as when her magic curled around him with a sensual, loving caress. To go without it now was unthinkable.

Another. Another. Another.

It didn't happen all at once. In fact, it was slow enough that he barely noticed the extent to which he'd integrated her into his life until she was already everywhere.

And he didn't even know her name.

For seven years, he'd indulged himself. For seven years, he'd rigidly upheld his rules, his distance, for fear of what would become of him if he gave in.

Until the day Theodore Solbourne, his unwilling elvish protege, made headlines all over the world with his shocking elopement. Taevas had nearly spat out his coffee when the headline crossed his morning briefing.

"Sovereign and Healer? The Match of the Century!"

And there the elf was, pictured with his gloved hand on the nape of a young witch's neck. They only had eyes for each other as they climbed into the back of a town car. Their marriage sigils were fresh, and the symbol of a union that shattered generations of destructive elvish dogma. Elves hadn't been free to take outsiders as mates in a thousand years, but little Teddy had just gone and done the damn thing.

Taevas had been proud. He'd bugged the boy to throw that shit out from the moment he came to power. It took some serious balls to do it the way little Teddy had, but Taevas couldn't fault him for style — or taste. Margot Goode was lovely, if one liked breakable-looking, somewhat-spooky witches.

But that pride faded quicker than Taevas would've liked. He was left staring at the happy, improbable couple. Something in his chest went missing. Maybe it had never been there, but its absence had been a comfortable habit. Staring at their smitten faces, he felt it keenly for the first time in nearly a century.

Loneliness, he'd realized, thumbing the crimson stitching of his shirt's cuff. His artisan had outdone herself with a new geometric design, and he loved tracing each little loop of thread.

He counted the stitches and thought of her as he looked at Teddy's boyish grin. That hollow feeling grew and grew until it swallowed up the last pitiful reserves of his decency.

It was perhaps a cruel but justified turn when the atelier's associate refused to give him her name. *"It's a matter of privacy, sir,"* they'd explained, oozing unctuousness. *"But I'd be happy to pass a message along."*

What could he say? Taevas had hung up, irritated with himself and the associate and even his artisan, his *metsalill.*

The Isand's precious, elusive wildflower.

He tried again, a few weeks later when the sting of his weakness had faded, but received the same answer. The next attempt, his pride gave way and he did what they suggested. Taevas sent along a message, asking if the artisan would be willing to speak to him personally.

A day later he'd gotten a response — from the owner of the atelier himself. *"I'm so sorry, Isand, but she's a very private person. While she appreciates your patronage immensely, she prefers to communicate via the Atelier. I'm sure you understand."*

Rejection was an unfamiliar and galling experience. Who was she to refuse to speak to *him*, Taevas Aždaja, Lord of the Dragon Clans and Isand of the Draakonriik, war hero, the youngest leader to sign the Peace Charter, the patron who'd spent hundreds of thousands of dollars commissioning her over nearly a decade, the man who spent every waking hour trying not to think of her—

He'd been forced by pride and self-preservation to remove himself from the situation. A large part of him was relieved, believing that he'd finally found his limit and the obsession would die off, but it didn't last.

It *never* lasted.

It only took another one of her notes, delivered with a parcel he hadn't ordered.

I know this isn't your usual style, but the flowers in my garden are in bloom. They made me think of your colors. Thank you for all your support over the years. I look forward to every new project more than I can say. I hope you're well. -A

It was a gift. His artisan had sent him an oval-shaped embroidery hoop. The fabric stretched within it was nearly translucent. The stitches were so small, so fine, that they were only tiny flashes of jewel tones holding real pressed wildflowers in place. It was the single most beautiful piece of textile work he'd ever seen — and he'd beheld her skill with real gold and scarab beetle shells and crystal beads. Nothing compared to it. To what she'd chosen to give *him*.

He crumbled. The great Isand, with his immense pride, was felled by the petals of a few wildflowers.

Some rules had to remain in place, for his sake and hers. He couldn't allow himself to use the full force of his influence, nor his resources. It would violate the sacred thing that had bloomed between them. Taint it. He didn't want to force his way into her life by demanding the atelier divulge her information or having spies track her down.

Not only would it be a horrific misuse of his power, but it would violate her right to keep him away. It was more than likely she was one of his citizens. Using his position to find her felt ugly. Taevas was obsessed, but he wasn't a monster. More than that, he wanted *her* to come to *him*.

So he continued, little by little, to needle the atelier. In return, they continued to demure, alternating between respecting her privacy and simply brushing off his requests. After a time, he got the feeling that their refusal wasn't entirely based on his artisan's wishes, which ignited a cold, quiet fury, but he didn't dare press too hard, lest they cut him off entirely.

It seemed unlikely, given his patronage over the years, let alone his position, but he couldn't risk it. The out of control thing in him wouldn't allow it.

He began sending gifts. Bolts of the finest fabric and silk thread for her own use. Art that reminded him of her work. A new chair and work table designed specifically for sewists, to save their backs. He would've sent diamonds the size of robin eggs, gifts of food, blankets made of the finest materials, exotic flowers, or even money — if only he could be certain any of it would make it to her.

As it happened, he could only believe what the atelier told him, which was that they passed everything along. His artisan's notes never mentioned his gifts, however, so he couldn't be certain. The notes were sweet, always thanking him for his patronage, and usually included some tiny, abstract detail about her life.

This design was inspired by my grandfather.

This color reminded me of my favorite tea.

I know you asked for maroon, but I'm sure you'll like plum better. It's my favorite color.

He didn't care what she sent him anymore. He'd wear anything. He *did* wear anything. Taevas wore her creations as often as he was able, and he tried his best to make sure he was photographed. Over the years he began to develop an even flashier reputation than he previously possessed, but he didn't care. It was all part of the plan to get his artisan's attention, somehow, someway.

Look at me, he demanded, flashing a wink over the rim of his sunglasses at a photographer. He always imagined it was her behind the lens. *See how proud I am to wear your work. Talk to me. Please, gods, just talk to me.*

Three years he'd been holding onto the fraying threads of his decency, his control, waiting with bated breath for her to reach out to him.

Never, in the decade of imaginings, did he think that he would simply... stumble across her. And never could he have dreamed that she would be more beautiful, more interesting, *more mysterious* than the phantom he'd crafted to fill that hollow place in his chest.

Nothing about it made sense. How could fate have worked so perfectly, so cruelly, as to thrust them together *now?*

Chapter Ten

Hours after they came to an understanding in the kitchen, Alashiya sighed, "I hate being behind."

Stalton had withheld her payment for a month the last time she'd asked for an extension. She couldn't afford to take that kind of hit again, or worse — risk the atelier cutting ties with her altogether.

Her grove had been doing business with them since her grandparents first came to the UTA. The atelier sold her grove's work and took a cut for their efforts. Once, their work had been in high demand from many shops and designers, but now the demand for handmade embroidery was much lower.

She was lucky that Stalton still commissioned her, and even luckier that Adon continued to request her work. Alashiya couldn't risk alienating either of them.

So she worked into the evening, until she was forced to turn on a lamp, and then worked some more, pretending all the while that she wasn't hyper-aware of the dragon that watched her from the doorway. The tips of her right thumb and index finger grew red and sore from the constant push and pull of the needle. Her back ached. Her eyes began to burn from the strain of focusing on such small details for so long.

It wasn't until the dragon made a low rumbling noise that she realized she was hungry, too. She'd missed dinner again.

Alashiya sat back in her chair with a low groan. Flexing her right hand came with some difficulty. Her muscles were locked in position. Trying to massage some life back into them, she dared to glance at the dragon, whose snout just barely touched the threshold of the door.

"I don't make for good entertainment," she dryly noted. "I bet watching me work is a bit like watching paint dry."

The dragon's great head tilted. She had no idea if it was an agreement or not.

"I embroider things for a living. Clothing, mostly. My specialty is goldwork — embroidery with threads wrapped in gold wire. My family has been doing it for centuries. I do other things too, but this is what I'm best at." She watched the light reflect off the gold the atelier sent with the order slip and the garment, her tired mind caught in a swirling current of memory.

The spirits of her grove, many ancient beyond reckoning and those she'd known in life, twined their stories and their skills into a branching silken thread. It was her duty to guard that thread, to add her own fiber to its length, and to pass it on to another.

And it was the greatest grief of her life to know with perfect certainty that she would fail.

Shaking off the familiar thought, she continued with false cheer, "I learned from my mother's line. My father's people come from the seaside, so they did things differently. They were famous for their dyes, and were some of the first to make purple. Our cloth dressed royalty for thousands of years." A smile quirked the corner of her mouth when she cast the dragon a look. "Not everyone comes by it naturally, you know."

He said nothing, of course, but something in his eyes caught her. They held each other's stare for what felt like a long time. Too long.

The hook in her chest jerked. She looked away, breathless and alarmed by the near-physical pull that overcame her whenever he was near. Alashiya chalked it up to nerves, but that didn't make it tolerable.

Flushing, she shook herself. The dragon had no interest in listening to the story of her ancient line, their triumphs and the failures that led to her. To the end. It was even less likely that he had any desire to hear about her work. No doubt a dragon lived a far more exciting life than hers. She lived safely by design, but that didn't mean it was anything he wanted to hear about.

Gods, *she* didn't even want to hear it.

Levering herself up from her chair, she stretched her tired muscles before approaching the doorway. The dragon graciously moved aside as much as he was able, allowing her to enter the kitchen.

The kitchen had been expanded to accommodate her grove, meaning it was far larger than she'd ever needed it to be, but only just big enough to accommodate a huge dragon and herself at the same time.

Trying to cast aside bleak visions of the future, she squeezed around her guest to begin fixing herself a late dinner. "Anyway, I'm behind on a commission. I've got to finish that project this week or I'm screwed."

The dragon's low rumble made itself known over the sound of sauteing onions. Alashiya had no hope of figuring out what it meant, so she pretended he'd made a noise of interest and continued her one-sided conversation. "I've never met a dragon before. I bet you have an interesting job. Everyone around here is either an outdoor recreation guide or a farmer. The most exciting job I know of is being a ranger, but I wouldn't want to do that, personally."

Chopping up the bounty from her garden using an ancient cleaver and a well-loved butcher block, she wryly added, "Not that they'd want a nymph, of course. The rangers are almost all shifters — mostly wolves and bears. A couple of elk. They're the scariest, I think. There are some humans, too — arrants and witches both. They have to be really tough to keep up with all the shifters. Every once in a while, an orc does a rotation here, but that's about as exciting as it gets."

Alashiya scraped her vegetables into her cast iron pan and gave them a good stir. Wooden spoon in hand, she half-turned to give the dragon a questioning look. "Have you met any nymphs before?"

He lay on the kitchen floor, his chin propped on his forelegs and his gaze locked on her. He blinked slowly before shaking his head.

"Figured as much." She hid her dismay by quickly turning back around. It wasn't like she was surprised, but it pained her to think of how few nymphs there were in this part of the world. How disconnected they all were.

Once, they'd all been part of a vast, intimately intertwined network. They'd all been linked by that silken thread. Now they were little islands struggling to survive as time and change eroded the sand beneath their feet.

"We're very private." Alashiya's gaze lowered to the pan. She cleared her throat. "I wish you could talk. I'd love to hear about dragons. I've embroidered them before, but I've embroidered all sorts of things over the years. I've never gotten the chance to meet one before you, and they don't star in any of the books I inherited from my aunt. She had a preference for orcs, then gargoyles and harpies."

The dragon made a derisive sound deep in his throat. There was no way to know whether she was correct or not, but Alashiya thought he was a little offended.

"Don't get upset. *I* don't have a preference."

It was true enough. Her image of Adon swung wildly between beings. Depending on the day, she could imagine him as a gargoyle at breakfast, a merman at lunch — particularly unrealistic, that one — and an arrant by dinnertime. For dessert, she might picture an elf, just to shake things up a bit. She knew from his garments that he had wings, but what did that matter when he could be anything in her imagination?

Moving away from the stove, she missed the way the dragon's violet gaze followed her with rapt attention, his eyes narrowed and nostrils flared.

"I'd love to know what your life is like," she continued, her focus on whipping up a sauce with yogurt she made from scratch every week and the massive garlic bulb she cut down from a braid hanging in her window. "I only know what I learned in school, but that was ages ago now. Well, school and what Debbie tells me when she recaps her soap operas. I can't imagine that's too reliable, though."

Peering over her shoulder, she asked, "Do you all live in skyscrapers?"

The dragon moved slowly across the floor. His great body sprawled until one side pressed against the cabinets by where she stood. A peculiar tingle swept through her when she realized he was trying to get closer to her.

Fortunately for her, a soft rattling noise drew her attention away from the flush in her cheeks and down to his tail, which curved around the edge of the room to lay near her feet.

Resting his chin on his forelegs, the dragon nodded twice.

"Oh, is that a *some do, some don't* kind of answer?"

He nodded.

Alashiya concentrated on her sauce as she tried to picture what that would look like. Casting him a quick look, she asked, "Do you?"

She really wasn't sure how he managed it, but the dragon looked downright *haughty* when he nodded again. His upper lip curled, too, like he was offended she even had to ask.

"I've never seen a skyscraper in person," she admitted, leaning over him to stir her vegetables and add a splash of olive oil. "I wonder what it's like to live so high off the ground." She flashed him an embarrassed smile. "But you can fly, so I guess it all seems really second nature to you, doesn't it?"

The dragon said nothing, of course. He watched her silently, his great body occasionally wracked with tremors. The bandages she'd painstakingly reapplied stood out starkly against his dark skin. It was really difficult to remain wary of him when he was sprawled on her kitchen floor like that, but his expression was hard to decipher. She really couldn't tell if her chatter was annoying him or not.

Hunching her shoulders a little, she focused on finishing her dinner. "Sorry if I'm bothering you. I should probably be letting you rest in quiet, not talking your ear off and asking questions you can't even answer right now." She flicked the dial on the stove, turning off the gas, and then began to spoon her dinner into an earthenware bowl. "I don't get visitors and I don't have any pets, so it's nice to be able to talk to someone."

Lifting her bowl off the counter, she sucked in a quick breath and turned to give the dragon a nervous smile. "You really should get some sleep, so I'll eat in my room."

She'd only taken a step or two when that coiled tail snaked across the floor to drape across the doorway, barring her exit. Alashiya shot the dragon a confused look over her shoulder and found him peering at her intently, his lips peeled back from his teeth and a low rumble emanating from his throat.

"What?" She looked back and forth between the dragon and his tail. "Do you not want me to eat in my room?"

He shook his head. The small action seemed to cost him, as he almost immediately laid his head back down on his forelegs. His gaze went in and out of focus for a moment before he blinked and let out a chuff.

A rush of weightlessness made her head spin a little when she whispered, "Do you want me to stay with you for a while?"

The dragon gave her a tiny nod and dipped his chin toward the floor in front of him. Alashiya hesitated a moment. He seemed to be telling her that he wanted her to sit with him, but she'd been wrong about reading him before. The urge to ask for clarification prompted her to open her mouth, but it closed just as quickly when another set of tremors shook his powerful frame.

Empathy squeezed her heart in a vice.

"Okay, I'll just..." Alashiya shuffled toward the dragon and slowly lowered herself to the floor. She didn't dare sit *too* close, but she didn't sit as far away as she could've, either.

The floor was cool under her bare legs as she folded them beneath her. Settling the warm bowl in her lap, she got into a more comfortable position and peeked at the dragon through her lashes.

He watched her from beneath lowered lids, his pupils huge and quivering against the backdrop of his violet irises. His nostrils flared with every breath, and as she arranged her skirt over her thighs, his tail dragged sluggishly across the floor to loop loosely behind her. She could *just* feel it against the base of her spine.

Goosebumps broke out along her arms whenever she felt that glancing contact, but she didn't move away. Flustered, Alashiya tried to ignore it as she picked up her fork and began to eat.

It was more than a little awkward, sitting there in silence and being watched while she ate, but the dragon looked more relaxed than before, so she hoped that meant he was happy. A warm glow suffused her at the thought that she'd brought a little comfort to him.

Pushing her food around her bowl, she said, "You know, you really scared me when you first got here, and you were definitely a little rude, but I'm sorry you're in pain right now. I wish I could do more to help you."

The dragon made a soft rumble deep in his throat. It was a comforting sort of sound, though she couldn't exactly put her finger on why that was. His tail pressed more firmly against her back. Alashiya looked away quickly, embarrassed by the way her eyes went misty. It felt a lot like a hug.

It'd been a very long time since anyone hugged her.

Clearing her throat, she set aside the remains of her dinner. Her stomach did somersaults as she scooted just a bit closer to him. The dragon's gaze sharpened with interest. Lifting his head as much as he was able, he gestured toward the spot on the floor right beside his foreleg.

"Um..." She hesitated, already embarrassed that she wanted to be near him at all. He was a stranger who couldn't even communicate with her properly. It wasn't appropriate to get up close and personal, let alone *safe*. Who knew what he was really capable of? Sure, the evening had been pleasant enough, but anyone could pretend to be friendly. It didn't mean she should ask for a cuddle.

The dragon's tail nudged her. When she still didn't move, he let out a huff and made what looked like a great effort to roll slightly to one side and stretch his neck toward her. Before she'd properly grasped his intentions, he'd laid his head in her lap.

It was damn heavy. Alashiya grunted and adjusted the position of her legs under his bulk. Her heart lurched just as it had that morning, when he did the same thing as she changed his bandages.

Her bruises still ached and her knee was painfully swollen from their rough introduction, but it was hard to square *that* dragon with *this* one, who seemed to crave comfort and her nearness so openly.

It was a little strange to think that a being so fierce could need those sorts of things. She'd always thought that if she had claws or could breathe fire, she'd never fear anything again, but that didn't appear to be the case. Apparently even dragons needed soothing every once in a while.

At least, that's what she thought he was after. It was entirely possible he just needed a pillow.

Not really knowing what to do but drawn toward him anyway, Alashiya hesitated for only a few seconds before she tentatively traced the shape of one great, arcing horn. Her breath stalled as she followed its elegant curvature.

Seemingly pleased with her nervous exploration, the dragon pressed one side of his face into her middle like a great, attention-seeking cat.

A breathless laugh escaped her. It quickly changed into a squeak when the dragon didn't stop with a nudge, but rather used his considerable bulk to tip her backward onto the floor.

She squeezed her eyes shut, prepared for the jolt and explosive pain of her head cracking against the tiles, but it didn't come. Instead, she let out an *oomph* when her head landed on his tail, which had swung around to cushion her fall. She thought it was a small miracle she hadn't hurt herself on one of its spikes, until she glanced backward to find he'd tipped it to the side.

Startled, she pressed a hand to the floor and made to lever herself up again, but was stopped by the dragon laying his head flat on her middle, his chin touching her collar bones and the weight of him pressed down on her breasts and stomach. His breath huffed loudly beneath her chin and stirred her hair.

Very aware that she was now in an exquisitely vulnerable position not unlike when he had her pinned by the trough and seemed seconds away from *roasting her alive,* Alashiya gasped, "What are you *doing?*"

The dragon let out a deep, thrumming sound. She hadn't the slightest clue what it meant, but he didn't seem like he had any immediate plans to attack her.

Good gods, she thought, watching those massive eyes close, *he really is using me as a mattress.*

"You know," she muttered, "if you wanted a pillow so bad, I could've gotten you one. And I'm only giving you five minutes like this. We're *not* doing a repeat of when you got here. You're not keeping me on the kitchen floor all night, okay? My back can't take it."

The dragon cracked an eye open. It looked a little glazed, but she thought she spied some acquiescence there, too.

Bit by bit, she relaxed beneath him. The dragon seemed to only be seeking some comfort, so she tried not to let worry consume her as the minutes passed. It certainly wasn't the most comfortable position to be in, but she didn't mind it so much when she passed the time gently tracing the fascinating shapes of his face with the tips of her fingers. She probably shouldn't have, seeing as he was a person and not an animal to be petted, but he didn't seem to have any complaints.

A content rumble filled the kitchen, and for reasons she didn't want to examine too closely, Alashiya lingered there beneath him long after the five minute limit passed.

Eventually the discomfort won out, though, forcing her to nudge him until he reluctantly lifted his head off her chest. Feeling shy, she said nothing as she worked some blood back into her sleeping limbs by hobbling out of the kitchen. She still couldn't quite look at him when she returned with the things he said he didn't need: a few plush pillows and a blanket.

Whatever he meant about not needing blankets before didn't seem to apply anymore. Almost as soon as she laid the pillows down, he pressed his snout into them and closed his eyes.

Feeling that familiar tightening in her chest, she draped the blanket over as much of him as she could reach before tiptoeing out of the kitchen.

Considering how she'd spent the last half hour on the kitchen floor with him, Alashiya felt silly for closing the door into the hallway, but he *was* still a stranger. One good, oddly tender evening didn't mean she wanted to sleep with her door open and wake up to find him watching her or something.

Alashiya could hear his breathing as she settled into her slightly depleted mound of blankets, pillows, and mattresses by the hearth. It was too warm for a fire, so she stared past the iron grate and strained to listen to the beast in the other room. There was the distinct sound of his tail *swush-swushing* across the tile before the dragon let out a long, gusty sigh.

She listened to the air whooshing in and out of those massive lungs for a while before the sound lulled her to sleep.

CHAPTER ELEVEN

THE FOLLOWING DAYS MOVED AT AN ALMOST IDENTICAL rhythm. Alashiya got a little bolder. It was nice having someone to talk to, even if they couldn't talk back, and she didn't mind taking her meals on the floor or even how heavy his head was when he pushed it into her lap.

When they had their one-sided conversations, she said nothing of importance but chatted with him in the way she would with Debbie down at the general store or the less terrifying rangers. She spoke of how nice the weather was, how happy the plants were with the summer storms, and speculated about whether they'd get any tornadoes this year.

"One nearly took the barn last summer," she told him, "and a few years back, a big chunk of the house's roof was torn off. Luckily it was the side I don't use."

That was one of the rare times she caught the dragon looking anywhere but her. He'd stared at the pans hung up on the kitchen wall for nearly ten minutes, a deep, terrifying growl rumbling from his chest. His tail rattled violently, too, which was always a little unsettling, since one swipe of those spikes would see her needing more than a few stitches.

When he turned his attention back to her, she reassured him,

"Don't worry. I'm sure you'd survive a tornado, and I have a storm cellar, so I'd probably be okay."

She hoped it'd make him feel better — if she was reading his body language correctly — but it might've done the opposite, because he looked at her like she'd lost her mind for a while after that.

Alashiya didn't like to talk while she worked, since she was so used to silence, but during her minimal breaks, she enjoyed asking him yes or no questions. That was how she discovered he was over a century old, that he enjoyed sweets, and that he liked his job.

She avoided tougher subjects that would require more explanation, like how he ended up in her barn, what danger he was in, or what his name was. Truthfully, she didn't need or want to know those things. His trouble wasn't hers. She'd done her part, and she didn't think the gods would find fault in her treatment of her guest, considering the circumstances.

Every hour saw his wounds healing faster than hers ever would. While she still sported a cut on her brow, his deepest wounds were already scabs. Perched on one of the pillows she'd lent him, Alashiya carefully cut away his stitches after only three days.

She knelt before him on the kitchen floor and gathered up the old, bloody thread. "That's done, then," she announced, trying to sound pleased. "No more stitches. Unless you've got other issues I can't see, I think you should be good to go. Do you think you'll be able to shift soon?"

The dragon nodded once. A pang of loss struck her, but it was there and gone in an instant. It was nice having another being around. Really nice. She knew that she'd been lonely, but she hadn't quite realized how much until an injured dragon burst into her life, demanding her attention.

That didn't mean she wanted the dragon to stay, especially when he was for all intents and purposes stuck in her kitchen, but she didn't exactly want him to leave, either.

Climbing to her feet, she moved to dispose of the old

bandages and thread in the trash. "You know, I think I'll get a cat when you leave," she announced. "A big tomcat who likes to walk with me in the garden and sleep by the fire."

Padding to the sink, she soaped up the soiled bowl. Speaking with no small amount of false cheer, she continued, "I can walk you into town when you're ready. It's not too far. Only about an hour away. There's a ranger station, a library, and a general store. You can use the phone or computer at the library to contact your people. We can also walk to the Thompsons' farm, but they just have a phone, so that limits your options—"

A strange current of air buffeted her back. There was a shuffling sound, an unsteady gasp, then: "No one can know I'm here, *metsalill.*"

The bowl slid out of her slippery hands and crashed into the basin of the sink. Shards of glass exploded around her, which was only half as surprising as hearing a man's throaty voice.

Alashiya tried to twist around, but strong hands clasped her upper arms, holding her still. "Don't move," the voice commanded. "Some glass got on the floor. You'll cut your feet."

"Better than having a stranger at my back," she croaked. Her soapy hands trembled against the lip of the sink. That hook in her chest tugged hard, back through her ribs and spine, toward *him.*

"I've slept in your dwelling. You've cleaned my blood off your hands and threatened me with a wooden spoon. I hardly think I'm a stranger."

Alashiya begged to differ. She hadn't put much thought into what it would be like when the dragon could shift back, only that it meant he'd be able to leave at last. Her guest being a *person,* a living and breathing and sapient man, had been an entirely abstract concept.

It was a bizarre thing to realize she'd become so very comfortable with the fire-breathing dragon. Now he'd been replaced by a person, and Alashiya was once again wrong-footed.

"I..." Her throat, lips, and tongue were all out of sync. She couldn't form a sentence, but even if she could, she had no idea

what she'd planned to say. A part of her maintained a wild hope
that if she stood still and silent for long enough, he'd disappear as
quickly as he'd come.

"Easy." It was a husky whisper above her head. Warm breath
stirred the curly wisps there. "You're safe, my Shiya."

Am I? That sounds like something a murderer would say.

How was it that she felt so much safer dealing with a dragon
than a man? Her heart thundered in her chest and a clammy sweat
broke out along the length of her spine.

"Um... I don't— I'm sorry. I don't know what to do." She
shuffled back half a step and froze when her back met a solid wall
of warm muscle. Alashiya tensed. The hands on her arms did too.
Clawtips pressed into the soft flesh of her upper arms, but they
didn't prick her. Yet.

She glanced warily down at one of the hands. It was the same
night-time color as the dragon — a deep, velvety black with a
crimson sheen wherever the light hit it. It was also about three
times the size of her own. A wave of dizziness overcame her as she
imagined how easy it would be for hands like that to destroy a
nymph.

"Shiya, I said don't move. You must learn to listen to me.
There's glass." The voice had lost its soothing tone and instead
became very stern.

She cast a wild-eyed glance to the ground. Shards of glass glittered around her and a pair of alien feet. They weren't shaped
quite like hers. The arch was a lot higher, and there were only four
toes. Alashiya stared at them in bewilderment for a moment
before she noticed something else.

Snapping her head back up, she squeaked, "Are you *naked?*"

A deep, familiar rumble tickled her back. "Not if you don't
look."

"You're either wearing clothes or you're not," she protested.
"It doesn't matter if I see it!"

"I thought nymphs were free spirits who didn't care about

nudity. You told me yourself that your grove used to walk through the woods nude."

The feeling of being cornered began to tingle like static beneath her skin. She'd told that story to the dragon, not to this man. In hindsight, she'd told the dragon a lot of things she probably wouldn't have told a strange man.

Alashiya shot a furtive look at the kitchen door. "I care about it when a strange man without pants is in my house."

"There are many people in this world who'd be delighted to find me naked in their house."

She honestly couldn't tell if he was joking or genuinely bragging. Either way, it didn't endear him to her in the slightest. Leaning toward the sink, she primly replied, "Go find one of them, then."

Appearing not to hear her, the dragon let go of her arms in favor of cupping her waist. His hands were so big, his fingertips nearly touched when they spanned her ribs. "I'm going to lift you over the glass, *metsalill*. I'm still not as strong as I should be, so don't wriggle too much."

Alarmed, she sputtered, "Wait, wait—" Her protest ended in a small squeal of surprise as he hoisted her into the air.

The kitchen blurred as he spun her around. For a moment, her world was all dark skin and long raven hair. Then he settled her on her feet across the room. Alashiya blinked rapidly, trying to clear her head of dizziness, and angled her neck to peer at the towering form of the dragon.

He stood there, trembling wings mantled, broad shoulders pushed back, and violet eyes glinting in the low light. The smallest, anticipatory smile revealed a sliver of shockingly white teeth. His nose was proud, almost hawkish, and the rest of his features were just as bold. Thin streaks of gray framed his temples and ran down the length of his long black hair, the majority of which was held back by an intimidating set of four horns.

Alashiya had never seen, let alone imagined, a being like him.

Even riddled with scabbed-over cuts and the shadow of

bruises, he was beautiful. More than beautiful. He was the kind of stunning that evoked a deep and instinctive urge to fight or hide or destroy the thing that was too beautiful to exist.

And he was *terrifying*.

The dragon's gaze roved across her face, the whites of his eyes flashing with every pass. Those massive hands still held her waist. They flexed when he grated, "You have no idea how long I've waited for this, my Shiya."

CHAPTER TWELVE

Taevas hadn't anticipated anything more than this moment in his entire life. It felt bigger than the day the clans finally selected him as Isand of Isands, Dragon of Dragons, Lord of the Clans. It was more momentous than the day he signed the Peace Charter. It was the culmination of a decade of self-denial, yearning, and frustration. It was *her.*

Taevas attributed the way she stared up at him with wide eyes as being star-struck. It happened enough. He was the Isand, after all, and he could only imagine how shocking it would be to have someone like him in his home unexpectedly. She clearly hadn't been able to recognize him in his other form, but there was no possibility of that now.

Hoping to give her a little time to recover herself, he forced his hands away from her waist. "Easy," he murmured, looking her over hungrily. He couldn't touch her, but gods, he could *look.* He'd become an expert at it.

"Take deep breaths now, *metsalill.*"

His fingers flexed. The urge to stroke her arms, to soothe, to feel the heat of her on his palms again, was almost impossible to resist. He managed it, but only barely.

Hoping to distract himself, he asked, "Maybe you would feel more comfortable if I had something to cover myself?"

Dragons didn't bother themselves about nudity. Clothing was for decoration and status more than anything else. He was lucky that he could afford to have much of his wardrobe imbued with magic that allowed it to survive his shift, but many dragons either couldn't afford such luxuries or didn't bother. They lived in the nude half the time anyway, so what was the point of being ashamed of it when they had two legs rather than four?

Taevas had vague memories of his clothing being exchanged for little more than rags during his captivity, which explained why he currently stood nude in Alashiya's kitchen. It was a smart move on his captor's part, considering his clothing could've had tracking devices sewn in, but it filled him with a deep, keen-edged rage at the thought that other beings had laid hands on what his nymph made just for him.

Alashiya gave him a blank look. "Cover..." She blanched. "Oh, yes! Um, I have— I should have something."

She looked harried as she scurried out of the kitchen, her eyes always carefully averted from his cock. Taevas watched her go with a chuckle. It was for the best. He didn't think it would do her any good if he explained why he was half-hard.

Would she bring him the robe he'd commissioned? He had mixed feelings about the garment now, after having seen her work her fingers to the bone on it. It bothered him badly that she worked so hard, but it was undeniable that the piece was a marvel. He could already imagine how grand he'd look with it on — and the pride with which he'd display her skill.

But his nymph didn't bring him the robe he'd paid for. She crept back into the kitchen with what looked like a bundle of off-white linen. "Here. This should fit," she muttered, thrusting it into his arms.

Taevas took it with an arched brow. Shaking out the bundle, he discovered a breezy pair of pants. They appeared to be about the right size, though his tail would prove problematic. He'd just decided to use his thumb claw to split a small hole in the fabric when a troubling thought occurred to him. Turning a sharp look on her, he asked, "Who do these belong to?"

It wasn't unreasonable to assume they might be a commission for someone else, or perhaps something equally innocuous, but Taevas's riotous instincts weren't in the mood to be reasonable. It didn't matter that there were no fresh scents of anyone else in the home, nor that he hadn't seen Alashiya so much as pick up a phone to speak to another person since he'd arrived.

My territory, the new, unreasonable thing in him growled. *My nymph.*

She'd said what he thought was a man's name once before. *Adon.* Were they his? They'd be having a tense discussion if so.

"Does it matter?" Alashiya gave him a peculiar look. "They should fit."

It was on the tip of his tongue to snap that it *did* matter — very much, in fact. If he was going to wear another man's clothes, then it had damn well better not be an ex-lover. Just the thought made him itch to shred the pants into ribbons.

Ridiculous, he scolded himself. Taevas Aždaja didn't get jealous. He didn't throw temper tantrums. So he clenched his jaw and moved to put on the damn pants.

Alashiya made a tiny squeaking sound. "I, uh— I'll give you some privacy!"

He looked up in time to see her rush out of the room again. The hem of her skirt fluttered as she slipped through the doorway, as soft and pretty as her. His annoyance took a backseat to a bloom of warmth.

This is the same woman who threatened a dragon with a wooden spoon, he thought, shaking his head. *And yet she runs when her man puts pants on. Oh, my Shiya, we will have so much fun together.*

It was almost unbearably charming. He fought a smile as he listened to Alashiya move about somewhere just out of sight.

Resigning himself to his task so he could more quickly reunite with his nymph, Taevas delicately sliced a hole suitable for his tail before he slid his legs into the pants. The fly was the old-fashioned button-up kind, which he detested, but after some cursing, Taevas managed to get the pants up and suitably fastened over his needy cock.

His body screamed from the effort, but he ignored it. The soreness, the acute pain of his still-healing wounds, the nausea that churned in his gut, the fever that still burned beneath his skin, and the deeply concerning stiffness of his wings — all of it could wait until he had Alashiya in his sights again.

"I'm decent, *metsalill,*" he called out. When he didn't receive a reply after several beats, Taevas blew out a breath. *So shy.*

Smoothing his hair back behind the points of his ears — and making a note to braid it as soon as he had a proper shower — he padded out of the kitchen and into the hall. The darkness didn't hinder him as he peered down the length of it, wondering what lay beyond. Alashiya never went that way. She seemed to exist entirely in the garden, kitchen, converted living room, and bathroom.

He only vaguely recalled the shape of the house from his delirious trek up the hill and wondered at its size. From where he stood, he could make out four closed doors and then another one at the far end, which presumably led to more rooms. It was quite a large dwelling, though it was painfully low to the ground and in hideous disrepair.

His young cousin Artem had told him horror stories about his Chosen's dwelling, which had needed to be nearly torn down to the studs to be suitable for a dragon's mate and young, but Taevas suspected Alashiya's home was far, far worse off. It was a good thing he wouldn't be wasting his time repairing it, since she'd be much better off in the 'Riik.

Trying not to show his disgust, he turned away from the dark hallway to cross into the living room. Hiding his opinion on the state of things got harder.

He'd only been able to inspect it from the doorway while he

recovered in her kitchen, and from there it hadn't seemed so bad. Stepping over the threshold changed his opinion.

The only saving grace was that it was, without a doubt, entirely *her*. The very walls were saturated with her scent. He could see her touch in every square inch — from her cozy nest to her chaotic workbench to the antique armchair in the little nook by the window and the stack of ancient paperback novels at its feet. It was a cozy little burrow for a woman straight out of a fairytale.

Unfortunately, it was also entirely unacceptable.

Dragons took tremendous pride in their roosts. In fact, a dragon could not be considered grown until they'd left their parents' nest and made their own dwelling. The quality of their roost told the world how much they valued that which was most precious: their nest. The nest was the heart of the home, where Chosen and young were kept safe. One could not have a Chosen without a good nest, and they couldn't have a nest worthy of a Chosen without a fine roost.

A good roost was required to be high up from the ground, for ease of take-off and landing as well as security. They needed to have strong walls, preferably made of stone or more modern materials like steel and concrete, to keep out the weather and enemies alike. Of course, they had to have a nest — the primary bedroom — which came with even stricter requirements like dragon-grade bedding, low light, easy access to a nursery, and more.

Alashiya's home met exactly none of those requirements.

The walls were flimsy wood and chipping plaster. It was a single level on what could only generously be called a hill. Electricity had clearly been added after it was built, because the wiring was on the outside of the walls and evoked old memories of the transition from gas to electricity. What little insulation it possessed appeared to be supplied primarily from fanciful quilts that had been strung up via pins in the plaster. The only source of heat was an old iron stove in the center of the room, which was such a terrible idea it nearly drove him to madness.

Not only was it dangerous merely in its design — the gods knew the last time the chimney had been serviced — but Alashiya *slept beside it* in a pile of flammable bedding. The walls of the home itself were covered in fabric. The room was full of piles of yarn, thread, and just about every flammable thing he could imagine.

As a dragon, fire couldn't harm him, but he balked at the damage that could be done to Alashiya with one stray spark on a blanket. He knew what it was like to lose everything to flame, the complete devastation of one's entire life being reduced to ash. To think that might happen to her was utterly unacceptable.

Taevas surveyed the room with a clenched jaw, his claws curled into tight fists, and tried to get a handle on his revulsion. It was then, of course, that he realized what he'd been too distracted to notice: Alashiya wasn't there.

He turned on his heel and, one hand on the door jamb, swung into the hallway. The door to the bathroom was open, the inside dark. The kitchen was empty. He held very still as his heart began to pound. Straining to listen to a sound, *any* sound, Taevas held his breath.

Nothing.

"Shiya, where did you go?" Dread made his tone harsh, very much the bark of the Isand, when he demanded, "Answer me!"

There was only silence. Alashiya walked with featherlight steps, but even they would've been heard in the complete quiet. He was attuned to any slight rustle of cloth, the rasp of breathing, the shift of weight on old floorboards. There was nothing but a whistle of wind from down the hall.

Ignoring the rising discomfort in his battered body, Taevas took off. The home got stranger as he went, but he barely noticed anything beyond the closed doors as he chased the lingering scent of her in the air. He barreled down the hall, through the door at the far end, and past another string of closed doors. Moonlight came through a ragged, barely covered hole in the ceiling — no doubt a result of the tornado that could've killed Alashiya before he ever got the chance to meet her.

The length of the hall seemed to be somewhat U-shaped, with the kitchen and the living room at one end. At the opposite end there was a tiny entryway with the patina and cobwebs of an abandoned room. The front door, with its peeling paint and rusted fixtures, was left open.

Taevas stood there for half a heartbeat, too stunned to do much else besides stare into the darkened treeline, before instinct kicked in.

His focus narrowed into a familiar point. It was the mindset of a dragon who'd spent his formative years fighting for his life in the sky, where an enemy could appear from above or below in an instant. He didn't think about *why* she might've run, only that she was out there in the dark woods, alone and defenseless. Distantly, he also recognized that she couldn't be allowed to tell anyone of his presence, but that concern took a backseat to his immediate worry for her safety.

Her scent was a faint thread in the air. It nearly blended in with the smell of sun-warmed soil, green things, and fresh air. But even diluted by the summer air, he had no trouble picking it up.

He followed that instinctively, the claws on his toes digging into the soil with the force of every step. She'd gone for the trees. Taevas hissed with pain as he tucked his wings close to his back, wary of getting them caught on spindly branches. Dragons were shit in tight places. Their wings were exquisitely sensitive, and his were injured, making the hunt through a birch forest even less desirable.

But he forged ahead, chasing that wild scent. Her name bubbled up his throat and pressed against the backs of his teeth, but he suspected calling for her would only send her deeper into hiding.

He couldn't risk that. All he had was his nose and the hope that she'd slip up. Nymphs were wild creatures built for this terrain. If she hunkered down somewhere, he doubted he would ever find her.

He hadn't spent ten years pining after her ghost only to lose her the very moment he finally held her in his claws. Taevas Aždaja didn't give up. He didn't *lose*. The needy beast in him refused to let it happen.

He was the motherfucking Isand, and she belonged to *him*.

CHAPTER THIRTEEN

CRASHING THROUGH THE UNDERGROWTH AND heedless of the noise he made, he ruthlessly chased her familiar scent. It clung to leaves that had brushed her curls and the scraggly vines that had the privilege of touching the hem of her dress. There was no visible trail. She appeared to barely bend the foliage even when she must have walked directly through it.

While she apparently floated through tangles and over thorns, Taevas wasn't quite so lucky. It was like the forest fought his every step. Vines snared his ankles, every small opening between trees seemed to shrink into nothing before his eyes. It wasn't long before even his tough skin began to chafe from the constant abrasion of branch, thorn, and weed.

He lost track of how long he searched for her. Pain and fever ravaged his body. It didn't matter. It'd been a long time, but he'd been through far worse. The war had seen to that.

He had no intention of giving up. The only time he paused was when he nearly reached a break in the damn troublesome trees. The wavering image of a wooden fence appeared in the gaps between leaves, and when the wind changed, he could clearly make out the pungent farmyard smell of cows nearby. Alashiya's wards were strong enough to distort the air at the boundary of her land, making it shimmer like heat radiating off a blacktop.

The Thompsons', he thought, pulse jumping. Alashiya had said something about her nearest neighbors being dairy farmers. If her scent trail led to their fence, it stood to reason that she'd gone to them.

Fuck. He slowed down to a pitiful limping gait, one hand propped on his side like it might help ease the pain there. Several ribs had been broken at some point, he suspected, and he hadn't done them any favors by hauling ass through the woods.

If she went to the neighbors, I need to leave. Now.

Even if his wings could hold his weight — *doubtful* — he'd need a damn good head start to give his enemies the slip. It stood to reason that with his injuries, he hadn't flown terribly far when he escaped. If he wanted any chance of getting word to his Wing, then he needed to start moving.

He had to leave her behind.

Taevas came to a halt by an old, straight birch. He braced his palm on the trunk and hunched his shoulders. His wings drooped.

"Damn," he hissed.

To have spent so long hungering for a phantom, only to be forced to give her up... Instinct and pride balked. He wouldn't just be leaving her to her own devices, but in that fucking hovel, perhaps even at the mercy of the enemies that might track him back to her land.

It occurred to him that perhaps this was all a ruse, that she could've been part of the plot in some roundabout way, but he immediately shook that thought loose. He couldn't see any logical reasoning behind using her, nor how they might've predicted where he'd land. If she *was* part of it, her participation would likely only be after he crashed through her barn, which seemed unlikely. He'd done nothing but watch her for days. The woman barely had electricity. It was hard to believe she had any place in an assassination plot, no matter how small.

Even attempting to cheer himself up with the knowledge that he now had her name and could find her again didn't help. What use was her name when his first impression on her was so bad she ran into the woods?

He'd been desperate to know her before, but now it was a real, physical craving. Taevas had no idea what he'd do if she refused to see him again. He'd been very, very careful with his boundaries, with the lines he couldn't cross as Isand and as a decent man, but he feared what he might do if that foreign animal in him gained control for longer than a moment.

Dragons had worked hard to dispel the public perception of them being seen as greedy, possessive mates who'd snatch their Chosen off the street without warning, but that didn't mean it wasn't *true*.

Their instincts were forged in the great fire of life or death competition, during a time when healthy mates, good roosts, and resources were scarce. They came from a time when young died before they ever got the chance to flourish, and stealing a mate from another's nest wasn't uncommon. It was primordial, the pull to guard and to preen, to seduce and to provide.

Taevas had never felt it before, but centuries of desperation resonated in his marrow. It called him a fool for even thinking of leaving her on her own, where another dragon might snatch her up. It called him irresponsible for allowing her to remain in such a poor roost. It called him unworthy for even considering abandoning her.

I must get back to the 'Riik, he reminded that new, irritating voice in the back of his head. *I'm not just Taevas. I'm Isand. I need to know what happened to my Wing, and I need to let my people know I'm alive. I can't abandon them, either.*

He didn't realize he'd squeezed his eyes shut until he opened them again. Taevas glared at the trampled underbrush, at the stupid, judgmental eyes on the white trunk of the birch tree across from him, and at the single green thread tangled amongst the paper-like bark.

His shoulders tensed. Focus narrowing on that familiar color, he slowly bent his knees until he was nearly level with the thread. He took a deep breath. Alashiya's scent was strong there. Very strong.

Hunting instincts roared to life. His clamoring thoughts and conflicting desires went silent as he crouched low, until he was on his hands and knees amongst the greenery. Somewhere overhead, an owl hooted. Its call was accompanied by the low buzz of insects hidden behind leaves and amongst the grass.

Taevas could almost see a trail now. The way her scent was concentrated, he was almost certain she'd crawled, which made it harder for her to disguise her weight in the underbrush.

Had she heard him coming and dropped low? Taevas bit back a rumble of displeasure. There was no thrill of the chase, only the all-consuming need to find her as quickly as possible.

She ought to be in the nest, that age-old instinct bemoaned. *Not here. Not in the dirt. Not where she can get hurt. Not without me.*

He didn't realize he'd struck up a low crooning note in the back of his throat until it silenced the insects around him. It was a comforting, coaxing sort of sound — one he'd never made in his life but recognized all the same. It was the call to the nest, the courting song.

Before he could dwell on that new development, the sound of a breath made him freeze. It was just one breath. A short, nearly silent gasp.

A ripple of exhilaration coursed over his skin and through the fine membrane of his damaged wings. Her scent was all around him, and despite the fact that he still couldn't see her, he *knew* she was close.

He'd crawled into a small dip in the forest floor. One side rose up higher than the other and was topped by a line of birch trees. Their roots, exposed by the earth eroding from the sides of the depression over time, created something like a hollow.

It, along with the rest of the area, was densely packed with vegetation. He could hardly see more than a foot in front of him, but he struggled to imagine she was as close as he knew her to be and still managed to be unseen. Alashiya was no waif. She was made of luscious, soft flesh and long legs. While she was small compared to him, he didn't think she was anywhere near small enough to simply disappear into the undergrowth.

But she was there. She had to be.

Instinct propelled him to tear the greenery apart until she'd been revealed, but Taevas fought back control. He'd scared her enough. It didn't matter that *he* knew he only wanted to keep her safe. If he started using his claws to destroy her hiding place, she'd be well within her rights to be absolutely terrified of him.

But revealing that he knew she was there *without* acting was a gamble. The gods knew what tricks she had up her sleeves. His nymph was clever and resourceful. If she got away again, he didn't think he could take another chase through the woods. And if she made a break for the farm just beyond the fence...

Praying that he wouldn't lose this gamble, Taevas eased back onto his haunches and swiped a hand across his sweaty brow. "Shiya," he rasped, "I'm sorry I scared you. I don't know what I did, but whatever it was, I never intended to frighten you off. I just want to talk, okay?"

He held his breath and waited. There was no response.

"If there's something I can do to make you feel safe, I'll do it. I understand that it's alarming to have me in your roost, *metsalill*. I should've been more reassuring. I want to fix that. Please let me."

When a full minute passed, he asked, "Are you all right? You didn't hurt yourself, did you?"

Could she see him? Without access to the internet, there was no way for Taevas to know how good a nymph's night vision might be. A chill ran down his spine at the thought of her running blindly through the woods. She could've tripped and broken her leg. She could've hit her head on a rock, and the only reason she wasn't replying to him was because she was bleeding out somewhere just beyond his sight. Or worse.

Growing more alarmed by the second, Taevas struggled to

keep the gentle facade up. *If she doesn't answer me in the next minute, I'm tearing this place apart.*

"Come out, *minu metsalill.* Please."

There was no response. At least, nothing verbal. Taevas couldn't say whether it was a choice she made or simply an involuntary reaction on her part, but there was the smallest movement in the ferns and tangled vines directly before him. Without thinking, his right hand shot into the foliage.

His claws closed around a delicate ankle.

Her flesh was petal-soft and warm beneath the pads of his fingers. As soon as he made contact, Taevas was astonished to see her shape resolve itself in the depths of the shadows in the hollow beneath the birch trees. A chill ran down his spine.

He'd been staring right at her from less than a foot away.

Alashiya didn't jerk her leg to be free. She didn't make a sound and hardly seemed to breathe. She watched him from her hiding spot, her arms wrapped tightly around her knees and the whites of her eyes visible within the shadows of the roots. They almost appeared to cage her in. Now that he could see her clearly, Taevas got the uneasy sense that the plants and roots in the hollow were leaning toward her, like they were trying to block her from view — or draw her into the depths of the earth, never to be seen again.

The hair prickled on the back of his neck. It was hard to banish the feeling that he was being keenly observed by an entity that hadn't yet decided if he was an enemy or not.

Swallowing, Taevas said, "Shiya, are you hurt?"

"Not yet." Her voice was as soft as the brush of leaves against one another.

"Not yet?" Taevas glanced around sharply, straining for any sight or sound of an enemy. "What are you afraid of?"

When he turned his attention back to her, he discovered that peculiar look on her face again — the one that said she had absolutely no idea what to make of him.

"You," she answered, at last pulling her leg from his grip.

Alashiya pressed herself deeper into the hollow. To his great alarm, he noticed the edges of her began to blur, as if the very earthen wall of the hollow was beginning to close around her.

Taevas lunged for her. The scent of crushed and broken greenery perfumed the air as he wrestled her out of the hollow as gently as he could. It didn't seem to matter. Alashiya was a soft creature, but she had a belly full of fire. When threatened, she lashed out with everything she had.

It was unfortunate for her that even with his current weakness, her nails and teeth and blows didn't stand a chance against him. Only when she went for his injured wings did Taevas have to put some real effort into restraining her.

"Stop this!" he barked, pinning her wrists beside her ears. His knees sunk into the loamy soil on either side of her hips. Alashiya lay splayed out beneath him, her curls tangled in the fans of ferns. Her chest rose and fell with every panting breath. Electricity buzzed in the air around them — a nearly tangible chemistry that set his blood on fire.

His cock, always deeply rebellious when it came to her, jerked behind the damn button-up fly of his borrowed pants. He wanted to tear her pretty dress down the middle, free those perfect, heavy breasts, and feast on her until the last of his strength left him. Taevas wanted her wet and squirming beneath him. He wanted her soft hands on his cock. He *needed* to spread those perfect, full thighs and rut between them like a beast, and then he needed her to arch her back and scream when she came, so she'd never, ever run from him again.

But none of it would happen when she looked at him like *that*.

"Alashiya," he growled, voice roughened by need and exhaustion, "I am *not* going to hurt you."

"Then why did you chase me?"

Taevas's brow furrowed. "Why? Shiya, you *ran*. You could've gotten hurt."

She shook her head. "So?"

"So? I was *worried.* I'm grateful you took me into your home. You treated my wounds. You've been kind. We've sat together for hours. You've told me about your life. You've stroked my skin and whispered soft things to me. What *possible* motivation could I have to hurt you?"

Her throat, glistening with a thin sheen of sweat in the moonlight, bobbed with a nervous swallow. "I don't know. It didn't seem so bad when you were— when you were the other thing, but now you're a man. It's different."

Under normal circumstances, he'd agree. The idea of Alashiya inviting strange, nude men into her home threatened to give him a heart attack. But he wasn't some random man. He was *her* client. They'd known one another for ten interminable years. And even if that wasn't true, he was the Isand of the Draakonriik.

That had to lend him *some* measure of credibility, didn't it? A little bit of trust?

A creeping sense of unease skittered up his spine. Easing his hold on her wrists, Taevas scrutinized her face for any hint of recognition, any sign at all that she *knew* him.

His fingers trembled. "Tell me you know my name. Tell me you know me."

Alashiya's heavy brows lowered. Confusion flashed in her eyes, so big and sad in her perfect face. "I... How would I know that? You couldn't tell me."

That familiar empty sensation carved a deep space within his chest. It was a cavern made by a terrible movement of feeling — first of disbelief, then of horror, and finally a monstrous sort of impotent outrage.

Was I wrong? Is she not my artisan?

No, that couldn't be right. He'd seen his robe. He recognized her work. If nothing else, he'd know her by scent in any place, time, or setting. This was *her.* His artisan. His treasure. His mysterious *metsalill.*

So how could she not *know* him?

"You know me." A sharp edge made its way into his voice. It

was a command. An order from her Isand, from the man who'd yearned for just a glimpse of her for so very long. "You must. Look closely, my Shiya. Look at my face. Touch me, even. You *know* me."

She let out a startled breath when he dragged one of her hands to his cheek. Her palm was cool against his flushed skin, and her fingers shook when he guided them over the curve of his jaw and the heavy line of his brow.

A hoarse whisper escaped him. A plea. "Recognize me."

Some of the fear bled away from her gaze. It was replaced by confusion and no small amount of concern.

He imagined he must have seemed out of his mind to her. Taevas had begun losing his grip on his sanity the day he opened that first package and now... now he knelt in the dirt, begging a frightened woman to say his name.

How far the mighty Isand has fallen.

Alashiya didn't take her hand away from his cheek when Taevas released her wrist. She held it there, just barely touching. In a gentler voice than he probably deserved, she asked, "Have we met before?"

"No," he choked out.

"Then how would I know you?"

A lifetime in the public eye flashed through his mind. Hundreds of interviews. Countless press releases, photoshoots, and headlines.

He'd been the leader of a fierce, wealthy territory for well over a hundred years. Nearly his entire life was documented in pictures and video, thrown out into the ether to build his reputation — all in the name of making the 'Riik stronger, safer. His presence on a street drew crowds no matter what territory he was in, and his choices changed the fates of millions every day.

Despite all of that, he saw no recognition in her eyes. He was as much a stranger to her as she'd been to him.

He hunched his shoulders. "Taevas," he whispered. "My name is Taevas Aždaja."

The words drifted in the air between them, normally so heavy but in that moment as light as one of the fireflies that danced around their heads. They didn't seem to land anywhere in her memory. She absorbed them quietly, with neither gasp nor reflexive, nervous smile. To her, it was a name like any other.

Alashiya's fingertips skimmed his cheek as she slowly lowered her hand. She sucked in a deep breath through her nose. Appearing to come to some tentative decision, she asked, "You're not going to hurt me, are you, Taevas?"

"Never."

"How do I know you're telling the truth?"

Taevas was a lot of things. He was arrogant, wry, and domineering. There were plenty of character flaws one could criticize. But never, not once in his long life, had someone accused him of going back on his word.

"My name is Taevas Aždaja," he rumbled, eyes locked with hers. "I am the Isand of the Draakonriik, Lord of the Dragon Clans, and head of Clan Aždaja. My word is law, *minu metsalill,* and I say you're safe from all things."

Alashiya blinked. Her expression was nonplussed. "I don't think anyone can make a promise like that."

He let out a breath. "My Shiya, I am not just anyone."

Chapter Fourteen

She was being foolish again.

It wasn't the whisper of her grove's ghosts that admonished her. They had been curiously silent since the man appeared in her kitchen. Even when she ran into the woods, seeking shelter amongst the roots of her trees as her people had done since the dawn of time, they said nothing.

She thought, perhaps, that they might have something to say about her leading the man she'd been so frightened of back to her home, but they murmured no warnings, no urgent instructions to run. That gave her a tiny bit of hope that she wasn't making a colossal mistake.

A *very* tiny bit.

Taevas stomped behind her, his footsteps heavy and uneven. When she risked a glance back, she found his face heavily grooved with exhaustion, discomfort, and some other nameless thing that made her pity him. He looked lost — and not just because he had no idea how to get back to the house.

There was something unnatural about seeing a dragon in the forest. He didn't appear to understand how to move. He was clumsy, loud, and tense. Those impressive wings were folded tightly against his back and his tail remained coiled around his thigh like he worried a creature might pop out from behind a bush to bite it.

The forest didn't seem to know what to do with him, either. The two beings — one small and one a vast, interconnected network — appeared at odds with one another on a fundamental level.

"You don't walk in forests much, do you?" she observed.

Taevas's eyes, a violet so bright they nearly glowed in the night, fixed on her with hair-raising intensity. "Dragons don't like tight spaces. Even if I had the time to go for hikes, I wouldn't choose a setting where I can't spread my wings."

She nodded, though she couldn't relate. "You must like mountains."

"Not as much as gargoyles do, but yes. I prefer cities, personally."

"Ah." Alashiya faced away from him. Her pitiful attempt to understand Taevas had failed with impressive swiftness.

There was a long stretch of tense silence before he asked in a strained voice, "Do you like cities, Shiya?"

"I've never been to one."

They sounded wretched to her. Her books sometimes made them out to be places of wonder and activity, but the concept of living so close to strangers, with no green land to connect to, made her skin crawl. She'd tried to imagine it many times, what it might be like to live in an apartment, to ride a train, to raise a child in a place where they couldn't run with their shoes off.

Must be miserable.

Taevas's tone was as bemused as she felt when he replied, "Not *once*?"

"No," she said, giving him a quick look. "I've never needed to leave home. Why would I?"

He appeared to be at a loss for a moment. Gathering himself, he asked, "Ah, where is home, exactly? I haven't been able to put that together. You told me the town is Birchdale, but I've never heard of it before."

"Didn't you fly here? How could you not know where you are?"

"I was drugged and injured. My sense of direction still isn't right. Even when I try to pinpoint which direction my roost is in, it keeps guiding me back here." The skin around his eyes and mouth tensed. "I have no idea how long I've been gone or where I am, so I need you to tell me."

Alashiya rubbed the pad of her index finger along the edge of her thumbnail, mimicking the hold she used for needles. A nervous habit. "This is my land. It's part of Birchdale Township. The outskirts of it, anyway."

"And where is that? What territory's jurisdiction does it fall under?"

"It's the border between the Northern Territories and the Shifter Alliance," she answered. "Minneapolis is about five hours south by truck. And if it helps, it's July fifteenth."

There was a terrible crash behind her. Alashiya swiveled around just in time to see the dragon catch himself against a tree. He'd tripped over a fallen log, half-rotten and nearly hidden by ferns.

Alarmed, she deftly navigated the forest floor to reach him. He'd seemed terribly fearsome when he chased her through the woods, but now he appeared breakable. Touching his arm, she asked, "Are you all right?"

Taevas shook his head. His eyes were wide when he rasped, "Over two weeks? I've been gone over *two weeks.*" He let out a sound that was very much *not* a laugh, but something like its evil twin. "Good gods, they probably think I'm dead."

Her stomach sank. "Were you *kidnapped?*"

She hesitated to believe anything a stranger said, but the distress on Taevas's face was extremely convincing. "Yes," he answered, his voice weak.

It seemed obvious, but she had to ask, "And your family has no idea where you are?"

"No, or my people would be here already."

"Is it possible they think you've gone on a trip or something?"

"My people would *never* think I'd abandon them without a word," he snapped.

She shrank back a step. "Sorry. It was just a question."

Taevas thrust a knuckle into his left eye and rubbed hard. There was no softness, no understanding in his voice when he said, "I'm *Isand.*"

He said the word like it explained everything. *Ee-zand.*

The trouble was that she had no idea what it meant, let alone the weight it apparently carried. He'd called himself Lord of the Dragon Clans, too. Taevas seemed to be someone of importance — or that's what he said, at any rate. She wanted to believe he was who he said he was, and that everything that had happened to him was the truth. She wanted to help him in what small way she could.

But even she, a woman who'd never left the bounds of Birchdale proper, knew that people lied.

Plenty of people thought they were important when they were really just like everybody else. Or worse. Rich recreationists often thought themselves above the people who lived in Birchdale. In her experience, there was very little more dangerous than a man who believed in his own importance too much.

Alashiya's heart went out to Taevas for his clear suffering, but she also felt a deep, instinctive distrust of his attitude. Being *Isand* meant nothing to her, and she was fairly certain she didn't want to dig any deeper than she had. His world wasn't hers and they were all better off for it.

Decision to not pry any further firmly made, she turned and began walking again. He said something under his breath, but it was in a language she didn't understand, so it wasn't meant for her ears.

Taevas continued his clumsy, limping steps behind her. Hearing his obvious struggle, Alashiya slowed her pace. They walked for a long time before he said anything more.

Breathing heavily, he murmured, "I'm sorry I was short with you."

"It's fine," she replied, eyeing the familiar break in the trees that indicated they were near home.

"It's not. I'm exhausted, in pain, and unhappy — but you aren't to blame for any of that. You are someone I respect, Shiya. That means I should treat you as such."

"It's already forgotten."

And it was, for the most part. Alashiya had shifted her focus to figuring out what the next several hours would look like, how she could help Taevas without getting burned in the process, and, most importantly, when she'd be able to get back to work.

Her lips pursed at the thought of what she had to do next. It was all well and good when he was a dragon trapped in her kitchen, but now he was a man. He'd need a proper place to sleep. There were many rooms on offer, but none of them had been lived in for nearly twenty years, and all of the usable bedding had been pilfered. Some of the rooms weren't suitable for habitation at all, even for a night, after so much neglect.

She wove through the gap between two young birch trees and stepped out into the grassy field just beyond her garden. Her home sat on the small hill above them, its hulking form slouched and dark against the star-strewn sky.

Working out how she was going to safely cohabitate with her guest for the night took up so much of her focus that she barely noticed Taevas had stopped halfway up the hill. Frowning, she glanced over her shoulder to find him standing stock-still. He'd dug his fingers into the long hair by his ears and appeared to be staring at her home with abject astonishment.

Raising her eyebrows, she asked, "What?"

"This is where you live?" She wasn't sure what to make of how his baritone went up an octave when he asked his question.

Looking back at the house, then at him, she answered, "Yes? You've seen it, haven't you?"

"I don't remember looking that closely when I..." He made a

high, crooning noise she'd become familiar with during her time with the dragon. "But... but why is it— Shiya, why does it look like the ground is trying to *swallow* it?"

She supposed it did look a bit like that. There wasn't much of the walls left visible these days. Some of that was intentional. Her grove had worked hard with shovels and wheelbarrows for over a week, building up the earthen barrier along the walls. Nymphs preferred to be as close to the earth as possible when they slept, and modern housing didn't support that. A compromise was made by raising the earth around the house, with space made only for doorways. The converted barn would've gone the same way, but the grove hadn't survived long enough to do it.

Over time, as was always the hope, nature moved in step with their work. Grasses, vines, ferns, and even some small saplings took root in the berms, shielding the home even further. Then moss began to dominate the home itself. It crawled over the roof and across window panes. She gently scraped it away once every few years, since she liked natural light when she worked, but never completely.

The overall effect was that of a home built into, and indeed swallowed by, Burden's Earth.

For the first time she considered how strange it must be to a dragon, who lived in towers and on mountaintops. She wondered if *his* home would feel as alien to her as hers did to him. Even trying to picture it was impossible. It was as fantastical to her as the idea of standing on a cloud.

Not knowing how else to answer him, she said, "It's how we like it."

Taevas made a curious noise in the back of his throat and tugged at his hair. "I..." Whatever he was about to say, he swallowed it with considerable effort. After a visible struggle, he muttered, "I've never seen anything like it."

"I'd probably find your home strange, too," she generously offered.

"Dragons are proud of their roosts. It's the mark of a good

mate and a happy home. We build ours high and strong and—not this."

Tired of standing in the yard, Alashiya resumed her trek up the hill. "Nymphs are just as happy sleeping on the forest floor as a bed. One of our many differences, I suspect."

Taevas lengthened his noisy stride to catch up to her as she rounded the house. "You don't really do that, do you? Sleep outside?"

A familiar, sick feeling coiled its slimy body into a knot in the pit of her stomach. Swallowing, she answered, "I have, yes. We hibernate under the soil during the winter — or when hard times come."

She reached for the kitchen door, but Taevas's long arm beat her to it. He swooped in over her head and pulled it open for her with a slight smile. Giving him a bemused look, she stepped inside.

Following after her, he remarked, "But you don't do that alone, do you? What if someone were to find you out in the forest all by yourself?"

"The same thing that's happened to most nymphs in that scenario: I'd be killed. Eaten, maybe. Or worse. It's a good thing that normally we're very hard to find." Padding across the kitchen floor, she went straight for her small tea collection. If any situation called for a cup of something comforting, it was this one.

"Why would anyone hurt a nymph? You're basically defenseless."

Alashiya kept her focus on filling her kettle and pulling down a couple of cups when she answered, "Why does anybody hurt anybody? To gain something, to take something away from someone else, to right a wrong, or just for fun."

Movement in the corner of her eye at last drew her gaze to Taevas, who braced his palms against the edge of the counter beside the stove. "That explains why you live in a fortress of wards, I suppose. But is that why you ran? You thought I might try to hurt you for fun?"

She shrugged. Alashiya didn't feel like explaining that she had no idea why he might've wanted to hurt her, only that the likelihood was high enough that the urge had been too hard to resist. An opportunity had presented itself, survival instincts kicked in, and she'd gone.

She wasn't proud of it. After all, hadn't she stood up to him when he was the size of a truck? But something about facing *him*, a real man with unknown motives and those burning violet eyes, had seen all her courage drain away into nothing.

Monsters were easier to face than men, apparently. But then again, monsters had never hurt her.

Selecting a blend of her own dried herbs, she quickly prepared a cup of tea for both of them. The weather was a little warm for a hot drink, but the comfort made it worth it.

"Here," she muttered, passing a cup to Taevas. His hands were so much bigger than hers that when he accepted it, his palms nearly engulfed hers. There was an odd moment, just the span of a few heartbeats, where they both held still, his hands over hers, the warm cup nestled in her palm.

Taevas had long, sooty lashes. They fanned out over the tops of his cheeks when his eyelids lowered, shielding those penetrating eyes from view. His voice was a low, low rumble when he said, "Thank you, *metsalill*. For this, and for your trust. I promise you, it's not placed in the wrong man."

A warm sensation bubbled in her veins. It was a bit like the tingle that came with a kiss from a much-loved one, or the sensory joy of cool, running water over naked skin on summer's hottest day.

She'd felt its echo several times during his stay in her home, but it was much more potent now that he was... him.

Unsettled, Alashiya gently extracted her hands. She couldn't quite manage to look at him, so she grabbed her tea and made her way over to the kitchen table, which had been mostly unusable when the dragon occupied the room.

Her knees were weak. She sank into her favorite seat gratefully, her tea held close to her chest, and tried to get her thoughts in order. "I suppose we should figure out how to get you back to your people," she mused.

"Yes." Taevas gingerly lowered himself into the chair catty-corner from hers. His legs were so long that one of them bumped hers beneath the table. He didn't move it, but rather rested his knee against her thigh until she scooted self-consciously away. It was one thing to cuddle with the dragon, but it was quite another to be touched by *him*.

Everytime it happened, her body and mind went haywire.

Oblivious, Taevas pressed a few fingers to the space just before his right ear and stared into the middle distance for the span of a few heartbeats. Closing his eyes, he muttered, "Damn."

"What?"

"They took out my communication implant, which means I need access to a secure, private line," he explained, eyes opening. His proud features sharpened in a way she couldn't quite put her finger on. One moment he seemed worn, his exhaustion apparent, and the next his jaw was firm and his broad shoulders straight. "I have to get word to my people that I'm alive. They'll send an extraction team."

"I'm not sure I know what you mean by *secure, private line,*" she admitted.

"I mean any phone on a private network or that uses an encrypted line. A satellite phone would do as a last resort." Taevas glanced around the kitchen with a knowing look. "Shiya, do you even *own* a phone?"

"No. Why would I?"

"To talk to people."

Giving him a narrow-eyed look, she replied, "I know what phones are *for.*"

Taevas stuck a knuckle in his eye again. "Then why don't you have one? What if there's an emergency? What about your business?"

"If there's an emergency, I can go to the Thompsons' farm.

And I do business how my grove always did it: through the mail. The atelier sends me the orders and the supplies, I send the order back to them, and they forward it to the client. Easy."

He looked quite keen then, though she hadn't a clue as to why. There was an avid gleam in his eye when he muttered, "That — I want to talk about that later. I have to stay on track right now, but *later* I want to hear everything about your business."

"Okay," she replied, openly dubious.

"Back to the phone— What if you want to talk to someone who doesn't live in Birchdale? Most people don't write letters anymore."

That was an easy one. Alashiya took a slow sip from her tea before answering, "I don't talk to anyone."

"What? No family? No friends?" He didn't sound like he thought she was a liar, exactly, but it also didn't feel like he *believed* her.

"I never had many friends," she explained, "and the few I had left Birchdale decades ago. We exchanged letters for a while, but you know how things go — you travel, you have babies, you get busy. All untended things wither in the end."

The ball of his throat bobbed with an audible swallow. "And family?"

Alashiya's gaze roved around the kitchen, where her grandparents, her parents, her cousins, and all the members of her grove had once cooked, eaten, loved, cried. As she often did, she imagined what would happen to it and the rest of the home when she joined them by Grim's riverbank.

All untended things wither.

It was not a sorrowful mantra, but one of studied release. It was a beautiful thing to wither. To fade. To return to the earth and be remade.

She took a sip of her tea. "My family is dead."

CHAPTER FIFTEEN

TAEVAS STARED AT THE CEILING OF THE ROOM Alashiya had given him, unable to sleep. He could scarcely close his eyes. Everytime he tried, the darkness closed in on him, the shadows seething with everything he'd learned, every worry that bit and scoured his mind.

He needed to *focus*. His people needed him more than anything, and getting back to them was his first priority.

But he couldn't stop circling the mystery of his artisan, his *metsalill*. She stood in his mind, unmoving, while he went around and around her. He'd spent so long imagining her that now he felt over-full, as if he'd gorged on a feast he had no right to touch. But his hunger hadn't been sated. A bone-deep craving gnawed at him to keep going, to know *everything*.

Perhaps it was the fact that her real life was so far removed from his imaginings that threw him off-kilter. He'd pictured a free-spirited creature in a New York apartment surrounded by eclectic decor and a social circle of artists. He pictured a woman of boundless creativity and curiosity living her life unchained, unwilling to be pinned down by even his admiration. He pictured exactly the opposite of Alashiya.

She was lush and golden and vital and rooted to the earth. She didn't live in a small city apartment, but a half-rotten house being slowly consumed by nature. She didn't have friends. She didn't have *family*.

Where had all the money he'd paid her over the years gone? It was easily a quarter of a million dollars, though he'd long since stopped keeping track. It certainly hadn't gone into her home or anything else he could see. And why didn't she *know* him? If not as Isand, then she ought to be familiar with his name, his requests, his many, many gifts.

But he'd seen none of those gifts around the house. Most notably, the custom chair and workbench he'd sent her was nowhere to be seen. She was forced to wedge flattened cushions behind her back as she worked, and often had to stop to stretch when the discomfort became too much.

Had she sold his gifts? It was possible she had some incredible debt or other expenses, but that seemed a less likely conclusion than the obvious: that nothing, including the vast majority of the money he'd spent over the years, had ever gotten to her.

Rage tightened the powerful muscles of his jaw. It wasn't the time or place to be worrying about whether a skilled embroiderer had been properly compensated. His priority couldn't and *shouldn't* have been Alashiya.

And yet he stared at the ceiling, the pain in his wings almost unbearable, and strained to listen to the softest sounds of her breathing from the next room, as he had every night since the drugs began to wear off. Taevas was a protector by nature, so it was one of the great challenges of his life, learning to prioritize everything and everyone who needed his help.

His people, the 'Riik, had to come first. Usually he could, after some small internal struggle, accept that. But now...

Alashiya could not be put aside.

She's part of this now, he decided, as something of a compromise with the ravenous beast in him. *My presence here puts her at risk, which means she's owed my protection. I can get back to my people and take care of her. I'm motherfucking Isand. I can multitask.*

He'd get back to his people, and he'd satisfy the thing that drew him to Alashiya. At the very least, he owed her for her hospitality, reluctant though it might've been.

His decision didn't make it easier to sleep. A nagging sense of unease demanded he get out of the old, musty bed to check on her. A permeating sense of *wrongness* didn't just seep from the sad little room Alashiya had tried in vain to make nice for him with fresh linens and a quick cleaning. It came from the closed door. The six feet of hallway. The nest on the floor, unguarded, unscented, unclaimed by him.

Taevas wasn't an idiot. He wasn't ignorant of what his instincts demanded of him. He just didn't want to listen.

A cold, slushy wave of fear churned in his gut. It was one thing to crave, but quite another to give in to that craving. That would mean relinquishing control over everything he'd so carefully safeguarded over the years — an utterly unthinkable path, no matter what his instincts howled for.

His mind never stopped spinning, but sleep eventually claimed him anyway. Like a switch flipping on and off, Taevas couldn't recall closing his eyes, only opening them again to a room lit with pale morning light. A strange shape of it was cast on the floor by a small gap in the fabric pinned to the window frames.

He watched it on the floor for several moments, disoriented, until awareness came back to him. The scent of coffee and the soft sounds of cooking prompted him to move before he'd properly assessed whether that was possible.

Taevas nearly stumbled out of the bed. He caught himself just in time to spare himself the fall, but he still landed hard on the bed. His head spun. Bile crept up the back of his throat. A full-body quake overtook him. It was as if his body couldn't decide whether it wanted to shift or not. Every muscle seemed to slither under his skin, unsure of their places.

Taevas gasped, claws curling into the bedding, and fought it hard. He barely heard a soft knock on the door, but Alashiya's voice came through. "Taevas? Are you okay? It sounded like you fell."

A pitiful noise left his throat. Not a moment later, the door swung open. His vision was too blurred to see her clearly, but he'd know the shape of her, the golden tones of her skin and hair, anywhere.

Alashiya rushed into the room, bringing a waft of rich coffee and cypress with her. "Whoa, whoa," she muttered, bending a little to brace her palms on his shoulders. "Easy. Don't move. Are you hurting?"

"I'm okay," he rasped, muscles shuddering as they finally settled back into their proper places. His mouth filled with saliva as an impression of memory surfaced, one of complete helplessness as he was pricked with a needle again, a threadbare bag thrown over his head and his limbs bound.

I couldn't shift, he suddenly recalled. *I couldn't control it.*

"The drug that was used," he found himself explaining around gasps of exertion, "I think it was a shift inhibitor. It must still be in my system, doing gods know what."

Petal-soft hands smoothed over his shoulders and down his arms, tracing invisible but unforgettable paths down the naked skin of his biceps. "Is a shift inhibitor like medicine? Will it wash out of your system on its own?"

Taevas ran a hand over his clammy face. "Most do, but they could've used anything. And I was injected so many times..."

I could've died.

The thought came to him as clear as day. Of course, he'd recognized that he was likely to be murdered, but there was something more unsettling about the possibility of a careless, accidental death. A senseless one.

Most inhibitors were safe, used only in rare cases where two-formed beings needed to be restrained for their safety or that of others. But they weren't meant for long-term care, and those that were more potent were far more dangerous. *None* were meant for repeated use.

Snatches of memory, a muffled argument here and there, drifted from the foggy mass of his memories. "They didn't know what they were doing. I don't remember what they said, but I got the sense that they weren't supposed to have me for as long as they did. Something went wrong."

Alashiya hovered close. It calmed him, though a new urgency asserted itself when she pressed the silken skin of her inner wrist to his forehead. "You're warm. Really warm, Taevas. I don't know what's normal for a dragon, but you feel feverish to me."

He opened his eyes. Gods, the sound of his name on her lips was the sweetest thing he'd ever heard. It was on the tip of his tongue to command her to say it again. Just one more time.

She was so close that he could count her lashes. He might've even been able to count the hidden freckles across her nose. Breathing deeply, he wrapped his fingers around her wrist and gently guided it down.

Settling her hand on his shoulder where it belonged, he muttered, "I overexerted myself yesterday."

He expected a wince and maybe an apology for her disappearing act, but he got neither. Instead, Alashiya arched her brows and peered down her nose at him. "It was stupid of you to chase me."

Taevas opened his mouth, but it was an ancient instinct who replied, "I'll always chase you, *metsalill.*"

There was a taut moment of silence as they stared at one another, a scant few inches between their faces. A wild thing beat in his chest — his heart, he thought, though he didn't recognize the new rhythm it struck.

His claws curled into the bedsheets again. It was a reflex, but not one he'd ever struggled with before. Dragons were grabbers.

Acquirers. They often snatched things on impulse, and it took the work of years to train their young to manage it.

It was a humbling regression — *one of many,* he thought bitterly — to struggle against the urge as a grown man.

If Alashiya noticed his internal battle, she didn't comment on it. No doubt it appeared to her as yet another of his many oddities and improprieties. She eased back, taking the comfort of her touch with her. "Definitely feverish. You should stay in bed."

Appalled, Taevas exclaimed, "I will *not.*"

"You're sick and clearly not as healed as you thought you were," she argued, hands on her hips. She wore the strangest outfit that day, composed of what looked like repurposed men's overalls, and still somehow she managed to be the single most appealing creature he'd ever laid eyes on.

With her curls tied up in a colorful scarf and her eyes as bright as polished cedar, she looked the very picture of robust health when she ordered, "Back into bed. I'll bring breakfast, then you'll rest."

"I don't need bedrest," he growled, tail thrashing against the sheets. "And I don't like this room. I need to get out and—"

"Contact your people. Yes, I *know.*" Alashiya jammed a thumb over her shoulder. "That's why you are going to stay here and *I* am going to walk into town to see if I can find some way for you to reach them that isn't the Thompsons' phone or the library's computers."

Alarm flashed down his spine. Nearly rising from the bed, Taevas slashed his claws through the air in one clean sweep. "Absolutely not. You aren't going anywhere alone."

Alashiya looked distinctly unimpressed with him when she replied, "All right, so let me get this straight: You need to make a call. That has to happen as soon as possible, but it has to be on a special phone. I need to find you that special phone and you need to come with me, except you don't want anyone seeing you or knowing you're here. Please, mighty dragon, explain to me how this is supposed to work."

Taevas eyed her with a combination of annoyance and secret delight. "I really don't appreciate your sarcasm."

"And I don't appreciate you being bossy," she quipped.

Exasperated, he declared, "I *am* the boss."

Alashiya didn't miss a beat. "This is *my* land, dragon. Whoever you might be out there, *I* am the queen of this grove. No one is the boss of me."

He opened his mouth to reply, but for the life of him, he had no idea what to say to that. It was true. He wasn't in charge of her. If anything, he was in her debt and ought to be on his best behavior.

But he was Isand, and moreover he was a dragon in the clutches of instinct that thrilled at the challenge she represented. Dragons appreciated strength and bravery above all things, so when Alashiya stood so regally before him, shoulders back and expression serene, while telling him to shove his orders up his ass, Taevas was forced to drag a blanket into his lap.

Half-dead and she can still make me harder than fucking steel. It hardly seemed fair.

Interpreting his silence as having won the argument, Alashiya flashed a satisfied smile that would've left him weak at the knees if he'd been strong enough to stand. "I'm going to town," she reiterated. "And you can't stop me. I think I have an idea of how to get you a secure phone. And besides, I need to visit the shop if I'm going to be cooking for two."

Alashiya turned to leave the room, but was stopped by his tail looping around her wrist. She gave it, then him, an exasperated look. "What?"

"Shiya," he rumbled, "I'm serious. This isn't an exaggeration or a joke or a lie. I'm telling you that the people who're looking for me are dangerous, connected men. They kidnapped and held the most powerful dragon in the UTA for weeks. If anyone finds out I'm here, it won't just be bad for me. They'll hurt you, too, and they won't think anything of it."

Gently prying his tail from her wrist, she replied, "Most

powerful dragon in the UTA, huh? All the more reason for no one to notice me, then."

"What do you mean?"

Alashiya gave him an odd look. "Important people don't come to Birchdale, dragon, and they certainly don't know nymphs like me."

CHAPTER SIXTEEN

ALASHIYA WAS FIFTY PERCENT SURE TAEVAS WAS A criminal on the run. The other fifty percent was actually foolish enough to believe his story.

She couldn't put her finger on exactly *why* even half of her believed his grandiose declarations, but she suspected it had something to do with his bearing. If he were lying, wouldn't he let down his guard occasionally, allowing the mask of superiority to slip? But no, Taevas held himself like a king even when it looked like he was on the brink of puking.

And he *was* really sick, at the very least. Even the best liar couldn't fake a fever, cold sweat, or the way his eyes wouldn't dilate the way they should've.

He could just be a spectacularly arrogant, ill criminal, she thought as she picked a familiar path through the dense woodland that bordered her land. She could've used the dirt road, of course, but it was more likely she'd encounter recreationists that way, so she normally chose the safer route through the trees.

The dragon would've hated it. The walk was long, hot, and involved navigating dense undergrowth that found it amusing to disorient wayward travelers. Alashiya had long since come to an agreement with the birch forest, which allowed her to pass through it relatively unchallenged, but a clumsy oaf like the dragon wouldn't stand a chance.

Alashiya cast a glance over her shoulder, though her land was too far in the distance to see. She wondered what he was doing without her there. A nervous twinge made her shuffle her feet. It wasn't like there was much to steal, but if he touched Adon's things... Just the thought was nearly enough to send her walking back the way she came.

No one was allowed near her work. It was a sacred thing to her for many reasons — not least of which was the rich fantasy of her imaginary relationship with Adon. The robe, like all his commissions, was the only tangible link she had to him and to the dream that sustained her. It made her skin crawl to think of an outsider getting their grubby hands all over that vital tether.

Swallowing back her impulse to return to the house, she adjusted her bag over her shoulder and doubled her speed. The quicker she got her errand done, the better they'd both be. Taevas would leave and she could return to her work.

A twinge of guilt pinched her. Taevas wasn't so bad, really. Hadn't they shared a nice cup of tea? If she could get over her discomfort of having a strange man around, then she thought she might even be able to enjoy his company. Maybe. If she could keep her head on straight whenever he so much as looked at her, which she didn't have high hopes for.

Is 'enjoy' the right word?

Alashiya slipped between the fronds of an old fern. The leaves caressed her calves in a gentle greeting, but she barely registered it. Her mind was consumed, for reasons beyond her, by the image of the dragon's face. *Taevas's* face. And other things.

It was hard not to be, with the height of his horns, the proud jut of his nose, the hard jaw, those *eyes*. Add his impossibly wide shoulders, his fascinating wings, and the eyeful she'd unwittingly gotten of his cock... She supposed she could understand how one might grow an over-inflated ego. It didn't make his bossiness more tolerable, but it did mean she snuck looks at him when he wasn't paying attention.

The forefinger and thumb of her right hand pinched the shaft of an invisible needle as she imagined stitching his striking profile. She saved all her scraps of silk thread from her commissions. Usually she used them for her veil, but a small, painterly portrait wouldn't use too much—

There's no time, she firmly reminded herself. *Work needs to be done. I can't keep Adon waiting.*

But no matter how hard she tried to divert it, Alashiya's focus continued to wander back to the moment they'd shared in his room. She'd never experienced *wonder* in the way she had when the heat of him touched her. And when those dark lashes lowered over his unsettling eyes, the compulsion to lean closer had been a living thing under her skin.

She was still thinking about the scent of him — something rich and earthy, like smoke and spices — when she finally made it to town.

Calling Birchdale a town was, by most estimations, a stretch. It was more of a pit stop for hikers, hunters, and boaters than anything else. Once, it'd been a thriving trading town, where the border between the UTA and the Northern Territory blurred. Fur trappers, loggers, and farmers had made a go of it for a while, and though the town had never been exactly metropolitan, it had a tight community, a main street of shops, a schoolhouse, and even its own all-god temple, where many priests and priestesses had passed through in their travels.

The war had destroyed most of that, and the reshuffling of the territory into shifter hands had done the rest. Opportunity had moved elsewhere and the people along with it.

That was why her grove had been able to buy their land so cheaply. It was also why, when Alashiya stepped out from behind an old, shuttered storefront onto the main road, it was into a town that consisted of one general store, a community center/library, and a post office that only opened on odd days of the week.

The rest of it consisted of vacation rentals and the scant few locals who remained to maintain the dying town during the off-season.

An enterprising soul had once tried to open a small restaurant, aiming to feed the hungry tourists who made the mistake of forgoing snacks at the last rest stop two hours down the road, but the seasonal flood and drought of customers had ended the venture after only one year. It was big news for a while, but every local knew it was doomed before they'd even opened the doors.

As always, Alashiya looked both ways before she hustled across the road, her arms held tightly to her body and her awareness of the world around her stretched taut. There were a handful of new but mud-flecked vehicles parked in front of the general store. She eyed them with dread.

Hitching her bag over her shoulder, she firmed her jaw and pushed the door open. A riotous tinkling of bells announced her entrance into the old store. Its shelves were mismatched, the walls covered in hunting trophies, decades of promotional displays, and various bits of dusty hiking gear. A wall of ancient refrigerators chugged along at the far end of the shop, full of a minimal selection of perishables and fishing bait.

Alashiya rarely needed much from the store, as she grew most of her own food, however, things like flour, baking soda, cleaning necessities, and cooking oil had to be purchased. She'd been going to the shop all her life and had even attended school with Debbie's kids, but she still dreaded the inevitable greeting that drew every stranger's eye in her direction.

"Morning, Shiya." Debbie, the old woman who'd run the business since Light and Darkness created the Earth, probably, waved a liver-spotted hand stained yellow by tobacco in Alashiya's direction.

She met only Debbie's rheumy gaze, but she was aware of the three men standing at the counter. It was impossible not to be, when she could feel their eyes on her like a bunch of sweaty hands.

"Good morning, Debbie," she muttered, offering the quickest

smile. Picking up an old wire shopping basket, Alashiya moved quickly toward her relevant aisles, her head down.

"You outta that flour already?" Debbie croaked, content to ignore the customers standing right in front of her. "Oh, I meant to ask you last time if you had any of those plums in yet. Mike won't shut up about it."

Without looking up, Alashiya answered, "My first crop of plums got eaten by birds, but I can bring you and Mike some of what's coming in next week, I think." Cruising down the medicine and toiletry aisle, she hastily gathered some fever reducers and anything else she thought might help the dragon.

What can aspirin do against being drugged for weeks? She grimaced and put another bottle in her basket.

The strangers at the counter talked amongst themselves. Their voices were too low for her to make out what they were saying, but she was happy their attention had moved off of her. Quickly gathering eggs, salt, and a few other essentials to avert any attention to her other purchases, Alashiya paused by the small selection of shampoos and pretended to browse.

A furtive glance at the counter found the group of men still standing there, their heads bent as they continued their discussion in more hushed tones. They were all dressed in typical hiking gear and appeared, to her untrained eye, to be human. Their body language was stiff, their backs almost unnaturally straight.

Uneasy about moving closer to the group but lacking a choice, Alashiya ducked her chin and shuffled down the aisle.

As soon as she stepped away from the shelves, the men went silent. Startled, her gaze snapped to them reflexively. All three men were watching her again. That wasn't altogether unusual.

Nymphs were desirable to many, if only because of their perceived vulnerability. Eyes followed her whenever she dared to venture into the town. But this was different. A chill ran down her spine when she met the eye of the tallest one. He was average looking, with light skin and closely-shorn hair. He could've been her age, or perhaps a little bit older. He was powerfully built, like many of the more enthusiastic recreationists who came through Birchdale.

Nothing about him was extraordinary, save for the way he looked at her.

Alashiya's fingers curled tightly around the handle of her basket. Her gaze skittered between the three faces. They wore identical expressions — or rather, non-expressions. Their eyes were blank. There was no desire, no interest, no malice or even polite curiosity when they watched her. There was... nothing.

When they continued to stare, their large bodies completely still, Alashiya tore her gaze away and forced her feet to move. Debbie didn't appear to notice the strange exchange. She was busy watching a program on her tablet, which was propped up by a cheap tackle box, and occasionally spitting into a can with the tab torn off.

Alashiya's grandmother had once told her that people were drawn to nymphs because they radiated the stuff of life, all the carnal things they might reject and yet crave. Maybe that was true, but she didn't get the sense that the men watched her like they craved something. They looked at her like she was an insect they'd never encountered before, with neither disgust nor true interest. She was just *there,* and at any moment they might deem her unimportant enough to trod on.

"You done?" The sound of Debbie's familiar, put-upon croak made her jump.

"Um, yes," she answered, accidentally thumping her basket down on the chipped formica countertop. Cold sweat slicked the back of her neck as she forced her attention away from the strange men.

Debbie muttered a token complaint about something Alashiya didn't catch — probably something about Mike, or the weather, or her children, who were all a pain in her ass. There was an uncomfortable buzzing in Alashiya's ears as she watched the old woman carefully ring up every item. She needed to ask Debbie a question, but her mouth was too dry to form words.

"...don't forget the plums next time. I'll trade you those noodles you like, but only for the good ones."

Alashiya blinked as Debbie handed her card back. "Right," she breathed, shoving her wallet back into her pocket. Her hands shook as she stuffed her purchases into her canvas shoulder bag. Clearing her sticky throat, she asked, "Debbie, have you seen M—"

She was interrupted by the clang of the bells over the door. Tensing, she looked up in time to see the very man she intended to ask about.

Monty Howard had looked the same all her life. Tall, rail-thin, with a shaved head and deep lines grooved down his cheeks, he would've fit in with the unhappy men of any era. He usually wore sunbleached baseball hats pulled low over his eyes, layers of baggy clothing that needed a good wash, and a pair of boots she suspected were older than her.

He'd never spoken to her until one awful day at the start of hunting season several years ago, when he'd approached her about opening up her land for killing. The Shifter Alliance put harsh restrictions on when and how much hunting could be done on public land, but there was more leeway on private property, so long as she allowed the surveyor to keep an eye on things once a year. Since her land was almost entirely wild, it'd become a haven for deer, elk, rabbit, and the occasional moose — an irresistible buffet to a man like Monty.

He hadn't liked her answer. She thought turning him down had sparked some resentful interest in her. She'd been more or less beneath his notice before then, but after, she couldn't seem to escape it.

Unfortunately, it was Monty who she suspected would be able to get her what Taevas needed.

Like always, Monty's watery blue eyes fixed on her the second he spied her by the register. Adjusting the brim of his hat with one dry, work-worn hand, he said, "Look at that — the little princess has graced us with her presence again, huh?"

Debbie brought her can up for a covert spit of brown tobacco juice. "Morning, Monty. Don't be a dick."

"Deb," he grunted, releasing the door. It didn't swing shut, however, as a hand caught it just before it made it to the jamb.

Alashiya had opened her mouth to force out her question about getting a satellite phone like the one she knew Monty had, but the words died on her tongue when a pale blue arm pushed the door open again.

Monty glanced carelessly over his shoulder as he shuffled inside, making way for the much bigger man to follow him in.

It was remarkable how one could go from never seeing a dragon in their life to seeing two in the span of a week.

Alashiya stared at the man who stepped into the shop with wide eyes. He had to duck to accommodate his height, which was added to by a set of short gilded horns. His hair was dark and carefully styled out of his eyes. Heavy-set in the way people with natural muscle often were, he was perhaps the single largest being Alashiya had ever seen. Even slightly bigger than Taevas, though they had to be close. Her dragon was a bit leaner and ever-so-slightly taller, but it was a near thing.

Dressed in what looked like brand new hiking gear, sans the boots, he made a bizarre image there in the narrow doorway.

"Move, princess. You aren't the only one who has shit to do," Monty barked.

He nearly elbowed her away from the register, but she stepped aside just in time. There was suddenly hardly any room to move in the space between the register and aisles. With the three men, Monty, and the huge dragon, Alashiya had the thought that she might actually get stepped on.

"That's not very nice," a deep, smooth voice rumbled. "Give the lady some room."

Alashiya tensed when the three men immediately stepped aside, their attention moving in sync to the dragon, who'd shoved his massive hands into the pockets of his expensive-looking hiking pants. He smiled at her, showing off pearly fangs and the webbing of crow's feet around his dark eyes.

The motion of his tail slowly swishing back and forth behind him drew her eye. The hair on the back of her neck stood up. It moved in the way a cat's tail did just before they pounced on an unsuspecting bluejay.

He was handsome, in a mature, dangerous sort of way, and he appeared to know it when he gave her a slow perusal with a smile. "Where have *you* been hiding, pretty thing? Never thought I'd find a treasure all the way out here." He flashed her a wink. "The gods have sent me a blessing in my time of need. What's your name?"

Monty, who'd already begun arguing with Debbie over the price of a week's worth of MREs, drew his back up to level a glare at the dragon. "Why'd you need to know that?"

The dragon's easy smile didn't fall, exactly, but something cold slithered in his gaze when he briefly turned his attention to the hunter. "I'm not paying you to question me, arrant. I was speaking to the lady."

Fear was suddenly a hard, spiky lump in the pit of Alashiya's stomach. The dragon hadn't done anything. He didn't raise his voice or even take his hands out of his pockets, but he didn't need to. The menace was in his eyes.

What if he had something to do with Taevas's abduction?

She shuffled her feet in an effort to dispel the urge to run. There was no evidence of that. He hadn't explained who kidnapped him. It was strange that she'd see another dragon so soon after finding Taevas in her barn, sure, but more improbable things happened.

But that menace lingered in her mind's eye like a stormcloud on the horizon. Goosebumps broke out across her arms. *Whoever he is, I want nothing to do with him.*

Monty was either too irascible or too stubborn to take the hint from the dragon. Alashiya would've wagered it was equal parts both, if she weren't fighting her instinct to run with everything she had.

The old hunter gave her a scathing once-over and made a derisive sucking sound with his teeth. "Oh, she's a lady all right. Too good for anybody or anything in this town."

"Shut the fuck up, Monty," Debbie groused.

Eyeing the dragon in the way that meant she was estimating just how much money she might be able to wring out of him, Debbie explained, "This is our Shiya. Born and raised here, never been trouble for anybody in her life. Comes from a real old, royal family, her grandma told me — Grim guide her soul. This grouchy fuck's just bitter she doesn't want an old man breathing down her shirt and killin' things on her land."

Alashiya's lips tightened. *You just love to gossip, Debbie.*

The dragon tilted his head slightly. The whole time Debbie spoke, he hadn't taken his eyes off Alashiya, who stood frozen by a stand full of miniature bags of chips. A hideous sensation of exposure, like Debbie had peeled Alashiya's skin off to show the dragon her insides, made her heart jackknife against her ribs.

"Tell me your family name, Shiya. I come from an old family myself, so who knows? Our kin might've crossed paths." He gave her an indulgent look, like he knew she couldn't possibly be anyone of importance but was choosing to indulge her anyway. To *flatter* her.

Alashiya swallowed a bitter taste on her tongue. "It's Ardz."

He gave her another one of those polite, infuriating smiles. "Hm. How old is your *royal* family, exactly?"

"The oldest," she answered, briefly throwing caution aside to meet his dark gaze. Her ghosts whispered in her ear, their pride a wave of prickling heat under skin, in the blood that pumped through her heart and the silver roots that marked her body as sacred.

The oldest of the old. As old as creation.

The dragon made a thoughtful sound in the back of his

throat. "Ardz doesn't ring a bell, but I'll look into it." One step put him into her space. He towered over her.

Swallowing her useless pride, she dropped her eyes and felt for the first time what it was to be a mouse in the shadow of a hawk.

He opened his mouth to speak again, his head bent as if he intended to whisper in her ear, but the dragon was cut off by Monty's impatient bark. "You're paying me to take you hunting, not to stand around and watch you hit on some fuckin' nymph. You want me to go?"

It was breathtaking, seeing the change in the dragon's expression from so close up. One moment his smile was soft, beguiling, and his handsome features were set in an expression of pure invitation. Within the span of a heartbeat, those same features had contorted into an animal's snarl.

He whirled on Monty, huge wings mantled high enough that his talons scraped the yellowed popcorn ceiling. "Watch your fucking tongue, *arrant*," he snapped. "If I want to waste my money speaking to a beautiful woman rather than this fucking shit show, I will. And you'll mind your language in front of the lady. I know it's hard for you, but show some respect."

Monty sucked his teeth again. "You only paid for a week of huntin', rich boy. You want me to watch my fuckin' mouth, too? That's extra."

The dragon took one threatening step toward Monty. Alashiya saw her opportunity and took it.

Gripping the strap of her bag until her knuckles blanched white, she ducked her head and slipped behind the dragon. Avoiding his swiping, rattling tail took a dexterous twist of her hips. A handful of quick steps saw her to the door. She moved so fast that no one, including the silent group of men, seemed to notice she was on her way until the bell clanged. By then she was already out the door.

Chapter Seventeen

She ran until she hit the border of her land. Even then, it wasn't until the familiar, comforting weight of her wards closed over her that she felt she could breathe freely again.

It wasn't unusual for her to leave town feeling uncomfortable, even unsafe. But this particular encounter left her shaken to her core. The sense that she'd narrowly escaped something ugly was a shadow over her mind. It chased her all the way back to the edge of her forest, which seemed to hum with concern all around her.

Pausing to catch her breath, Alashiya placed a hand on a tree trunk. Its energy, the thrum of its very soul, chorused through the sensitive pads of her fingers and palm. Plants couldn't speak, but they held a consciousness of their own. Their language was one of pulses, *feeling*. Trees were especially aware and tended to communicate as a unit rather than individuals.

So it was the whole forest who wondered what had so disturbed her. It was an impression rather than words, but Alashiya didn't need words to understand.

"I'm fine," she muttered, stroking the papery bark reassuringly.

The forest wasn't a pet. It wasn't soft or kind or forgiving, and it didn't necessarily ask her out of any concern for her wellbe-

ing, but rather that of itself. The forest had viewed her as one of
its own since the night her grove died, when it'd sheltered her and
stood guard for days, until her grieving grandparents dug her out
of the soil and the tangle of roots that had sustained her.

A threat to her might well be a threat to the collective and
ought to be dealt with swiftly. To the forest, she was just another
sapling. It didn't necessarily need or even understand her affection, but she thought the forest enjoyed her attention. Even
though it never told her as much, it might even like it when she
petted a trunk every now and again.

Sensing that there was no imminent threat to itself, the
ancient consciousness of the trees retreated back into itself, its
attention drawn to more important things.

The air was warm and heavy with moisture. It clung to her
skin, promising another summer storm. She breathed it in and
willed her heartbeat to slow.

The house stood unchanged on the slight hill. Her garden
glowed with life in the sun. If she slipped her shoes off and dug
her toes in the soil, she would've been able to hear the happy,
wordless chattering of her plants all the way from the forest's
edge. Being so close to home helped calm her at last.

They could've just been hunters, she reasoned, grunting with
discomfort as she switched her bag to her other shoulder. *Monty
takes groups out all the time, though gods only know why anyone
hires him.*

But two dragons in a week? Alashiya couldn't dismiss that.

*Their gear looked brand new, too. And those three men... They
didn't act normal. They didn't even speak.*

All of it felt off, though she couldn't say anyone besides
Monty had done anything wrong. But that was normal, in its own
way. She sometimes thought that he believed he could eventually
wear her down with his cruelty and she'd just give in to whatever
he wanted. It'd worked for him in the past. Most folks didn't say
no to him because it was too much trouble.

It was unlucky for Taevas that Monty was the only man she

knew who owned a satellite phone. And it was even more unlucky for her that she hadn't even gotten the chance to ask him about it.

Feeling defeated by it all, Alashiya wiped the sweat from her forehead and trudged grimly across the yard. She was stepping through the kitchen door when something Monty said registered in her mind at last.

"You only paid me for a week," he'd reminded the dragon. And he'd argued with Debbie about the price of a week's worth of MREs, the pre-made meals hunters often took on long trips.

"No," Alashiya moaned, dropping her bag on the kitchen table. A bottle of cooking oil tumbled out and rolled onto the floor with a mocking thump. "He's going to be hunting for a *week.*"

Which meant that he wouldn't be able to lend her his phone for that time, and Taevas was left high and dry.

Silently cursing her foul luck, Alashiya took the time to splash cool water on her face and the back of her neck before she sought out her guest. It was with a nasty jolt of surprise that she found his bed empty. She'd barely noticed that he'd taken the blanket and pillow off before she darted back down the hall to the living room.

Fear clamped itself around her throat, holding tight, as she imagined what he could've done with Adon's robe, with the only precious things she possessed. Almost none of it would be of value to him, but that had never stopped people from destroying or stealing things before. And her commission for Adon *was* valuable, at least in the gold she sewed on it.

Imagining every worst case scenario, including finding him dead of whatever ailed him, Alashiya rushed into the living room.

"Taevas?" she called, frantically taking stock of her quilts, her work table, and all the other things that wouldn't have value to anyone but her.

Nothing appeared disturbed. The robe lay on her workbench in exactly the way she'd left it. The blood rushed from her head in a dizzying wave. Thinking that perhaps he was in the bathroom, she turned to leave the room. "Taevas, are you—"

A faint rustling drew her back into the living room.

Alashiya stepped inside slowly, her gaze moving in a careful sweep over the room, until it landed on her bed.

At first she didn't notice anything amiss. Her bed consisted of three mattresses sewn together on the floor, piled high with every bit of bedding and pillow she could find. After long days of hunching over her work, it was a luxury to be able to lay completely flat or in any position that eased her aching muscles, necessitating a large, customizable bed.

So it took her a moment to notice, amongst the many blankets and cushions, the shape of the dragon, his large body sprawled across the mattresses. He lay on his front, she thought. Most of the dragon was obscured by blankets he'd pulled haphazardly over himself, but a fall of raven black hair over a white cotton pillowcase gave him away.

Alashiya took all this in with a galloping heart. *Thank the gods.*

It was annoying, certainly, but compared to what she'd imagined, finding the dragon taking a nap in her bed really wasn't that bad.

The bed in the other room *had* been quite small for him, she admitted to herself. And if he'd been in pain or feeling ill, perhaps he'd sought a more comfortable place to rest. Her chest squeezed with empathy.

It wasn't good guest behavior, but it was at least understandable. And if she were being honest, there was something secretly thrilling about seeing him in her bed. No man had ever slept there before. To know he was sprawled across her sheets was oddly tantalizing. A blush heated her cheeks when she found herself wondering if her blankets would smell like him now.

Kneeling beside the bed, she gently peeled away some of the blankets from around Taevas's face. He stirred a little. Groaning, he clutched a blanket and drew it to his nose. The deep furrowing of his brow eased after a deep breath.

Something went tight in her chest as she watched him. Taevas had seemed very fierce, and she didn't doubt he *was,* but there was nothing besides softness to him as he lay in her bed, the lines of exhaustion around his mouth and eyes erased. She didn't want to wake him — and not only because she had bad news.

It was... nice, seeing him so relaxed. She'd gotten used to the dragon in her kitchen, and though it seemed impossible only a day before, she thought she could get used to seeing *this* man in her home. For a little while, at least.

In the end, it was her concern over his health that forced her hand.

Alashiya gave his bare shoulder a gentle shake. His skin was blazing hot under her palm. Her concern mounted when he didn't rouse right away, but groaned a complaint and kept his eyes closed.

"Taevas," she whispered, patting his hot cheek. "Taevas, you have to wake up. I have some medicine you need to take."

Her alarm spiked when he still didn't respond. Leaning in close to check his breathing, she ordered, "Wake *up,* dragon!"

Glazed violet eyes snapped open just as something snaked around her waist and cinched tight. "Naughty. You left," he muttered in a hoarse voice, upper lip curling to reveal his fangs. "You're not allowed to leave. I forbid it."

Alashiya blinked rapidly. There'd been no basis for comparison before, but now that she'd met two dragons, she realized that *this* one didn't scare her. Not in the way the blue dragon had — like one wrong move would see him tearing her limb from limb, that charming smile fixed on his face all the while.

Trying to process that revelation while Taevas glared at her through narrowed eyes, she replied, "I got medicine. I think you should take it."

"I don't want medicine," he complained. "I want to go home. I *need* to go home."

Realizing that she was dealing with someone not quite in their right mind, she gentled her tone. "I know you do, but taking the medicine will help us figure out how to get you there."

Taevas's look turned downright mutinous. "Not *you*. Us."

"Huh?" She tried to sit back a little, but his tail held her there. Unwilling to jostle him too much, Alashiya held still. "Can you let me go? I've got to—"

"Never, *never*," Taevas hissed, eyelids drooping. The end of his tail rattled violently against her.

Sensing that she was getting nowhere fast, Alashiya tried a different tactic. "Okay, dragon. Okay. If I promise to stay here with you, will you let me get the medicine from the kitchen? I'll come right back."

He squinted at her for several long seconds, his expression grave. "Promises can be broken, *metsalill. Minu metsalill.* How do I know you'll come back? You're rebellious. Always hiding from me. I just found you. No more hiding."

That tight feeling returned, though she hadn't a clue as to why; only that he looked so sad, so expectant, that she couldn't stand it. Her pulse quickened when she dared to stroke the curve of his cheek with the tips of her fingers.

"Some promises are harder to keep than others. This is an easy one, *argaman mlk.*"

He turned his face into her touch, seeking her fingers with a long, relieved sigh. "Don't break my heart, please."

The hook in her chest threatened to pull her heart out and show it to him. "I won't," she whispered, stroking his brow. "I promise."

Chapter Eighteen

He woke to the soothing sound of a needle and thread being pulled through fabric. It was a perfectly rhythmic sound composed of several parts: a barely audible pop of metal through the weave of taut fabric, the draw of the thread, a slight pause, then another pop.

It wasn't a sound he was used to anymore. When he was a boy, living in a shack on a mountain with parents fighting for the family's survival, he'd often heard it in the evenings as his father mended clothing by the fire. His *isa* didn't sleep until his mate came home from her service to Isand Jaak and he needed to keep his hands busy.

Taevas had never seen the appeal of sewing, though he appreciated the skill. His focus had gone to training as a carpenter. Like his father, he enjoyed having work to do, and carpentry connected him with his childhood hero, the greatest dragon of the Aždaja line: Isand Vanasarvik. Taevas idolized the dragon who'd begun life as a lowly carpenter, only to Choose a princess threatened by warring dragons greedy for her lands and become the greatest of the Aždaja line.

It'd been good for Taevas to have a trade, it connected him with Vanasarvik, and it calmed his young mind when fear for his mother sought to drive him mad. And then, like the sound of sewing in the evening and everything else he cherished, it was taken from him.

Taevas opened his bleary eyes. It took him several slow seconds to comprehend where he was. Exhaustion and a dull ache permeated every cell of his body. He knew that he ought to spring up, to summon the urgency his situation demanded, but whatever reserve he'd drawn from to chase his nymph had been utterly depleted.

He could only blink slowly, his gaze drifting until it found the most important thing in the room — Alashiya.

She sat at her workbench, her back to him, as she labored in the soft yellow light of a lamp. Everytime the rhythm of her sewing paused, it was because she'd stretched the thread to its limit, allowing him to glimpse the flicker of silver as her needle just crested the rise of her shoulder.

The air was rich with the scent of something savory. A brief pang of shame struck him when he recalled where he lay, but it was gone as quickly as it came. Crawling into her nest while she was away wasn't the same as being invited, but he hadn't been able to help himself. Being in a more comfortable nest would help him recover faster, he'd reasoned, so it was in fact necessary.

Another failed negotiation with the hungry beast inside him. Another concession to parts of him he'd believed were locked away for good.

He'd been upset with her when she left. It burned something vital in him that he'd been powerless to protect her, that she'd defied his authority and waltzed out like she had — ignoring his command *again.*

It didn't matter that he wasn't the ruler of her territory. People respected him. They did what he said whenever he said it. It was galling to be defied by such a soft, breakable creature, and it was even more troubling to realize he could hate something and find it arousing at the same time.

But he wasn't angry at her anymore. How could he be? Taevas

gazed at the perfect, soft lines of her form with a raw sort of longing. He wanted her nearer. He wanted her in the nest.

Swallowing that instinctive urge, he croaked, "Did you find a phone?"

The rhythm of her sewing halted. Alashiya twisted around in her old wooden chair. Her brows were drawn low over her sad eyes. She looked concerned when she stood up from her chair and crossed the room. Kneeling down beside him, she reached out to touch his forehead with her inner wrist. "Fever's gone down a bit and you seem more lucid. How are you feeling?"

"Like I was drugged for two weeks," he replied, a touch crankier than he knew she deserved. "Did you find a phone, Shiya?"

He had vague memories of her return to the house and of being coerced into swallowing a few chalky pills, but no memory of what she'd told him. It vexed him that she'd gone into town on her own, but it might've been worth it if she'd succeeded in whatever plan took her there.

Removing her wrist, Alashiya sat back on her haunches. The concern in her eyes didn't lessen. "You're still warm. We should get some food in you and then more pills. If your fever doesn't go down by tomorrow, I really think we should call the ran—"

"Metsalill," he interrupted, "the phone."

She shook her head. "I'm sorry. I went to the store to ask, and the only man who I know owns a sat phone was there, but I wasn't able to ask him if I could use it."

Frustration made his tone harsh when he demanded, *"Why?* Damn it, Shiya, you have no idea how important this is!"

Taevas didn't often raise his voice. It wasn't necessary. The times he did need to make an impression on someone or intimidate them into submission, he never let his emotions get the better of him. If he shouted, it was a precisely aimed strike, not out of some explosion of emotion.

But this was different.

Alashiya recoiled as if he'd struck her. Aghast, Taevas tried to reach for her, but she evaded his seeking hand. "I apologize. I didn't mean to—"

"I tried," she explained, small fists curling in her lap, "but Monty is— It doesn't matter. I tried to ask, but he was busy with a hunting party. He's a guide. They were getting supplies for a trip. When one of them started talking to me, Monty and the guy got into an argument. I didn't feel safe, so I left."

Trying to muddle through the sick feeling of guilt that turned his insides to sludge and the details of her story at the same time, Taevas attempted to rise onto his elbow. Struggling, he demanded, "Who's Monty? And what the fuck do you mean you didn't feel safe?"

She wouldn't look at him, but she didn't hesitate to slip a few pillows under his shoulders to help him sit up. Because she was a sweet soul. Taevas cursed his short temper to the vilest pit in the underworld. *I must be better than this for her.*

"Monty is a hunter who lives about an hour from here. He's one of those anti-government nuts who lives off the grid. I know he has a sat phone, so I thought I could ask to borrow it."

Aware that it wouldn't be wise to mention that Alashiya herself lived off the grid, Taevas pressed, "And you couldn't ask because he got into an argument with some guy at the store?"

"It was his client," she replied, nervously smoothing a curl behind her ear. "He said they were going out for a week-long hunt. But the guy started talking to me and Monty got— how Monty gets. The client got mad and I didn't want to get in the middle of a fight between the two, so I had to go."

She said the last part quickly, defensively, like she thought he would get angry at her for leaving when she felt threatened. Taevas supposed that was fair, if inaccurate.

"Good girl," he praised, meaning it with everything in him. A tightness took up residence in his chest at the thought of Alashiya being stuck between two brawling idiots when he wasn't there to protect her. His breath hitched at the mere thought.

"That was the right thing to do, *metsalill*. If you ever feel threatened, you should run."

"Didn't do me a lot of good with you."

He offered her a small, sharp smile. "The rules are different with me. You should always run *toward* me, never away."

Alashiya gave him a dubious look. "I thought you were angry."

"I'm frustrated and worried about my people," he explained, shaking his aching head, "but your safety is worth more than a phone. We'll find another way."

"Well, Monty should be back in a week."

Rubbing his stinging eyes, Taevas muttered, "A week is a very long time when a people are missing their leader."

"I understand better than you probably think. I'll try to think of something else." Alashiya rose from her kneeling position. Speaking almost to herself, she added, "Honestly, I'd really rather not ask Monty if I can help it."

His eyes narrowed. "Why?"

She moved toward the kitchen. He couldn't see her face, but the line of her shoulders was tight when she answered, "We have a history."

"What kind of history?"

But she was already out of the room, leaving his question unanswered until an unbearable length of time later, when she returned with a tray laden with two earthenware bowls, a dish of what looked like flat bread loosely wrapped in cloth, and a pair of glasses.

Kneeling gracefully enough that she hardly rattled the dishes, she set the tray in his lap before removing what had to be her portion. Settling on a cushion, she placed her bowl on her lap and answered, "After my grandfather died, Monty asked me if he could use my land for hunting. I said no."

Whatever it was she'd made for dinner smelled mouthwatering. Taevas glanced at the bowl — some sort of green stew swirled with cream or yogurt — but he couldn't unclench his muscles enough to allow him to try it.

"Is that all?" he asked, tail rattling softly beneath the blankets of her nest.

Men, he knew, could do a great many terrible things when their demands weren't met. It made his blood run cold, thinking of Alashiya being alone on her wild land, at the mercy of any greedy being who might turn his eye toward her.

Alashiya leaned over to tug at the cloth covering the bread. Steam, carrying the heavenly scent of the bread, filled the air as she plucked one from the pile.

"No." She tore a piece off the bread and dipped it into her stew. "He also wants me to marry him."

If his wings hadn't been damaged, they would've been mantled over his head the instant the words left her mouth. Speaking in a hard, flat voice, Taevas repeated, "He wants to marry you."

"My land is better than his," she explained, shrugging. "And he's a mean, lonely man. I think he wants a woman to take care of him, and I think he's tired of not having sex."

Alashiya didn't seem at all concerned by this, only a little uncomfortable as she quietly ate her stew. It was Taevas who found it alarming. Possessiveness was a roar in his blood, yes, but it was a deeper concern that made him want to hunt Monty down and handle him right then.

Trying to find his usual cool pragmatism, Taevas asked, "Does he harass you?"

Alashiya didn't answer him directly. "I avoid him whenever I can."

"So that's a yes." Fire, icy cold and infinitely dangerous, surged up his throat to lick at the backs of his fangs.

He wouldn't dare if she had a mate, the beast in him growled. *He wouldn't even look at her if this were my roost, if she smelled of me, if my ash were laid.*

Sensing there was far more to the story, he grated, "What happened at the store, Shiya?"

She eyed his untouched dinner with pursed lips. "You should eat. You've hardly had anything since you shifted, and nothing at all before that."

"Tell me."

"Monty likes to pick on me," she explained with a sigh. "Sometimes I think he believes if he does it long enough, I'll eventually cave. Or maybe he does it because he just hates me. I don't know. But he was doing it when his client came in, and the client started talking to me, which made Monty worse. He gets nastier when he sees other people, men especially, being nice to me."

I bet he does, Taevas thought, fists clenching.

"He was rude to his client about it, which didn't go over well," she continued. "They started to argue, so I left."

"You will not approach Monty without me again." Taevas waited for her to meet his eyes before he repeated, slowly and with every ounce of authority he possessed, "You will *not,* Alashiya. That's an order from your Isand."

Alashiya lifted one shoulder in a half-hearted shrug. Dragging her bread through the stew, she replied, "I can handle him. It's the dragon I'm not so sure about. He gave me this awful feeling."

Taevas went still. "What dragon?"

"The client." Apparently fed up with his disinterest in eating, Alashiya set her stew aside and leaned over to grab another piece of bread from under the cloth. Tearing it in half, she stuffed it into his hand and guided it to the bowl. "Eat, Taevas. You haven't had anything for days and days."

It wasn't the time to explain to her that dragons could go a very long time without meals. They were designed to be able to fly for weeks at a time, never touching the ground or stopping for water, let alone food. It wasn't without consequence, of course, and usually involved a dragon gorging themselves to replenish their resources when they landed, but it was a system that worked well enough.

Since he'd spent the last few weeks more or less immobile rather than burning through his fat stores in flight, Taevas didn't *need* the meal she'd made him. He wanted it, though, as soon as he got his answers. Alarm bells clanging in his mind, he asked, "The client was a dragon?"

"Yes. I thought that seemed strange. We don't get dragons here. You weren't kidnapped by a dragon, were you? I don't know what a kidnapper looks like, and I don't want to assume your own people would try to hurt you, but... I don't know. He felt wrong to me."

She pulled her bowl back into her lap and crossed her ankles in front of her. At another time, he would've admired how at home she looked, sitting beside him, enjoying a bit of dinner by the nest.

His heart lurched painfully. He *also* didn't want to believe his own people would attack him, but being Isand meant he had enemies, and many of them had been gunning for him since he was a teenager. Jaak had a lot of friends, after all, and some still wished to return to the old ways — and it was a dragon that had tangled with him above the summer storm clouds the night he crashed into Alashiya's barn.

But what Taevas found most upsetting was the fact that she'd been so very near danger. Of course he knew that he'd put her at risk just being there, but he hadn't dared to think his enemies would find her so quickly, let alone when he wasn't at her side, protecting her.

Wracking his mind for the most likely suspects, he demanded, "Did he say his name?"

She frowned. "I don't know. He didn't say."

Nervous energy made his tail rattle menacingly beneath the blankets. "Tell me everything, Shiya. Every single detail."

"Only if you eat a little," she haggled.

Dipping his bread into the stew, he growled, *"Fine."*

She looked very pleased with herself when she watched him shove the bread into his mouth. It vexed him further that it was, of course, delicious, and he couldn't hide his pleasure from her. A dimple appeared in her cheek when she gave him a smug smile. "I was going to mention it to you anyway because it's not normal for dragons to pass through here. I'd never even seen one before you. I always heard the land is too flat, so your folk avoid it."

Taevas was too busy with his stew to answer properly, so he merely grunted. It was true. His people had traditionally settled in mountain ranges, since takeoff and landing required a leap. They only tended to compromise on that when it came with large economic trade-offs, which was why they took New York's harbor and the Great Lakes. In the flat places, they built skyscrapers and perches from which to leap off and land, which solved the problem well enough.

Nodding at her to continue, he tore another piece of flatbread in half and returned to his stew. It was rich with spices and drenched with a garlicky yogurt sauce that made him want to lick the bowl clean, dignity be damned.

"Like I said, I didn't get his name. But he was a big guy. His skin was light blue and he had dark hair. His clothes looked new and expensive, so I figured he was another one of those bored rich people who come through every summer. Oh, and his horns had metal on them." Alashiya soaked up the last of her stew with a small corner of bread, her eyes lowered. "He wasn't unpleasant, but something about him didn't sit well with me. I don't know what it was."

The description meant little to him. There were many blue dragons in the world, and even more big ones. The only unique detail she'd offered was that he had gilded horns. That was a sign of a noble birth which had more or less been destroyed by the war, when metals couldn't be spared for something like vanity or a display of rank. Afterward, it was seen as a mark of an old-timer, someone who was stuck in the past. The only people he knew who still sported gilded horns were either on the old continent or those few who still clung to the old ways.

It didn't mean anything necessarily, but it also didn't bode well at all.

Of course, it was possible it was just a coincidence. Dragons weren't confined to the Draakonriik. They could live anywhere and do whatever they liked, including hiring someone to take them on a hunting trip in the Shifter Alliance.

But the odds of a dragon appearing not long after Taevas landed on Alashiya's land weren't great. He'd never met a dragon who liked to hunt on foot. They were aerial predators. Most would find a walk in the forest about as pleasant as Taevas had.

But if a dragon lost something in the woods...

CHAPTER NINETEEN

A CHILL RAN DOWN TAEVAS'S SPINE. "YOU SAID HE hired Monty for a week?"

"That's what it sounded like, yeah." Alashiya grabbed her bowl and stood. He watched her make a quick trip back to the kitchen with his heart jammed in his throat.

There was a chance the dragon had nothing to do with his capture, but he knew for a fact that at least one had been involved in it. The idea that Alashiya might've been in the presence of that person, stuck between them and a man who thought nothing of harassing her, while *he* remained confined to the nest, filled him with a terrible, impotent rage. Not at the situation, nor even at the aggressors, but at himself.

What was he good for, if not protecting the people he cared for?

He needed to warn her again, to make absolutely certain that she understood the risks of encountering that dragon or telling anyone he was with her, but Taevas found his ability to speak hampered by his shame.

How long had he dreamed of meeting her, only to find that when the time came, he was a burden, unable to so much as defend her from the threats he'd brought to her door? He was

Isand of the Draakonriik, but he'd been reduced to complete dependence on her for everything — shelter, food, and now defense.

The delicious food curdled in his belly. He'd set the tray aside by the time Alashiya made her way back into the room. She gave him a small, nervous smile and made to settle at her workbench again, but this time Taevas found his voice.

"You work too hard, *minu metsalill.* It's late. You should stop."

"I need to get this done," she replied, head already bent over her task. "I'm behind, and I can't deliver it late."

Guilt gnawing at him, he soothed, "I'm *certain* your customer won't mind."

"I would."

"It is good to be proud of your work," he argued, "but not if it hurts you. Come sit with me. I want to speak to you more before my body betrays me again."

He expected her to immediately refuse, but she surprised him with a long, thoughtful pause. "I really have to finish this."

"Then bring it with you. Show me how you make such beautiful things. I've watched you work for days. Now I want to know everything about it."

It felt like a victory when she eventually replied, "I can't bring the whole thing over there, but... I could bring a smaller part, if you *really* want to see."

"I do," he emphatically replied.

She didn't move right away, and he got the sense that she was warring with herself, like she was trying to talk herself out of it but couldn't quite manage the task. At last, she gathered her things and slowly made her way back across the room. He wanted her, *needed* her in the nest beside him, but she settled on her cushion again — near enough to touch but too far for comfort.

Settling her various tools beside her on the floor, Alashiya spread a fine velvet sash across her supple thighs. The ends were pointed, and from each fell a delicate gold tassel. Across its length was a collection of celestial motifs wrought in gold, half-finished but unmistakably beautiful.

Taevas's fingers itched to touch it. Without thinking, he reached for it, but Alashiya snatched it away. "Don't touch," she ordered, sounding appalled.

For a moment, he forgot that she had no idea who he was, nor that the sash already belonged to him. It didn't matter. It was still his and he wanted it.

Drawing himself up as much as he could, he demanded, "Why not?"

"Because it's for *him*, not you." Alashiya eyed him suspiciously, like he might try and snatch it out of her lap again.

"Who's *him?*" he asked, knowing full-well that sash went with *his* robe, which he'd had handmade and shipped to the atelier months ago.

He was fascinated to watch her cheeks darken with a flush. "He's— It's for my favorite customer. I've been making things for him for ten years now."

"You started to say something else there," he pointed out. "Was it his name?"

She shook her head. "I don't know his name."

He'd put that much together, but it still pissed him off to hear it confirmed. "Why not?"

"Because I work for a shop," she explained, taking up her needle. "They handle the clients and send the commissions my way. I don't need to know anyone's name."

Trying not to speak through clenched teeth, Taevas pressed, "And what do you call him, if you don't know his name?"

"I call him Adon," she murmured.

He wanted to focus on the skill with which she worked, the graceful tug and twist of her wrist as she threaded designs into the garment, but he couldn't. Taevas had to flatten his hands in his lap to thwart the urge to touch it.

Mentally adding up all he'd paid in the last decade against her patched clothing and tumble-down house, Taevas asked, "And does this *Adon* pay you well for your hard work?"

Alashiya shrugged again. "The atelier pays me, not him. I get by."

I get by.

Throat tightening with righteous anger, he forced himself to take a deep breath. It didn't help. "What about gifts? Surely someone as skilled as you receives gifts of thanks for your work. Your Adon must have sent you something to show his appreciation."

Where are my gifts, Shiya?

She gave him a funny look. "I've never gotten any gifts. Why would I?"

"Because Adon is grateful. And he understands how difficult your work is, how much time it must take, how your body must ache after so many hours. It's the least he could do, sending you something to show his appreciation."

Alashiya blinked several times, as if she struggled to imagine her favorite customer caring so much. Taevas ground his teeth together with such force, his molars squeaked.

"I doubt he thinks of me," she replied, shaking her head. "Why would he? For all I know, he probably doesn't even commission his own clothes. Maybe he has a stylist who does it, or a partner." She swallowed thickly. Her needle flashed in the light, the movements of her right hand turning a tad less graceful than before. "He doesn't know I exist."

His anger was momentarily knocked off-kilter. Watching her closely, Taevas asked, "Do you want him to?"

Alashiya's needle stilled. She didn't look up when she replied, "Like I said, he probably has no idea who I am and almost certainly has a partner."

"Why would it matter if he had a partner or not?"

Her needle began to flash again, its flicker picking up speed as her hand moved more quickly. "I never said it did."

"But you brought it up twice."

"So?" Her jaw jutted out at a stubborn angle.

"So what if he did want to know who you were — and he was *very* single?"

Alashiya sucked in a deep breath and held it for a second. After a measured exhale, she answered, "Then I would still just be the woman who embroiders his clothes and makes up silly stories about him being her husband so she doesn't feel as pathetic as she normally does. It wouldn't matter."

Silly stories about him being her husband? Taevas's stomach somersaulted. He had plans to hear those silly stories, her shyness be damned.

Husband. She makes up stories about me being her husband! Taevas wanted to crow with victory. The giddiness of it made him feel nearly drunk. And aroused. Very, very aroused.

"What's the difference between doing this for work and sewing for your *husband?*"

Alashiya looked like she'd rather he asked her to pull one of her teeth out and show it to him, but she still answered. "I take my time. I make it perfect."

She was holding something back. He could see it in the stiff set of her mouth and the way she stalwartly refused to look at him. "Is that all?"

"I..." She let out a slow breath. Looking down at the sash, she stroked the gleaming stitches with reverence. "There are some things that are reserved for kin. For spouses."

Feeling like he couldn't get enough oxygen, he whispered, "What things, my Shiya?"

Her fingertip traced a tiny, sigil-like pattern he'd seen on his clothing many times. "Blessings. Prayers." She skimmed the loose thread until she found the shiny silver needle again. "The strongest protection I can offer."

Without hesitation, she pressed the tip of the needle into the pad of her thumb. Taevas hissed, reaching for her instinctively, but was stopped by the sight of a single drop of her blood slipping down the shaft of the needle and into the gold thread.

The faintest sizzling sound filled the air and the heavy press of magic compressed his lungs for the span of a heartbeat — just long enough for the blood to disappear completely.

A buzzing took up residence in his ears.

No wonder her magic has felt different for a while now.

Alashiya hadn't just imbued his clothing with powerful wards and spells. She'd bound her magic to them with her *blood.*

He couldn't catch his breath. It wasn't just work for her. It was like the mending his *isa* did by the firelight — an act of care for her *husband.* It was a visible, tangible, *real* display of her claim.

His mind shot back to an image of his expansive closet. Stomach swooping, he tried to wrap his head around how much of her blood she'd put onto each garment. Too much, certainly, but also... He really didn't know how to parse the conflicting feelings of pride and dismay over her hundreds of tiny sacrifices.

It was a sweet relief to know he'd cared for every piece like the treasures they were, but even so, he couldn't help but feel like he hadn't appreciated them enough.

He wondered when it'd begun for her. What was the first garment that wasn't just for a client, but for her *husband?* He needed to know exactly which jacket, shirt, handkerchief, or sash it was. He needed to know so he could get it framed.

Gods, she claimed me with blood and magic and stories. I'm her husband. I'm her husband *and the luckiest dragon in the fucking world.*

Dragons took little more seriously than courtship. They were forward, focused, and almost impossible to dissuade once they'd laid their claim. But there was nothing, no higher compliment or greater honor, than for a dragon to be claimed *first.*

She didn't know his name. She didn't know his position. She'd claimed him as her husband by instinct alone.

Somehow, they'd known one another. They'd always known. A swelling sense of *rightness* threatened to expand his chest past the limits of his ribcage. It was too good to let anything else in —

no doubt or fear or the instinctive revulsion that'd kept his instincts in check for over a century.

Taevas had never felt a rush like this one. He doubted he ever would again.

Whatever his problems were, there was nothing that could diminish the pure, unfiltered triumph of being *hers*. Already knowing the answer, he breathed, "You don't give your blood to just anybody, do you?"

"Of course not," she muttered, tucking the needle into the fabric so it couldn't accidentally stick her. "That's reserved for kin."

"And you decided this Adon was kin without even knowing his real name? Without *asking,* at the very least?"

She shook her head. "It's just a story I tell myself. I decided a long time ago that if I knew the truth about him, it'd probably ruin things anyway. What's the harm if all I'm doing is adding extra protection?"

It took work to keep the feeling out of his voice when he asked, "Come on, you aren't curious about him at all? Your *husband?*"

At last losing her patience with his prodding, Alashiya set her needle and the sash down to fix him with an exasperated look. "Of course I am! I've embroidered dozens and dozens of garments for him. I imagine what his face looks like when he opens every box. I think about him *constantly*. But I'll never know Adon, and he'd never care to know me, so it's a sad little fantasy I shouldn't have told you."

He watched her with open wonder. An incredulous laugh escaped him. "You claimed him! All without knowing anything about him. Your *husband,* Adon. Do you have any idea how lucky he is?"

She stared at her lap, the fingers of her left hand curled into a fist. Speaking in a quieter voice, she said, "Once, my grove was something, but now we're nothing. I don't have friends. I'll never have a real husband or a family or a grove again. *This,* the silly fantasy and my work, is all I have. I'd really appreciate it if you didn't mock me for it. I'm very aware of how pathetic it is."

He was so wrapped up in his discovery that he nearly let her stand up and run out of the room. Gathering his wits just in time, he lunged for her free hand and held tight. "Shiya," he breathed, craning his neck to peer into her flushed, averted face. "My Shiya, no. I'm not mocking you. I wouldn't do that."

"Why not? I know what it looks like. Just a lonely woman making up stories about a man who'll never even— It's sad."

"It's not," he argued, tugging on her hand. She held herself stiffly and refused to move, but he wasn't done. "I know better than you think I do."

"Uh-huh." She cast him a flat look. "Let go."

"Only if you'll stay."

She shook her head. "I'm tired, Taevas. I'm going to sleep in the guest room."

"Good gods, woman, I won't kick you out of your nest," he protested, appalled.

Alashiya let out an exasperated sigh. "Then *you* go back to the guest room."

"Stay and speak to me, *metsalill.*"

"I don't *want* to."

"Why?"

"Because I'm embarrassed." Her voice cracked. "I don't know why I told you any of that, but I wish I hadn't. I just want to go to bed and forget it."

Sliding his fingers over the silken skin of her wrist, Taevas gently turned her hand until her palm was facing him. Easing his fingertips over the lines, tracing their unique pattern so he could picture them in his mind later, he asked, "What do you have to be embarrassed of, *minu metsalill?* You think your husband doesn't think of you, too? Do you imagine Adon thinks nothing of the artisan who presses her magic into the weave of his most precious possessions?"

Gently but firmly, he used his grip to reel her back toward the nest. Alashiya watched him with a guarded expression as she allowed him to guide her reluctantly down, until she knelt on the mattress beside him. This close, he could see every minute shift in color of her dark eyes — the same shade as waxed cedar wood, full of reds and browns and golds.

Whispering now, he asked, "Do you think your Adon doesn't breathe in the smell of you whenever he opens a new package? Do you think that he doesn't save every pressed flower, or sleep beneath the hoop you sent him whenever he's home? Do you think he doesn't get *painfully* hard whenever your fresh scent hits his nose? Do you think he isn't dying to know you? To have even something as simple as a name to cling to?"

Alashiya's lips parted. "Taevas, what— How do you know I sent—"

The corner of his mouth lifted in a self-deprecating smile. "Because I'm a pathetic man with a silly little fantasy, *metsalill.*" Allowing himself the indulgence of brushing his knuckles over her cheek, he whispered, "That sash and robe is mine. If you must leave me for the night, I'd like to keep them with me. Your husband is a greedy man, I'm afraid. Terribly hard to please."

"What are you talking about?"

He skimmed his thumb over the soft pillow of her lower lip. "You aren't the only one with a claim, Shiya. I'm afraid your Adon might be a bit more demanding in real life, but you'll get used to it." Taevas pressed his lips to the corner of her mouth — not quite a kiss, but close. Painfully close. "You'll have to, seeing as he's in your nest."

CHAPTER TWENTY

THE SASH SLID FROM HER HAND AND POOLED ON THE floor. The bristles of the velvet tickled the pads of her fingers as it fell, but she hardly noticed. Alashiya sat there, unable to move or speak or even breathe.

The whispers of her grove filled her ears, but she couldn't hope to understand what they were trying to tell her when they all spoke at once. It wasn't like she could focus on anything besides him, anyway.

Nymphs were physical creatures. They were lovers of the senses, of touch and sound and taste. They were present in their bodies more than most could hope to be — aware, at all times of their flesh, their impermanence, and the unlikely privilege of existence.

And yet Alashiya had never in all her years been as aware of her body as she was then, when Taevas ran his claws over the curve of her jaw. She swore she could feel the spark of life itself in the infinitesimal gap between their flesh.

"You can't be Adon," she whispered. "That's impossible."

Taevas nodded. "I know. It's the most impossible thing to ever happen to me, I think. But my name isn't Adon. It's Taevas Aždaja, Isand of the Draakonriik, Lord of the Dragon Clans, head of Clan Aždaja..." He paused to give her the gift of a slow, hungry smile. "And lover of beautiful things."

When she said nothing — *could* say nothing — he trailed the very tip of one claw through the spiral of a wispy curl by her ear. "Do you need me to prove it to you, *metsalill?*"

It was like her brain had stalled out. He said the words, and she didn't know how he'd know about the flowers if he wasn't telling the truth, so it all seemed like something she should be able to understand. It didn't work that way, though.

She tried to think through it logically, looking for any way he might've known, and came up with nothing. She hadn't packed any orders since he'd crashed through the roof of her barn. She definitely hadn't shared her habit of sending tiny gifts to her favorite customer with him. There wouldn't have been any reason to, since she hadn't gotten to the point of packing anything yet, and it was such a private thing...

That was perhaps proof enough, but she couldn't make herself believe it. She could hardly get her mind to work enough to *disbelieve* it. Instead, she simply sat there, blank, stuck between the two states of being, as Taevas's tail slowly curled around her waist.

He spoke in a low, hypnotizing murmur when he continued, "The first time I saw your work, it was in Stalton's Atelier. That was ten years ago. Since then, I've commissioned just about everything I could think of from you — pillowcases, jackets, handkerchiefs, robes, shirts. And everytime an order arrived, you sent me a card with a pressed flower."

He sat up a little. Slowly, like he was trying not to spook her, he curled his right hand around the nape of her neck and drew her closer, until she could feel the warmth of his breath on her skin. "I keep them in a crystal dish on my desk, so when I'm working I can always see something beautiful nearby."

"They're just flowers," she croaked, like it even mattered.

Taevas's smile turned wry. "I've told myself that many times. They're just flowers. It's just embroidery. She's just a faceless artisan. But I couldn't bear to throw them out. I had to commission more. I couldn't stop imagining the woman behind the needle, with her wild magic and perfect scent."

What could she possibly say to that? Alashiya trembled all over, though she wasn't entirely sure why. It was a lucky thing that Taevas didn't need her to reply. Once he'd begun to talk, he couldn't seem to stop.

"I've been trying to find you for years, Shiya. I practically begged the atelier to give me your name, a phone number, *anything*. I've sent a dozen messages and even more gifts." A flinty look replaced the softness in his eyes when he commanded, "Tell me honestly now: Did you receive *any* of that?"

She could only shake her head.

He sent me gifts? A sick sensation rolled around in her stomach. He'd tried to contact her, to write to her, and the atelier had just... failed to tell her. She couldn't even begin to understand why.

Her heart jumped when his fingers tightened around the back of her neck. It wasn't a painful hold but an intimate one. It was like she could feel every tiny shift in his emotions through the smallest twitch of his fingers against the sensitive skin of her nape.

"When everything is back to how it should be, I will be making a visit to Mr. Stalton and his sons," he promised. Alashiya hadn't seen a look like the one he wore before. Not on him, at least. It was one of pure, icy menace.

"What does it mean to be Isand of the Draakonriik?"

They were both surprised by the question when it came tumbling out of her mouth. Alashiya wasn't sure why they were the only words she could muster up, but it felt important; like she couldn't begin to unravel the rest of her thoughts until that particular knot gave way.

It was the first time since they'd begun their conversation that Taevas looked away. His jaw clenched as he stared at some point in the distance she couldn't see. "It's complicated. Technically, the word means *lord*. But it's an old thing, with a traditional meaning closer to *the one who sits on the tallest mountain.* It means that the dragon who sits above others is responsible for all below them."

Her mind had begun to work again. Alashiya could tell by the way it felt like the earth started to shift beneath her, sliding slowly away until she could perceive some terrible opening creeping closer. Her stomach plunged.

"You sit above all others. You're... the leader of the Draakonriik."

Taevas flashed her a huge, brilliant-white smile. It was genuine, she thought, but something in it felt practiced, like he was posing for her rather than truly joyful. "I told you this, didn't I?"

He had. It was simply his misfortune that he'd fallen into the lap of the one person in all the UTA who didn't pay any attention to what happened outside the borders of her tiny haven.

Of course she knew where the Draakonriik *was,* but what use did she have for learning the frivolous titles for every leader of the territories? From what she recalled in school, there were heaps of them. *Sovereign. Matriarch. Alpha. Congress. Queen.* The list was endless. It was enough to know that those important people existed, she thought. It never occurred to her that the path of her life would *ever* cross with one of them.

The opening in the earth beneath her was rapidly approaching. She could feel the slip-slide of it speeding up as it rushed nearer.

Speaking in a whisper, she told him, "Adon means *lord.*"

Taevas's smile fell. The striking features of his face softened into an expression of wonder as he slowly, slowly inched their faces closer. "And *metsalill* means *wildflower,*" he murmured. "*Minu metsalill.* My wildflower."

It's him. He's here. It's been him this whole time.

The floor fell out from beneath her.

She'd imagined him many times. Too many times to count. As she fell asleep at night, she'd picture what it would be like to meet him. He'd be handsome and kind and sensitive. They'd recognize each other instantly, and he'd sweep her away to some other life not so full of fear and grief as her own.

He was wealthy, since that was the only thing that made sense in context, but not *important*. He'd never been a dragon, but the head of a sept of gargoyles, maybe, or a loner. He was a harpy, too, with grand feathered wings and penetrating raptor eyes.

Why hadn't it ever crossed her mind that he could be a dragon? Gods, not just any dragon. *The* dragon.

Taevas's soft look bled into one of concern. "Shiya, what's wrong?"

"I don't know," she answered honestly. Her voice was breathless with a nameless kind of panic. "I never imagined— You weren't supposed to be—" She clutched at his sturdy arm like it was the only thing that could pull her out of the hole she'd fallen into. "Was this all a plan? To— to meet me?"

"No, of course not." He gave the back of her neck a firm squeeze. "Look at me. Remember how injured I was when I landed in your barn. How would I have faked that? And even if I had — *why?* You think I wanted to meet you at my lowest? Alashiya, I dreamed of *impressing* you, not imposing myself on you."

Yes, of course. That all made sense. But the panic wouldn't leave her. She wasn't let down by the revelation that her Adon was Taevas, leader of a territory, but there was a staggering sort of loss in the revelation.

Keeping him as a dream, the husband of her heart, had kept her safe. Now that he was real, her husband was banished to the place where all fantasies went to die. She was left behind in the cold reality of it. Him.

Real people could hurt you. They could let you down. They could crash through your barn and steal your bed and make demands. They could break your heart without even trying.

Taevas's tone was back to being that stern, worried one that simultaneously annoyed and delighted her. "Shiya, tell me what you need."

Her skin prickled as age-old instinct moved in a wave inside her. "I—I want to hide. From this. You. I don't know why."

Looking truly alarmed now, Taevas cupped her cheeks and pressed their foreheads together. Rather than give her space to calm down, his solution always seemed to be to bring her closer. "I'm so sorry, but I can't let you hide from me. I'm too damn weak to hunt you down again so I must keep you here. Breathe, *minu metsalill.* You must breathe for me now. There's nothing to fear."

She tried to, but it wasn't easy. A great weight had settled on her chest. It pressed down on her so hard, it squeezed all the air out of her lungs and made her eyes water. The more her thoughts spun, the worse the weight became.

Out of the corner of her eye, Taevas's wings arched and flexed. It didn't appear he meant to do it, and as soon as they began to move, they stopped. The appendages jerked back into position behind him, the elegant bones and gauzy, veined membrane twitching uncontrollably.

Taevas's dark skin went ashen. A curse hissed from between clenched fangs. "What kind of dragon am I, that I can't do even *this?*"

She had no idea what he meant and couldn't ask. Whatever had upset him, he seemed to come to a compromise when he snatched a blanket from his lap and, in a series of sharp, urgent movements, wrapped it around her tight enough to make her squirm.

Tugging her into his arms, Taevas pressed her face into the juncture of his shoulder and neck. "If you must hide, my Shiya, I will be your shelter, even now, when my wings fail me."

The long curtain of his raven hair blocked out the light. His skin was feverishly warm under her cheek. Had the fever reducers done so little?

Worry nagged, but his scent, something warm and rich and *him,* closed in around her as tightly as the blanket. He wrapped her in his arms, two iron bands over her back. She was strewn haphazardly across his lap, rendered entirely immobile, and it was the single most comforting embrace she'd had since the night her grandfather died.

Her heartbeat began to slow. Pressing her face into his skin, she felt the frantic thrum of his own pulse against her lips. Her eyes closed.

Adon.

Was this not what she'd imagined when loneliness clawed at her belly in the night? The scent of him. The warmth of his skin. The baritone of his voice as he whispered her name into her curls.

This is my Adon.

And it was Taevas, too.

A tentative calm crept over her the longer they stayed like that, so tightly intertwined that she could hardly perceive any distance between them. The existence of Taevas didn't mean the death of Adon, though that was, she realized, what her mind had instantly fixed on. It was so very used to loss that it could imagine little else.

Or at least, it didn't *have* to mean that. Maybe.

"You're Taevas," she whispered, mostly to herself.

"And you're Alashiya." His breath caressed the curve of her ear. One large hand skated up and down her spine. His throat bobbed with a hard swallow before he asked, "Why did you want to hide from me?"

"It's what nymphs do when we're threatened. It's how we survive."

A beat of tense silence passed. "Do I threaten you?"

"Yes," she answered honestly, though she believed it wasn't the answer he wished to hear. "This is terrifying, isn't it?"

"I'll be honest, I'd hoped for a happier reception. Or even a more neutral one. But I suppose nothing has gone according to plan so far, so why would it start now?" Taevas stroked her spine again, slow and careful, as if he were counting the beats of each pass in his mind.

"What did you imagine it'd be like?"

"I hoped our meeting would go a very different way. I thought that eventually you'd agree to see me, and I would take you to dinner in the city. You'd offer to show me your studio. And then—"

Her heart skipped a beat. *And then...*

There was so much in those two words, but no matter how long she waited, it didn't appear that he intended to finish the sentence.

"And then?" she whispered.

Taevas cleared his throat. "I never let myself think past that part."

"Why?"

A heavy sigh stirred her hair. "A question with too many and too few answers, *metsalill*. Maybe you could tell me what *you* expected."

Alashiya would've happily pulled her teeth out instead. She'd been married to her imagination for so long that it felt disloyal to even entertain the thought of— well, she didn't know what she was doing with Taevas just yet, but it felt like *something*. She grappled with the urge to refuse until it quieted down.

This is Adon, she reminded herself. *Don't you want to know him? To be known by him? Isn't that all you've ever dreamed of?*

"I never cared how we met. I just liked imagining you. Pretending Adon was— *you* were here," she admitted, speaking into the dragon's hot skin. A tiny quake rippled through him, making her pause. Was it the fever or could he possibly be reacting to the touch of her lips on his skin? The possibilities were thrilling. A little scary, but thrilling nonetheless.

"I... I've been alone here for a long time. All the men I might've married left years ago for better jobs in the cities, or just because Birchdale has been in its death throes for as long as I've been alive. If I didn't want to take Monty up on his offer or be a hunting season fling for a recreationist or become a ranger bunker, then companionship was up to my imagination."

"Ranger bunker?"

Alashiya shrugged as much as she was able under the circumstances. "The rangers are mostly made up of shifters who know exactly how attractive they are. People are drawn to them and will hang around the barracks, waiting for a bunk to open up. The name for them in school was ranger bunkers. It's not a bad thing, but it's not for me."

That was how some of her tiny class of schoolmates had found their partners, so she supposed there was a chance she'd been missing out on something, but most of the stories she'd heard had made her shudder. Contrary to popular belief, nymphs were, in general, a romantically monogamous group. Some viewed sex as being part of that and others didn't, but Alashiya had always associated romantic partnership with an exclusive sexual partner.

She had no desire to hop into a shifter's bunk to lose her virginity in a wild night of passion, only to leave cold and sticky the next morning. Or worse, have to sneak out not long after the act, as she'd heard a number of her classmates had to do. She had even less desire to go from bunk to bunk, searching for the shifter who'd catch the mating fever for her.

Alashiya wanted to be wed, as her parents and grandparents had been. She wanted to grow strong roots with her husband, to have a dozen fat, squirming babies, and watch a new grove flourish in the sun. She might've been able to make that life, too, if only she wasn't such a coward.

"My imagination filled the gap," she continued. "I loved getting Adon's— *your* orders because each one told me a little bit more about you. The things you liked. How you lived. It was hard for me to picture how we'd meet, but I could imagine a handsome gargoyle introducing me to his sept, or a harpy—"

"A *sept?*" Taevas gripped her upper arms and put enough space between them to give her the full force of his incredulous look. "You thought I was a gargoyle and I'd share you with my *sept?*"

Alashiya's cheeks went hot again. "What's wrong with that? Septs are great."

Taevas made the oddest gurgling noise in the back of his throat. "Do you want multiple mates?"

Truthfully, it had always sounded like a lot to deal with. *"Too much upkeep,"* Debbie had once commented as she watched one of her soap operas behind the register. *"One Mike is enough. Imagine a stable full of 'em!"*

There was certainly appeal in being the center of a wheel of devoted mates, but Alashiya had never taken the idea too seriously for herself. A sept would've been something of an instant replacement for her grove, but she knew in her heart that she could truly only devote herself to one person.

No, in her imagination, he'd most often been one of the rare loners, as desperate for companionship as herself. Maybe someone who could understand what it was like to have so much, only to lose it all.

Feeling exposed, Alashiya stared over his shoulder when she answered, "That wasn't... Having a sept wasn't my ideal, no."

If she expected him to relax, she would've been disappointed. Taevas sat rigidly beneath her. His voice was tight when he pressed, "A harpy, then. That's what you wanted."

"All I knew was that my Adon had wings. I pictured what fit that description."

"And you never, not *once*, imagined he— *I* might be a dragon? That *your* Adon, your husband, might be a fine, strong, powerful dragon who could protect you from all things? Who'd give you the best nest, the softest life, the most— *Really?*"

Alashiya squinted at him. "Have I offended you?"

"You have!" he confirmed, throwing up his hands in exasperation. "I am *Isand*. Hundreds, maybe even thousands of people go to sleep dreaming of becoming my— being *mine*. And yet the one woman who occupies every waking thought never even *pictured* a dragon."

Taevas looked away sharply. The muscles of his jaw flexed as he ground his teeth. "A fucking *sept*. Honestly!" A deep, thunderous growl shook his cavernous chest in time with the rattling of his tail.

"As if any half-decent mate would share you. You'd get a *sliver* of the attention you deserve. A fucking harpy is barely better. Good gods, what were you thinking? They like to be fought for control in bed, and they practically sleep outside, rain or shine. Don't forget feathers everywhere! For fuck's sake, Shiya, think of your *skin*."

There was much to process there — *thousands, really?* — but all Alashiya could focus on was a small, electrifying part right at the beginning of his tirade. In a tentative whisper, she asked, "I occupy every waking thought?"

"And the sleeping ones, too," he snapped, pinning her with a glare. "I wear your magic against my skin every day. Your scent is ingrained in my *roost*, Shiya. It's in my *nest*. Do you have any idea what that does to a dragon? I live for the essence of you. I have a fucking territory to run, a clan to wrangle, inter-territory politics to navigate, wars to thwart, trade negotiations to win. But I *still* think of you, a faceless, perfect creature, with every beat of my insipid little heart."

"Oh, I—"

Taevas tangled his claws in her curls, pulled her in, and crashed his mouth down on hers. Shock held her still as he pressed them together. Taevas molded their lips together and *breathed*. He sucked in soft, panting little breaths through the tiny gap between their mouths, as if he was trying to sip the air from her lungs.

Chapter Twenty-One

It had been a very long time since she'd been kissed, but her memories were vivid. It wasn't unusual to have someone swoop down on her like a bird of prey, and it had always been swiftly followed by a wet, thrusting tongue and wiggling lips. Sometimes she liked it, other times she hadn't.

But this... Maybe it should've been awkward, just sitting in his lap as they breathed together, their skin flush and eyes closed, but it wasn't. It felt nice. Better than nice, even.

It was *thrilling*.

Alashiya inhaled sharply through her nose before she dared to place a hand on his naked chest. His heart thundered under her palm. Hardly believing that *she* was the one making a move, she shyly rubbed her lips against his. Just a little. Just enough.

This is Adon. My Adon.

Without thinking, the very tip of her tongue darted out to dab at his lower lip. The faintest hint of his taste was a shock to her system; as heady and rich the first time she tried red wine. Her breath hitched.

Nothing in all her life tasted as good as he did.

Taevas's claws tightened in her hair, making her scalp tingle.

He said something in a language she didn't know. It was a low, pained murmur into her mouth that she didn't need to translate to understand. Slowly tilting her head to one side, Taevas parted his lips and began to coax her into a languid rhythm of soft, sucking kisses.

In the beats between each one, he'd often mutter something under his breath. It reminded her a little of the blessings she spoke when she stitched his garments. Every word was full of wonder and longing and a hunger for things that were too good to be named. Prayers, of a sort, to the Hungry God who gave love and madness in equal measure.

Eventually, his hands skated down her arms, pushing the blanket aside, and fit into the divot of her waist. His tongue darted out to tempt her. Alashiya found herself leaning into him, chasing the taste of him and the heat of his skin.

She had no idea when her hands found his thick hair. It was pin-straight and heavy in her grasp. He groaned when she tugged it, urging him closer. Big hands began to rearrange her in his lap, throwing one thigh over his so she straddled him. A sweet ache took root in her stomach and expanded into a pressure that sank lower, to the juncture of her thighs.

It'd been decades since anyone touched her. It was barely a thought anymore, the longing faded into an old bruise, but now... Now she felt it. Sharp. Needy. *Immediate.*

A new urgency crackled to life between them. Taevas let loose another thunderous growl and nearly bent her in half to stoop over her, his lips and tongue and fangs working hard to make her forget the loss of her fantasy, or even her own name.

Lust was a hot wave through her body, making everything bubbly and too bright, until it felt like something inside of her was going to float away. Only Taevas's increasingly hungry lips and roaming hands held her there, tethered to the Burden's Earth.

Alashiya wasn't naive to desire, nor sexual pleasure. Even if she hadn't done just about everything except the final act with a handful of local boys available, she had her grove's experiences to explain what she was missing. Individual memories weren't accessible, thank the gods, but the accumulated knowledge of them was.

Her sexual education was complete, if not practiced. She knew how to bring herself pleasure quickly. She remembered the taste of seed on her tongue. She knew how a partner ought to curl their fingers or use their teeth just-so.

But she'd never felt *this.*

It was desire in a new and evolved form; one that made all previous incarnations appear pale and watery in comparison. Alashiya got drunk on it. Gorged herself on it. Let it eat her up from the inside out.

She couldn't tell if she wanted to rip her clothes off or begin giggling uncontrollably as the thrill of it rushed through her. Her hands moved restlessly over his hair, the strong cords of his neck, the tantalizing slopes of his chest and arms. She wanted to touch all of him. She *needed* to.

Like he could hear her thoughts, Taevas's hands moved to the buckles of her overalls. "Too many fucking clothes," he gasped, fumbling with them. Without even a hint of caution, Alashiya pried her hands from his feverish skin to help him.

She'd gotten one unbuckled when he growled, "I've dreamt of this for a decade and still, somehow, it's already better than anything I could imagine."

Her breath wheezed out of her. The next buckle proved more challenging due to the fact that her fingers had begun to shake. Grasping her hips, Taevas dragged her into a better position in his lap. They both jolted when the juncture of her thighs met the straining bar of his cock beneath the blanket.

A flicker of logical thought came and went, saying something about how they probably should slow down a bit, that they had a lot more to talk about. It was soundly ignored, of course, as she finally managed to pop open the second buckle. Taevas hissed out something that sounded like praise.

Pressing another hungry kiss to her lips, he growled, "I've dreamed of what your cunt will taste like. What you'll feel like wrapped around my cock. How you'll whisper my name when you come."

He hitched her closer. Their hips rocked together again, more deliberately this time. Alashiya closed her eyes as a sharp jolt of pleasure snapped down her spine.

Sliding one hand into the front of her overalls, Taevas grated, "Tell me you've dreamed of me. Touched yourself to the thought of me. Craved me even half as much as I've craved you, my Shiya."

She wasn't certain how he expected her to respond when his fingers found the hot, slick skin of her aching cunt. Alashiya was only capable of breathy sounds of what she hoped was encouragement.

"No panties?" Taevas delivered a sharp bite to her lower lip. It felt more like a reward than any kind of punishment. "Good. I fucking hate those things. I never want a barrier between me—" His fingers curled downward to cup the whole of her possessively. "—and what's mine."

The heel of his hand ground down, creating a delicious, inescapable friction. She rocked into his hand helplessly, mindless, completely lost to sensation. It was too fast. All of it was too soon, too much, but she didn't want to stop.

It'd been so long, and it was *him*. It was Adon. She'd dreamed of this. Couldn't she enjoy it for just a moment longer before rationality returned?

"Adon," she whispered, digging her nails into his shoulders. "Please, I—"

He moved his fingers back up to caress her slowly, feeling how wet she was, how needy. "Your Adon has you. Your husband is here, *metsalill*, and he wants you more than he's wanted anything in his life." He paused to glide his lips over the curve of her cheek. Whispering in her ear, he told her, "I've waited a very long time for this, Shiya, but I'll stop if you ask me to."

Alashiya hadn't felt so alive in... ever, probably. She chased the feeling with everything she had, even though she was almost certain it couldn't end in anything except disaster.

Digging her nails in a little harder, she found the courage to rasp, "Keep going."

His groan reverberated through his deep chest and into hers. "I don't have the energy in me to take my time like you deserve, but I'll be damned if I don't see what it looks like when you come. Now."

His fingers, which had been fairly gentle in their exploration, began to move in a way she'd never experienced. They shuttled back and forth with breakneck speed, so fast it was almost like they were vibrating.

Alashiya gasped, her back arching until her arms were straight between them. Taevas supported her with a grip on the back of her neck. When she could open her eyes for a handful of seconds, she found him staring avidly at her, his expression a mask of pure determination.

Sweat broke out across her body as he settled into a pattern of overwhelming speed and gentle, circular strokes. Everytime he paused, he'd growl something she could barely hear over the buzzing in her ears.

"A dragon is what you need. Nothing and no one else," he muttered as he ramped up the speed again. "A dragon is *all* you need. Can't you tell? Your body knows. Look how well it responds to me, Shiya. Look how much it needs me."

It wouldn't have taken much to get her off, but Taevas was right. She did respond to him in ways she never had to anyone else. It felt like it took only seconds before she began to tense.

"Yes, yes, yes," he chanted, drawing her in close again, but not too much. She didn't even need to open her eyes to know he was staring at her face. She could feel it just as much as she could feel the glide of his fingers.

When her orgasm crested, it was sharp, fast, and everything she needed. Alashiya tossed her head back and let out a soundless cry as it swept her under. All the while, Taevas continued his relentless back and forth motions, until she finally slumped in his arms.

His chest rose and fell rapidly under hers as he gathered her close. He didn't seem like he really wanted to, but eventually he extracted his hand from her overalls, too. Resting his cheek against the crown of her head, he breathed, "It's a good thing you didn't agree to meet me."

It took a lot of effort to follow what he was saying, but she tried. "Why?"

"Because if you'd gone to dinner with me, I would've done that at the table. If you'd showed up at my office, I would've done it on my desk. If you'd met on the fucking street, I would've done it there, too."

"That's..." She had to work hard to find her voice again. "That doesn't sound like something the leader of a territory should do." *If he's telling the truth.*

"You're right. It's not." Taevas took in a shuddering breath. "But here I am."

Alashiya's heart hadn't stopped racing even as the sweat began to cool on her body. Embarrassment edged in, forcing her to turn her face into his shoulder again.

He made a *tsking* sound. "Are you hiding again?"

Instead of answering, she asked her own question. "Would you really do *that* in front of other people? Where they could see?"

Taevas tensed. "I'd hide you. No one but me is allowed to see that face. You'd be where you belong when I made you come. You'd be *here*—" There was an odd *whooshing* noise, a displacement of air, and then a sudden darkness beyond her closed eyelids. Surprised, Alashiya opened her eyes to find a great pair of leathery wings enclosing them — for all of three seconds.

Taevas jerked backward, severing their connection. He didn't say anything, but rather made a breathy, choked sound deep in his throat. Alashiya watched, alarmed, as his skin went chalky.

His wings trembled violently before they tried to fold into

position at his back, only to slump into two undignified heaps behind him. Sweat dotted his brow and his eyes went glassy as he collapsed into the pillows.

"What happened?" she demanded, lust cooling even faster than the sweat on her skin.

"My wings are damaged," he gasped. "I knew they were, but I hadn't extended them all the way before."

Eyes wide, she gripped his shoulders and craned her neck to peer at the trembling appendages slumped behind him. "Do you have a broken bone?"

"Don't think so. It feels—" He swallowed hard. The light glistened off the sweat that had begun to coat the column of his throat. "It feels like a muscle. Or a nerve. I don't know."

"You need a healer." Alashiya raked her fingers through her disheveled hair. Worry beat hard at her chest. The golden glow of her orgasm vanished. "I have to call the rangers," she announced, moving to clamber out of his lap. "They can send a medical evac team to—"

"No, Shiya." He grabbed her wrist and held on tight, refusing to let her leave his lap entirely.

She tried to shake him off. "Taevas, look at you! You're in pain. I can't take care of you the way you need. I *have* to get you a healer."

Wrestling with her until he could place her hand on his pounding heart, he explained, "If you go to a healer now, with that dragon around, we might both be dead, but I will not die of this, *metsalill*. Broken wings are better than bolts to the head. You must *not* tell anyone I'm here."

"Then how can I *help* you?"

Rubbing her wrist with his thumb, Taevas gave her a shaky smile. "Stay with me. Don't leave so soon after giving me such a gift. Change into one of those pretty nightgowns and lay with me in the nest, my Shiya. It will ease my pain better than any medicine."

"That's bullshit," she scoffed, unable to stop the watery smile that tugged at her lips.

Taevas dragged her hand up to kiss her palm. Murmuring against her skin, he agreed, "You're right. I should probably take more medicine. But I stand by the rest."

Chapter Twenty-Two

HE HADN'T WOKEN UP BESIDE MANY WOMEN BEFORE. None had ever been welcome in his nest, but when he was young and flush with hormones, he'd taken just about every woman he could to bed. He was the youngest Isand, a war hero, and only in his twenties. Eager to drown his sorrows and the poison of war in pleasure, he'd taken offer after offer.

The intricacies of how to navigate those temporary relationships had taken a while for him to understand. He didn't realize at first that sleeping over implied permanence, nor that women talked. His father never thought to explain to him that it was best to kindly but firmly explain his boundaries, setting expectations *before* sex so no hearts could be broken. These things he had to learn on his feet and, occasionally, through the well-meaning but often contradictory advice of the older men in what would become his Wing.

He did learn, though, and eventually he came up with a system that worked for everybody involved. It was one built entirely on clear communication, non-disclosure agreements, and a predetermined time limit. No woman slipped into bed with him without knowing the score, and therefore no woman left disappointed — outwardly, at least.

It made things easy, impersonal, and safe. Taevas couldn't get attached to someone he could lose, and the women weren't led to believe they'd caught the Isand after a night of passion.

He never meant to build a reputation as a player, but it was inevitable. Especially during the early days.

It bothered him at first and still did on some level. Taevas didn't love the thought of being known as someone who disregarded lovers like yesterday's laundry, but he quickly realized that, inexplicably, people seemed to like the idea that he couldn't be pinned down. There was some strange draw to being the UTA's most eligible bachelor and an incorrigible ladies' man. Even as his appetites waned with maturity, the image stuck in the collective mind of the populace and took on a life of its own.

Sometimes he wondered what people would say if they knew he hadn't slept with a woman in years. Would they even believe him? He imagined sitting down for an interview to explain that he'd been in a committed relationship with a figment of his imagination built on little more than a scent.

The Isand's Finally Lost It, the headline would read.

His Wing wouldn't be surprised. They'd been looking askance at him for years, ever since he stopped taking partners for the night.

Vael, perhaps his closest friend and most recent addition to the clan since his mating to Taevas's cousin Hele, had been watching him even more closely than normal lately. The big, scarred dragon was too damn observant. Despite the fact that he'd been on sabbatical from the Wing for over a year, busy traveling with Hele to find her fellow elementals, he still somehow managed to notice that Taevas couldn't seem to stop checking when his next package would arrive.

For ten years, Taevas had managed to keep his obsession mostly under wraps, but he'd been slipping more and more.

In fact, he'd slipped so far that he landed in Alashiya's nest. It should've been nothing but a triumph, with copious amounts of carnal delights to celebrate the occasion, but fate wasn't that kind.

He'd finally gotten to touch her, to watch her as she came on *his hand,* and he was too damn injured to do anything else.

Taevas gritted his teeth against the chills that wracked him. At some point in the night, he'd crawled out of the nest to throw up in the bathroom. Alashiya had drowsily fetched him his toothbrush, a glass of water, and several more fever reducers before she helped him back into bed.

Not how I imagined my first night in the nest with her.

It was definitely not what *she* probably had in mind, with her dreams of Adon the gargoyle. *Ridiculous.* As if even a football team of gargoyles could satisfy the hungry thing he'd glimpsed in his nymph. Only a dragon could do that.

Only a dragon *would* do that.

Possessiveness bubbling in his gut like last night's vomit, Taevas opened his bleary eyes to search for her. He lay on his stomach, his miserable, useless wings folded against his back and his head turned toward her. Alashiya lay on her side facing him. Her body was tucked into a tight ball beneath the blankets and her curls were a scattered explosion across the pillows.

Judging by the thin shafts of sunlight that made it past her curtains and all the moss on the windows, gods help him, Taevas judged that it was well past her normal wake-up call. She was typically up and moving at dawn, but he supposed that he *had* kept her up far later than normal.

It was another humiliation that he hadn't done so for any pleasurable reason. After he'd made the colossal mistake of trying to embrace her with his wings, as instinct demanded, he'd been in too much pain to continue where they'd left off.

He wanted to. By all the gods, he *needed* to. He'd soared with clouds. Seen where the domains of the gods touched at the very edge of the horizon. Fucked every kind of woman in every kind of way. Fought to the death and experienced the high of somehow making it out alive.

And none of it compared to *her.*

Kissing her and watching her come had been without a doubt the best experience of his life.

It was like sipping from the river of life itself. He tasted the very essence of vitality when she blessed him with her touch. When she breathed against his lips, he felt a kinship with the gods as he finally understood what it must have been like at the beginning of all things.

The urge to tear something from himself, to hand over an offering of flesh and bone in exchange for a moment of her radiance, had consumed him. His rational mind fled. It left only the devotee, the supplicant desperate to get his fill of the divine, and in that moment, Taevas as he'd known himself was lost forever.

In the light of morning, he didn't want to think of what that meant. He couldn't, until everything was back as it should be. Only then could he consider what it meant that he would never be able to sleep in a nest without her by his side again, or that when he thought of home, his internal compass had permanently reset itself to point to her.

Taevas sucked in a deep, shaky breath and reached across the infernal gap between their bodies to trail the tip of his claws over the curve of her exposed shoulder.

You shouldn't be so far away, he silently scolded her. *You should be under my wing always, metsalill.*

He tried to pull her in during the night, but she'd stubbornly refused, too worried about accidentally jostling him in her sleep. And yet her head had somehow ended up close to his, her body coiled tight like she had to restrain herself from crossing the gap completely.

Taevas knew that even given a thousand years, he couldn't have pictured a being as perfect as his Alashiya. It was a vicious blow to his ego to be so weak during their courtship period, when by rights he should've been showing her his fitness in all things.

Perhaps that was why it bit him so badly, the revelation that she'd fantasized about a *sept.* Did she truly believe that it would take a group of gargoyles to take care of her? He wondered if she'd dreamed of being whisked off to some cave stronghold or grotto, where a gaggle of hard-headed mates would fumble around her, trying to please her with no appreciation for her delicacy, her vibrancy, the elegance she wore like a cloak of silk over her shoulders.

Or perhaps she mostly dwelled on the image of a harpy, though only the gods knew why that might be. Did she understand that they liked to scratch, claw, and bite? That they were violently territorial? At a cocktail party, he'd once witnessed a male harpy rip two fingers off a man who touched his mate in passing. As if that didn't get the message across, the harpy had calmly offered one finger to his mate as a gift.

He ate the other.

Alashiya was too gentle for someone who could explode into violence at any time. His *metsalill* deserved a life of softness and luxury. One where she could be adored and fawned over and pampered and showed off proudly at a moment's notice.

She was a being meant to be worshipped by all, not hidden away by clumsy gargoyles or jealously guarded by a harpy.

It was decided. A dragon was the only choice for her, because only a dragon could appreciate the finest treasure.

It was a truth he felt in his marrow, and yet he couldn't peer too closely. The future seemed to play in front of him, so bright and full of life, but he refused to pull back that last gauzy curtain that separated him from it. Once he did, there would be no putting it back.

So instead, he contented himself with the knowledge that she was his, nameless and yet known in the core of every cell. He stroked the soft flesh of her arm, down to her crooked elbow, and up to where her hand lay on the pillow between them, fingers softly curled in sleep.

Such hands, he marveled. *To make so much beauty, to coax life from the earth with just these fragile fingers... I could admire them for hours. Days. A lifetime.*

Gently, trying not to wake her, he pressed the pad of his

thumb against the edge of one of her nails. A frown creased his mouth. *That's no good. It's not sharp at all.*

And her skin... Gods, he was always thinking of her silky skin. It was so soft. He could feel its delicacy under even gentle pressure with his clawtip. He shuddered to imagine how fragile her bones were. He knew nymphs were delicate creatures, but it was one thing to read about it and quite another to *feel* it.

She'll need her own Wing. Six men, at minimum, just for right now. Well, maybe even after we find the assassins. It couldn't hurt to be extra safe. I should assign Radek as Wing leader. He's a crazy old fuck, but he's the only one who will truly understand what's at risk.

Radek had lost his mate in the war, though to this day he refused to accept she was dead. Every chance he could, he scoured the UTA for her. They all knew it was no use. The internal compass all dragons possessed had simply malfunctioned in him, its needle pointing to a woman long-dead, making him believe she might still be out there somewhere, just waiting for him.

Poor, mad Radek, people whispered. *Better to be dead than to outlive a Chosen.*

Nausea swelled up his gullet to splash acid against the walls of his throat. Taevas promptly wiped that thought away. He wouldn't think of it. He wouldn't.

"Are you hurting?"

Startled by the sound of her sleepy voice, he looked up from where he'd been experimenting with her hand to find her gazing at him. Soft brown eyes gleamed beneath a dense fringe of lashes, and a frown puckered the skin between her dark brows.

"I'm fine," he lied, now free to pet her outright.

"Then what's with the look?"

"What look?"

She lifted a finger off the pillow to wiggle it in his general direction. "That one. You *look* like you're in pain."

"I'm only thinking of how to care for you, *metsalill,*" he answered smoothly, trying to cover up how uncomfortable his own thoughts made him. "I love how delicate you are, but it concerns me. I don't think even an army of guards would take that worry from me."

The audacious woman had the gall to roll her eyes at him. "Yes, yes. Nymphs are weak. I *know.*"

Taevas narrowed his eyes. "Did I say that word? Being delicate is not the same as being weak. A weak creature would *not* have stood her ground in front of an injured dragon."

Alashiya scrutinized him like she couldn't be sure he was telling the truth. After a beat, she whispered, "Thanks, I guess."

His gaze lingered on the scab and fading bruises, nearly unnoticeable now, that marked her forehead. He'd never meant to hurt her, not even to scare her, but that was the side-effect of losing the tightly held control he valued so much.

"I'm sorry," he rasped, stroking the backs of his claws over her brow. Alashiya's lashes fluttered. "I was out of my head with pain and drugs. I didn't know what I was doing, but I hurt you. It upsets me to think of it. I would never hurt you, *minu metsalill.* Knowing I did anyway shames me."

She had the grace to shrug. "Don't beat yourself up about it. I got some good shots in."

He quirked a brow. "Shots?"

Miming a slashing motion with an invisible weapon, she succinctly explained, "Scissors."

Her ferociousness thrilled him all the way to his toes. The almost instant hardening of his cock distracted him for all of five seconds before the horror of realizing she'd confronted a fully grown, out-of-his-mind dragon with only *scissors* for protection eclipsed it.

Taevas's hand shot out to clasp the back of her neck. She yelped in surprise, but his firm grip held her still when he growled, *"Never* do that again, Alashiya. Never! If you're threatened, you run. You hide and wait for me or your guard to handle the threat. You don't fight. You *never* fight! Gods, what if it'd been another dragon? What if I hadn't recognized— My Shiya, I could've killed you! What could've ever fucking compelled you to confront me all on your own?"

Scissors, he internally raged. *Fucking scissors.*

He wondered if she could've successfully dispatched even an arrant with a weapon like that, let alone a dragon, elf, demon, or orc. All his hair stood on end at the thought. It traveled over his skin in an electric current, the acute anxiety of Alashiya *fighting* caused him.

He opened his mouth to rail some more, but no words made it through the pillow that walloped him in the face several times in quick succession. Between each hit, Alashiya bit out, "This— is— my— *grove!*"

Taevas sputtered. It took an embarrassing amount of attempts for him to snatch the pillow from her hands and toss it aside. Sitting up on her knees, Alashiya pointed an irate finger at him. "It was a bad idea, but I'd do it again. You know why? Because running doesn't always save you. Wards don't always save you. Hiding doesn't save you. *You* caught me, remember?"

It was misery to turn onto his back, but he managed it by gritting his teeth and keeping his eyes on Alashiya. "I'm different. You should never run from me. I'm your Isand."

She gave him a wide-eyed look of annoyance. "So I'm not supposed to run from you and I'm also not supposed to fight you. What *am* I supposed to do, mighty Isand?"

He didn't think he liked the way she stretched out his title like that. Normally he enjoyed being called Isand, but when she said it, it struck a discordant note in his mind. No, to her he ought to be Taevas, or *my darling,* or Adon, if the mood struck her. But never should she address him as all the rest did. But that still didn't mean she had the right to ignore his commands. Not when she mattered so very much.

Giving her a stern look, he replied, "You will stay under my wing and do as I say."

"Why on *Earth* would I do that?" Alashiya, looking rumpled and increasingly angry, clambered out of bed. Taevas reached for her, cursing under his breath, but she was far quicker than him. Dancing out of reach, she shot him a glare over her shoulder. "I'm not your subject, Taevas. If you think you can boss me around because you pay me to make your clothes pretty, thinking it somehow makes you better than me or— or because of last night, then you should crawl out my door right now."

Taevas forced his body into a sitting position. "That's not what I meant—"

She was nearly to the hallway when she whirled around. Pulling her shoulders back, she snapped, "I'm queen of this grove, Isand. That might mean nothing to you or to anybody else, but it's all I have left. I'll defend it with my life if I have to."

"You *don't* have to," he argued, slashing one hand through the air. "You have *me* now. This is what I'm saying to you, my Shiya. You never have to worry about defending yourself or your land again. But I can't do this if you don't listen to me."

She gave him such a look, then, but he was helpless to decipher its intricacies. "We just met. You think it was reckless for me to face a dragon on my own? I think it's worse to put my trust in a strange man who plans to leave at the first opportunity he gets."

It was on the tip of his tongue to explain, in detail, how he had no plans to allow her to remain here once he'd made contact with his Wing. It was too dangerous, for one thing, and for another, he couldn't imagine a world where he was separated from her for even a moment. It simply didn't exist. It could not, *would not,* be allowed.

But he couldn't explain that to himself, let alone her, so instead he growled, "We're not strangers. I'm your Adon. I'm your husband."

Alashiya turned to leave the room. It wasn't quite fast enough to hide the staggering sadness in her eyes when she replied, "I'm not married, and Adon isn't real."

CHAPTER TWENTY-THREE

HE UNDERSTOOD THAT HE NEEDED TO GIVE HER SPACE, but it wasn't easy. Taevas could only stew in their nest, his body in open rebellion against him, and listen as she moved in and out of the house. No doubt she was plucking their breakfast from the bounty of her garden. He could smell strong coffee brewing. The urge to call out to her was immense and only got worse as the minutes ticked by.

By the time an hour had passed, Taevas worried he'd begun to truly lose his mind. He stared at the ceiling, his body one great, useless ache, and tried to get his brain to work as it usually did.

Normal Taevas wouldn't have had the issues he currently did.

He would've taken charge of his Alashiya, charmed her into doing exactly as he wished, and figured out how to get home by now. Normal Taevas would've had her neck-deep in the marble soaking tub already, her troubles as light as the bubbles covering the surface of the water as he handled the fucks who'd tried to kill him. When that was done, he'd return to find her soft and even sweeter-smelling in the nest he'd built them, ready to greet him with drugging kisses.

They'd have dinner in the sprawling atrium, and when it was

done, he'd lay his napkin in his lap, finish his wine, and order her to ride his face until he suffocated.

But Normal Taevas, the one in control of all things, was dead in a ditch somewhere. That left Weak Taevas to pick up the pieces. It was a miserable job. The more he thought of how in the gods' names he was supposed to get out of Birchdale with his Alashiya safely beside him and get back to the territory that so desperately needed him, the more he felt like he was drowning.

My wings are useless, he thought with brutal practicality. *They might be* permanently *useless. I can't shift. There's a dragon around, no doubt hunting me as I lay here. I'm ill and wounded. My Shiya doesn't understand that she's mine now, or that she's in danger every second we linger here.*

If he dwelled on the horror of what had been done to his wings, what might've been taken from him in those weeks of captivity, Taevas knew he'd lose what little remained of his control.

A dragon's wings were his pride, the shelter of his mate and young, the thing that allowed them to soar higher than any other creature. To have them damaged beyond repair... It was more than a physical blow. It was psychological torture.

He swallowed. *Vael does fine, and he was a child when his wings were broken, which is even worse.*

Crushed beneath his family's bombed dwelling during the final, pitiful years of the war, Taevas had pulled Vael out himself. He never mentioned it, but the sight of the boy's mangled wings and the shellshocked look on his face after days in the rubble surrounded by the shattered corpses of his clan haunted Taevas still.

He'd personally seen that Vael received care from a healer, who painstakingly knitted the delicate membrane, nerves, and fragile bones back together. It'd gone as perfectly as it could've, and yet Vael still struggled with pain, spasms, and regular physical therapy all these years later.

It hadn't stopped him from becoming a soldier, then an elite member of the Isand's Wing. Although his resilience wasn't the most important reason Taevas admired Vael, it was one of them. He'd never said it, but Taevas considered Vael one of the strongest people he'd ever met — far stronger than *him*.

After the war, despite the rare assassination attempt here and there, Taevas had never considered that he might be similarly injured. The loss of his wings, even temporarily, was yet another reality he flinched from. However, since it wasn't something he could hope to fix with the resources at hand, it was cowardice he was content with.

His other problems were not so easily shoved aside.

Clenching and unclenching his claws in the nest's blankets, he thought, *If I can't access a phone, then we have to leave. We'll drive somewhere far from here and find a place to make the call.*

An m-gate, a tear in space-time wielded by a select few witches-for-hire, would be arranged immediately, given the right code words. If for some reason he couldn't get through to his people, then he'd settle for Lee Seymour, the de facto alpha of the Shifter Alliance and old... well, friend wasn't the right word, but it was close enough to do the job.

The only problem was that he hadn't seen any hint of a vehicle outside. He tried to remember if he'd seen one, but came up blank. Alashiya had walked to town, hadn't she? Taevas let out a low groan.

A soft rustle of fabric made him crack open his eyes. Alashiya stood in the doorway, her expression unreadable. In her hands were a steaming mug and a shallow bowl with a spoon sticking out. His chest tightened.

Even angry with him, she'd brought him breakfast.

Taevas was used to luxury. He spent his days surrounded by people tripping over themselves to give him his every whim. But that wasn't the same as being cared for. He couldn't remember the last time he'd allowed anyone to do that.

Maybe not since Isa died, he realized. How very long ago that was, too.

"I made you yogurt with oats and wild honey. I figured something simple would settle in your stomach better," she told him, bare feet whispering across the old wood floor. She managed to avoid any creaky boards as she wound her way around drapes of fabric, boxes of bobbins, and antique furniture in the crowded room.

Wanting her smile more than any food, Taevas replied, "You spoil me, *minu metsalill,* but the only sweetness I crave is you."

Alashiya pursed her lips. "Does that line work on the *thousands* of other women you mentioned?"

Damn you, Weak Taevas. Normal Taevas wouldn't have made such a profoundly foolish strategic blunder as to mention *any* other women, let alone thousands of them, in the presence of the one he wanted above all. Now that his Alashiya was angry with him, of course she used the conversational dagger he'd given her.

Sounding a mite strained to his own ears, he answered, "Is it pushing the limits of your tolerance to ask that you forget I said that?"

She knelt down with his meal and set it on the floor beside the nest. Several curls tumbled from the ribbon she'd wrapped around her hair, obscuring her expression as she dipped her head, her focus on the task. "Probably."

Desperate to pet her, to feel her warmth against his palms and paint his scent on her skin, he clenched his fists in his lap. He wanted a repeat of the previous night, but he'd take anything she gave him.

"Then I will tell you this instead, *metsalill:* I haven't been with a partner in years. Everyone else became irrelevant to me the day I sent word to the atelier that I wished to speak with you."

She froze there, one knee on the floor and her eyes hidden from him. In a soft, disbelieving voice, she asked, "Really?"

"Really." He dared to loosen one fist. Using just the tips of his claws, he guided her curls out of her face and back behind her ear. Their eyes met and he swore he saw the spark of the divine in her gaze — some raw, nameless magic that made him so pale and weak and needy for her.

To think she believed even for a second that he thought he was better than her!

Swagger, confidence, power — these things he had in spades, but Taevas had never, in all his life, been blind to his failings. He'd always considered it an intensely valuable skill. Ego clouded judgment and made tyrants.

It was the thing that made him loved amongst his people, he believed. The fact that he understood he was no better than any of them, only in the right place at the right time with the perfect amount of righteous outrage, was what made him Isand.

In fact, he was keenly aware that after all he'd said and done, there wasn't a chance he was worthy of *her*. He would claim her even if the blood on his hands never washed clean, but he would always know he'd stolen a treasure from the gods themselves.

"You were right earlier. Adon isn't real," he murmured, letting his hand fall, "but Taevas is — and he worships you, my Shiya. I would kiss your feet and make a sacrifice of myself for you if you'd let me. Is it any wonder I become a terror when I think of you being threatened?"

Alashiya's expression softened for a moment before she shook her head. "This is crazy. You know that, don't you? What we have is chemistry and an extremely unlikely coincidence. It feels more meaningful than it is. Than it *can* be."

Normally, Taevas wasn't religious, but when it came to her, he couldn't make sense of any of it without the divine. "I don't believe that," he protested. "And I don't think you do, either. We've been tied together for a decade, *metsalill,* and the gods simply got tired of us fumbling around, trying to follow the thread. Now we're together. There's no going back."

"Why not?"

He stiffened his spine, ignoring the pain, and leaned in to press a kiss to the shell of her ear. "Because I won't allow it."

CHAPTER TWENTY-FOUR

HER GRANDFATHER HAD ALWAYS HOPED SHE'D END UP with a nice nymph boy. He'd talked of little else in the last days of his long life, when ghosts crowded his mind and the only thing that troubled him was the thought of her being left on her own.

"You need a nymph to build your grove," he'd insisted, his voice gone dry and reedy no matter how she plied him with sweet tea and homemade lozenges. *"You need a partner who'll weave himself into you, support you, so you can wear the crown without all this sorrow."*

Historically, male nymphs acted as the support system for the women of the grove, who were tasked with leading the group, carrying out traditions, and making the major decisions that could, in a dangerous world, lead to life or death. In her grandfather's view, her ideal partner would be gentle, steadfast, disciplined, and submit to her authority in all things, as he'd done with her grandmother and his forefathers had done since time began.

Of course, nothing was ever that simple, no matter what her grandfather believed. The rules had changed many times. Having a queen was traditional, but it was just a name tacked onto a greater, older thing that did not define itself by imaginary limits.

To be queen was to *tēq*, to carry. To bear.

To be the partner of the queen was to follow, no matter how treacherous the path. To ease the burden, no matter the sacrifice.

These things didn't rely on strict, imaginary lines of gender or sexuality. They were a partnership, neither existing without the other, each unwaveringly essential in their contributions.

Her grandparents had that perfect partnership, and it grieved her *pappous* that Alashiya didn't, especially now that she bore the burden of *tēq*. He'd urged her to leave the land, to strike out into the unknown in search of other groves, where a husband might be found who would take some of the weight from her.

Knelt on the floor beside a powerful dragon, a king in his own right, Alashiya didn't have to wonder what her grandfather would think of him.

Too bold, she could almost hear his ghost whisper. *Too hard-headed. He's not soft enough for you, my joy. You need to send him away and find a nice nymph who will know his place.*

Everything about Taevas was wrong. When she looked up at him through her lashes, she was struck once again by the shocking boldness of his hard features, the power of his body, the burning violet of his eyes.

If there was such a thing as a direct opposite of the perfect nymph, it was Taevas, the perfect dragon.

Was there something wrong with her? There must have been, since nothing stirred in her at the thought of a diffident, soft-spoken husband and never had. Her grandfather and her father's examples should've been enough to mold her expectations, but something had gone wrong along the way, apparently. Even in her imaginings, Adon had never been a nymph.

It wasn't the softness of a nymph but the power of the dragon that quickened her blood.

Was it not its own kind of softness, the worship that Taevas promised in that low, bass murmur? Surely even her grandfather and the generations of queens' partners who stretched behind him couldn't find fault with that.

Alashiya gave herself a swift internal shake. Her dragon had a way of casting a spell on her, pulling her in despite her very real concerns. That was its own form of danger. Her gut told her that he was genuine, but what did it matter when they were so completely incompatible? If it wasn't their traditions that made the case, it was their lifestyles.

Taevas wasn't Adon. He did not belong safely in her imagination. If he was telling the truth, then he had responsibilities that were so much bigger than she could imagine. He couldn't stay with her, serve her, or help her rebuild that which had been broken beyond repair.

He wasn't *safe*.

"You need to rest," she told him, cutting her gaze away. "Eat and go back to sleep. You need your strength."

The hand that so gently brushed her curls back behind her ear skimmed her shoulder before it fell away. "My Shiya—"

Setting his breakfast down, she climbed to her feet once more and turned to leave. It was unnatural to abandon her work, but the idea of sitting in the room with him for a moment longer, doing that sacred act of care for a man who did and did not exist, made her stomach curdle. It was too intimate. Too close to all the things she longed for.

She was at the door when his voice stopped her. It wasn't just the sound, but the tone which froze her steps. Speaking in a low, dark voice, he told her, "This is the last day, Alashiya."

Her heart lurched. *Last day?*

Was he leaving already? A hot wave of panic washed over her. Of course he wanted to leave. He had to, and really, she wanted him to go, too, didn't she? But in an instant, she realized how awful the prospect was.

To lose Adon *and* Taevas in the span of a day— She braced one hand on the door jamb, trying to anchor herself so she wouldn't fall into that dark hole beneath her feet again.

"What are you talking about?" she asked, risking a wide-eyed look over her shoulder.

Taevas sat in her bed like it was a throne. It didn't matter that his hair was disheveled, nor that his skin still hadn't regained the flush of good health. His spine was straight, his brow lowered, and his jaw firm. He balanced one wrist on a raised knee and fixed her with a dark look.

"You have today, *metsalill*, to run. To hide from me in your garden, or wherever else you choose. When it's done, it's done forever."

Relief made her momentarily dizzy. *He's not leaving. Yet.*

Taevas reached for his coffee and raised his cup to her, promising, "After today, I will chase you. No matter how broken my body is, no matter where you go — I will follow. You are queen here, but I am a dragon, and we do not let treasure escape us."

Something whispered along the paths carved into her flesh. It was the hum of thousands of minds, her ancestors, her grove, as individual and collective as the trees in the forest. It was rare that they stirred all at once, and she wondered fleetingly what had roused them so.

Was it the way her heart jackhammered against her ribs? The flush of her skin? Or was it how easily, how unknowingly Taevas had stepped into the path trodden by so many of her kin before her?

I will follow.

It was what a nymph would say. So why did it feel so much like a threat?

～

She suspected he was judging her, but Alashiya spent most of her day doing exactly as he seemed to know she would: avoiding him.

Oh, she checked on him, of course. She brought him lunch when she made it and forced more medicine down his throat. Occasionally she popped her head in to find he'd gone back to sleep, or to find that he'd filched books from her collection and buried his nose in them. But for as often as she saw him, they didn't truly speak, and he made no further overtures or grand declarations.

He appeared content to wait her out, though she suspected a lot of his blasé attitude was an act. Alashiya couldn't claim to know him well — though it *felt* like she did — but she saw something in the tightness of his jaw and the tension around his eyes that spoke volumes.

To avoid that, she spent most of the day doing chores around the land that she'd been putting off in favor of getting her work done as quickly as possible. After all, what was the point of that work now? If he'd been commissioning her just to feel close to her, perhaps he didn't even want the robe. Or worse, she'd put him off her *and* her work entirely.

Alashiya didn't want to think about what the future held, but she couldn't seem to stop herself. One seemingly unrelated thought after another tumbled ass-over-tea-kettle into Taevas. Even thinking about work, normally a safe zone for her mind to wander, led her to questioning what things would be like going forward — whether Taevas would still order from her when he returned to his life, if she even wanted him to, and what she would do if he didn't.

For a decade, his commissions had been nearly her sole source of income. What if all that had been said and done in her home made him feel uncomfortable in continuing? Her stomach bottomed out at the thought.

Mrs. Thompson had once offered to help her set up an online store for her work, but she'd shied away, intimidated by the barrier technology posed. She'd never had cause to use it before, and she'd left school before they did little more than learn to type on mechanical typewriters. Trying to navigate the internet, of all things, in order to make a livelihood sounded as attainable a goal as flying to the moon.

But she might have to try, once Taevas left. Because he had to leave. He wanted to leave. He *needed* to.

By the time the sun began its descent into the fiery horizon,

Alashiya was dirty and sweaty from a day outside mending fences, checking on the trees, and shoring up her wards, which were now more important than ever.

Anticipation curled in her belly as she pried the broken door from its place and stepped into the kitchen. It was probably her imagination, but she could smell a hint of him in the air as soon as she walked in. A flush warmed her from her toes to the tips of her ears.

Suddenly nervous, Alashiya ducked her head and made a beeline for the bathroom, avoiding any glances in the direction of the living room.

"*Oh,*" she breathed, stopped in her tracks as soon as she pulled open the bathroom door. Steam billowed out in gauzy waves. That was where the scent was coming from. The bathroom was positively redolent with it and the water vapor smell of a recent hot shower.

He must've just stepped out. Fog still clouded the old mirror over the medicine cabinet, and a slow drip of water made a steady beat when it fell from the head of the faucet.

The temperature of her skin heated as the steam cocooned her. Without thinking, she sucked in an even deeper lungful of air, pulling in the essence of the dragon she'd sought to escape. Instantly, she was overwhelmed with images of her dragon in the shower, his powerful body bathed in warm water and the scented oils she kept on the shelf. The memory of his fingers between her legs rushed in, teasing her with how good it could be when neither of them wore clothes.

She imagined the look he'd give her if he was standing in it now — all dark eyes and slow, hungry smile. Her thighs clenched.

From somewhere in the other room, his silken voice called out, "My Shiya?"

Startled, she slammed the door shut. Her cheeks heated to a humiliating degree as she pressed her back against it. Her pulse was almost too fast to be a proper beat anymore. It thrummed between her thighs like a live wire, insistent and dangerous,

begging to be touched by someone unafraid of the consequences.

Alashiya took a cold shower.

Unfortunately, whatever calm it gave her was immediately
negated by the fact that she'd forgotten to bring a change of
clothing with her. All she had was her summer robe, which hung
in its normal place on the peg behind the door. She was too used
to living alone. It hadn't occurred to her that she should bring a
change of clothes *with* her.

The robe wasn't necessarily *intended* to be indecent, but it
wasn't something she'd ever planned on wearing in front of
another soul, either. It was overflowing with repurposed fabric
she couldn't bear to cut more than absolutely necessary. Mrs.
Thompson had offered it to her, and she'd fallen in love with the
nearly transparent gold voile. Made of light-weight cotton
blended with silk, it'd been a perfect and luxurious addition to her
summer wardrobe.

Mouth bone-dry, Alashiya donned the robe and tried to
arrange the fabric in such a way that it wouldn't be quite so
obvious that it was, save for the spots in which the fabric overlaid
itself, decidedly sheer.

Maybe he won't notice? She stared at her reflection in the
mirror for a while, fingers combing oil into her curls in nervous
little twists. *It's just a body. One he's already been more or less intimate with. Who cares if he sees?*

Swallowing to try and replenish some of the evaporated moisture in her mouth, she stepped out of the relative safety of the
bathroom. By the time she tiptoed into the doorway of the living
room, her heart had attempted to jam itself into her throat. She
braced herself.

It took only a second to realize that it was pointless, because
Taevas wasn't in the bed.

A sound behind her prompted her to turn and pad the few
feet down the hall to the kitchen. Her near-nakedness was
momentarily forgotten as she stood in the doorway.

The dragon stood over a well-loved cutting board, his broad shoulders rounded as he painstakingly sliced a cucumber and put the pieces in a bowl with oil, salt, and the hard, crumbly cheese she ordered special from Debbie.

Had he noticed that was her favorite snack after a long, hot day in the garden? That tingling sensation ran wild in her chest again.

His hair was loose and damp. It hung in dark tendrils between the astonishing array of muscles that made up where his wings met his back. He'd found another pair of loose pants from the stash of old clothing she'd put in his room — now unoccupied, of course — and they hung dangerously low on his square hips. A passing thought that she ought to modify where his tail rested on the waistband for him rather than continue letting him crudely slice through it, came and went.

The strain it took him just to stand, let alone stay upright for as long as he must've, was apparent in the tremor of his hands, the odd, wrong-looking slump of his wings, and the way his tail rested on the ground behind him.

Alashiya surged into the kitchen. "What are you doing? You need to be in bed!"

He set down the knife and wiped his hands on one of her threadbare but lovingly decorated dish towels. Taevas propped the heel of one hand on the edge of the counter, using it to support his weight, and half-turned to address her. "If I can run you down in the woods, I can feed— What on Burden's Earth are you *wearing?*"

She stopped just short of touching him. Alashiya flushed to the roots of her hair. "It's just a robe. I forgot to bring my clothes into the bathroom with me."

Out of the corner of her eye, she thought she saw his claws curl into the countertop. His tail began to swish slowly behind him.

"That's not a robe," he rumbled, hooking a single finger into the tassel that held the whole gauzy thing together to draw her closer. His nostrils flared with a deep, deep breath before he continued, "That's *bait.*"

Alashiya shook her head, but she was nothing except pliant and trembling when Taevas pressed the length of his body against hers. Considering what had happened the previous night, it *was* probably provocative, but for some reason, she opened her mouth anyway. "It's just a robe I made from some old fabric Mrs. Thompson didn't want anymore. It's not— No one's ever—"

Taevas's hand spanned the width of her back. The heat of him blazed through the thin material of the garment like it wasn't even there. Hunching his body over hers, he pressed his lips to her ear. "No one's ever seen you wrapped up in shimmery gold like a pretty little present? That must mean you're a gift just for me."

Between one shuddering breath and the next, Taevas had her on the counter, her knee just kissing the corner of the cutting board. Alashiya yelped and grasped his shoulders. "What are you *doing?* You shouldn't be—"

A deep rumble cut her off. "You will not confine me to the nest any longer, *naine.*" The hair on the back of her neck rose. The knowledge that he was dangerous — really, truly dangerous — danced like skilled fingers across every nerve. "I've been forced to watch you swan in and out all day, so beautiful and maddening and indifferent to me. If I must use what little strength I have to prove to you that you aren't, then so be it."

Taevas slotted himself between her legs. Passing his hands up from her knees to the tops of her plush thighs, he whispered in her ear, "You didn't answer me last night. Did you ever dream of Adon making you come, *naine?*"

Chapter Twenty-Five

THE COLD SHOWER HADN'T DONE HER A DAMN LICK OF good. The embers of desire roared to life in the pit of her stomach. Alashiya didn't know how to answer him — *yes,* but also *no,* because she could never have imagined the intensity of *this* — so instead she gasped, *"Nie-nah?* What does that mean?"

Something curled around her calf. It was his tail, she realized, only to be immediately distracted by the way his fingers glided up and over her hips to find the belt at her waist.

For a long moment, the only sound in the room was that of fabric rustling as he slowly, painstakingly unwound the knot. "It's what I'll call you when you're being naughty with me," he coolly informed her. "My little *naine,* who wants to test my limits, just to see how far my devotion goes. *Tsk.* You'll understand."

"I really wasn't trying to do anything!"

"No?" The sensation of the tasseled belt falling away made her jump. Alashiya's thighs trembled as she tucked her heels against the lower cabinets.

She braced herself, but Taevas didn't immediately pull the sides of the robe apart. He cupped the span of her ribs with both hands. Ducking to trace the tip of his nose over her cheek, he challenged, "You couldn't have asked me to bring you something? Or even told me to look away for a moment while you grabbed your nightgown?"

"I..." Alashiya hadn't realized she was still clinging to his bare shoulders until his muscles flexed under her fingertips. "I didn't think of it."

And maybe there was a small, needy part of her that had wondered what it would be like to be seen. To *let* herself be seen.

There'd been more than pent up sexual tension between them the previous night. There was an awakened craving to be *looked* at, to be admired without fear or revulsion. If she were being truly honest with herself, it was that craving that had propelled her out of the bathroom in little more than a sheer drape.

As if he could read her mind, Taevas sucked in a ragged breath and asked, with what sounded like a deep drawing of restraint, "How long has it been since you were admired, *naine?*"

What a question.

It was one with many answers, and all of them various levels of sad. Alashiya tried to pick apart the best of the bunch. "I... don't think I've ever been admired in the way you're implying."

She didn't want to say more, but with her body urging her in the way it was, and *his* body doing what *it* was, Alashiya knew it wasn't the responsible thing to ignore the elephant in the room — even if she was the only one who could see it.

"And if you're asking when the last time I had a partner was, then—" She cleared her throat and maintained eye contact with the hard line of his clavicle. "I had two boyfriends and we did— things. But I've not— I've been waiting to..."

Warm fingers firmly cupped her jaw. They tilted her head back and up, forcing her to look into the dragon's incredulous gaze. The movement made the sides of her robe slip until they rested on the upper swells of her breasts.

Taevas's gaze darted across her features when he rasped, "You're a *virgin?*"

"Is that a problem?" she demanded, stiffening her spine.

Taevas looked like he was trying to piece together a particularly challenging puzzle in the dark. "It's not a *problem,*" he answered after an amount of time that suggested it was, in fact, a *problem.* He looked pensive. Uneasy, even. "I'm more concerned with the *why* of it."

Feeling altogether exposed, she huffed, "I don't see why that's any of your business."

She thought the mood had been pretty thoroughly slaughtered there on the kitchen counter, but Taevas didn't seem to agree. Despite the almighty frown that pulled at his mouth, his hands began to travel again. They slipped into the folds of her robe to slowly expose her chest an inch at a time.

"I heartily disagree, *naine,*" he rumbled in that deep, stirring bass. "As the man who intends to have, at minimum, his fingers inside you by the end of this night, I believe it is very much my business."

Mood's definitely not dead, she thought, painfully aware of the whisper-soft drag of his fingertips against the curve of her breasts. The image of Taevas's night-dark fingers sliding between her thighs made her cunt clench with the echo of the previous night's orgasm.

Compared to her flushed skin, the summer air felt cool on her suddenly bare chest. Taevas's gaze dropped. He hissed something low as he skimmed the very tips of his fingers over her puckering nipples.

A string of muttered words, unknown to her, were finished with a growled demand. "Tell me. If it's dislike that made you avoid it, I need to know. If it's past experiences, I need to know. If it's because you were saving it for—" He sucked in a deep breath, the muscles of his powerful jaw flexing hard. "I really fucking *need* to know."

Was it the fact that it'd been nearly a century since another person had touched her with desire that made even the simple action of his thumb brushing the peak of her nipple painfully erotic or was it just *him?*

Not knowing what to do with her hands, she dropped them to the edge of the counter, which she clutched so hard her blunt nails sank into the gritty particle board on the underside. "I wasn't exactly *saving* it. It just didn't happen when there were other people my age still around, and then there were only rangers, and I thought, well, if I've waited this long, I might as well try to make it mean something and— *Oh!*"

Taevas cupped her breasts. They nearly overflowed even his large hands. "There is no good or bad reason to do or not do something with your body," he said, thumbs stroking her sensitive skin with exquisite slowness. "But I need to know your boundaries, my Shiya. I need to know what you will and won't allow, because if it was my choice, I'd give you everything."

He hovered his lips over hers, stroking back and forth in the suggestion of a kiss. For someone who was so hard-looking, the dragon was shockingly tender with her. His hands were firm but gentle as he slowly rolled her nipples between his fingers and thumbs, and when he kissed her, it was the most delicate, sipping kind.

It was easy to get swept under the spell. It might not have been if he was terribly demanding, if he grabbed and pinched and thrust his tongue into her mouth. There was passion in that and a certain thrill when she considered it, but *this...* Alashiya couldn't escape the feeling that she was being molded in expert hands. She didn't want to.

She couldn't say what else she wanted from him, but she knew without a doubt in that moment that she needed to know what it was to be *admired.*

Alashiya forced one hand away from the edge of the counter. Placing it on the thick cords of his neck, she traced the throbbing pulse she discovered. His hitched breath stuttered against her lips.

He's leaving at the first opportunity. I'll never see him again. I may never even get another commission. Shouldn't I take the chance while I have it?

All things wither. This moment was fleeting; the lushness of sensation was ephemeral. Perhaps she wasn't quite ready to take the final step, but what harm would it be to explore him, *them*, in the moments she'd been granted?

"I want you to touch me," she whispered.

One of Taevas's hands slid into her damp hair. "Thank you, gods."

To be kissed by a dragon, *really* kissed, was to be devoured. Alashiya discovered this when Taevas tilted her head back and set upon her like a starving man, his lips and teeth and tongue meeting her own in a luscious dance. All thoughts of the future were swept away as sensations took their place.

Her attention bounced back and forth between their mouths, the scent and taste and *feel* of him, and the way sparks of electricity sizzled beneath her skin whenever he slowly pinched and rolled her nipple. Pressure built low in her stomach with each firm turn.

Just when the feeling bordered on true discomfort, he switched to the other side, starting the process all over again until her breasts felt heavy and hot and too sensitive. She made a small sound in her throat when his fingers finally slid away to tickle the deep valley between her breasts.

Separating their mouths with a lingering, restrained nip of his fangs, Taevas grated, "I've seen the divine in these breasts. Gods help me, I'll never be the same again. I want to lay my head here and die a happy death."

She'd always viewed her heavy chest as more of a nuisance than anything, but when he looked at her like that, she suddenly didn't care about back pain or sewing in extra support in her clothing.

Taevas grabbed her hand from his neck and gave it a lingering kiss. Giving her a molten look over the ridge of her knuckles, he ordered, "Lean back for me."

Under that violet gaze, self-consciousness didn't exist for her. She didn't hesitate to do as he asked. Alashiya placed her trembling hands behind her, heedless of the dozens of jars and containers arrayed against the wall, and arched her back.

"Fuck. *Fuck.*" Taevas wiped at his mouth. His gaze roamed her exposed skin and over the layers of her frothy robe, which spilled out around her waist and across her thighs. His eyes weren't the sultry half-mast she'd read about in books, but almost too wide, like he was trying to take everything in at once and afraid that a single blink would dispel the image.

It was with the utmost delicacy that he finished unwrapping her. Taevas picked at the edges of her robe, touching as little as possible as he pulled it completely apart. She stopped breathing when he took a measured step back.

This, she realized, was what it was to be *admired.*

Taevas stood with his palms braced on the back of his head, his expression the picture of sheer disbelief as he looked and looked and *looked.* For someone so used to hiding, to wishing not to be seen, it should've been uncomfortable. But Alashiya was shocked to discover a wild, fiery thrill at his silent observation.

She liked it. She liked it *a lot.*

Alashiya watched his face contort into a visage of agony when she slowly raised one leg and rested her heel on the edge of the counter. The warm air kissed the slick flesh between her legs. The feeling of exposure, the possibility that this might be a humiliating failure of seduction, ratcheted up her lust until the ache grew to a nearly unbearable level.

"*Naine,*" he growled at last, "I think I've already died."

Her gaze dipped. It fell down the slabs of strong flesh that made up his chest and stomach and settled on the straining shape of his cock tenting the thin material of his pants. A shiver of trepidation ran through her. Perhaps she wasn't ready for *that* yet, but the thought of it, of him wanting her so badly with just a few touches and a look... Alashiya took another risk.

The dragon's gaze somehow managed to grow wilder when he

tracked the progress of her right hand over the softness of her stomach to the dark curls of her mons.

He made a low moaning sound and lurched forward until he stood between her legs once more. She had no idea what compelled her to do it. The gods knew her last fumbling attempts at intimacy nearly a century prior hadn't exactly primed her for boldness. And yet she found herself placing her foot above his pounding heart, stopping him abruptly when he reached for her.

They both stared at each other in surprise. Taevas didn't move. His normally smooth voice had gone rough as sandpaper when he said, *"Naine?"*

Praying she wasn't making a massive fool of herself, Alashiya swallowed hard. "I like it when you watch me."

Taevas's mouth snapped shut. A muffled sound, a little bit like the whistle she'd heard that first night in the barn, came from somewhere deep in his throat. His attention zoomed back to her right hand, which had begun to slowly part her slick, swollen cunt.

"Can I touch you?" There was an edge of desperation in his voice now, but no frustration, no pushiness. He *wanted* to touch her, had no problem expressing just how much he wanted that, but he would only do so if she agreed to it.

He was always so bossy, but now... Now he seemed ready to beg.

A heady sense of power overcame her. She'd dared to command a dragon, a *lord,* and now he asked *her* for permission.

"You can touch my legs," she allowed, following the familiar path over skin that begged to be stroked. Alashiya was an old-hat at self-pleasure, but she didn't think any experience going forward would compare to how it felt to swirl her fingers under Taevas's ravenous gaze.

One of his hands instantly banded around the delicate bones of her ankle, while the other pressed into the plush skin of her thigh.

"Let me help," he breathed, voice ragged, as he stepped closer.

Gently, he slung the leg she'd propped against his chest over his elbow. The other he lifted and pushed up slightly, taking her weight off her thigh so it didn't cut into the counter.

Having him so close, the feeling of his pants brushing her inner thighs, the way his eyes never wavered from where they watched her... She knew how to get herself off quickly, but that wasn't what she was after. Just to see what he'd do, Alashiya observed him closely as she slid one finger inside her slick cunt.

Taevas had a full-body reaction to the sight. The hard lines of his face went even starker than normal, and he lifted her leg to press an open-mouthed kiss against the smooth skin of her thigh. He left his lips there, moving restlessly, as he stared unblinkingly at the finger that slowly went in and out of her with wet, sloppy sounds.

She slid another finger in to join the first and ground the heel of her palm down, providing just enough friction to ease the ache. His fangs scraped her skin. A shock of pleasure, made sharper by the tiny bite of pain, made her gasp.

"You're so fucking beautiful," he breathed into her damp skin. "A work of art. I want to make you come so bad, *naine*. I want to show you what it's like to be worshipped. Let me do it."

Forcing him to watch was all well and good, but when it came down to it, Alashiya didn't actually want to do everything herself. She'd had a lifetime of that, after all.

But she wasn't *quite* done yet.

She lifted her chin in the direction of his hips. "I want to see you, too."

Taevas let out a husky laugh. "Haven't you already? That's why you ran, if I recall."

"Not like this." She slowed her movements down. Curling her calf over his side, she pulled him in just a little closer. "I want to see what you look like when you're hard for me, *argaman mlk*. I... want to see my husband come first."

All the hard lines of his body stood went taut. "Keep calling me that, *naine,* and I'll give you anything you ask of me."

Her heart stuttered. Licking her lips, she whispered, "My husband."

He groaned. "You have no fucking idea what that does to me."

"You could show me."

A soft, amazed breath left him. Taevas gingerly set her leg down and hurried to free himself from his pants. The linen tie came away with a frantic jerk, and the waistband, its structure weakened by his customization, fell almost instantly.

Alashiya's mouth watered. She couldn't claim to have an abundance of experience or opinion on the matter, but she knew Taevas was a gorgeous specimen in all ways. In this he was truly spectacular. Thick, veined, and standing proud with a livid erection, his cock was at once intimidating and perfectly formed.

Taevas took himself in hand with a hiss of pain or pleasure or both. The tip of his cock, the deep color of his night-shift and flushed with blood, glistened with moisture that looked like little stars against a night sky. She watched as a hard stroke sent a bead of pre-come onto the floor between them.

Too distracted to continue her own side of things, she slapped her damp hand on the counter behind her and settled in to watch as he pumped his fist. A part of her was in disbelief that it was happening, that he was touching himself *for* her, *to* her.

She thought that maybe she should say something, but no words came. She had no practice with any sort of dirty talk, and even if she had, the sight of him had completely knocked any thought from her mind.

He wasn't particularly gentle with himself. She wondered if that was his habit, preference, or a consequence of being so worked up. At last finding some words, she murmured, "Easy, *argaman mlk*. Don't damage what's mine before I even get the chance to enjoy it."

Taevas's rhythm stuttered. More moisture beaded and slid down into his stroking, squeezing fist until he, too, was making slick noises. His expression was pained when he groaned, "My Shiya, my Shiya. You've already ruined me."

Too tempted, she nudged him just a bit closer, until the bumps of his knuckles skimmed her mons with every pass. Taevas sucked in a sharp breath. "I can't— I can't take this. Where?"

It took her brain a moment to catch up to what he'd asked. It was hard to focus on anything other than the sight of him stroking himself between her legs like he was desperate to do exactly as she asked.

"Hm?" She lifted one hand to smooth her palm over the hard plane of his stomach, mere inches from the base of his cock. "Where, what?"

In a tight voice, he clarified, "Where do you want it, *naine?* Tell me where to come."

It? What does— Oh! Alashiya's eyes opened wide.

Yes. She remembered this part. She *wanted* this part, but it was so easy getting caught up in the act itself that the finish seemed unimportant. In her memory, she couldn't recall it ever being that way with someone else, but with Taevas, everything was different.

To cover up the fact that she really didn't have an answer, Alashiya stroked his stomach, fascinated by the way the muscles contracted at her touch, and answered, "Why don't you choose?"

"Ah, my generous goddess," he panted, shoulders hunching as he stroked harder, faster, and completely ignored her admonishment to go a bit easier on his poor flesh. "You give me too much. Don't you know that it only makes me want more and more and more? I want you covered in my seed. I want to watch it spill out of you and stain our nest, just so I can fill you up again. I want your thighs sticky with it every— fucking— day."

Before she could think of what to say to that, Taevas rolled up onto the balls of his strange feet. Already tall, the added height allowed him the perfect angle to come in thick white spurts across her soft stomach and thighs.

A sound unlike anything she'd heard rumbled from the

depths of his chest as he did it. It was a great tearing noise, definitely not human and yet not entirely beast, either. It fell somewhere in between, and when it rolled through her, her toes curled with delight.

Alashiya barely had a moment to register the cooling seed that dripped down her thighs before Taevas swooped in on her again. His kiss was frantic, and the way he batted her hand away from where it accidentally blocked the entrance to her body was urgent, determined.

He ripped his mouth from hers, but it wasn't to give her time to catch her breath. Taevas dropped to his knees, that terrifying rumble still rattling his chest, and slung her thighs over his broad shoulders. He muttered something guttural in that lilting language as he gently pried the folds of her cunt apart, exposing everything to his avid gaze.

A choked sound was all she was capable of when he pressed the flat of his tongue against her opening and licked upward in a hungry sweep. He didn't seem even a little bit bothered by the splattering of seed already there. If anything, it made him wilder.

Taevas swirled the very tip of his tongue around the taut pearl of nerves of her clitoris and through his own release. His rumble turned into a deep, bass purr. It vibrated through his tongue and straight into her, making her eyes cross.

"Oh," she gasped. "Oh, Taevas— I'm—"

She squeaked when he slid two fingers deep inside her with no preamble. Not that she needed one, but his fingers were considerably larger than hers, and she really wasn't prepared for the way he curled them *just so,* allowing the pads to massage her inner wall.

Her hips jerked. She found herself clinging to him as he set a frenetic, relentless pace.

Taevas could move with extraordinary speed and power, at precisely the right angle, and when he closed his lips around her with a hard, fluttering pull of suction, Alashiya came with a violence she'd never even imagined.

Her back bowed as a cry tore from her throat. She gushed over his hand, marking him like he'd marked her. He didn't stop his frantic touches for even a second. One powerful orgasm bled into aftershocks that broke her down to her foundations.

It took her a while to realize he was speaking to her. She'd tilted her face up to the ceiling, as if the pleasure was sunlight and all she wanted was to bask.

Dazedly tilting her head just a little toward him, she caught his satisfied growl. "Next time, you'll do that sitting on my face."

CHAPTER TWENTY-SIX

HE WANTED HER TO SIT IN HIS LAP WHILE SHE ATE HER dinner, but his Alashiya was shy. She chose to sit on the opposite side of the little table, tempting him with everything she was. There was a high flush in her cheeks. Her damp curls were beginning to dry in the warm air. She still wore that ridiculous, sumptuous robe made of *scrap*, of all things, which provided him with tantalizing glimpses of the dark shadows of her nipples and the deep line of her cleavage.

Alashiya had the dazed, glowing look of a woman well-fucked, and it drove him absolutely mad.

Pain was a constant, grinding presence in the back of his mind, but he forced it away, into a tight little room where its presence could still be felt but not nearly so keenly. He refused to let it steal this moment from him.

Taevas had little appetite, so he sat back and watched as his nymph picked at the light dinner he'd cobbled together. It was the first time he'd cooked in any capacity in... fifty years, probably. The cucumbers were roughly chopped and he had a feeling he'd over-salted them, but she didn't complain.

She appeared relaxed, even outright *pleased* with him, when she dipped her bread in oil and laid a thick slice of tomato — her own addition to the spread, which he made careful note of — before taking a large bite.

He'd been proud of many great things in his life. He'd signed the Peace Charter, which ended the Great War that tore the continent apart, and he'd united the dragon clans — *really* united them, rather than rule them under an iron fist like Jaak had. He'd met kings and queens, seen the world, helped cultivate mind-boggling new technology, and watched his clan flourish once more.

But when Alashiya gave him a shy, rosy-cheeked smile over her slice of bread, her nose wrinkled with pleasure and her eyes gleaming like the sun on polished cedar, he was the proudest he'd ever been.

A different kind of hunger grew in him. He thought it might've been at least temporarily satisfied by their interlude on the kitchen counter, but like true dragonfire, it'd only grown bigger and more destructive as it was fed.

Taevas's tail found its way beneath the table, where it coiled possessively around her perfect ankle. He tried to offer her a nonchalant smile when she gave him a quick amused look.

Let her think it's nothing. That it's a cute little game, the beast in him purred. *Let her think there's a chance she'll ever be rid of me. By the time she realizes it's a lie, she won't want to be free anyway.*

Dragons, like many beings, had forged their most distinctive characteristics in a time of horrific strife. Taking what you want, being the kind of person who felt no compunction with stealing resources, roosts, *mates,* often made all the difference between being one who survived and one who didn't.

It was deeply ingrained in them, that singularly covetous nature and decisiveness. In the modern world, it was often deemed unacceptable — a relic of evolution that ought to be left by the wayside. An arrogant, demanding dragon was one who endured the test of time and adversity, but not necessarily one who succeeded in the new era of the world.

Dragons had a reputation for being selfish, jealous lovers who would decide, with little input from their partners, that theirs was a permanent union. It was instinctive as well as cultural and had resulted in a reputation that sent many prospective mates running in the opposite direction. So they course-corrected.

Modern dragons, aware of their reputation, tended to use a combination of inherent charm, humor, and carefully crafted nonchalance to make the world think they weren't exactly as they'd always been. It was the easiest way to get what they wanted with the least amount of resistance, and necessary to successfully cohabitate with all the different beings of the world.

And when the time was right, they could drop the mask — and snap the trap shut.

Taevas offered Alashiya a slow smile as the tip of his tail stroked the contour of her calf. "You're beautiful, *metsalill*. I could watch you for hours and only ask for more."

Catching the double meaning of his words, Alashiya ducked her head to hide the fierce blush that radiated beneath her skin. She looked terribly maidenly, like a nymph from a classical painting, so pure and unaware of the watcher as she dipped her naked body in a burbling stream.

What a change it was from the vixen who'd planted her foot on his chest and commanded him like it was her due. Looking so bashful, it wasn't hard to believe she was a virgin.

A virgin, he thought, briefly stabbed with dismay at the thought. The concept itself meant nothing to him. There was no triumph in being her first, as he was certain he would be, but rather an upwelling of such grief, he couldn't stand to look at it head-on.

His nymph was a deeply sensual being. He'd seen it with his own eyes. He'd felt it with his blessed, greedy fingers. To see how she'd bloomed with just the slightest bit of sunlight... It was something he'd never forget.

And yet she'd been left in isolation for so long. Why?

He'd heard her explanations — about the school boys and the rangers and the lack of choice mates around Birchdale. But he'd sensed something deeper, darker, lingering around the edges of her life from the moment his mind came back to him. To discover that such a creature had been locked away in isolation for so long made his protective instincts bristle.

What could compel a lush, lively creature like Alashiya to hide herself away for so long?

Despite clearly longing for it, she'd foregone finding a mate, having offspring, or keeping friends. She lived in a crumbling house with too many empty rooms, all shut off like their occupants had simply walked off one day. She did little more than work, day in and day out, for whatever tiny percentage of money the atelier deigned to give her.

And the wards. He couldn't forget the wards.

His nymph lived in a wild fortress of her own making. She didn't leave. She didn't seek out another kind of life. She seemed to have contented herself with silence, with never finding a mate, and Taevas couldn't think of a single reason *why*.

As much as it killed him, he knew all of that would have to wait. They would have plenty of time for him to unravel her mysteries — and that depended entirely on his ability to get them safely back to the 'Riik.

He waited for Alashiya's blush to cool before he broached the subject. "My Shiya, can you drive?"

She swallowed a sip of water before she answered, "Oh, sure. I started driving when I was nine. It's been a while, though."

He wasn't surprised to hear it. Many children in rural areas learned to drive country roads and across farms as soon as they could reach the pedals, but it did raise several more questions. "Do you have a car?"

"My grandfather's old truck is in the barn, I think," she replied, brow furrowing. "But it stopped running in the 2000's. Once my grandmother got sick, we couldn't afford to fix it and Mike — Debbie's husband — never followed through with his offer to help, so we just left to rust. Gods know what state it's in now, especially after the roof caved in. Why?"

Taevas restrained himself from bombarding her with more questions. Reminding himself that her safety had to be the priority, he answered, "Because the safest option for us is to drive to the 'Riik, or at least as close to it as possible."

Alashiya looked up from where she'd speared a ragged chunk of cucumber on the end of her fork. "I thought you needed a phone?"

He shook his head. "With that dragon hanging around, it's too risky. I won't send you out on errands that might get you hurt. It's better if we just leave. I can find a way to contact my Wing when we're no longer in immediate danger."

Slowly lowering her fork, she replied, "I don't have a working car."

"Then we must find one," he sighed, hating to add yet more trouble onto her plate. Taevas had already silently promised her that he would pay her back in ways she couldn't imagine, but that didn't make his pride smart any less everytime had to ask yet more of her.

Alashiya's gaze lowered to the table. She didn't respond right away, and something in her expression made the hair rise on the back of his neck. "Well... I could maybe borrow one of Debbie's trucks, but it'd be a hard sell."

Entirely unused to normal people saying no to him when he asked for things, Taevas frowned. "Why?"

"Because the Draakonriik is a thousand miles one way, first of all. And second, I'd have to lie and tell her I was the one taking it." She sat back in her chair and began to make an odd, apparently unconscious motion with her right forefinger and thumb.

She's sewing, he realized, gaze sharpening as he recognized the barely perceptible swoop and pull of an invisible needle and thread.

Protective instincts stirring, Taevas rearranged his chair so he was sitting much closer to her, his body turned toward hers so that their knees brushed. Bracing one elbow on the dinner table, he laid his hand on the warm skin of her arm and reassured her,

"It's actually only about seven hundred miles, I think. If we're where I think we are."

Her arm went stiff under his. "You say that like it's practically next door."

"Well, isn't it?" He rolled his gaze to the ceiling as he reassessed the distance. Assured that he was correct, he said, "Yes, it's very close."

Alashiya gave him a long look that he didn't enjoy at all. It was like she'd just realized something, and whatever it was, it had completely dashed that gorgeous, post-orgasm glow he so admired. "Seven hundred miles *isn't* close."

"For a dragon it is."

"I'm not a dragon," she replied, pulling her arm out from under his hand.

"I've noticed." Taevas tried to ease her worries with a smile and a long, admiring look. "I love this about you, *minu metsalill.* I hope to continue to show you just how much when we're in our nest."

The smile didn't work, and he was fairly certain the compliments had the opposite of their intended effect.

Alashiya crossed her arms and inhaled in a way that suggested she was summoning patience. "I don't even know why it matters. It's not like I'll be going. But getting you a car for that kind of a trip—"

Taevas sat up straight, his tail tightening reflexively around her calf as the tip gave a menacing rattle. "What are you saying? Of course you're coming with me."

They stared at each other in mutual incomprehension for a beat before Alashiya asked, "Why would I do that?"

"Why wouldn't you? I can't stay here."

"So... you'll leave." She didn't appear very happy about that, which was somewhat gratifying, but the fact that she said it at all made him cranky. "Wasn't that always the plan?"

She thought I intended to leave without her? Taevas leaned forward to cup her cheek, a soothing rumble starting up in his chest. His chest tightened. *That explains it. She must've been hurt, thinking I'd abandon her. My sweet Shiya. Never.*

"Ah, I see where the miscommunication happened, Shiya. You thought I would call in my Wing and they'd whisk me away without you. I wouldn't allow this."

The immediate relief he expected to see in her eyes didn't come. If anything, she appeared more uneasy than before. "Why not?"

"For one thing, it would be dangerous to leave any trace of me here that might lead my attackers back to you. Until I know for certain that they've been dealt with, you are at risk simply for having harbored me." Taevas's voice dropped as he became distracted by the smooth skin of her cheek under his stroking thumb. "And for another... sweet Shiya, I've found you at last. I've wanted you for ten years. Do you expect me to give you up so soon?"

"But my wards will hide me," she protested, gaze moving restlessly across his face like she thought there might be some answers there. "And... and can't you just come back to visit me?"

The possessive thing in him snapped its jaws. Feeling his muscles tense, one by one, Taevas informed her, "Any wards can be broken with enough force. You aren't safe here, Alashiya. You said this yourself. And what of that man who harasses you— *Monty?* You expect me to leave you here on your own when he could escalate his behavior at any time? You don't even have a *phone,* Shiya. You're completely isolated and easy pickings for anyone who might get the wrong thought in their head."

He recognized the familiar rebellious glint in her eye when she protested, "I've done just fine on my own."

Not wanting to rehash the argument from that morning, he shook his head. "I won't fight with you on this again. This is non-negotiable."

"You expect me to leave my home?" Her expression grew even more incredulous. "For how long?"

Trying not to sound evasive, Taevas danced around her second question. "I wouldn't ask this of you if it weren't absolutely necessary, but Shiya, you aren't safe here, and I am Isand. We are tied together now. I know you feel this. I *know* you do. And that means we can't stay."

"I can't leave," she insisted, sounding truly alarmed now. "I've *never* left."

"What?"

Alashiya stood up from the table. His tail slid reluctantly away from her leg as she began to pace. Her right hand bounced and twitched by her thigh — *dip, pull, flick.*

"I've never left Birchdale," she explained in a rush. "My grove bought this land just before I was born. I went to school here. I've only ever been to town and back. I can't just— You expect me to go out there? I'm a nymph, Taevas. We aren't built for that world. *I'm* not."

To someone like Taevas — indeed, to any dragon — the concept of being confined to a few acres of flat land, to a tiny rural town, was wholly inconceivable. It was the stuff horror movies were made of.

A dragon could glide fairly early in childhood. They began leaping from carefully placed platforms around the roost at around four, sometimes as early as two. By the time they were ten, they were expected to take short flights with their parents and to leap fearlessly from many story-high launching platforms or roofs. By their teens, average dragons could fly hundreds of miles without needing to touch down for food or water, guided unerringly by the magnetic field of the Earth.

Adults could fly for much longer, much farther, making all the world seem quite small. Their limitations were contained to the bands of the atmosphere that clung so delicately to the face of the planet and, in the modern world, by the political landscape, which could make finding a safe spot to land tricky.

Borders and laws didn't exist when soaring through the clouds, but they had an annoying way of popping up when one touched down.

To roam was an innate part of them, culturally and biologically. So much so that they could get what they called the roaming sickness, an insidious, often random disease that messed with a dragon's internal compass. It made it so they couldn't land, driven by the impulse to just *keep going* until they found the perfect place to roost, and tended to result in unchecked aggression, confusion, and death as exhaustion simply dropped them from the sky.

Taevas's own cousin had fallen prey to the sickness a few years prior, but it had all worked out for Artem, since it led him to his Chosen, Dr. Paloma Contreras, who dwelled at the top of a mountain in the Sierra Nevada range.

To fly, to chase, to *roam* — it was in their blood. Taevas couldn't imagine a life where he stayed in one place every day. To hear that Alashiya had done exactly that for the gods knew how long was horrifying.

Afraid that he was getting some of the answers he'd craved in the worst possible way, he pressed, "You must have left at *some* point. There is a whole world out there, Shiya. I understand not having the money to travel, but to never leave Birchdale— *Why?*"

"What's out there for me? I have no one and nothing except this house," she answered, heartbreakingly matter-of-fact. "I don't know how to live out there. I was never taught. And nearly every person I've met from the outside, everything I've ever read or heard, has only made me more certain that I wouldn't survive ten minutes on my own in a city. I can't risk that."

Good gods. If this hadn't happened, I never would've found her.

The idea that the only way he might've met her was if he'd finally broken those final, ethical rules he'd laid down for himself so long ago made his stomach drop. What if he hadn't? Alashiya would've lived out her days in complete solitude, never appreciated for her kindness, her gifts, her strength, until the day Grim came for her with death's sickle and veil.

A cold trickle of unease slid into his veins. He'd been so certain that he was doing the right thing by clinging to his control.

He'd convinced himself again and again that abiding by his made up rules was the best choice.

For me. I only ever thought of what I wanted. What I fear. If I continued on that path, we never would've met.

Putting that disturbing thought aside for later, he tried to quickly reorganize his argument. Taevas truly hadn't considered that it might be difficult to convince her to go with him. It was a foregone conclusion in his mind. They were together. Since he had to return to the Draakonriik as soon as possible, of course she would come with him.

Only now, staring into her ashen face, did he realize he had another fight on his hands.

"You're scared," he realized, stomach twisting.

Alashiya's right hand bobbed against her thigh as she began to pace the length of the kitchen. "Of course I am! I can't leave. It's impossible."

"Why is it so impossible, *metsalill?* Explain it to me."

"What's there to explain? I just can't."

Taevas rose slowly from his chair. He had to support himself against the table as pain lanced through his fractured ribs and wrapped around the base of his wings like hot barbed wire.

Fighting to keep his voice even, he asked, "Is it because you have some connection to the land? I once heard a rumor that nymphs will die if they're separated from their land for too long."

She tossed him an impatient look. "That's ridiculous. Yes, we bond with land and become attached to it, but it's basically the same as becoming attached to a community over generations. It's based on relationships, on tradition. My grove once looked after the greatest forest in the world, but times changed and we had to leave. We didn't die. Not because of that, at least."

"The greatest forest in the world?"

Alashiya paused her pacing. Looking away from him, she explained, "The God Forest, where all beings were made. My mother's line stretches back to the very first nymph, who Blight made from a foundling left among the roots of the first trees. I'm the last one left."

Taevas wasn't religious, but he knew the place she spoke of. It was hard not to, when every version of the great creation myth began there. It was an unspeakably ancient, sacred cedar forest whittled down to hardly a sliver of greenery after ten thousand years of necessity.

But that wasn't what interested him most. *My mother's line stretches back to the very first nymph,* she'd said.

Something clicked in his mind when he looked at her then, something she'd been telling him all along and he had waved away without thought.

Even he knew the stories of the nymph queens of the old world, when everything was new and wild. They were the dispensers of wisdom, of prophecy, and it was often a chance meeting with one of those queens that would send a great hero on their journey. He vaguely recalled that they had once had their own powerful trade networks built of thousands of interconnected family groups — *the groves she spoke of?* — and vast wealth.

But time had come for them, as it always did, and nymphs had little by way of defensive abilities. At some point, they'd gone from legendary queens to ethereal dancing figures in paintings, their power lost to the erosion of history.

"You're a queen," he breathed, astonished that he'd been so blind.

Alashiya gave him another impatient look. "Yes, I'm queen of this grove. We've been over this."

"No." Taevas limped over to her and stopped her pacing by cupping her shoulders. "No, you're a *queen,* Alashiya. If you're a direct descendant of the first nymph, that means you're— what? Queen of *all* nymphs?"

She looked at some spot over his shoulder. "That title has been defunct for thousands of years."

"And so it means nothing?"

"Exactly."

"That can't be true," he insisted.

"It is." Her eyes closed. The fight bled out of her. "I say that I'm queen of this grove, Taevas, but that doesn't mean much. I was princess of something once, when my family was alive, but now I'm queen of nothing but memory."

The empty rooms. The crumbling house. The queen of memory.

Taevas skimmed his hands up until he cradled Alashiya's jaw. She seemed so fragile, but that wasn't true. It couldn't be. Not if she'd survived on her own for so long.

In a hoarse voice full of dread, he asked, "What happened to your grove, *metsalill?* Why are you all alone?"

It broke something in him when she leaned forward, bending like a flower in the wind, until her brow touched the dip between his collar bones. His breath hitched. Members of his clan often came to him for advice and even comfort, but it had never felt like this.

It *hurt.*

CHAPTER TWENTY-SEVEN

TAEVAS WRAPPED AN ARM AROUND HER SHOULDERS. His other hand cradled the back of her head, holding her to him as firmly as he dared. The wretched, useless wings folded against his back twitched with the instinct to wrap her in the dragon's embrace, where she would be sheltered from all the evils of the world. The embrace was a sacred thing reserved for closest kin and Chosen. For a dragon to let a person into the embrace was to expose their greatest vulnerability, the hyper-sensitive membrane and delicate bone of their wings, and offer them the protection of their shelter.

An embrace meant sacrificing their wings in the event of an attack. It meant letting a person under your guard, where they might slip a knife between your ribs or snap a fragile bone. It meant family and love and choice.

It made him angry — so, *so* angry — that he couldn't give her that which was her right, her *place*. Because of the decisions of a few faceless men, he couldn't give her the embrace when she so clearly needed it, and he would never, ever forget that.

But when Alashiya slid her arms around his waist and clung to him like that, a little of his rage was tucked away, saved for another time and a better use. She pressed her face into his throat, where her eyelashes tickled his skin. Her breath warmed him in tiny distressed puffs.

"I don't want to talk about this anymore," she whispered. "I just want to go to sleep."

She was hiding again. Running from the conversation. He felt as though he'd forced a door open that had remained shut for too long, and the memories that had escaped weren't the sort that could be dealt with in a single night.

But he couldn't let this die. As much as he wanted to, as much as it killed him to push, he had no choice. He couldn't allow her to suffer in silence any longer. She was his to protect, and that started now.

"I don't need details," he explained, "and I won't push any further than this, Shiya, but I have to know."

"Why?"

"Because I can't care for you properly until I do. I can't know how to ease your pain, what to avoid, how to help you. A healer can't cure what they don't see, and your husband can't soothe what you don't share."

Her breath hitched. "You're not really my husband, you know."

"I am," he answered without hesitation. "You decided this, my Shiya. It's done. Now tell me what happened to your grove."

Alashiya leaned into him. "A rogue band of shifters came through. Rovers released from the army after the war. They were looking for a place to settle their little pack — or that's what they said, at least. My grove welcomed them in, fed them, let them sleep in the barn. But they overstayed their welcome. Got pushy, then violent. When my parents and some of the others decided they had to go..."

Ice tipped into his veins. "What'd they do, *metsalill?*"

"They killed them." Her fingers dug into the dense muscles of his back. A fine trembling ran down her spine. "It was so fast. I was in the kitchen with my grandma when it started. We all felt it as soon as the killing started. Everyone scattered to hide in the woods, but most of them were hunted down. Just for fun, I think. It wasn't like we had anything to steal or were any sort of threat."

He could hardly get the words out, but he managed to ask, "What happened to you?"

"I hid in the place you found me," she answered, soft and matter-of-fact. "I was so scared, and I could hear screams close by. So I dug deep and let the roots take me. I hibernated for days, until my grandparents managed to find me and convinced the forest to let me out again."

A shiver ran through him. "Shiya..."

"Not everyone was killed by the shifters. Some of them were so damaged by the horror they chose never to come out again, or went into hibernation afterward, when the grief got too bad. The forest chose to keep them. That's what happened to my mother. The forest made its choice and... and I never saw her again."

Sickness churned in his stomach. He knew what slaughter looked like, and he knew the devastation couldn't always be counted into carnage. Most often, the true cost was paid by those left behind.

Dreading the answer, he asked, "The forest isn't just a hiding spot, is it?"

"No. It can hide us, it can sustain us, and if it chooses, it can end us."

He closed his eyes. Swallowing hard, he grated, "The shifters. What happened to them?"

"We weren't the only victims. They'd done it before, and they were caught not too long after they ran from here," she answered. "Rangers got them. They're gone."

He wished it satisfied him. Even knowing how swift and brutal shifter justice tended to be, it didn't make him feel any better.

Taevas wanted details. He wanted to know they suffered for what they'd done to Alashiya and her family. He wanted to avenge her like he'd avenged his parents and everyone else terrorized by Isand Jaak.

But he couldn't. All he could do was take care of her *now*.

"That's enough, *metsalill*. I don't need more." Stroking his claws through her fragrant curls, he murmured, "Go lay down in our nest. I'll clean up the dishes and then join you."

She didn't move right away. They lingered there for a while longer, their bodies swaying ever-so-slightly to the music of crickets just beyond the windows, until at last Alashiya's arms fell away.

It pained him to let her go. Taevas pressed a lingering kiss to her forehead. "Rest," he breathed into the fine, wispy curls at the edge of her hairline. "I'll be in soon."

She nodded. Saying nothing, her eyes downcast, Alashiya stepped away from him. The feeling of loss was instant.

He watched her wrap her arms around herself, the extravagant sleeves of her golden robe trailing from her elbows, and slowly walk out of the kitchen. A queen in finery made of scraps, off to a nest on a floor.

A queen of memory. A queen who belonged to him.

He found her curled up in what had become his spot.

She'd changed into one of her pretty pleated nightgowns and tied her hair back in a loose braid. It snaked over the pillows in a thick, mahogany coil. Her back was to him, but he sensed that she was awake.

Dread was heavy in his gut. Exhaustion and pain made him crave the soft embrace of the nest, but it was the desire to shield her that propelled his steps across the darkened room. Taevas lifted the blankets and slid in behind her.

"Your wings, Taevas. You should lay on your stomach, not on your side," she whispered in soft protest. Her voice was rough. Had she been crying? The faint scent of salt in the air made his chest clench.

He slipped his left arm around her waist and tucked his right beneath her pillow. "I would trade them for a chance to hold you without hesitation."

A watery laugh escaped her. "You're very smooth, *argaman mlk.*"

Pressing his lips into the curve of her shoulder, he asked, "What does that mean?"

A soft huff escaped her nose. "Purple king."

He hoped she could feel his smile against her skin. "You are my wildflower and I am your purple king. I don't think either of us gets points for creativity."

"I like that you call me *metsah-leel.*" She slowly slid one hand beneath the pillow until she found his fingers. Twining them together, she whispered, "I never imagined what your voice would sound like."

He gave her fingers a small squeeze. "How is it?"

"Good."

"Just good? Ah, my Shiya. You love to wound me."

The softest, most precious laugh popped like champagne bubbles in the dark. "It's *very* good. I like it even when you're being bossy."

"I fear I will always be bossy," he wryly informed her.

Alashiya was quiet for a beat. "My grandfather wouldn't approve. He always said I needed to find a nice nymph for a husband."

Taevas stared into the darkness beyond the nest, the weight of her tragedy pressing down on him from the shadows. "Do you think I could've won him over?"

He felt her deep breath as she drew it in and let it out. "Yes."

Surprised by that, he noted, "You sound very certain. He must not have had his mind set on a nymph after all."

"He did," she insisted. "It's all he talked about at the end. He was so worried about me being alone, and he blamed himself for not having done enough to make sure I wasn't when he passed. But he's not so anxious anymore. At least, I don't think so."

Taevas's brow furrowed. "What do you mean?"

"It's *tēq*. I carry his ghost."

"I don't understand."

"A queen isn't just a queen. It's not just a title. It's *tēq*. To carry. To hold memory, knowledge, and the souls of those who passed." She clutched his hand beneath the pillow and curled a bit more tightly on her side, like she needed to protect herself against something unseen.

Speaking in the rhythmic cadence of a storyteller, she whispered, "The first nymph survived because she was given to the Earth by Blight. He couldn't provide her with milk, so he dug a hole at the base of the oldest cedar tree and placed her inside, where the roots and the soil itself could provide for her. They burrowed into her skin, her bones, her heart, and twined themselves into every part of her. When she was strong enough, he dug her out again and showed her how to live in the forest he'd made. He told her that the knowledge was hers to hold forever."

"I'm not used to Blight being the hero of a story," Taevas murmured.

The god of disease, decay, and wilderness wasn't widely spoken of for being kind or nurturing. He was known as the scorned lover of the goddess Glory, the being who lurked in the dark and whose image was never shown, lest his gaze rest for too long on an undeserving soul.

"The gods aren't heroes. They simply *are.*" Alashiya pulled the arm he'd slung around her waist up so she could cradle it against the plush warmth of her chest. "Blight disappeared, leaving the nymph to fend for herself. Eventually she found a husband and had many children, who went on to have children of their own. When she died, her knowledge passed to her oldest daughter, and then again to *her* daughter."

Taevas blinked. "Wait, what?"

"All nymphs are descended from the first. A few years ago I did some research at the library and read that she was most likely a normal arrant woman who somehow became infected with a strain of mycelium that grows on tree roots — Blight only knows how, I suspect. That mycelium allows information and nutrients to transfer from tree to tree, and, with time and the mutation of magic, from nymph to nymph. We all have it. We all live and die and make our mark in the hyphae, the network — but only queens *carry* it."

He wondered if this was what it was like to be truly, completely gobsmacked. "I... You have a *hive mind?*"

"No," she replied, rubbing the line of his knuckles against the underside of her chin in slow, soothing drags. "We have a connection. We share memory and knowledge. How to survive in the wild, what berries are safe, and what caves have bears. Over the generations it deepened, became more complex. I can't speak to my ancestors through it, but I can feel them and access the knowledge of their lives through impressions. All nymphs can, to some extent, but only queens can reach back as far or hear them as clearly as I can."

"Queen of memory." Goosebumps prickled his arms.

Alashiya nodded. "Each grove has its own queen, its own branch of the hyphae, but all nymphs are connected by the root, the first. And now me."

"And you... You became queen of your grove when your mother died." She hadn't said it, but he couldn't imagine how else it could've gone.

"My grandmother, actually," she replied, her voice tight with emotion. "My mother never got to be a queen. My grandmother outlived her, and then when she passed, it became my responsibility. But by then it was just me and my grandfather. When he died, there was no grove to guide or family to share the memories with. Nothing but ghosts and the end of a line that saw the beginning of all things."

Taevas wanted to say something. He wanted to offer her some profound words of comfort or a speech about how she was a fucking *queen,* and that meant something even now. But the words wouldn't come.

It was nearly impossible for him to comprehend the enormity

of what she'd told him, what it *meant* to her, to the world, or the ocean of grief that rippled in slow, dark waves beneath every word.

No wonder she didn't want to speak of how she'd ended up alone in Birchdale, cut off from the world.

Taevas tightened his arms around her. "You're not alone anymore, Shiya. You'll never be alone again."

"You can't make promises like that. We barely know each other."

He let out a shaky breath. "I think we know each other better than anyone else in the world."

The fresh scent of salt tinged the air. Alashiya was crying, but she didn't make a sound or shake in his arms. She simply wept in the way one might bleed — silently, continuously, until eventually it stopped, one way or another.

"I'm sorry," he rasped. "I'm so sorry."

Alashiya sniffed. "What for? You didn't do anything."

Regret curdled his stomach. The sour taste of it climbed up his throat to settle on his tongue and the backs of his teeth in a thick, toxic film. It tasted like salt and cowardice.

He closed his eyes. "For making you wait so long."

CHAPTER TWENTY-EIGHT

ALASHIYA WOKE BEFORE DAWN. WHEN SHE BLINKED, her eyes stung. Her body was faintly sore, as if speaking of her past had taken a true physical toll.

She watched as a tiny sliver of pale light began to take shape on the floor, cast by a gap in her thick curtains, and tried to summon some embarrassment for how she'd fallen apart in front of a stranger-who-wasn't-a-stranger. There was none. There wasn't much of anything, save a sense of peace as soft and new as the little sliver of light.

Taevas's arm was heavy over her middle and his breath tickled the top of her head with every slow exhale. They hadn't moved an inch in the night. Alashiya couldn't remember a time when she'd slept more deeply. There were no dreams. She didn't wake, as was her habit, whenever the old house made one of its favorite noises, thinking that an intruder had come at last.

She slept in the deep-dark, the hidden gap between life and death, and when she woke, it took a long time for her to settle back into her body.

Taevas slept on, no doubt exhausted by his exertion the previous day. Not wanting to disturb him, Alashiya took her time getting out of bed. She suspected he was normally a light sleeper, which would've made the maneuver more difficult, but when she peeked at his face, she found it relaxed in the deep sleep of the ill.

She rearranged the blankets so they covered him before she tiptoed out of the room.

Her mind remained blissfully blank as she shrugged on her robe. The sun was just kissing the horizon when she stirred her sugar into her coffee, and the sliver of light had taken on a gold hue when she returned to the living room a little while later, mug in hand.

Whispers, always so close and yet so far, filled the silence in her mind. She took a sip from her coffee as she padded across the room, to the opposite side from the bed and her work area. Her destination was the little sitting nook, with its antique loom and spinning wheel beside the two ratty loveseats she and her grandfather used to sit in. Tucked behind one of the chairs, *her* chair, was a cedar chest the same color as wild honey.

Alashiya quietly set her coffee down on the small, doily-covered table between the chairs, ever-aware of the slumbering dragon across the room. The chest had always seemed so big to her, so precious, when she was a child. When she lifted it from its hiding place behind her chair, Alashiya was struck, as she always was, by how very small and fragile it seemed to her now.

She sat in her chair and placed the chest on her lap. It was an heirloom all on its own. Her grandmother said it was made from wood gifted by Blight's cedar, the one who held and fed the first nymph. Alashiya had her doubts about that, but they didn't matter. It was a good story, and when she brushed her fingers over the silk-smooth surface of the wood, she felt the generations of her family doing the same.

The latch had been replaced many times, but it was still old enough to squeal a bit when she eased it open. Alashiya cast a worried look at the bed and was relieved to see that Taevas hadn't so much as twitched. Satisfied that his rest hadn't been disturbed, she peered inside the chest and found all the familiar shapes she expected.

There were old photos from the various places her ancestors had lived. Dried flowers pressed between yellowed tissue. Two golden arm bands formed to look like branches, undoubtedly more ancient than the chest and the only gold the grove could never bear to part with. A coiled ball of purple silk was the unassuming shape of an ancestral gown made of several yards of pleats so small, each fold was only as deep as the tip of a pencil.

And above it all, neatly folded and perpetually unfinished, was Alashiya's veil.

She extracted it from the chest with the utmost care. The silk was so fine it fell through the gaps between her fingers like flowing water. In the blushing glow of dawn, she could make out her hands through it.

It was a deep, luminous green shot with strands of shimmering gold. Her mother had ordered the fabric for it the day she discovered she was expecting, and when Alashiya was born, the oldest woman of the grove had cleaned her and wrapped her in it before she was presented, as all babies were.

Her parents had sewn the gold around the scalloped edge. Her grandmother's skilled hands had added tree branches and wildflowers. Over the years, when she had scraps from her commissions and the will, Alashiya had added her own designs in silk thread: blue robins, fat honeybees, a proud stag, and so many other creatures that had become her companions over the decades. Between those beloved creatures were tiny designs in various jewel tones, all of them miniature replicas of work she'd done for the dragon who slumbered in her bed.

It was unfinished by design. It was supposed to remain that way until after she married. The story she'd been told was that an unfinished garment confused the spirits who brought bad luck, and since she would only wear the veil again when she died, then such things wouldn't matter.

She sometimes wished, as she did then, that the tradition wasn't to bury the veils with the bodies. Alashiya thought wistfully of her grandmother's, and her mother's, and those of the

other women in her grove who'd been given back to Blight. Each
garment was the story of a life, from conception to death, and she
would've liked to hold them again. Especially now.

It was one thing to feel their spirits in the hyphae, to know
their stories with a touch of the invisible web that connected them
all, but it was another to run her fingers over the stitches that
marked every great and terrible event of their lives, to feel their
presence in the warp and weft of the fabric.

Alashiya touched the large empty spot at the end of the veil. It
was framed by the other designs and clearly reserved for a centerpiece that she could never decide on. The shape of the negative
space was a little odd — an upside down triangle, almost. She'd
puzzled for years over what ought to go there, or if she should risk
making the empty space smaller by adding more designs around
the edge, which would change the shape somewhat.

But now her fingers traced the path around the border of that
empty space knowingly.

A dragon could go here, she thought, throat tightening with
emotion. *If I wanted to, I could fit a dragon with its wings spread
in this space without any trouble at all.*

Violet and crimson threads, a hint of navy here and there...
Yes, a dragon would look very fine as the centerpiece. But putting
one there could mean many things, not all of them good. If she
were to sew Taevas into her veil, would she look at it years later
with joy or regret?

The silk was too fine for *maybe's* or *let's see's.* Once the needle
had passed through it, the delicate fabric was forever altered,
making any room for error or second-guessing almost non-
existent.

Alashiya gazed at the empty space for a long time, her coffee
cooling on the table by her elbow. *Would I regret it?*

It wouldn't be such a strange thing to sew him in. No matter
what happened, he'd made a mark unlike any other on her life —
as Adon, but also as Taevas. Perhaps he'd earned his place there.

But if their relationship, such as it was, ended in heartbreak, would she wish she'd never sewn a dragon? She imagined it could be something of a memorial for hopes gone fallow, or a path she was too cowardly to tread.

He'd sworn to follow her wherever she ran, but that couldn't possibly be an oath he would fulfill. Their lives were too different. How could he just expect her to pack up and leave with him, to strike out into such a hostile world with just his word on which to cling?

He didn't understand. He *couldn't* understand.

It all made perfect sense to her. She would stay, as she always had, and be the guardian of her grove's memories, of the first Queen's legacy. It was the safe option, and the only one that didn't make her feel like she was stepping off a cliff just because a handsome man had asked her to. All things withered, including her proud line. She'd accepted a very long time ago that she would be the last.

And yet...

And yet she could see the dragon there in the empty space, and when she pressed her fingers against the cool silk, her ghosts' whispers rose in a great swell of urgency, defying their usual calls for caution. *Do it,* their echoes seemed to say. *Jump, Alashiya. You might just fly.*

"What is this?"

Startled, she looked up to find a drowsy dragon frowning down at her, pillow lines creased in his cheek. He knelt before her chair, his hands on the armrests, and peered curiously into the chest. Her veil had spilled out of it in a waterfall of green silk.

"These are my heirlooms," she explained, gently gathering the veil back into a protective coil. "I was feeling— I wanted to be with my family for a little while."

Taevas glanced at her through the dense fringe of his lashes. She thought for a moment that he was going to press again, to insist on knowing everything in that infuriating, endearing way of his. Alashiya steeled herself for it, but he didn't ask.

Instead, he said in his sleep-roughened voice, "It's good you have these things. I don't."

"You don't have heirlooms?"

"Only one," he answered. "A tapestry. Almost everything we had, we sold or abandoned when my family fled the Collapse. What little we managed to save was burned when my mother defied Isand Jaak. The only reason the tapestry survived was because my father made me take it when he sent me away."

The Collapse was something she knew well. It was the great age of calamity that had struck mainland Europe and Asia — a time of terrible disease, famine, and war. It was ultimately what had pushed her grove out of the God Forest, up through Europe, and ultimately to the UTA over the course of generations.

But she didn't know Isand Jaak. The hair on her arms stood on end when Taevas said his name.

Alashiya tentatively touched the hard line of Taevas's jaw. "Tell me about the tapestry."

He tilted his head into her hand without hesitation. "Don't you want to hear about the rest?"

"Yes," she replied, offering him a small smile, "but I won't pry. Especially before you've had any coffee."

The crow's feet deepened around his eyes, but his mouth didn't curve in a real smile. Defying her weak attempt to lighten the mood, he said, "I've asked everything of you, Alashiya, and offered nothing because right now I *am* nothing. If I can give you my story and have it be the real start of this thing between us, then I would like to."

She recalled how he'd touched her the night before, and the long thread of familiarity that had connected them for a decade. "I thought we started ten years ago."

Taevas moved his hands from the armrests of her chair to her knees. Despite his inherent grandeur, he looked subdued, some-how. Gentled. It was hard not to look that way, she guessed, when he was on his knees before her, his head bowed.

"Adon and his *metsalill* started ten years ago," he gravely replied, "but Taevas and Alashiya start today."

Her heartbeat quickened. All at once, the whispers went silent. The ghosts, like her, waited for him to speak.

"My clan is Aždaja. We have never been entirely noble or noteworthy. Some of my ancestors did well and others were paupers. We were lords one generation and thieves the next." He used his practiced, rakish smile. His violet eyes glittered with warmth when he continued, "My most famous ancestor was a carpenter who became Isand after he saved a princess besieged by two evil dragons."

Alashiya huffed a soft laugh. "I'd say it runs in your family, but the only dragon I've ever been besieged by is you."

Giving her knees a squeeze, he said, "Let's keep it that way, yes?"

"You're the only dragon I have eyes for." She intended for it to come out far lighter than it did, but there was truth in the words, and it was a heavy thing.

Taevas sucked in a deep breath. "I'm not an easy dragon," he warned her, seemingly against his better judgment. "I think you've figured that out by now, but I need you to be sure. I'm stubborn, arrogant, and need to be in control at all times. I'm also... There are parts of me, parts of being a dragon, that I've locked away for a very long time, my Shiya. A better dragon, a less scarred one, would—"

He cut himself off and looked away, his expression tight with self-recrimination. Mindful of the precious cargo in her lap, Alashiya leaned forward to brush her fingers over his hair in a soothing stroke. "What, *argaman mlk?*"

Taevas closed his eyes. "When I was five, my family fled the end of the Collapse. Our wealth was gone, food was scarce. My parents worried about what would happen to me. Like many others, they petitioned Isand Jaak, the wealthiest dragon in the UTA, for help in setting up a new life. The deal was that they pledged allegiance to him and would fight for him in the Great War in exchange for it."

Alashiya's stomach tightened. "That sounds like an easy way for a powerful man to exploit the desperate."

"It was." Taevas opened his eyes. Anger, old and deeply-rooted, glowed in them. "And if you didn't hold up your end of the bargain or became more trouble than you were worth, he'd abandon you. If you suddenly found your new roost on enemy lines? Tough. He wouldn't send help or evacuate you. We were entirely expendable. *Dragons have wings,* he'd say. *Why don't you fly?* As if it's ever so easy when you've got young, or a mate, or..."

Speaking in barely a whisper, she asked, "Is that what happened to you?"

"No." He wouldn't look at her, then. His eyes roved around the room, restless and seeking, while his hands remained locked on her knees, like he had to hold on tight or he'd float away.

"Toward the end of the war, Jaak took on a scorched earth policy. Instead of targeted attacks, he'd command his dragons to burn whole cities from above. United Washington was one of them, Baltimore another. There were countless towns along the border, too — all destroyed so that the Orclind's troops or the shifters wouldn't have a place to hide or a scrap to eat."

Echoes of memories from her ancestors rippled through the threads in her mind. While she had never experienced the fury of dragonfire, someone in her line had. She could almost hear the terrible roar of blue flame as it consumed everything and everyone in its path.

She found his hands on her knees and squeezed. He wasn't the only one who had to anchor himself in the present.

Taevas twined their fingers together. In a lower, thicker voice, he said, "My mother was one of his soldiers. When the order came down to her— She couldn't. She had young at home, and a Chosen. Knowing that there were families in those towns, how could she follow his order?"

Horror gripped her throat and squeezed. "What did he do?"

"I was fifteen. To keep me out of trouble and away from fighting, my father had sent me off to apprentice with a carpenter. I only allowed it because I wanted to emulate my ancestor, Isand Vanasarvik. I was living and working in a shop a few towns over when Jaak sent his men to our house."

Taevas brought one of her hands to his lips. When he spoke next, it was into the palm of her hand, like he wished to give the words to her, to let her take them far away. "He had my father, a teacher who never fought a day in his life, beaten and executed in front of my mother. Then he burned our home down. The goal was to kill me, too, but he couldn't find me. That was another one of his policies: defiance had to be answered with complete annihilation."

Sickness churned in her gut. "Oh, Taevas. I'm..."

He kissed her palm. "I know. Thank you, *metsalill.*"

CHAPTER TWENTY-NINE

ALASHIYA UNTANGLED THEIR HANDS. QUICKLY putting away her veil and closing the box, she set it on the table. When her lap was clear, she leaned forward until she could cup his cheeks. "I know this kind of pain," she whispered, pressing soft kisses to his cheeks, the bridge of his nose, and his bottom lip.

Taevas bowed his head toward her, accepting her touches. "I wish you didn't."

"Tell me what happened to you," she murmured.

"I went into hiding for a while. But I was so *angry*, Shiya. So, so angry." He let out a long sigh. "I never meant to start a rebellion. I didn't think that far ahead. Not until it was already happening, anyway. I kept meeting other people like me, who'd been conned and exploited and punished by that asshole. I started going after his inner circle on my own, but others wanted in on it. Things just started happening naturally after that. Everything seemed to escalate overnight. Next thing I knew, clan leaders were seeking me out, looking to help, and I was Jaak's number one target."

Alashiya's lips parted with surprise. She leaned back a bit to look into Taevas's face, trying to imagine it as a teenage boy, lost without his parents and waging a war against a dragon with an army at his disposal.

"But you were so young," she whispered.

Taevas gave her an ageless, sorrowful look. "I was, and then my father died, and my mother went mad in solitary confinement, tortured by the loss of her Chosen. I stopped being young very quickly after that."

"Chosen?"

Something stirred in his eyes then, but she couldn't define it. "It's what we call our mates. When a dragon Chooses, there is no other. There is no going back. There is no tolerable separation. The same parts of our minds that can navigate the Earth's magnetic field realigns to make them the center of our world. To lose one is... fatal."

Ice dripped down her spine. "We have something similar," she told him. "When we marry, we twine ourselves together and become symbiotic. Losing a spouse isn't always a death sentence, but it can be. When my grandmother passed... my grandfather didn't live well. He got sick, and no matter what I did, he only ever got worse. I watched him wither away until one day he was just gone."

Taevas searched her gaze for what felt like a long time before he said, "Then you know how terrifying it can become, thinking of tying yourself to another when you've seen what can happen when it goes wrong."

It occurred to her then, in a slow drip of realization, that she and Taevas were very much alike. The similarities weren't confined to the sadnesses of their past, but to how they'd reacted to them.

Alashiya sucked in a sharp breath. Gripping his hands, she rasped, "Is that the part of you that was locked away?"

"I thought so," he answered. "Life is easier when you can control these things."

"What things?"

"Becoming attached. Falling in love. The specter of loss."

Her heart squeezed in painful recognition. "I understand."

"Do you?" Taevas tilted his head to one side. His expression was softly troubled. "Do you really understand, my Shiya?"

"I understand what it means to hide from the world," she answered, "and I think you've been hiding for a very long time, my dragon."

One corner of his lips kicked up in a small, wry smile. "Only you would think that."

"Maybe I'm the only person who sees you clearly, then."

He leaned forward to press a soft, seeking kiss to her lips. It was all tenderness, all longing, and when it was over, Alashiya was left boneless and warm. "Of that I have no doubt," he murmured into her lips. "Now, my beautiful *metsalill*, shall we make some breakfast?"

Thinking of the hideously chopped cucumbers from the previous night, Alashiya wrinkled her nose and teased, "Do you even know how to make toast, great Isand?"

"I breathe fire, remember? Toast I can do. Eggs... might be beyond me." Taevas gave her another kiss. This one was sweeter, lighter, like he wanted to offer her a reward for supporting him through such a harrowing tale — or perhaps make her forget. "But I am *excellent* at making coffee."

"I already made my coffee," she protested as he levered her out of the chair.

Taevas cast the mug a disdainful look. "It's gone cold! I'll make you a new cup if you make the eggs."

Despite the heaviness of everything they'd talked about and all the worries that dogged her, Alashiya couldn't fight the smile that pulled at her cheeks when he gave her that haughty look, like the idea of her drinking lukewarm coffee personally offended him.

"I'll make breakfast," she promised, letting him lead her out of the living room, "but only if you sit and tell me about that tapestry. I want to know every detail."

Taevas didn't turn his head to look at her when he replied,

"I'll tell you everything you want to know, *metsalill,* but I promise, you'll see it yourself soon enough."

There were two versions of the story — one told to the rest of the world and one heavily debated amongst the clan.

The argument stemmed from the rumor that his ancestor, the princess Saara who'd needed saving from two feuding dragons vying for her noble seat, was not an arrant princess, but an elf.

Taevas had scoffed at that version of the tale many times growing up. He'd slept beneath the tapestry that told the story all his life. Wouldn't he notice if she'd been rendered with pointed ears?

Nevermind the fact that the tapestry had been commissioned long after her death, when elves had formally forbidden the taking of non-elvish mates, making the depiction of her as an elf... not risky per se, but less than socially acceptable. Regardless, it seemed too outlandish to be true. He'd certainly never seen any elvish traits in his uncles or his father — or he thought he hadn't, at any rate.

It wasn't until he met his first elf on the battlefield that he began to wonder if there was some credence to the story. If, perhaps, the famous Aždaja coloring — vivid crimsons and violets — couldn't be traced back to a jewel-toned elf somewhere down the line.

Not that it mattered, really. Dragons had notoriously dominant genes. If there was an elf somewhere down the line, their traits would've been lost within a generation. The question of Saara's identity was little more than an idle curiosity for all his life. The greatest effect it had on him was that he had something of a soft spot for those proud beings who held themselves so apart from the world.

He watched with satisfaction as Theodore Solbourne willfully defied a thousand years of tradition to marry his pretty little witch, thinking that if Saara was an elf, she'd be proud to know that Taevas had played some small part in nudging Theodore to free her people to love again.

But it wasn't until a couple years later, when all the rumors of how elves found their mates began to trickle in, that Taevas began to wonder. *Really* wonder.

As he told Alashiya the story of his famous ancestors, he considered what it would've been like for Saara. If the rumors and old stories were true, she would've known that Vanasarvik was her mate the instant she caught his scent for the first time. Elves were incredibly sensitive to pheromones and found their mates with their noses. Once found, they relied on their mate's pheromones for nervous system and hormone regulation — making them an extreme weakness.

It was no wonder elves had kept their secrets for so long. A dragon would go mad without their mate, to be sure, but an elf's body would shut down completely in a miserable, slow-acting death.

Taevas watched Alashiya drift across the kitchen on her bare feet, her golden robe fluttering around her as she sliced cheese and plump tomatoes. Sunlight touched her curls, her soft cheeks, and the tips of her eyelashes. The scent of her, cypress and warmth, permeated every breath he took.

He recalled how he felt when he smelled her for the first time. He forced his mind past the instinctual recoil he experienced whenever he thought of how out of control he'd been, how ashamed and afraid.

He hadn't dared probe any deeper into his suspicions, all those silly family rumors about an elvish ancestor, until he sat in Alashiya's kitchen.

She asked a dozen questions about what the tapestry looked like and how it was made, completely unaware of the monumental step Taevas was silently taking. He did his best to answer her, but his mind was in that instant ten years ago, when everything in him had shifted so violently.

Saara had lived many generations in the past, and dragon genetics tended to dominate whatever they were mixed with. If there was any trace of her left in the Aždaja line, it couldn't be seen at a glance.

But perhaps it could be felt.

He wasn't certain why it was so much easier for him to consider that possibility than the other certainty — the thing he knew in his bones, in the part of him that grew fiercer and fiercer every day. But there was no running from that nameless thing any longer.

Because Alashiya was right. He'd been hiding for a very, very long time. He'd hidden something essential away, hoping it would die in darkness, but it'd only been dormant, awaiting her sunlight.

Now it was alive, and it would never allow itself to be hidden again.

Whether they were drawn to one another by fate or some genetic predisposition didn't matter. He couldn't be without her. He didn't *want* to be without her, despite his fears.

Taevas wanted her presence pressed into the grain of his life. He wanted to make a new nest with her. He wanted to show her that the world wasn't only full of terrors, but beauty, too. He wanted to make up for everything that had been so cruelly ripped from her — from them both.

But it wasn't those wants that urged him to confront what he'd been stubbornly ignoring. Rather, it was the certainty that he couldn't force any of it. He couldn't demand anything from Alashiya, least of all her blind trust.

As much as he needed to get back to his people, Taevas came to the sobering realization that if it came down to it, he would choose Alashiya over returning to the 'Riik. He'd choose her comfort, her autonomy, and her grief over everything he'd worked for over a century.

He'd choose her.

He'd *Chosen* her.

Taevas let out a slow breath. *There it is.*

The filmy curtain he'd placed between himself and the truth was pulled away, revealing what he'd known for a very long time.

He wasn't giving up on getting her to safety, nor the 'Riik, but Taevas was forced to accept that he couldn't rush it or force her hand without risking her loss.

Guilt and urgency gnawed at him, but it was muted by the sudden and profound peace he felt when he accepted what was done. There was nothing gained without sacrifice, he knew, and if he had to give up a little more time to earn her trust, then so be it.

He tilted his face up for a kiss when Alashiya bent to place a plate in front of him. She shyly met his demand, her touch light and sweet.

"Will you show me more of your work while I rest today?" he asked.

She pulled back a little to examine his face. He wondered what she expected of him. More demands, probably. More pressure to help him, to leave the only home she'd ever known. It must've been a surprise to hear he only wished to spend time admiring her for the work that had drawn their threads together.

A slow smile spread across her face. "If you promise to *really* rest, I can work in bed."

Voice pitched low, he honestly replied, "For you, *metsalill,* I'd do anything."

Chapter Thirty

The following days were the happiest of her life.

Alashiya wasn't sure what had stalled Taevas's urgency to return to his people, but for the next three days, he didn't say a word about it. Instead, he became a calm, often disarmingly charming presence in her home. Where she went, he was determined to follow, whether his body would allow it or not.

His health improved, and his fever at last seemed to disappear, but she wasn't blind to the fact that he often hid his pain from her. While his cuts and bruises had healed, whatever had been done to him during his captivity didn't appear to improve with bed rest and over the counter pain medication. She often caught him grimacing when he thought she wasn't looking, and he suffered most in the evenings, when his strength finally fled.

She worried about him, but he did his best to distract her. Taevas waved away her concerns with practiced ease, as if he was used to reassuring people that he was fine when he wasn't. Perhaps that wasn't far off the mark, considering who he was. She imagined that the leader of a territory rarely got the chance to rest. It sounded like he was close with his clan, which she hoped meant there was always someone around to pester him about that.

Alashiya still struggled to grasp the idea that Taevas was as important as she knew him to be. Of course she believed him, but it was a hard thing to conceptualize from her tiny corner of the world.

What did it do to a person to have so many lives dependent on your judgment, your ability to know what's right in a crisis? Of course she had her hyphae to draw from, all those generations of queens who made hard decisions for their grove and the many, many families who depended on them once upon a time, but for *her,* Alashiya the Princess of Nothing, it was foreign as another planet.

Taevas had been Isand since he was a teenager. She wouldn't have been surprised to learn that the days he spent lounging in her bed or watching her work in the garden were the closest thing he'd had to a vacation in his entire life.

They were aware, she thought, that they were living on borrowed time, and so it appeared they were both intent on making the most of it.

If she stopped to think for too long, Alashiya experienced an existential sort of all-consuming guilt for not doing more to help him get back to his people, so she did her best to not think at all. Instead, she basked in the glow of his single-minded attention, and in the conversation that flowed so easily between them.

He insisted that she didn't need to work on his commission, but when he told her he'd ordered it as a birthday present for himself, she was determined to finish it for him as quickly as possible. She really didn't mind, especially when he began to fill the silence with stories.

Taevas was a magnificent storyteller. Almost too good, really. Alashiya often found her needle frozen mid-stitch as she became engrossed in whatever tale he wove. When it happened, he'd give her one of his cheeky smiles and a small nudge.

"Are you going to finish that?" he'd ask, leaning in close to tease her with a kiss.

It always took her an embarrassingly long time to focus after that, but not even his kisses could stop her. She enjoyed his stories too much.

It was her sneaking suspicion that he told them as often as he did so that he could tempt her into leaving. Taevas loved to tantalize her with vivid descriptions of his homes — skyscrapers, he told her, built to his exacting specifications for luxury and privacy — and of all the faraway places and fascinating people he'd met.

But her favorites by far were the stories of his clan. The stories about his uncles and his cousins and their children were full of quiet joy. She could imagine them all vividly, and often found herself mouthing their names so she wouldn't forget. He told her all about the people of his Wing, too, which he explained was his elite guard. Vael, one of those powerful dragons, had recently married — or Chosen, as her dragon always phrased it — Taevas's cousin Hele.

Hele's story was one of the few that completely outmatched Alashiya's embroidery. She'd had to set it aside almost as soon as the story began. It was intimately intertwined with the tale of how his cousin Artem had met his wife, which had been engrossing enough, but as soon as Alashiya discovered that Hele was an *elemental*, her work was put away.

Taevas took great pleasure in telling her how he'd flown in the storm that had created Hele, a being of pure magic forged in the atmosphere, but it was the detail of how Vael had caught her when she fell from the sky that made Alashiya sigh. It was one of the most romantic things she'd ever heard. It beat anything she'd ever read in her aunt's old books by a mile.

"They're off hunting down elementals all across the continent, trying to bring them all into a new kind of clan," Taevas told her, smiling fondly. But that smile faded after a while. In a more somber voice, he'd added, "Though I suppose they're probably looking for *me* right now. They won't stop. Not until they see a body."

Guilt had closed up her throat and forced her to look away from him. He'd never said it, but she knew he was holding himself back because of her. Taevas wasn't the sort of man who gave up on anything easily, so she didn't believe that he had dropped his insistence that she leave with him. For some reason, he'd made the choice to spend more time with her.

And that meant that he was delaying his return to his people because of *her*.

Alashiya tried not to think about it, or at least to not take the blame entirely on herself. Taevas could've left at any time, or insisted she find him a vehicle, but he hadn't. He'd made some sort of choice without consulting her, and so that wasn't on her.

But that wasn't how reality worked. She knew he'd delayed leaving because he wanted her to come with him, and she also knew that she intentionally didn't bring it up again because she didn't want him to go where she couldn't follow. A more selfless person would've encouraged him to leave at every opportunity, but after being alone for so long, Alashiya just couldn't find it in her to do what she knew was right.

With every day that passed, it got harder and harder to bear the thought of being left again. The thought of returning to her silent life of work and watchfulness kept her up late into the night, and so did her guilt.

It came for her whenever she found him staring out into the woods with a dark look on his face, like he expected some threat to melt out of the treeline whenever he wasn't paying attention, and when he asked her if there was any way for her to get news — even from a radio. She felt sick with it when she had to explain that she had nothing. She'd offered to go into town or to the Thompsons', but he'd merely sighed and shaken his head.

"I won't let you endanger yourself for me," he'd firmly informed her. *"Not now. Not ever."*

It was easier during the day, when they distracted each other with soft touches and stories and the quiet contentment of a shared task. Despite his pain, Taevas's boredom drove him to seek out the old tools in the partially-destroyed barn so he could repair the kitchen door — and find her lost sheers, which were found in a bush near the trough. With his tools, she quickly learned that he wasn't lying about being trained as a carpenter.

They moved around each other with the ease of long-familiarity. When they bickered, it was good-natured and almost always ended in a kiss. They slept wrapped up in one another. Every meal was eaten sitting beside each other, and their evenings were full of stories.

Intimacy was slow and indulgent. They flirted relentlessly, and Taevas's eager fingers always seemed to be somewhere on her body. His tail, too. If they were within touching distance, his tail was looped around some part of her. She got used to its weight around her wrist or waist or ankle. The only time it wasn't holding her was when he used it to sneak under her skirt or blouse.

Alashiya wasn't ignorant to the fact that Taevas wanted her. He made it very clear. *Every* part of him made it clear. The power that gave her was heady. To have a mighty dragon so used to being in charge watching her, waiting for the word to pounce...

She often debated with herself over whether she was squandering their time together with games and petting and teasing him until he came in her hands. An invisible clock ticked down their time, no matter how much she tried to ignore it. Shouldn't she take the opportunity to enjoy sex while she had him?

But everytime she thought of rushing it, just getting it out of the way, she recoiled. The precious, fragile thing they'd begun to build together deserved more than that. *They* deserved more than that. And what was the harm in keeping things as they were? She certainly had no complaints about learning that Taevas enjoyed having his face ridden, or discovering that she hadn't lost her skills when she took him into her mouth in the middle of the garden.

He'd been a begging, leaking mess on her tongue, his hands fisted in her curls as she knelt there in the dirt. She could hardly breathe around his girth and didn't care at all. With the air heavy with humidity, surrounded by the hum of life all around them, and drunk on the power his pleasure gave her, she'd never felt more alive in her life.

Every twist of her fist on the base of his cock had been an indulgence. Every hard, sucking pull of her lips and tongue was a treat. To watch his expression contort in pleasure as he whispered *thank you* over and over again was an experience she wouldn't trade for anything.

And when he came on her tongue, her name a deep, resonant prayer on his lips, she didn't feel like she was missing something. Everything they did together as an exploration. Every kiss and whisper and giggle and orgasm was another brick added to the foundation they'd laid ten years ago.

Sex would happen when it was meant to happen, but neither of them were in a rush. Because rushing anything, even pleasure, edged too close to confronting what they both knew was coming.

～

Alashiya perked up at a dismayed sound from Taevas.

"What is it?" she asked from her place by the stove, where she'd been frying some eggs.

He turned to show her the old tin where she kept her coffee. There were only a few specks of dark coffee grounds caught in the seam at the bottom of the tin. "There's nothing for tomorrow," he told her.

"Oh. I don't normally run out this fast." She wrinkled her nose, teasing, "You use too much!"

Taevas gave her backside a swift tap with his swishing tail. "I use *exactly* the right amount of those terrible quality beans, *metsalill*. You just prefer your coffee as weak as tap water."

"I do not!"

"You do," he insisted, rattling the tin at her. "This is barely even real coffee. I can't wait to show you what it should taste like."

Alashiya rolled her eyes. "Well, that's all I can get at the store that isn't instant. Would you prefer that?"

That earned her another swat. "I'll accept instant coffee over my cold, dead body."

"Then I don't want to hear any more complaints." She batted at his tail, which had decided to curl around her hip, all affection now. "I'll pick up *totally fine* coffee from Debbie's today."

Out of the corner of her eye, she caught Taevas's sudden stiffness. His tail tightened around her hip, drawing her attention to the way he'd stopped stirring sugar into her mug in favor of watching her closely. All the levity had left his voice when he asked, "You want to go into town?"

He can't come with me.

And just like that, the invisible clock stopped ticking.

Alashiya quickly looked away from him. "Yes. I have to, don't I? We're out of more than just coffee," she answered, her tone carefully neutral.

A tense silence descended on them. The atmosphere, which just a moment prior was soft and warm and cheerful, darkened. Even the air felt a little heavier in her lungs, making it harder to draw a breath in.

"Shiya, you can't."

She flipped the stove's dial, extinguishing the flame before the yolks were overcooked. "I did it before."

Taevas, the softer version of him she'd come to adore so deeply and so quickly, disappeared. The dragon, the *Isand*, took his place when he bit out, "That was before we knew there was a dragon and an unknown group of men searching the woods. It's too dangerous for you to leave here by yourself. I won't allow it."

"What am I supposed to do? Just never go to the store again?"

Taevas turned to her with a hard look. "You and I both know that's not the answer. You'll never have to think about going to the store again when we *leave.*"

She stepped back from the stove. A clammy sort of panic shuddered over her skin in awful little lurches. He wanted her to jump off a cliff with him, but her feet were stuck to the ground. All she could do was stare over the edge.

CHAPTER THIRTY-ONE

"I CAN'T," SHE HEARD HERSELF SAY.

Taevas's strong, hawkish features went tight. "I know you're scared. I know that I'm asking too much of you. But there's no other option."

She shook her head mutely. There was another option, but neither of them seemed willing to say it.

The tension in his body doubled. Gripping the edge of the counter with one huge hand, like he needed to anchor himself to something, Taevas tried a different tactic. "You think I *want* to rip you away from all that you know? This brings me no joy, Shiya. I know how important this place is to you. I know how much it would mean to *me* in your place. But you can't stay here. Not anymore. Not while a threat circles us every day. It's days and days, Shiya. Do you think they'll never come looking here? When the rest of the woods turn up empty, when there's only one place left to check, do you believe you can stop them?"

Her pulse throbbed in her throat. Words escaped her. What could she say? He was right, but denial could survive on even the smallest scrap of hope. *Maybe that dragon has nothing to do with anything. Maybe he really was just a tourist.*

But even if that were true, which she could admit was

unlikely, that didn't mean he could stay. That he wanted to. He had responsibilities to his people, his clan. To even ask him to was so blindingly hypocritical that she couldn't think the words. Nymphs were all about the collective. They were about sacrificing for the whole. That's what queens were *for*.

Perhaps it was a good thing the responsibility of being queen passed to her when there was no one around to see it. She would've made a terrible leader.

Taevas released the counter with a jerk, a soft curse on his lips. He came to her like a rolling storm cloud. She wanted to flinch away from his anger, his disapproval, but he wouldn't let her.

Two huge purple hands held her head in place when he growled, "I hate this. I hate that I have to take from you again and again. I hate that I don't have another option. I hate that you have no way of knowing that I'll be true to my word, my Shiya. That I'll return what you've given me one hundred fold."

He pressed their foreheads together. Angry breaths puffed against her cheeks. "I could give you anything. I *will*. You'll never have to worry about money again. You'll always be protected. You'll be *respected*. The 'Riik is safe for you. My clan will protect you. I swear, Shiya, if you just take this one last risk on me, you won't regret it."

A wild part of her, the part that was just a woman desperate to *live*, clawed inside her chest. She carved deep, bloody grooves into the cage of Alashiya's ribs, one for each day she'd been trapped.

But she couldn't only think of that girl. Alashiya had to think of *everyone*. Every ghost, every memory. She was all that was left, and if she stepped out of the little bubble of safety she'd crafted, the risk wasn't just to her.

I wish that was the reason I can't do it.

Shame made her skin crawl. There was honor in trying to protect the legacy she'd been left, even to its inevitable extinction, but there was none in the real source of her reluctance.

I'm scared.

She stepped away from Taevas, unable to stand the feeling of his hands on her skin. It was too stimulating. It was too good. It reminded her of her cowardice too much. Her chest was too tight. Her vision swam.

Leave? I can't leave. It's too dangerous. I have nothing out there. I am nothing out there.

"I don't understand why you can't— why you can't just leave and come back," she argued, voice trembling. Defensive anger flared up from the burning coals in her stomach, stinging her with little sparks again and again. "I can get a phone. We can talk. It doesn't have to be what it was before. You— you sound like you expect me to leave everything I know behind forever just because you say so. How is that fair?"

She couldn't look at him. She just couldn't. There was no doubt about what she'd find there.

"Shiya, you *know*. You have to know."

She paced away, their breakfast abandoned. "What do I know?"

Taevas's tone was utterly implacable when he answered, "That even if there was no threat, I couldn't leave you here. I won't. If I was another man, I would've already made this my roost — but I'm not and I can't. I'm Isand, Shiya, and you're mine. I'm sorry."

The way he said those last two words sent goosebumps up and down her body. *I'm sorry.* It was the kind of apology an executioner would give someone under their sword. They might mean it, but it doesn't change anything. They'll still swing.

She stepped back toward the kitchen door. "What will you do if I say no?"

"Are you asking me to choose between you or the 'Riik? My clan?" The question was so soft, so damning.

"No," she insisted, voice pitched high. Gods, she wanted to run so badly. She wanted to clamp her hands over her ears and scream until everything returned to how it was before, when he was just Taevas and she was just Shiya. "I would never do that. I can't do that to you. I know what your responsibilities are—"

"And I know what I'm asking of *you!*"

Not that much. Not really. He was asking for her to take a chance, to believe that even if things went wrong, it wouldn't be life or death. It might turn out okay. He was asking her to trust him *before* things went bad, because he knew better than her the odds that they would.

So why couldn't she just say *yes?* It didn't have to be permanent. He hadn't asked her to marry him or anything. The way he spoke made it all sound so dramatic and like it was forever, but that would probably die away the minute the shine came off their fantasy. Once they were in *his* world, they'd likely realize they had nothing in common save chemistry and coincidence.

Say yes. Jump, Shiya. See what happens.

She still couldn't meet his gaze. Hands trembling, she reached for the door knob.

"Don't."

"We need coffee," she muttered, turning away.

Taevas's hands gripped her waist. He pressed himself against her back. Tension radiated from him in waves. "I don't need fucking coffee. I need you."

That hook in her chest gave a painful jerk backwards, pulling her into the safety of his arms. Alashiya's shaking fingers splayed over his. The thought of never being able to touch him again made that ugly panicked feeling that much stronger. She couldn't bear to leave Birchdale, but she couldn't let go of him, either.

"Don't run," he whispered into her hair. "Don't run from this, *metsalill.* Hide here if you have to, but don't go where I can't watch over you."

"I don't want *you* to go." The words slipped out of their own accord, barely audible.

Taevas squeezed her waist. "And I can't be without you. How do we negotiate this?"

"Negotiate?"

He spun her slowly, careful to never put too much space between their bodies as he turned her to face him. His tail coiled around her leg with an affectionate, possessive squeeze.

Something in his gaze was different when he looked at her then. It was intent, almost cool. Like he was looking at a wily opponent rather than *her*. "I've been treating you like you're mine because you are, but I've neglected the other parts of you."

"What do you mean?"

"I'm Isand, but you're a queen. We're leaders. We do politics. We negotiate terms to make mutually beneficial arrangements. I need you and I need to get to the 'Riik. You need me and don't want to leave. Now we have to negotiate to find a compromise."

She sputtered. "I'm not a *leader*—"

"You are," he firmly interrupted. "You are a natural leader, Alashiya, and even if you weren't, you are by birth and by my Choice. So tell me your terms. What do you want?"

"I— I don't want anything!"

Taevas breathed deeply. "Believe me, I *know*. But I'm not asking you as Shiya. I'm asking you as Alashiya, descendant of the first nymph and queen of this grove. I'm asking you as *Isand,* not as Taevas, your husband."

"I..." She shook her head.

He didn't show her any mercy. In that same cool, professional voice, he said, "Your people are leaderless in the UTA, Alashiya. I've seen them. They haphazardly vote on a representative and send them to Congress every year, always a new one, never anyone who dares to speak up when it counts. No one thinks of nymphs when laws are made. They have no voice. If you could be that voice, what would you ask for? You said to me that people see nymphs as easy pickings. What would change that?"

He'd always seemed grand to her. A little larger than life, even before she grasped who he really was. But now he was something different. His expression, how he held his shoulders, the tone... Taevas wasn't humoring her. He wasn't indulging in her whims to get what he wanted. He really, truly wanted to know — not as her lover, but as a *leader.*

The sense of power it gave her was dizzying. Too much. Queasiness made her stomach turn.

"I don't know. I need to... I need to think about it."

"Then think. Come back to me with your terms." The mask of the Isand cracked a little, revealing the softness underneath. It gleamed in his violet eyes when he leaned down to press a kiss to her forehead.

"Would you really give me anything I asked for?"

His expression took on a strange, almost wry cast. "As my queen, I'm required to negotiate with you, purely on principle. But as *mine,* I'd give you far more than you could ever ask of me."

"What if this doesn't last?" The words came out of her all mangled and mashed up, like her vocal cords did their best to reject the very concept. Somehow they made it out, though she wasn't sure it was a good thing. The moment they hit the air, everything went very still.

Taevas took his time answering her. "Is that what you're afraid of, *metsalill?* That when we leave this place, I'll forget about you?"

She looked away, too exposed by the questions. "I just meant that if— There's a chance we won't— I have to know if your promises will hold if it turns out we're not..."

Gods, I really can't even string the sentence together. That hook in her chest, the bright, hot feeling in her blood — it wouldn't allow it.

"I owe you a life debt. If it wasn't for you, I would've been found and probably executed. I'll be indebted to you for the rest of my life, no matter what happens between us. The entire Draakonriik, every dragon under my command, my clan — all of them are in your debt, Alashiya. You don't know what that means yet, but you will."

If I could ask a leader of the UTA for anything for us, what would it be?

She thought that Taevas must be a bit of a liar, because a natural leader might've thought of it already. They probably would've considered how to angle their advantage, the favors they'd be owed by him for what they'd done. They wouldn't have tried their damnedest to chase him out of their house whenever the opportunity arose.

But the thought was there now, a seed planted in fertile soil. She could already feel the roots unfurling. Soon enough it'd grow into something real, something she could *do,* and then all her excuses about why she couldn't leave would mean nothing.

Nausea bubbled in her stomach, but for the first time, a little bit of excitement came with it. She couldn't dwell on that too long, afraid that even acknowledging that she *might* want to go would scare away what tiny amount of courage came with it.

Hands shaking for a different reason, she stepped out of his hold and moved to scoop up her basket from where it sat by the door.

"Shiya? Where are you going?"

"To pick some plums," she answered, swallowing hard. "I'm going to need them if I want any chance of Debbie saying yes."

Taevas followed her step for step. His big body hovered just behind her as she opened the kitchen door and jogged over the creaky porch and down the steps into the garden. "What are you going to ask Debbie for? Shiya—"

Standing barefoot in the cool, damp soil, she turned to peer at him from over her shoulder, one hand lifted to shade her eyes from the morning glare. He stood on the top step of the porch, his expression pinched with worry. He looked like he was bracing for something. It was a good feeling, knowing that she wasn't about to disappoint him again. For now.

"Her car," she answered. "I need something to trade."

He drew himself up instantly. In a deep, thick voice, he said, *"Naine,* is that a yes?"

She turned back to the garden. "It's the start of our negotiations."

CHAPTER THIRTY-TWO

SHE HONESTLY DIDN'T EXPECT DEBBIE TO SAY YES. IT wasn't that she sought out failure, but it didn't seem likely that her first attempt at getting them a vehicle would work. Alashiya thought she'd at least have to haggle more.

But Debbie didn't blink when she made the request. The old woman had only given her a disinterested look, her watery blue eyes illuminated by her tablet's screen. "Sure, but what'd you need it for?"

Setting the paper bag of plums on the shop's counter, Alashiya tried not to show how nervous she was. How *exhilarated.* Her head had been full of happy little bees the entire walk to town. They buzzed so loudly, it was hard to focus on anything else. She wondered if Debbie could see her nearly vibrating as she stood there.

Am I really doing this?

The thought was too hot to touch. She shied away from it instantly, but that didn't stop her from forging ahead.

"I need it for work," she lied. It surprised her how easily the fib came to her. "You know I take commissions for a shop in New York, right? Well, they asked me to go in. I know I could take the bus, but it'd be so many connections that it'd take me a week to get there."

Debbie looked away from her screen, startled. "You ever been anywhere 'sides Birchdale?"

"No."

"You goin' by yourself?"

Alashiya's palms began to sweat a little. Smoothing them against her skirt just below the counter, she answered, "Yes. I'll only be there a couple days. I doubt I'll want to stay long."

The hook in her chest tugged sharply in the direction of her land. Toward *him*. It was like everything inside her balked at even the thought of separation.

Debbie grunted and narrowed her eyes. "I don't like you goin' by yourself, Shiya. These are dangerous times. What if something happens to you? Or the car? Mike'll be a pain to live with if you mess up one of his shit-cans."

Alashiya knew all about Mike's obsession with collecting what could only generously be called cars. It was why she'd asked Debbie in the first place. They had at least a dozen, and some of them even drove.

But that wasn't what caught her attention. Brows furrowing, she asked, "What do mean by *dangerous times*, Debbie?"

"Don't you watch the news?"

The buzzing in her head was beginning to die down. An awful sort of quiet took its place. "No," she admitted.

One of Debbie's weathered hands, the nails yellowed by tobacco and veins winding like snakes across the brittle bones, flipped the tablet around. She placed it on the counter between them. *"Extremists."* She drew out the word with great relish, like she was about to launch into one of her recaps of the soap operas she normally watched. "Some crazies in Glory's Temple tried to take over the Elvish Protectorate a few weeks ago. Last month? Something like that. Same day a bunch of leaders were attacked."

Debbie leaned forward, her voice lowering. Her eyes gleamed with the maniacal sort of glee she normally reserved for the reveal of an evil twin plot line. "It's all connected. Queen Sigrid's death, Glory's Temple, Lee Seymour. And Taevas Aždaja— *I* think he was the brains behind it. He's been missing since the solstice, see? This theory that he's been kidnapped? Please. No one else was kidnapped. They were all attacked. My money's on him being the leader of the conspiracy, and when it went to dog shit, he disappeared to cover his tracks."

There were no more bees. No more exhilaration. There was only silence as Alashiya slowly dropped her gaze to the glaring brightness of the tablet's screen.

A familiar face stared up at her. It was a beautiful photo.

He stood on the steps of some grand building, dressed to the nines in a navy double-breasted suit, his hair swept back behind his horns and braided by his ears. Sunglasses with hot pink lenses obscured his eyes, but she'd recognize the lips, the hard line of his jaw, the arch of his horns *anywhere*. Even in the photo, surrounded by what appeared to be important people, he radiated the kind of power that made everyone else look small and colorless in comparison.

And he was wearing her work.

It might've been invisible to anyone else, but she remembered the crisp white shirt beneath the suit. She didn't often do whitework — embroidering with white thread on white fabric to make subtle, almost invisible designs — but she wanted a challenge, so she'd sewn the waves of an ocean she'd never seen with her own eyes onto Adon's shirt.

The man in the photo couldn't have been more different from the one who'd lived in her home the past week. But they were the exact same. There was no mistaking it. No disbelief. Alashiya stared at Taevas, at *Adon,* on that screen and felt the world give way beneath her feet.

She believed him. Mostly. But it was still deeply jarring to *see* it there. To look at his photo, to see the tattooed dragons standing guard just behind him, to look into those shiny sunglass lenses and *know.*

Good gods, he really is who he says he is.

A part of her was glad she'd never bothered to seek out the news before then. If she'd known that her Adon was the leader of a territory... Well, she had no idea what she would've done differently, except maybe shrivel up in abject humiliation at the thought of fantasizing about *him.*

"He's always looked too smug to me," Debbie sniffed, breaking the spell that shock had cast over Alashiya. "Just look at that smirk. He's plotting something right there!"

"No, he's not." The words came out quick and sharper than they should've. *He's a good man,* she wanted to rage. *He's good and kind and patient. He might be a pain in the ass sometimes, but I wouldn't trade him for anything.*

Fortunately, Debbie didn't appear to hear the real heat in Alashiya's voice. "Ugh, you girls are too easy. A nice jaw and some money. That's all it takes. Don't you see that's how they get you?"

Alashiya glanced down again, her attention drawn irresistibly to the web page Debbie had been scrolling through. It was hard to keep her attention away from the photo, from the *proof* — not only that he was who he said he was, but that he was her Adon.

The photo was part of an article, she realized. With a nervous, unskilled touch, she scrolled up to see the headline. Another picture popped up, this one of a wizened dragon in a dark suit addressing an audience of reporters. His face was grim and somehow familiar, though she had no idea how that could be.

ISAND STILL MISSING, PRESUMED DEAD: UNITED CONGRESS URGES DRAAKONRIIK TO HOLD SPECIAL ELECTION, REFUSED AGAIN—

"We won't appoint a new Isand until a body is found," Constantin Aždaja, First Advisor to the Isand and his paternal uncle, told the world at the latest press conference. *"Or until we have no other option."*

A month has passed since Taevas Aždaja's disappearance and the outside pressure for the gap in leadership to be filled, even temporarily, continues to grow. Following the assassination attempts on all the leaders of the UTA, the need for stability is rapidly growing.

Sophie Goode, leader of the Coven Collective, still hasn't made a public appearance after her release from the hospital, and the Orclind is in official mourning following the death of Queen Sigrid. Fearing what could become of the Peace Charter if stability isn't found quickly, many powerful voices in the United Congress are calling for someone — anyone — to replace Taevas Aždaja, filling what could potentially be a devastating power vacuum in the second wealthiest territory on the continent.

Alashiya couldn't read more. Her gaze skipped like a broken record needle over the words, blurring them. A part of her *wanted* to keep reading, but she couldn't stomach it.

This is my fault.

All that suffering, all that worry. Her stomach curdled. She knew she'd been selfish, keeping him with her. It didn't matter that he'd consented to it. She *knew* that he wouldn't leave without her, and she'd used that to play house with him.

It was all so abstract. A part of her hadn't grasped, hadn't *believed* that it was real. She'd waved off the realities of him being exactly who he said he was. If she couldn't wrap her head around it, living in the fantasy was easier. Being *scared* was easier.

Alashiya pushed the tablet back to Debbie. She thought her voice would be croaky, but it came out deathly calm when she said, "I'll be fine in the city. I just need a car."

"You got a valid license?"

"Yes. I updated it last year." She was good about things like paperwork and taxes and such. It was all part of keeping her world stable, her land protected. If she slipped up on something like her license, it was a slippery slope to making a mistake that might get her whole world ripped away from her.

"All right, I guess. You stop over at my place and talk to Mike. Tell him I said you need the blue car. It's one of the good ones. If he's a dick about it, come back and get the bat."

She shook her head. "Thanks. I'll head over there now. Enjoy the plums."

Debbie grunted, her attention already back on her tablet, on *Taevas*. It was a deeply bizarre, almost out of body feeling that came with knowing Debbie was aware of the man that had been her secret for so very long. Even before he crashed into her barn, he'd been hers. She never talked about her clients with anyone in town, never mentioned her imaginary husband.

But they'd *known* him. They'd known him far better than her.

She had just opened the door when Debbie called out, "You see any extremists in the city, run 'em over!"

"Will do."

Alashiya stepped out onto the street. Her skin was clammy. The warm summer breeze that had carried her into town now felt accusatory somehow, like everytime it brushed her skin it wanted to remind her that she'd done something wrong.

She wanted to rush home and vomit out an apology, but what good would that do? Taevas didn't need her to be sorry. He needed her to get a damn car. That was the only reason he'd allowed her to go into town at all, and she could only imagine that every second that ticked by saw his worry increasing.

He was worried about *her* when he had an entire territory to think of. *Gods, I'm an ass.*

Alashiya hustled down the street, her hand-me-down boots clicking on the cracked sidewalk. Normally she was extremely vigilant when she was in town, especially during the summer, but not now. All she could think about was that photo, and Taevas, and how badly she'd messed up.

It made his offer that much more weighty. It was one thing to imagine he could give her what she wanted, but it was another to *know* he could. He was the leader of the *Draakonriik*. The second wealthiest territory on the entire continent, with an army of dragons at his disposal.

And he'd looked at her like an equal. He wanted to negotiate with her like she was just as powerful, just as important as him.

If I had his resources at my disposal, what could I do? Not as Shiya, but as Queen Alashiya.

She stopped the thought before it could dig its roots any deeper. Guilt gnawed on her bones with a thousand hungry teeth. What right did she have to even *think* about taking anything he offered when she'd caused so much trouble? If she'd only listened to him and really tried to get him back to his people, his uncle wouldn't have been defending himself at that press conference, people wouldn't be asking so many questions, and Taevas's position wouldn't be threatened.

Her throat closed up at the thought. *What if we're too late?*

Was it possible that they might get him home, only to discover that his people had been forced to replace him? The idea that Taevas might return to *nothing* all because she was too scared to leave Birchdale was sickening.

Debbie and Mike lived close to town, at the end of a neat row of houses now owned by people who rented them out for recreationists. Alashiya remembered when those homes were full of families. Many of her friends had lived in them. But she also remembered when they'd gradually begun to empty out until one day there were only a handful of familiar faces remaining — a row of tarnished pearls strung on a broken necklace. Sooner or later they'd all fall off.

The homes that were left had slipped into disrepair, accelerating Birchdale's decay, until the investors came sniffing around. Seemingly overnight, most of the town was purchased by people looking to make a quick buck on vacation rentals. The homes were fixed up. They all looked like plastic versions of their old selves to her. Like someone had popped her friends' homes into a machine and extruded some cheap replica out the other end.

One of the few originals remaining was Debbie and Mike's house, which sat at the end of the lane. The detritus of their lives spilled out around them, into the trees and tall weeds that ringed their yard. They weren't untidy people, but Mike liked to collect things — cars and old farming equipment, mostly. He claimed to make a good living on reselling them, but Alashiya rarely saw anything leave their yard once it crossed the boundary, so she had her doubts.

She picked her way around the familiar winding path between machines to approach the side door. No one ever used the front except the mailman.

Mike took a while to open the door. Peering at her through the screen, his suspicious glower quickly melted away. "Hey, Shiya! What'd you need?"

Alashiya offered him her sweetest smile. She'd known Mike all her life. Though she'd never really been friends with his kids, they'd been thrown together often enough that he'd been something of a fixture in her childhood. He wasn't a particularly nice man, but he could be handled easily enough when he felt important.

Unfortunately, even the slightest hint of what he deemed *disrespect* could send him into a fit, which was probably why he and his wife never got along.

Debbie didn't have the patience to cater to him or anyone. Alashiya couldn't say she blamed her, but she did wonder how on Earth they'd gotten together in the first place.

"I'm so sorry, Mike. I know you're probably busy," she began, knowing full-well he was most likely spending the day glued to his recliner, just like always.

"Never too busy for you, honey." His ruddy face flushed with pleasure as he cracked open the screen door and leaned out. He was rail-thin, with bony shoulders and long, spidery hands. They'd scared the daylights out of her as a kid, even when he used to sneak her sweets or help her tie her shoes.

Widening her eyes, she softly explained, "I have a big favor to ask. I have to go out of town for work and I wasn't given any notice about it. I asked Debbie if I might be able to borrow one of your cars for a few days and she said yes, but I know how hard you work on them, so I wanted to be sure it was all right with you first."

She held her breath. Her bashful, pleading expression remained fixed in place as she waited to see what he'd say. Some days Mike would do anything she asked of him and other days he'd cuss her out for even stepping on his porch. She never really knew which one she'd get, but her odds were better if she acted a little helpless and deferential.

It'd never really bothered her before, but something about having to stand there and brace for his reaction grated. So much of her life had been spent making herself smaller, softer, more palatable to people like Mike, who might turn his claws on her no matter what she did.

It was just a fact of her existence, but all of a sudden it didn't feel quite as tolerable as it once had. Maybe it was because she was desperate, her patience thin. Or maybe it was because she'd spent so much time with Taevas. For some reason it'd never occurred to her to put on this act for *him*. She'd been entirely herself for the first time in a very long time, and now the deferential act felt like an old pair of shoes that didn't quite fit anymore.

He squinted at her and rolled his tongue over his teeth. "Which one'd she say you could use?"

Tensing, she answered, "The blue?"

"Where you goin'?"

"New York."

"Needs its oil changed if you're goin' that far," he grumbled.

Not sure if that was a yes or no, Alashiya shuffled her feet on the creaky boards of the porch and tried not to show her impatience. "I can pay for that," she offered. "You'd be doing me such a favor. I'm more than happy to—"

Mike's face went even ruddier than normal. "You don't think I know how to change my own damn oil?"

Alashiya's stomach sank. *Shit.*

"You're the best mechanic in town, so of course you do," she assured him. "I wouldn't even know where to start. I just don't want you working too hard for me, Mike. You've done so much."

It was only the truth if one counted the favors he'd half-finished, like how he'd promised to fix up her grandfather's truck and only ever changed a few spark plugs, or that time he said he'd help her repair the roof of the house, but just slapped a tarp over the hole.

A bit of the color drained from Mike's face. It was a good sign. Waving away her objections, he replied, "Nah, don't waste your money. I'll fix it up tonight. Come 'round tomorrow and get the keys."

Relief made her smile a little more genuine. "Thank you, Mike. Really, I can't tell you how much I—"

A squeal of tires cut her off. They both turned to look a little ways down the street, where a shiny black SUV with tinted windows had just careened into the driveway of one of the rentals.

Mike made an ugly spitting sort of sound behind her. "Fuckin' tourists. Too damn loud and don't even know how to drive!"

CHAPTER THIRTY-THREE

THE DRIVER'S DOOR POPPED OPEN, SPILLING A snarling voice onto the otherwise quiet street. "—fucking *useless*. What's the point of you? First you fuck up, and now you can't even follow orders? We can't waste anymore fucking time with — *Oh.*"

Alashiya's spine went stiff as the dragon's gaze fixed on her from over the hood of the SUV. He stood there, one huge fist clenched like he was a heartbeat away from slamming it down. She wondered if the hood would crumple under the force of it.

A chill swept through her as she watched his snarl melt into an easy smile. It was like a switch turning off. One minute he looked ready to wreck his own car, and the next he was looking at her like she'd made his day.

His wings had been held tight against his back, but now they lifted and raised a little, mantling around his shoulders like he needed to appear just a bit bigger. His tail swept around his thigh to curl in the air. She wasn't sure when she'd learned it, but Alashiya recognized the posture as one of interest.

Shit shit shit.

Quickly turning back to Mike like she hadn't seen the dragon at all, she rushed out, "I'll swing by tomorrow afternoon, okay? Thanks again."

She didn't want to look like she was running away, fearing that would only draw more interest, but there really wasn't anything for it. Alashiya hopped off the porch and moved at a swift clip around the cluttered yard. Her heart hammered as movement to her right caught her eye.

Don't come over, she silently pleaded, heart hammering.

If she could make it to the trees, she could probably lose him. It would take her longer to get home if she had to go around town, but her only other option was to walk back the way she came, which put her directly in the dragon's path.

"Shiya!"

She'd barely made it to the sidewalk before a clawed hand wrapped around her arm, halting her abruptly. Fear skittered down her spine as she was turned to face him.

The sun blazed behind him, casting his handsome face in shadow. She flinched, momentarily blinded by the glare. Smiling indulgently, the dragon lifted one wing a little higher, blocking the worst of the sun from her eyes.

"I was hoping I'd see you again." His gaze raked over her, taking in her soft wrap dress and leather boots. She wished she'd worn a dress with long sleeves. Feeling his skin on her arm was unpleasant in a way that had nothing to do with his firm grip.

"Where are you off to, pretty thing?"

"I... I was just heading home." She swallowed. *Let me go. Please let me go.*

The dragon's grip softened, but he didn't release her. His smile sharpened. "To a mate, I'm sure."

"Oh, no," she answered, hoping her voice didn't come out too strangled — and if it did, he'd read it as general nervousness. Normally she would've told him yes, she had a fierce mate at home, and hoped it dulled his interest, but the thought of even hinting at Taevas's presence made her wary.

Offering him a tight smile, she said, "I—I don't have a husband."

The words tasted like ash on her tongue, but they seemed to be exactly what the dragon wanted to hear. "Now, how's that possible? The prettiest woman I've ever seen can't possibly be unclaimed. I can't believe it."

I'm not, she thought reflexively. But that wasn't exactly true, either. Whatever she and Taevas were... Well, they hadn't named it, and now that she knew exactly who she was dealing with, she was even less certain that it was anything permanent. The leader of a territory and *her?* Not even her most outrageous fantasies were that deluded.

Not that she could explain any of that to *this* man.

Striving to sound normal, she replied, "Well, there's not exactly a lot of options. You've met Monty."

A flash of something dark crossed the dragon's expression. "I have. I can't say I enjoyed how he spoke to you. I'd never raise my voice at a woman. It really pisses me off when men pick on people weaker than them. And you'd have to be a monster to bully a nymph. Especially one as lovely as you."

Alashiya's gaze moved around his face to drift over the hard line of his shoulders and the rise of his mantled wings. Something about how he held himself made her instincts scream in alarm. She didn't get the sense that *she* was in danger, but there wasn't a doubt in her mind that *he* was dangerous.

Dropping her gaze like she'd been truly flattered rather than alarmed, she demurred, "I'm nothing special. I'm sure where you come from there are thousands of more interesting women."

The dragon's thumb skimmed her arm. She watched his tail swing toward her, like he intended to wrap it around her thigh. Disgust tightened the muscles of her abdomen. *Only Taevas is allowed to do that.*

It stopped just short. The rattle at the end brushed the hem of her skirt when he murmured, "Quantity doesn't mean quality. And dragons have an eye for all things quality, pretty Shiya. I knew you were special when I saw you, but I couldn't believe it when I looked up your family name. The Ardz line is older than mine — and that's saying something. Mine stretches back almost two thousand years."

He dipped his head, trying to meet her gaze. "Feels a bit like fate to have met such a treasure all the way out here."

Fate? This dragon had no idea. Whatever mistakes had brought him to Birchdale paled in comparison to the series of miracles that had come together to unite Alashiya and Taevas.

She had no idea how to safely respond to that, so she held her tongue. The dragon seemed to take her silence as bashfulness. His expression turned very self-satisfied for a moment before he asked, "I am curious, though— Why does that smelly piece of shit hate you so much? What did you do to him?"

"I..." Her brows drew together. "I don't think he really *hates* me."

The dragon leaned in close, until she could almost feel his breath on her ear. "Oh, he hates you. I know it when I see it. That old man wants to get his hands on you and make you hurt. I'm gonna handle that for you, all right? Once my business is done here, you won't have to worry about him again."

Her stomach turned when he pulled back enough to give her a look that said he was about to do her a big favor. "Nothing pisses me off as much as men who go after vulnerable women. And you don't have a mate looking out for you. I can't let that stand."

The sense that she was in an increasingly dangerous position increased. She didn't particularly care if the dragon went after Monty, but she didn't like the assessing gaze he leveled her way.

"Monty just wants my land for his business," she explained, trying to divert his attention away from her. "I refuse to give it to him. And if he wants more than that, then he's out of luck. One day he's gonna die all alone out in those woods, and when the buzzards pick him clean, I hope they shit him out somewhere worse."

Surprise lit up the dragon's face. He probably didn't expect the real venom in her voice, but it was barely a hint of how deep her disdain for Monty went. She didn't often let herself dwell on it, knowing there was nothing to be done, but sometimes that old rage burned through her carefully crafted restraint.

"Well, damn," he breathed. He dropped his hand, but not before he skimmed it all the way down the length of her arm. "The little princess has some claws. I like that. I'm Sergei, by the way. You ran out of the shop before I could introduce myself."

Alashiya shuffled back half a step. "Ah... It's nice to meet you, Sergei, but I should go."

The dragon matched her movements smoothly, his wings rising until they curved over his shoulders just a little. A picture from an old botanical book flashed in her mind — a diagram of a Venus fly trap ready to snap up its unsuspecting prey.

His brow furrowed. "Did you walk into town on your own?"

"Uh, yes."

"Do you normally?"

She cast a furtive glance at the trees. "Yes."

The dragon pursed his lips. Appearing to make some decision, he jerked his chin toward his car, where three men stood like statues around the back bumper, vacant-eyed and unbothered by the heat of the sun. Pitching his voice so they could hear him, he said, "Not anymore. I'll drive you home. You three — wait for me in the house. And don't fucking touch anything."

All the blood drained from her cheeks. "That's— It's really not necessary. I like to walk."

"It's dangerous," he shot back, a vein of ice in his otherwise friendly tone. "You don't walk anywhere anymore, understood? Anything could happen to you on the road by yourself."

There was nothing objectively wrong or threatening in what he said. She'd taken rides from townsfolk before, and it was true that there were risks in venturing out by herself — which was why she stuck to the woods and not the roads. But something in the proprietary way he spoke to her sent warning bells clanging in her mind.

It reminded her a little of Taevas's bossiness, but instead of filling her with an exasperated sort of warmth, all she felt was dread.

A vice constricted around her lungs. *This is bad,* the hyphae whispered. *Don't linger.*

She tried to gently laugh off his undisguised command. "I'm sure you have better things to do than drive some strange nymph around."

"Safety comes first." He gave her a slow smile. "I need a break anyway, and I'd like to get to know you better. So—" The dragon playfully tapped the back of her hand with the rattle at the end of his tail. "You're going to give me your phone number now, Shiya, and then I'm going to take you home. I'll be done with my business soon. You're going to stay there until I come get you."

It felt like she'd stepped on an invisible snare. The urge to gnaw her own leg off to be free was a wild, awful thing in her chest.

"I don't have a phone."

Sergei made an exasperated face. "That's inconvenient. I'll get you a phone when I'm done with this stupid fucking ordeal. I'll expect you to answer when I call."

Running out of patience at last, Alashiya snapped, "No, thank you. I don't want a phone. Or to spend time with you."

"That's about to change."

"I really don't think so—"

His pleasant expression didn't move, but something in his body language made her jaw snap shut on its own.

"You're a pretty, vulnerable treasure all on your own," he told her, like he was pulling from a deep well of patience. "There's more than just creeps like Monty in these woods, Shiya. There are big bad dragons, too. Trust me, you need a protector."

He can't mean Taevas. Please, gods, don't be talking about

Taevas. Hoping her voice would come out at least somewhat normal, she said, "Dragons don't come to Birchdale."

His expression darkened. "Some do. I did, and I'm plenty dangerous."

"Well, I—"

"Have you ever met a dragon before?" he asked, tilting his head to one side.

Alashiya's pulse was too loud in her ears. Yet another lie came easily to her. "No. Never."

Gently nudging her toward the SUV, he muttered, "That's too bad. You'll have to learn on your feet, then."

Chapter Thirty-Four

Taevas paced the perimeter of Alashiya's land for hours. Her absence was an acid drip in his veins, searing him slowly, drop by drop, until he was consumed by it. Relief, even elation, had buoyed him when she agreed to find a car, but it fled almost as soon as she did.

I've sent her out into the world alone.

Being helpless had gotten old days ago, but this powerlessness was completely untenable.

He knew it wouldn't make a difference if he stayed in the house or walked the perimeter of her property. It wouldn't make her show up any faster, and it wouldn't help either of them if something happened while she was gone. But he couldn't sit still and he couldn't fly, so instead he walked through the dense trees and undergrowth, pain echoing through his body with every step.

The birch forest seemed a lot less intimidating in the light of day. The air wasn't as oppressive, and he might've thought that overall the whole thing seemed less hostile than it had the night he chased her down.

But that didn't stop him from watching the trees as he walked, the back of his neck prickling with unease. He *felt* observed. Judged, even. The general air of hostility might've waned, but if there was some true sentience to the forest that hid Alashiya's home, it hadn't yet decided if he was worth a damn.

How could it? Taevas clenched his jaw as he wound a tight, circular path through the trees, heading back toward the overgrown main road that connected her property with the town.

He hadn't done anything but take and take and take from her. Taevas was a protector, a provider to the very core of his being. He hadn't given her anything in return for her hospitality or care. Nothing but his word. He hadn't even had the chance to lay down ash at the borders of her land, announcing it as protected by a dragon. It was the most basic fucking thing imaginable and the first step in declaring to all the world that she was Chosen. That she was treasured. That she was *his*.

Fire licked up his throat. Taevas had to swallow it down. It went against all of that raging, uncontrollable instinct, but he did it.

He'd never let himself imagine what he'd do in this position, but if he had, the concept that he might not be able to tell the whole world that he'd Chosen wouldn't have crossed his mind.

The air was hot and thick with the scents of soil, decay, and fresh, green life. All around him little sounds came together to make a wall of noise — a woodpecker working diligently on a tree trunk, a squirrel skittering across branches, bugs humming just out of sight, and greenery swaying in the warm breeze.

He didn't hear any of it. His world was silent as he let the word *Chosen* sink its teeth into him. He'd accepted it days and days ago, but it still nearly bowled him over when it popped into his head.

It wasn't a surprise. It wasn't something he could talk himself out of or deny. He'd just been ignoring it for years.

Looking back, he'd known it from the moment he opened that first package. If he didn't allow himself to dwell on it, to think the word, then maybe he could exist in a perfect middle space where fear couldn't get to him but he could have everything he wanted. It didn't have to be that singular thing to be *real,* to be the most precious part of his life.

But as he stared down at the loamy soil beneath his feet, Taevas was hit by a wave of shame so powerful, it pressed the air from his lungs.

It didn't matter that he intended to give her all the rights and privileges of the Isand's Chosen. Without the official title, she'd be leaving all she knew for nothing. The worst part was that she didn't even know it.

Alashiya was a queen and he wanted to… *What? Make her my girlfriend?*

The black eyes on the papery bark of the trees watched him balefully, like they *knew.*

It was a bitter pill to swallow, realizing that perhaps it'd been easy to pretend he hadn't Chosen because he subconsciously hadn't taken Alashiya as seriously as she deserved.

I'm an asshole, he thought, raking his claws through his hair. She didn't even know that she'd been disrespected, and he'd changed course before he did any real damage, but it didn't matter. He owed her more than just his life. He owed her an apology and an oath that couldn't be broken by anything now. Not even death.

Bile churned in his stomach at the thought, but it wasn't as bad as he assumed it would be. Taevas was resigned to it in the way one must be to all things out of their control.

The sun must rise. Death must come. A dragon Chooses. It can't be undone.

Alashiya is mine, he thought grimly, *and I'm going to give her everything she deserves. Even if it kills me.*

And it could. It'd killed his parents.

Choosing was a gift, but it was also a terrible weakness — one he'd done everything in his power to avoid out of nothing but pure, boyish cowardice. And look where it'd gotten him: He'd still ended up Choosing, only at the worst possible time.

His impatience and worry doubled. Taevas could give her

nothing now. He couldn't embrace her. He couldn't shower her in gifts during this most vital time. He couldn't even do his duty by guarding her when she left the nest.

Pathetic.

He roamed the woods once more, his mind a chaotic swirl of memories he'd long since shoved into a tidy little corner. Taevas thought time had taken the venom from them, washed them clean of all that could hurt him, but it turned out to be yet another lie he'd told himself.

With Alashiya gone, all he could think of was his father. His patient, loving, soft-spoken *isa*, who'd been left alone to defend the nest. He'd tried for a very long time to let go of his anger at his mother. It wasn't her fault, and the gods knew she'd suffered for her choices, but the fire of his grief had scarred him so deeply that he couldn't ever forgive her completely, as unfair as that was.

She'd done the right thing. The *honorable* thing. But her choice meant her mate died a hideous death and tore Taevas's life apart at the seams.

He'd sworn to never Choose, and if by some misfortune he ever did, he'd *never* allow his mate to pay for his mistakes. They would never be unguarded. They would never sacrifice for him. They would never, ever come to harm.

And there he was, nearing the obscured entrance to his mate's territory, as helpless as his own mother must've been when Jaak gave the order to execute his father.

When he came to the overgrown gravel path that might've been a road once, he followed it until he found the farthest edge of Alashiya's land. Taevas stood deep in the trees and observed the cracked pavement of the road that presumably connected all of Birchdale's little farms like a withered artery.

Lee, where is all your funding going? It's certainly not in infrastructure. He shook his head in disgust.

Standing there was a little surreal, and not just because the air shimmered strangely in front of him — a testament to just how strong Alashiya's wards were. This was the closest he'd been to the outside world in weeks. More weeks than he could reliably count, if one added in his captivity. The road seemed like a magical artifact from another life. If he touched it, if he followed it to hunt down his mate, it would instantly transport him away from the fairy tale world in which he'd taken refuge.

The narrow road was a pale, ashy gray and riddled with cracks. It probably hadn't been repaved in fifty years, and it certainly didn't have a branch of m-grid beneath it, which connected to all new cars to regulate speed. It was neglected nearly to the point of obsolescence, which seemed fitting.

Not even the road outside her home can be nice, he thought bitterly. Taevas forced himself to take a deep breath.

Promising himself that he'd make a call to Lee Seymour to personally complain when he returned home, if only for the principle of the thing, Taevas turned away from the road. He'd barely taken a few steps deeper into the trees when the roar of an engine froze him in place.

Whirling around, he watched as a dirt-speckled but clearly new SUV came around the bend. He expected it to keep going. There was no sign marking the entrance to Alashiya's land, and the wards obscured even the overgrown entrance from view. There was absolutely no reason for anyone, particularly *that* car, to even slow down as it passed.

But he watched, stomach dropping, as it slowed. It came to a rolling stop on the shoulder just past the entrance, where it idled for several long seconds.

Taevas eased back into the shadows, his wings nearly vibrating with tension against his back. They hurt no matter what position he held them in, but he forced the discomfort out of his mind as he watched the passenger door pop open and Alashiya practically leap out. The vehicle had barely come to a complete stop before her old boots were on the ground.

What the fuck?

Her face was pale as she shut the door behind her. Tension hiked her shoulders up high. She looked like she wanted to run.

The engine cut off and another door opened, though it was on the wrong side for Taevas to see it. A deep voice drawled, "You're supposed to wait for me, pretty thing."

A searing sort of familiarity hit him. It was like a ghost had spoken directly in his ear, conjured from his oldest, darkest nightmares. His body locked in place. A cold sweat broke out across his body.

No, Jaak's dead. I made sure of that.

Alashiya was already walking away from the car. Her head was held high, but her arms were stiff at her sides, like she was bracing for something. "No, thank you," she bit out, polite but stiff. "I appreciate the ride, but I can handle it from here."

The voice drew closer as the stranger rounded the bumper. "What kind of dragon would I be if I let you open your own doors? I was raised better than that."

A large dragon came into view, walking straight out of Taevas's nightmares.

Jaak.

In a heartbeat, Taevas was a teenager again. He froze in the shadows, horror binding him there, forcing him to watch as his mate attempted to evade a much bigger predator. She didn't stand a chance. The dragon closed the distance between them in a handful of long strides and clasped her hand, halting her by the edge of the road.

Jaak's blue face lifted as he eyed the trees. "Where are we? There isn't even a road here."

Alashiya's discomfort was clear to him, but it was obvious she was trying to hide it from the blue dragon. "I don't have a car, so why would I need a road? Thanks again for the ride, Sergei, but I really do have to go."

Sergei? Taevas blinked. His panic receded somewhat, slithering back into the dark, wet place it came from. The wards wavered in front of him, warping his view like hot air over blacktop, but if he squinted...

That's not Jaak.

It couldn't be, because he'd killed the old bastard with his own two hands. *This* dragon couldn't have been older than a century and a half, and he hadn't been prematurely aged by vices and indulgence like Jaak had been. But even so, the resemblance was uncanny. The color of their skin was identical, as was the shape of their noses and horns. And the voice... That was uncanny. The sound of it made Taevas's hair stand on end.

It filtered through memory, through the distortion of drugs and pain. He recognized it not just from the war, but from his captivity.

Sergei frowned down at Alashiya. Turning so his back was facing the forest, he said, "I'm trying to keep you safe. You don't know what could be in those woods. There are wild animals and worse out there. You shouldn't be alone."

All at once Taevas's senses sharpened. His focus honed in on Alashiya as his confusion and dread were pushed to the farthest corner of his mind.

That dragon has a hand on my mate.

Chapter Thirty-Five

Taevas wasn't normally quick to anger. It rarely served him in his day to day life, and he liked to think he had more control over his baser urges and reactions than most dragons. But when he did get angry — *really, really* angry — his rage was cold and deadly. Precise.

When someone fucked around in his territory, he handled it with swift, merciless action. When a dumbass elf stood his cousin Hele up on a date, he ruined the man's life with a single phone call and hadn't thought of it since. But when a dangerous dragon put his hands on his mate...

Taevas wasn't cool. He wasn't precise. He was a fucking bomb about to blow.

There wasn't any worry about consequences. Blood rushed in his ears, drowning out any other noise. He lunged for the treeline. Instinct compelled him to shift, but the moment he tried, his body rejected the change with an overwhelming wave of nausea and pain.

He staggered in the undergrowth. Alashiya's magic rippled across his skin in hot waves, but it wasn't the wards or the discomfort that stopped him in his tracks. It was the look on her face.

She stared at him with wide, horrified eyes. Her lips were

slightly parted and her normally glowing skin was gray. "No," she croaked, holding Taevas's gaze.

"*No?*" Sergei sounded genuinely surprised, not realizing that she wasn't even talking to him.

Alashiya's gaze flicked back to Sergei. She took a step back, away from the trees. Sergei followed her instinctively, his tail coiling around her ankle to keep her from going too far.

Absolutely fucking not.

Dragons didn't do that casually. It was a deeply familiar touch meant to mark territory and show clear intent to claim. Maybe not seriously — because even dragons could have casual liaisons, despite popular belief — but it didn't matter to Taevas whether Sergei wanted to Choose Alashiya or not. She was *taken.*

It didn't matter that it couldn't be Isand Jaak. The sight of his lookalike holding Alashiya...

Nausea swelled in a burning wave up his throat.

All of that rushed through his mind in a searing flash, urging him to act, to *move.* But he found his muscles locked. Taevas couldn't take a single step closer. A deep crawling sensation wormed its way beneath his skin to bore into his bones. Too late, he realized his feet had sunk into the soil. It held him fast as Alashiya's magic battered him like the waves of a furious ocean.

"N-no," she stuttered, keeping her gaze firmly fixed on the blue dragon. "That's not what I meant. I'm sorry. The path to my house is totally overgrown and would be uncomfortable for you. No one ever comes this way but me. That's all."

"Uncomfortable?" Sergei cast a suspicious look over his shoulder. He didn't appear to have any idea that he was looking right at Taevas.

Lips stretching into a thin, nervous smile, Alashiya placed a hand on his arm and drew his attention back to her. "Your wings."

Sergei's dark expression eased. "Ah, I see. You're probably right. I hate hiking."

Still keeping her gaze fixed on the other dragon, she asked in a slow, deliberate way, "You must've hated your hunting trip with Monty, huh? What were you trying to catch, anyway?"

Sergei made a derisive sound. "He's lucky I still need him, or I'd have ripped his throat out and left him to rot out there. We didn't find anything we were looking for."

Alashiya's eyes flicked back to Taevas. They widened slightly in a silent plea. *Go,* she seemed to say. But he couldn't go. He couldn't do anything except stand there and watch as his Chosen confronted a man from his nightmares. Even if the ground released him, what could he do?

Sergei could shift. Taevas couldn't. He wouldn't stand a chance.

"A lot of people feel that way about Monty." She took a few small steps to one side, away from Taevas. Linked by his tail, Sergei followed her.

Taevas caught a glimpse of his profile again as Sergei glanced at the forest. "He talked a lot about you when we were out hunting. Couldn't seem to stop himself. It felt a bit like he was trying to warn me away from his territory." A sharp smile revealed Sergei's pointed canines. "People never seem to grasp that dragons will take whatever they want — and if someone wants it too, it makes it even better. We love a challenge."

"Oh. Can't say I knew that either."

"You've really never met a dragon before?"

Alashiya licked her lips. "No. Never."

Something in Sergei's voice changed. "If you do see another dragon, will you tell me? I'm not actually out here on a hunting trip. My cousin was flying near here recently and we think he went down not too far from town. We've looked everywhere, but there hasn't been any sign of him. Or I *thought* we'd looked everywhere. Monty never said anything about there being a big chunk of land we might've missed."

Alashiya's voice was remarkably level when she replied, "I'm sorry about your cousin. That must be awful. But I haven't seen him. I have wards up to keep trespassers out, so he couldn't have wandered in without me knowing. Monty knows that, too, since they also keep *him* out. That's probably why he didn't say anything."

Sounding thoughtful, Sergei asked, "How much land do you have? Must be a lot to make him want it so bad."

She offered him a wan smile. "Not a lot. Just very well taken care of. Lots of game and places for it to hide."

Sergei looked over his shoulder again, his dark eyes narrowed. "I see. Are those..." He paused, assessing the trees with a sharpened interest. "Why do I feel wards?"

She waved the question off. "Nymphs always ward their land."

"And you're really the only one who lives out here?"

Alashiya cleared her throat. "Yes. It's just me."

"No clan? No visitors?"

"I live alone and I don't get visitors."

Sergei didn't sound entirely convinced. "I thought nymphs lived in big clans. I don't understand why you'd be out here by yourself."

Alashiya took a real step away this time. The dragon's tail slid down her leg to rattle quietly above the packed earth that lined the shallow ditch in which they stood. Her expression was shuttered when she bluntly explained, "My grove was small to begin with, but not long after we moved to Birchdale, a rogue shifter pack tried to take our land. Most were killed. Some left. It was just me and my grandparents until they passed away."

The air squeezed out of Taevas's lungs. It didn't matter that he'd heard the story before. It still hit him like a punch to the gut.

My Shiya, no wonder you're so afraid of the world.

And yet she stood there, staring into the eyes of a ghost who could tear her apart with so little effort, as bold and dignified as the queen she was born to be.

Moving toward his SUV, Sergei warned her, "Well, then it's clearly not safe for you to be alone in these woods. You have no idea who could be wandering your land. You'll pack a bag and be ready for me to pick you up tonight." Circling the front of the vehicle, he cast the woods another sweeping look, unaware that Taevas stared back at him.

Alashiya turned stiffly to face him. With her back to the woods, Taevas couldn't make out her expression, but he could hear the barely hidden revulsion in her voice when she asked, "Why would I need a bag?"

Sergei's smile was slow and full of heat. It was a look Taevas had never seen on Jaak's face, and instantly shattered the link between the two men in his mind, freeing him at last from the child's fear that held him prisoner.

This was no old, cruel despot who used the vulnerability of his people to control them. This wasn't the man who'd tortured and executed his *isa*. This wasn't the monster who kept his mother in solitary confinement for years, just to make sure she felt the death of her Chosen every day.

This was just a man. A dragon of no standing, no rank, no honor. His size was impressive and his horns were gilded, but Taevas had never heard of him. If he was related to Jaak, then that was his only claim to notoriety. And what a pitiful one that would be.

Fire replaced that bile that had scalded Taevas's throat when Sergei dared to give *his* Chosen that lustful, indulgent look. "Pretty thing, don't you want to get out of this shithole? I'm going on a trip and I plan on taking you with me."

"Where?"

Sergei winked. "That's a surprise."

"And if I don't want to go?"

He opened the driver's side door and shrugged dismissively. Climbing in, he replied, "It's not about what you want. It's about what you need." He gave her a stern look. "Pack a bag, Shiya. I'll see you tonight."

The roar of the engine was the only sound after that. Taevas stood there silently, shaking with rage, as the SUV pulled back onto the road and drove off at a reckless speed. Neither he nor

Alashiya moved until it was completely out of sight. Even then, they waited until not even the sound of the engine reached them.

As soon as it died off, the potent magic that held him in place eased. "Shiya!"

She whirled around, her boot heel kicking up dust, and ran for him. It was only a handful of steps before she crashed into him, her arms curled tightly around his neck. They were pressed so close together, he could feel her heart racing against his own.

"How could you *do* that?" she croaked, beating lightly at his shoulders. "What if he'd seen you? What if he'd smelled you or heard you or—"

Taevas's gaze roamed over the road as he hurried them back into the shadows of the trees, out of the blazing sun. Half dragging her and half stumbling himself, he walked them deeper and deeper into the woods. It didn't matter where they were going, so long as he got her as far from that dragon as physically possible. If he could've, he would've flown away with her right then and there.

"What *was* that?" he demanded. "That's one of the men who kidnapped me, Shiya. How did you end up in a car with him? What happened in town?"

"I don't know! One minute I was asking Mike to borrow a car, and the next he'd caught up with me in the street and started talking like— He just grabbed me and told me he was going to drive me home. I didn't know how to shake him off without making him more suspicious. I—" She cut herself off with a hard shake of her head. Peeling herself away from him, she grabbed his wrist and began to pull him down a path only visible to her.

Her voice was pitched high with panic when she continued, "It doesn't matter! None of it matters! We have to get you out of here, Taevas. *Now.* I don't know what that man wants with you, but he *is* looking for you. And I saw the news when I went to Debbie's! I'm so, so sorry. I've been keeping you here and the *car—*"

Taevas grabbed her arms, halting her frantic trek through the undergrowth. They were deep in her woods now, and had stopped in a small gap in the trees. Sunlight filtered in through the leafy canopy in streams that created abstract shapes on the forest floor.

It was a beautiful place, but he didn't see any of it. All he saw was Alashiya's pale face tilted up to look at him.

"Did he hurt you?"

Her lips parted with surprise. "I... What? What does that matter? Taevas, he's *hunting* you! And the 'Riik—"

Feeling like he was seconds from coming out of his skin, he ground out, "Answer the question."

"No! He just— I don't know what he wants with me. Not that it matters. Didn't you hear me? He has men with him, Taevas. There's no *cousin*. He's been searching the woods for you with Monty! You heard him. He wants to come back tonight!"

"Not what *matters?*" Taevas couldn't recall a time when he got so angry his mind simply *blanked*. Not even seeing Sergei put his hands on Alashiya just minutes before had the same effect. It was like that one simple phrase had robbed him of every thought he had or would have, save for one.

That great, serpentine beast of need and possession roared in him when he snarled, "You are *all* that matters, Alashiya!"

The 'Riik, his Wing, Sergei — they were all banished from his mind when he crushed their mouths together in a brutal, desperate kiss. Taevas slipped his claws into her hair and pressed her back against a tree trunk. She trembled beneath him as he swept his tongue across her lips, demanding she let him in.

Alashiya gasped. Her back arched when he slid his tongue past her teeth to glide it hungrily against her own. Her fingers pressed into his chest, her blunt nails raking gently. His cock jerked in his loose linen pants as he gripped one of her luscious thighs and hiked it over his hip.

No matter what he did, he couldn't seem to get close enough. To taste enough. To *feel* enough.

His tail coiled around her waist with a possessive squeeze as he stole kiss after kiss, each one needier, messier than the last. He wanted to mark her in every way he could. He needed her to taste him on her lips, to feel his hands everywhere, to endure the sharp pleasure-pain of his cock between her perfect thighs.

He needed her to know that she was his, that he was hers, and that whatever came next, there was no tearing them apart.

"Damn it, Shiya," he growled, hips rocking restlessly into hers. Alashiya made a shocked, breathy sound that sent a bolt of lust down his spine. "When are you going to get it? You're *everything.*"

CHAPTER THIRTY-SIX

IT WAS FEAR THAT DROVE HIM OFF THE CLIFF, AND IT was need that pulled him down to Earth. To her.

Taevas's muscles coiled so tightly they trembled as he devoured her, one furious kiss bleeding into the next. It was a nightmare. The nightmare of all nightmares — his worst fear come true in ways he could barely wrap his head around.

To have lost himself so completely to a mate, surrendering all aspects of himself to her, only to potentially lose her... Mating had killed his father. It tortured his mother. It threatened everything he valued in himself and what he'd built, but even that existential fear couldn't touch the raw, slithering poison of *losing her.*

He didn't think for a moment that Alashiya wanted Sergei, or even that the dragon was a real threat to his claim, but seeing Jaak's look-alike lay his hands on her— Taevas would be seeing that in his dreams for decades to come.

Urgency pumped through his veins with every frantic beat of his heart. The need to hide her away, the need to mark her, and the need to destroy anything that threatened her was a howl in him, so loud that it blocked out everything else.

"Tell me to stop," he begged. "Command me, Shiya."

He was already tearing at the simple tie that held her dress together at her waist. His hands moved without his consent, a flurry of action whose sole goal was to divest his mate of her clothing as fast as possible. Only a shred of Taevas the man, the Isand, the good, caring mate remained in him, and that shred needed her to push back, to tell him no.

She deserved better than a fuck in the dirt for her first time. She deserved his full attention, his care as he made it perfect for her. At the very least she deserved to be in their nest, not up against the papery bark of an old birch tree. He *knew* that, even if he couldn't seem to stop his claws from tearing through the knot of her dress or reaching greedily past its folds to cup the heavy swell of her breast.

Control was a thing of the past. That Taevas was dead. In his place was a mindless, rutting beast, and that beast could only be commanded by his queen.

The touch of her palm to his cheek was searing. For a moment, he was gutted, knowing that she was stopping him, *this.* It was the right thing, but gods, he needed it. He needed to seal this open wound that was his Choosing or the fear would see him burning the world to the ground.

"Taevas." His name fell from battered, swollen lips. Her cheeks were flushed and her eyes were wide when she put enough space between them to meet his gaze.

He held himself perfectly still, waiting for her to tell him what to do. Waiting for it to end as it should. But Alashiya didn't say anything for a painfully long time. Her eyes were clear, her emotions a vivid display in them as she came to some conclusion.

The hair on the back of his neck rose as instinct recognized something his mind couldn't. She'd decided on something, but he couldn't tell if it was in his favor or not.

"Why do you want me to stop this?"

His voice was a jagged edge when he answered, "You deserve better."

"Than what?"

"Than to be fucked in the dirt." His throat worked around

what felt like a shard of glass. "To have your first time be with me when I'm— I'm *this.*"

"This what?"

Taevas rocked his hips. A hiss slipped out from between his clenched teeth when their bodies connected, sending a jolt of sweet friction down his cock. Alashiya's breath hitched when he yanked the soft slip away from her breasts, letting them spill into the warm, sticky air.

Pressing his face into the soft flesh of her throat, he rolled one of her nipples between his thumb and forefinger with firm, continuous pressure. "This out of my fucking mind," he rasped, teeth scraping her throbbing pulse. "This lost. This ruined by you. For you."

She made a soft, needy sound in the back of her throat and rose up on her tiptoes, her back arching as he rolled her nipple in the other direction, never letting up the pressure. He could practically see her little toes curling in her boots as she panted.

"Tell me no," he ordered, more desperate than before. "Command me to stop, Shiya. You're the only one of us who can."

Her hands fluttered around his shoulders before they slid down, crossing his heaving chest until her fingertips settled on the waistband of his borrowed pants. "What if I don't want to?"

A high keening note left his throat. "You can't. You're worth more than this. You deserve *perfect.* Not this."

Even as the words left his mouth, he began to tear at her clothing with quick, efficient swipes of his claws. A twinge of guilt over the damage was a brief flare in the back of his mind, but it was gone as quickly as it came.

She'd never wear patched up clothing, hand-me-downs, or cheap fabrics again. She'd dress as she was always meant to — like a queen. He'd drape her in strings of pearls and silk so fine it stroked her skin with the same reverence he did. It'd be his honor to give her anything her heart desired from this day onward. Just the thought of her wearing what *he'd* given her for a change made a hot curl of lust tighten in his belly.

If Alashiya had a problem with his destruction of her clothing, she didn't mention it. Her breath came in quick little pants as she stood there against the tree in little more than her old leather boots, dainty and well-loved, but yet another sign of how much more she deserved.

"We don't have time for perfect," she whispered, slipping her fingers beneath his waistband. His cock jerked when she brushed the base with a fleeting, curious touch. "If this is all we get, then I'm not wasting the opportunity."

Something about the way she said that made a faint alarm sound in the back of his mind, but it was completely drowned out by the roar of victory in his ears.

She's not telling me no.

Some part of him was shaken by that. She was supposed to be the one in control, the logical one who'd keep their head when he couldn't. But she didn't appear to want that. The look in Alashiya's eyes was as desperate and frenzied as his was, like it was *her* who feared he'd be snatched away in a moment.

Never.

Taevas tilted her head back for another hungry kiss. *Never never never,* he silently chanted, pressing the word into her lips and tongue again and again.

The urge to reassure her was the final straw for that threadbare shred of control that remained in him. No, this wasn't as it should be, but it was what had to be done. This was the start and the end and the pivot point from which their life would change. Everything going forward would be different, but *they* would be a done thing.

Taevas ripped his lips away from hers and dropped to his knees. Without his support, she collapsed against the tree, her chest rising and falling as she stared down at him with dazed eyes.

She was fucking magnificent.

The dappled sunlight gilded her skin and curls. A faint sheen of sweat made her chest glitter. The tips of her heavy breasts were dark and jutting into the warm summer air, begging for more of his attention. When he palmed them greedily, he found her soft thighs trembling.

Nude and flushed with arousal, she looked like every fever dream of a nymph that had ever been had. She was wild with want, unbound by any shyness or coy games. There was nothing artificial or practiced about how she looked at him then — like she was just as out of her mind for him as he was for her.

Taevas hitched one of her legs over his shoulder. The joint of his wing screamed in protest when he moved it out of the way, but he shoved the now-familiar pain into a box and sealed it shut. Nothing, not even that, could distract him from his singular focus now.

Alashiya balanced herself by gripping the tallest pair of his horns as he pressed his face into the juncture of her thighs. The scent of her, musky and sweet, sent electricity skittering over every inch of his skin. A pleasant buzz filled his mind.

He barely recognized his own voice when he spoke. "If you tell me to stop, I'll stop." Taevas skimmed her slit and found her hot flesh slippery. He stroked her mindlessly, hungrily, stirring his fingers through the evidence of her need, when he growled, "If you don't, I'm going to ruin you like you've ruined me, *naine.*"

A shuddering breath escaped her bruised lips. "I think you've already done that."

No, he wanted to argue, *I haven't. Not yet.*

If he had, she wouldn't wear that avid, fearful look, like he'd disappear at any moment. She wouldn't doubt or worry. She'd *know* that they were a done thing, and that she ruled him now and forever. She'd demand her due without hesitation. She'd expect everything of him, and it'd be the greatest pleasure in his life to give all of himself to her.

Because that was the trade they made when a dragon Chose. It was not an easy thing to be a dragon's mate. They demanded everything, always, without remorse. They coveted what they treasured and would never compromise on that.

But in exchange they offered all of themselves, and the risk that should a Chosen leave or die, their lives would be forfeit in all the ways that mattered.

Taevas had never been willing to make that trade. He couldn't risk suffering as his parents had suffered, and the thought of his control unraveling was repugnant. But he was keenly aware that he was missing out on something that made life worth living.

And now it was done. It'd taken a decade of whittling down his willpower and an assassination attempt, but at last he'd offered himself up on the altar, sacrificing his own health and happiness to have her all to himself. He was aware that he would be a monster of a mate — more demanding, more troublesome, more selfish than any other. If he had any selfless love for her at all, he would've saved her from himself.

But he didn't. His feelings were as selfish as the fire that burned in his gut. It was all-consuming, ever-hungry, and so he knelt there in the woods, her thigh draped over his shoulder, and devoured her.

Alashiya choked out a gasp as he spread her and licked a hot stripe from her dripping entrance to the firm little pearl of her clitoris. The muscles of her thigh tightened reflexively as he savored the taste and feel of her on his tongue. It was pure bliss.

He didn't hear the sounds of the forest or feel the humid air pressing down on him. He barely felt the pressure building in his livid cock. Taevas normally prided himself on being able to get a woman off on his tongue with devastating efficiency, but that wasn't the goal with her. He drowned in sensation. There was no plan, no pride, no endgame. There was only the taste and smell and sounds of her as she ground down against him, chasing the pleasure his swirling tongue offered.

His name spilled from her lips over and over, blending in with strings of words from a language he didn't know. A heady thrill coursed through him when she began to direct his head with his horns, demanding more here, less there. It eased something tight in him to know that she held the reins, allowing him to fully lose himself in her.

When she began to rock herself restlessly against his mouth, he instinctively increased the pressure and speed, seeking to give her everything she needed from him.

He slid one finger inside her, then another. Her walls rippled around them, seeking to hold him there as he gently but urgently attempted to prepare her for what was to come. He eased the sting of a third finger with a long, sucking pull of his lips and tongue, which made Alashiya arch her back and keen with surprise.

Her grip on his horns became unrelenting, and there was precious little oxygen available when she forced his head hard against her. Taevas *loved* it. His skull felt too small to contain the rush that accompanied her taking control of him, using him to get herself off.

Every aspect of his life had been carefully curated, maintained, and ordered by him. Every partner, every sexual encounter — all of it was by his design, at his leisure, and ended exactly when he said so. It had never occurred to him that he'd fucking *love* being used, let alone commanded. He couldn't even imagine letting anyone but his Alashiya doing so.

And when she came on his tongue, panting and rolling her perfect, wet cunt into his mouth until his mind began to go a little fuzzy at the edges... *Bliss.* Pure, unadulterated bliss.

To everyone else he was Isand Taevas Aždaja, but to Alashiya he was simply *hers*.

CHAPTER THIRTY-SEVEN

HE BARELY REGISTERED IT WHEN SHE PUSHED HIM BACK by his shoulders, forcing him onto his elbows in the cool undergrowth. His tongue was a little sore, his lips and cheeks wet, and the taste of her lingered, making him feel almost dizzy with desire. He watched, eyes glazed, as she dropped onto the forest floor with him. Her breasts swung, heavy and full, drawing his gaze as she straddled him.

He loved her body. He loved absolutely everything about it. Every lush curve, dark curl, and dimple. He wanted the impressions of his fingers to live on her plush hips. He wanted to trace the strange, alien marks on her skin with his tongue and always keep one hand between her thighs, ready to please her at a moment's notice.

He wanted her more than he'd wanted anything in his entire life, and if he didn't have her soon, he was pretty sure he'd lose whatever was left of his mind.

Alashiya's hands settled on his tense shoulders and smoothed upward, until she cupped the underside of his jaw and tilted his head back. She breathed against his lips, "I used to dream of what it'd be like to be touched by Adon. But *you...*"

She pressed the tip of her tongue against his slick lower lip.

His mouth parted for her on a shaky breath. He felt her words whisper against his tongue when she finished, "You are more than I could've ever imagined."

His tail snaked around her waist, pulling her closer. Hips rocking upward until he could feel the slick heat of her seeping through the thin material of his linen pants, he panted, "Shiya, *pl*—"

He let out a strangled moan when she reached between them and freed his cock. It rested against her cunt, hot and throbbing and nearly unbearable. Her lips skimmed his, and she never looked away from his eyes when she began to gently explore what belonged to her.

"I know you probably want me to speed it up," she murmured, each word a gift between soft, sucking kisses. "But I like being gentle with you. I like touching you. Petting you."

The tendons on his neck stood out starkly against his skin as he strained to hold still, to let her do exactly as she pleased. She stroked him slowly, each pass punctuated by a reverent little squeeze of the swollen head of his cock that made his eyes cross. Sweat drenched his body.

"Keep this up and you'll make me come," he gasped, hips stuttering against his will.

He felt her smile against the sweaty skin of his cheek. "I *like* watching you come."

"Fuck. *Fuck.*" Taevas tossed his head back and squeezed his eyes shut. He tried to think of anything else, anything at all to stop the rising tide of his orgasm. "Please, *naine,* I want— I want—"

"Easy, dragon," she crooned, halting her torturous strokes. "I know what you need."

Alashiya gently pulled his head toward her, urging him to open his eyes and look at her as she rose on her knees. Taevas held his breath as he watched her position his flushed cockhead against her entrance. His claws dug into the soil as the muscles of his spine locked. The urge to whip his wings around and wrap her in them was a drumbeat in his mind, but he forced it aside, knowing that the pain would ruin this perfect moment.

He wanted to hold her hips, to help guide her down, but he was forced to keep his hands down, since they held his weight. The position left him totally helpless as she lowered herself down, inch by inch.

He'd tried to prepare her, but there was really nothing for it. He was big, she was tight. It was always going to be a struggle.

Taevas watched her expression change as she slowly fed his cock into her body. Her brows pinched and a little of her flush melted away when the head popped past the tight ring of muscle and closed hard around the shaft. She paused, her thighs shaking on either side of his hips, and took several deep breaths.

Desperate to ease her obvious discomfort, Taevas tipped his head to press a dozen fluttering kisses across her lips, her cheeks, and her closed eyes. "My beautiful, powerful *naine*. Yes, just like that. Go slow. Don't force it. I'm yours. There's no rush."

Alashiya leaned into his soft touches. Her arms circled his neck and a soft sigh feathered across her lips. The tension in her brow eased a little. Tucking her face into the rigid line of his neck, she rolled her hips downward.

Taevas sucked in a sharp breath. Every bit of progress was torture. Every pause was a test. He wanted to hold her, to comfort her, even as the beast in him raked his claws against his vulnerable insides, demanding he grab her hips and force her down, to get it over with so they could finish what they'd started.

But he couldn't — *wouldn't* — do that. His Alashiya was in charge now, and it was up to her how quickly her pain ended.

What he *could* do, however, was distract her.

Beads of sweat slid down his spine from between his bunched shoulder blades as his tail dipped between her thighs. The rattle at the end was a bit too rough to play with, but the side of his tail was smooth and dexterous. More than up to the task.

Alashiya jerked when it slid down to where they were joined. Taevas took a second to indulge himself, to feel the air-tight seal where their bodies connected and *relish* it, but no more than that. Putting firm pressure on the apex of her dripping cunt, he began to slowly draw his tail back and forth.

"*Ah!*" Alashiya's already tight walls clenched hard around him. He hissed, clenching his jaw hard against the white-hot flash of pleasure it caused.

Within a few moments she was rocking her hips again, taking him a tiny bit deeper everytime until, with a breathless sound, she seated herself completely.

They both groaned as she fluttered around him. He swore he could feel her heartbeat throbbing in time with his own. "Beautiful, brave, *gorgeous* creature," he rasped, grinding his hips upward. He resisted the violent urge to thrust, but only barely.

She shuddered. "Taevas..."

"I have you, *naine.*" He slowed the movement of his tail and changed from a sawing motion to a slow, gentle swirl. "Tell me what you need and it's yours."

Alashiya lifted her head from its hiding place against his neck. When she looked at him then, his heart broke and was remade in the span of a single breath.

Her dense lashes were heavy with tears that glittered in the dappled light. They streaked down her flushed cheeks and made her already bright eyes that much more alive. Her lips were swollen and red, and when a shaky breath escaped them, it smelled like honey.

The air around her shimmered, too bright, too vivid. The colors were dreamlike and unnatural, and the air itself seemed heavier than it had a moment before. It seemed to hum with the very thing of life.

Taevas stared at her in awe. He'd been adamant that he was doing her a disservice by allowing her first time to be in the *woods* of all places, but in that moment he became utterly certain that he was out of his fucking mind.

This was *the only* place it could've happened. The only place it *should've* happened. Not in the nest. Not in a luxurious bed or high up in his tower. It was *there,* amongst the earth and the plants and the living things that she was so very connected to that he saw the real Alashiya at last — broken down into her raw elements and the intangible substance of her soul.

To have her anywhere else would've dimmed her, diminished the sanctity of this holy moment.

"I only want you," she breathed, bracing her hands on his shoulders.

Taevas's chest heaved. He couldn't seem to catch his breath as she began to rock up and down, finding a rhythm that suited her. Their gazes never wandered, never wavered, as she rode him. It was all he could do to hold on, his hips canting to meet her, to make it easier to find that perfect spot and pace that would send her over the edge again.

He'd never worshipped the gods. He'd only ever been to ceremonies and services when it was absolutely required of him, and though he was careful to never say anything publicly, he thought that the obsession with beings who didn't exist was all a little silly on its best day.

On its worst, it led to endless strife and bloodshed.

But there, sat in the dirt and undergrowth of a birch forest, his cock buried in his mate's slick cunt and his name on her lips...

He understood worship.

He'd tasted the divine in her, and now that hunger would never be sated. It would never fade or dull. It was as a part of him as his fire was, and it was the new goal of his life to feed that hunger every chance he got.

They fell into a rhythm that gradually began to pick up speed. Taevas's hips kicked upward everytime she came back down, sending his cock as deep as it could go. Everytime it happened, her lips popped open in a surprised little *O* and her nails dug into his shoulders, urging him on.

"Yes, yes," she chanted, moving faster.

Taevas's hips left the ground completely on his next thrust. She gasped, her expression pinching, and her rhythm faltered as her walls began to ripple around him. Knowing she was close, he doubled the efforts of his tail and prayed he could hold on just a bit longer.

"Let me have another one," he begged, pressing their foreheads together so he could feel her breath across his cheeks. "Let me feel you come again, *naine.*"

He could feel the moment it began. Her muscles locked up one by one, stiffening her spine, her fingers, her thighs. It seemed to him to happen in slow motion, and it was the most beautiful thing he'd ever witnessed.

Alashiya went slack against him. She draped herself over his chest and shoulders, her face once more tucked into his neck, and shuddered with the aftershocks as his tail slowly rolled over her skin, prolonging them as much as he could.

Taevas's hips moved restlessly upward in shallow thrusts. Their bodies made wet, sloppy sounds as he chased his own pleasure. Feeling her so soft and sated against him was a heady thing. Knowing *he'd* done that and that he was now free to do as he pleased with her supple, willing body, was an unmatched thrill.

Hanging onto his sense by the thinnest thread, Taevas grated, "Where, my Shiya? Tell me where."

She nuzzled his neck. Soft, painfully loving kisses were pressed against his pounding pulse and the corner of his jaw. Her hands drifted over his shoulders and chest, petting him, stroking him, driving him past the point of wild and straight into madness.

"Inside."

At any other time, with anyone else, Taevas would've been humiliated by the whine that whistled from his throat.

White-hot need flashed through him, but he still somehow managed to choke out, "My Shiya, that's— We didn't talk about—"

She lifted her head again. There was no hesitation in her expression, just heavy-lidded desire and satisfaction. Holding him by the nape of his neck, she rocked into his thrusts — each one an explicit encouragement.

"It won't take," she assured him. "And I want to feel it."

He wanted to ask *why* it wouldn't. Taevas was fairly certain she didn't have a birth control implant, considering the general state of her access to healthcare. Of course, he knew that *he* had the shot. There was no risk of pregnancy from his end, but that wasn't the point. They hadn't discussed it. So she believed for a reason unknown to him that there wasn't a chance.

And that didn't sit right with him because he damn well wanted a chance. Not now, not when they were in danger and their mating was so new, but soon. The thought of Alashiya carrying *his* young was searing in its pleasure.

But all of his questions, his fantasies and his now crystal-clear desire for their future, fell to the wayside when she murmured, "Give it to me, *argaman mlk.* Now."

He was completely undone. There was no fighting it and no denying her. Everything he was, everything he would be, now rested in the palm of her hand — and the hot well of her cunt.

Taevas buried himself to the hilt and came with a soundless cry. Alashiya's back arched. She pressed their hips together so there was not even the tiniest space between them and held his gaze as his orgasm raked its claws through him.

Dazed, he could do little more than submit as she tilted his head back to press a gentle kiss to his lips. "That's it," she whispered. "That's everything, *argaman mlk.*"

CHAPTER THIRTY-EIGHT

THEY STAGGERED INTO THE HOUSE, SWEATY, A LITTLE dirty, and sated. Her body was satisfied, at least. And a little sore. A lot sore.

Alashiya didn't spare the burn between her legs or the pleasant ache in her muscles a thought. She wanted to, but there wasn't time. Even if there was, she wasn't certain she could've risked dwelling on what they'd done. The memory was already too bright, too hot to touch. It burned in the back of her mind, as perfect and dangerous as a new star.

"Mike will have the car ready tomorrow morning. If you can just hide until then, we should be okay," she told him, her mind already running through everything that would need to be done. A bag would have to be found and enough of her things packed to last her a week. She doubted she'd be gone that long, but—

Don't, she firmly instructed herself. Her throat spasmed hard, threatening tears. *Don't, Shiya. There isn't time.*

Alashiya couldn't bear to look at him, so she hustled into the living room, intent on finding some clothing to replace what he'd torn. She'd walked back to the house in the tattered remains of her slip. There was no way she could focus on what would need to be done if she continued to wear the reminder of the best moment of her entire life.

"Shiya—"

"I don't think he'll have it ready first thing tomorrow, but we should leave at dawn anyway, just to be safe. You can stay in the woods and I'll pick you up once I have the car." She yanked at the neatly folded bundles of clothing in her dresser, unseeing, barely even feeling the fabric under her fingers. Fear made it almost impossible to draw a complete breath in.

"He needs to change the oil," she chattered, blindly selecting a soft summer dress from the bottom of the pile. "It's— it's an old car, so—"

A large purple hand closed over hers, easing her death grip on the dress. "Alashiya," Taevas rumbled against her back, "stop this. Look at me."

It should've been easy. An hour ago she'd been impaled on his cock, demanding he come inside her as she stared unblinkingly into his eyes, desperate to memorize every minute shift in his expression. But now all she wanted to do was run again.

Not because she regretted it. Not because she felt awkward or shy.

She wanted to run because it'd been *spectacular*. More than anything she could've dreamed of, better than every fantasy.

A sense of impending doom had driven off her inhibitions and propelled her to ask for things she never would've otherwise. It heightened her pleasure, but when the sweat cooled and reality crept in, it made her stomach churn with nausea.

That was it, she couldn't help but think. *My one chance. I took it and now it's done.*

Because Taevas had to leave. Sergei was clearly the one hunting him, and even if he wasn't, Taevas had to get back to his people as soon as possible, or else the gods knew what would happen.

Once he was back where he belonged, this thing between them would end — one way or another. Alashiya had gotten caught up in the fantasy they'd woven together, but it was dispelled the moment she looked at Debbie's tablet.

There was no place for her in his world, no matter what he said. They had nothing in common save for a coincidence. Nothing held them together, except perhaps his gratitude for what she'd done for him and her desperation to keep him.

Neither of those things were the foundation of a lasting relationship.

Alashiya swallowed again. It was getting harder. She hadn't even lost him yet. Her thighs were still sticky with his release and his scent lingered on her skin. He was behind her, his hand covering her own, and yet it already felt as though she'd lost him.

Grief was a jagged piece of glass in her throat. *I don't want to be alone again.*

It'd been tolerable when it was all she'd ever known, but now... Now the idea of facing the rest of her life without him was like walking into a jail cell of her own making.

She didn't *want* to go a day without hearing his bossy voice. She didn't *want* to dream of Adon anymore. She didn't *want* to wake up to every tiny sound in the night, afraid that the worst had finally come to pass.

With Taevas, for the first time in her life, she hadn't been afraid. She'd been prepared to step outside the carefully crafted walls of her castle not simply because he asked, but because she finally felt like she *could.*

But that had been its own kind of fantasy. The reality was always that he would return to his people. Or worse. Sergei was definitely worse.

It was one thing for him to leave. It was another for someone to hurt him. Alashiya was sliced to ribbons at the thought of him not being a part of her life, but the threat that Sergei posed, the memories of what he looked like the night he crashed into her barn, the pain he still suffered... Intolerable.

All of those thoughts hammered her as she came down from the high of their coupling. Adrenaline coursed through her, giving her a frenetic energy that had no outlet. She didn't even realize she was trembling until Taevas wrapped his arms around her middle and drew her into his chest. A low, comforting rumble passed through him and into her, immediately easing some of the bone-shattering tension coiling her muscles.

"Be calm, *metsalill*," he commanded. Taevas pressed his lips into the curve of her shoulder and let out a long breath. "There is no need to panic. We will bathe, then we will pack your things and make our plan."

Alashiya gripped his forearms. "Sergei said he was coming back. We can't stay here. Taevas, he has men with him. Men who aren't *right*. What if you get hurt again?"

"Then I will be hurt defending what is most precious to me. There is nothing more honorable than that." He turned her slowly until they were facing one another. Still, she couldn't quite look at him, afraid that if she did, she'd burst into tears.

Taevas brushed her cheek with his thumb, wordlessly asking for her to look up. She couldn't. Instead, she stared at his collar bones, her vision blurring with tears she tried so hard to fight off.

"Why won't look at me, *metsalill?*" he rasped. "Are you embarrassed by what we did? Ashamed? Angry?"

An astonished breath escaped her. "What? No. *No*. Never. That was the best moment of my entire life. It was *everything* to me. I'm..." She fought to keep her voice level, to not let him hear how upset she was, but it was impossible to conceal. "I'm afraid, Taevas."

He pressed his cheek against her temple. Breathing the words into her ear, he grated, "I have asked too much of you, my Shiya, and given you nothing in return. To know that you are afraid even when I'm with you is— it guts me. You should never feel fear when we're together. Never."

Something in his voice changed when he continued, "Hear me now, *minu metsalill*: this will pass. You will never be put in this position again. You will never fear again. But for right now, you must trust me."

She could only nod. Words couldn't make it out of her throat even if she could think of what to say.

Taevas's sigh fluttered through her tangled hair. "We will bathe. You will let me care for you, and then we will figure out our next steps. Understood?"

A strangled laugh escaped her. "You're being bossy again." *Gods, I'm going to miss that so much.*

"Even a queen needs to be told what to do every now and again," he replied, already guiding her out of the living room and down the hall to the bathroom.

Yeah, she silently agreed. *But only if it's you.*

They barely managed to squeeze into the bathroom together, but Taevas was determined, so of course he made it happen. Alashiya watched him shed his dirt-soiled pants with a mix of fondness and anticipatory grief. He did it so shamelessly, so comfortably — like he belonged there, not just in her tiny bathroom but *with* her.

It was like they'd done this a thousand times. Taevas got the shower going while she slid off the tattered remains of her slip, and when the room began to fill with steam, he grabbed her hand and carefully guided her over the lip of the antique bathtub.

The water pressure wasn't great and there was barely an inch of free space to move around, but neither of them cared. Taevas placed her head on his chest and guided her backward until the hot water splashed down her spine. It should've been too warm for a summer afternoon, but at some point her internal temperature had gone haywire, leaving her feeling chilled to her marrow.

Big hands glided over her wet curves and delicately combed through her curls, picking out twigs, feathery bits of moss, and bracken. She shuddered at the ticklish sensation and melted into him.

"That's better," he crooned, sounding deeply self-satisfied. "Soft and at ease. Letting me tend to you makes everything right again. This is how it should be."

Her chest still felt too tight, that hook pulling constantly on her heart, but he was right. She did feel a little better. It was hard not to when his heartbeat thundered under her ear like the perfect drumbeat it was.

Closing her eyes, she turned her head just enough to catch a drop of water as it slid down his skin. It tasted just a bit sweeter for having touched him.

"Aren't you worried?" She couldn't help but ask. He was all urgency and terror when they met in the woods, but now he seemed worryingly calm.

"I am," he answered, reaching for her washcloth. Dabbing a bit of soap on it, he began to scrub the sweat and... other things from her skin. "I am *more* than worried. I am also fucking furious that we are in this position at all. I want nothing more than to steal away with you right this second and put you where you belong — safe in our nest."

Rinsing the cloth free of suds, he used warm water and gentle pressure to cleanse the apex of her thighs. A jolt of discomfort made her tense up, but Taevas made a soothing sound and held the cloth there for a moment, letting the warmth ease some of the sting.

"But you are my first concern in all things," he continued, his voice dropping into a hypnotic bass note that made her eyelids droop. She didn't realize how exhausted she was until he brushed her eyelids with wet fingers, urging them to close. "You are the beat of my heart and my fire and the joy of my nest. Without you, I have nothing. So I will always tend to you first. Everything else will wait."

She made a noncommittal noise. "You have a territory to get back to, Taevas. I'm not more important than that."

Instead of replying, Taevas set the wash cloth aside and cupped the back of her head, holding her even closer as the water pelted them both. "I have a question for you."

"Okay."

"Why were you so certain I wouldn't get you pregnant?" His

tone was perfectly level, revealing nothing. "Was it simply the heat of the moment? If so, we should discuss—"

Alashiya shook her head as much as their position allowed. It was a good thing the water was hot, or else he'd notice her full-body flush that accompanied the memories of what they'd done in the woods. "No, it wasn't. Nymphs can't have children with people outside of the hyphae."

"What?"

"That's why marriage is so important to us," she explained, properly drowsy now. "If I marry a nymph, it's more of a formality, but if I marry outside of the hyphae the ceremony brings them in. That way we can have children, and those children will be born in the hyphae, too."

Taevas's chest moved under her cheek with a sharp inhalation. "How does that work?"

"Blood," she answered, recalling all those times she'd sacrificed a drop to Adon's clothing. To keep him safe. To tie them together in the only way she could. Little sacrifices to bind her magic more tightly into the weave, yes, but also a shallow imitation of the connection she so craved.

The hook behind her chest tugged gently. A tiny push against the soft meat of her heart. For the first time since they'd met, she really examined the feeling — only to immediately shy away from what she found.

Blood calls to blood. Hyphae to hyphae.

"You have to be infected with the mycelium. When we— *I* marry, I'd give my blood to my partner and vice versa. When the hyphae takes, a pregnancy can happen. Otherwise the mycelium sees it as a threat and destroys it."

He was quiet for a long time. Long enough for her mind to drift, escaping the tumult that had tortured it since they left that perfect spot in the woods.

"I see." His wet tail slid around her thigh and gave it a proprietary squeeze. His whisper-soft murmur was nearly drowned out by the water when he said, "Another thing to look forward to, then."

CHAPTER THIRTY-NINE

SHE WOKE UP WITH A START.

Alashiya sat up in bed, her skin clammy and her mind off-kilter. She hardly recalled falling asleep, only that at some point Taevas had shushed her as he dried her skin with a towel.

But he was nowhere to be found now.

Alashiya's head swiveled as she strained to see him in the darkness. An acute sense of disorientation made it even harder to get her bearings. How long had she been asleep? It'd been mid-afternoon when they came back to the house after—

She had to suck in a deep breath. Even half-awake and anxious, the thought of what they'd done made her forget what it was like to breathe normally.

"Taevas?" Her voice was scratchy with sleep when she called out to him. She received no reply. Urgency whispered along the hyphae, sending a flurry of whispers through her mind.

Alashiya shook off the heaviness of her nap and crawled out of bed. Her muscles were sore and other parts of her protested loudly as she clambered to her feet, but she ignored it all. Her heart pounded in her ears as she hobbled over to her dresser and the mess she'd made of it.

Her hands shook. *He didn't leave,* she sternly told herself. *He wouldn't just— he wouldn't just leave me. He'd at least say goodbye. Something must've happened.*

But a small, disproportionately loud part of her couldn't help but run through all the reasons that might not be the case. Perhaps he'd done the smart thing and run as soon as it got dark. He'd stayed for her, but maybe he realized how foolish that was and took the first opportunity to slip out.

Her stomach swooped dangerously low, leaving her feeling sick in the aftermath.

Maybe having sex was a nice goodbye or— No. No, Shiya. *Don't try to ruin something good just because you're scared.*

Blindly throwing on her overalls and boots, she opened her mouth to call out again when a sound from the kitchen made her freeze. It was the soft squeak of hinges.

The urge to run was so strong, she nearly bolted for the open hallway door, but was stopped before she could make little more than a step in its direction. A pair of familiar violet eyes peered at her from the darkness of the hallway.

"Shiya?" It was an unspeakable relief to hear that familiar rumble.

Alashiya's knees went watery, but that didn't stop her from hurtling across the room. He caught her in his arms and squeezed her tightly to him, a concerned series of clicks and chirps emanating from his chest.

In that sharp, *I'm the Isand* voice, he demanded, "What's wrong? I was only gone a moment—"

"Nothing," she answered, cutting him off. She sniffled hard. "I just woke up and you weren't there and I freaked out a little."

Taevas hummed and bent to press a series of soft, apologetic kisses to her cheeks and forehead. "I see. I would be afraid too, if I woke and found you'd left our nest. I'm sorry, *metsalill.* I didn't mean to scare you."

The urge to grab him by the horns and just *hold on,* like she had to get a good grip on him or he'd disappear forever, seared her. Alashiya had to clench her fingers by her sides to stop herself.

Trying to not sound as out of her mind as she felt, she asked, "Where did you go?"

With his night time coloring, Taevas's expression was mostly lost in the darkness, save for his eyes and the occasional flash of his pearly white teeth. He sounded worryingly serious when he answered, "I had to prepare things. I packed your bag for you and fetched something from the barn."

Alashiya's brow crinkled. "You packed... But all my clothes are still here." She couldn't see much with the lights off, but she'd felt it when she waded through the mess of nearly all of her clothes spilled out across the floor.

"I packed your *important* things," he smoothly corrected. "Everything else we'll come back for, but I didn't want to risk anything happening to your keepsakes or your work while we're gone. I put your chest and embroidery kit in a bag on the porch."

"Oh. Okay." She blinked a few times, once more attempting to get her bearings. Another wave of clamminess washed over her. "Are we going *now?*"

Taevas stroked her hair with both hands, his huge palms swallowing the sides of her head with every pass. The violet disks of his eyes gleamed in the darkness when he looked at her for what felt like a very long time.

"No," he answered, slow and controlled. *"You* are leaving."

"What?"

"You are going to take your bag and walk as far from here as you can, then hide in the woods. You will stay in your hiding spot until morning, then make your way back to Debbie and Mike's to pick up the car. I will meet you at the border of the Thompsons' farm. If I don't come for you by noon, you need to drive toward Drummond Island. As soon as you cross over the border into the 'Riik, find a peacekeeper station and ask for Vael Orlov."

He said it all so coolly, so reasonably, that it took a moment for her mind to catch up with what he was really telling her.

Balking, Alashiya took a sharp step backward. "Wait, you want me to leave *without* you?"

Taevas let her go, but his tail followed her. She could feel it brushing her ankle when he replied, "I told you that you are my priority, Shiya. That means I have to put your safety above all things."

"But what about—"

He cut her off with a calmness that somehow frightened her more. "If nothing happens tonight, then there's no harm in it. But Sergei would be stupid to not search your land now that he knows about it, and I'll cut my own tail off before I let him near you again, my Shiya."

"Then come *with* me," she argued, feeling increasingly like she'd never woken up and was stuck in some slowly escalating nightmare. "There's no reason for us to split up. That's how people die, Taevas! We stick together and we live."

"You'll hide better and get farther if I'm not with you. We both know that." Finally, a faint thread of strain entered his voice, shaking that seemingly unflappable authority. "Everything will be fine, but you must do this for me."

"No." She clenched her fists and struggled to get her ragged breathing under control. *"Fuck* no. I'm not leaving you without a good reason, and you haven't given me one."

Taevas sucked in a deep breath. Whether it was for patience or something else, she couldn't say. "Sergei is the one who kidnapped me. I intend to find out why."

All the blood rushed from her head at once. "You— you want to *confront* him? Taevas, you're injured! And he outnumbers you. There are at least three men with him. How do you think you're going to take him?"

"I'll manage," he bit out, "but only if I know you're *safe.* "

She crowded close to jam a finger into his chest. "That's too bad, because I'm not going to leave you! If I run, you follow me. That's what you said. Remember?"

"If I don't do this now, there is every chance he'll go to ground and we'll never know what happened or who he's working with," he bit out, angrier than she'd ever seen him. His tail rattled in the darkness, punctuating every furious word. "I could maybe live with that, if only I didn't have you to think of. It's my duty to protect you. It's non-negotiable."

"So because of me, you'd rather put your life in danger than do the smart thing?" Alashiya couldn't make sense of it. She *refused* to. "If you cared about me even half as much as you say you do, you'd come with me! You wouldn't risk—"

Taevas's audible growl raised the hair on the back of her neck. "You want me to live, Alashiya? Then *go.* That's the only way I'll be able to focus. The only way I'll be able to keep you safe. I need you to trust me. One last time. Just trust me."

She staggered backward. Throat closing so tightly she struggled to draw a breath in, Alashiya shook her head. Echoes of the past made her head swim, but her heart hadn't hurt quite so bad when she was a child. Not until later, when the reality of loss finally settled in. Now it felt like he'd torn something fragile from her and crushed it in his fist.

He wouldn't run with her. History was repeating itself, and she'd be left alone again just when it felt like she'd found something worth living for.

Just because she could understand some of the logic of his argument didn't mean she wasn't angry. He swore he'd always follow her, but at the first opportunity, sent her away.

Bile crawled up her throat, scalding the walls. Echoes of that night so many years ago were loud in her ears. At least her parents had never made her promises. Not like Taevas had.

I should've known, she thought, stepping sharply around him to head for the kitchen. She didn't bother turning on any lights. She didn't want him to see how hard his words had hit her.

What are you, anyway? Nothing.

"Shiya." Her name sounded gritty on his tongue, like he couldn't force it out without discomfort. "Shiya, listen to me—"

She didn't stop to listen. If he wanted her gone, then she'd leave. Alashiya wouldn't be the thing that got him killed. He had a territory to get back to, after all.

The world was bathed in moonlight when she stepped out onto the porch. Her nose and eyes burned with unshed tears, but she found the bag quickly enough. He'd leaned it up against the mossy wall of the house beside an ancient double barrel shotgun.

The sight of it made her pause for just a moment as she reached for the old satchel. She hadn't seen, let alone *thought* of her grandmother's gun in decades. He must've found it when he was rooting around for tools in the barn, though what he expected to do with it, she couldn't say.

Her grandmother purchased it after the shifters came, but she'd been too unsettled by it to keep it in the house. Alashiya didn't think she'd ever even loaded it. Unlike modern guns, this one took bullets, which she doubted anyone could buy anymore. Had he found some alongside the gun? Would it even work after spending decades out in the decaying barn?

For his sake, she hoped so.

Alashiya didn't want this to be the last time she saw him. She just didn't have much hope.

Slinging the heavy satchel over her shoulder, she ignored the weight of Taevas's scrutiny as she stepped stiffly off the porch and into the garden. A corner of her cedar chest dug into her side with every step.

"Shiya."

Something in his voice stopped her short. She stood there, back to him and fingers locked around the strap of her satchel, waiting.

There was a tense beat of silence before Taevas rasped, "Trust me, *minu metsalill*. We'll be together tomorrow."

Grief was an angry, tearing thing in her chest now. It didn't leave any room for trust, let alone the idea of a *tomorrow*.

Chapter Forty

Taevas had made many hard decisions as Isand. He'd sacrificed. He'd done exactly what was necessary, no matter the cost, to make the world a better place for the people he cared about.

Nothing had ever made him feel quite so much like a monster as when he sent Alashiya away.

Yes, he knew she'd put up a little bit of a fight, but he never thought she'd actually *refuse.*

But no matter what hurt she felt now, at least she was safe. He could live with anything, so long as Alashiya was out of harm's way.

Taevas forced himself to tap into the part of him that had been honed in the Great War: the soldier, the general, the killer. He thought it might be harder to slip back into it, but it was like shrugging on an old, broken-in coat. He snapped into the role he'd happily left buried under the rubble of the old 'Riik with terrifying ease.

His mind was sharp. The discomfort of his body was unimportant. Nothing mattered besides ending the threat to him and, more importantly, his mate.

It didn't take long.

He'd only sat in the woods behind the barn for an hour, his mind adrenaline-sharp and full of possibilities, when Alashiya's wards rippled with warning. They were designed to disorient and hide rather than block intruders outright. Now that Sergei knew where the entrance to her property was, he could push through them with relative ease.

The sweet taste of her magic grew cloying, like the over-ripeness of decayed fruit on his tongue, and the world around him seemed to shudder violently long before the distant rumble of an engine reached him.

His jaw clenched, but his fingers remained loose and relaxed on the shotgun. He had a clear line of sight to the entrance of the property, but he doubted they'd be able to get a vehicle through there. They'd have to ram it through the undergrowth, which would announce their presence more than they already had. If they were smart, they'd abandon it and approach on foot.

He was counting on it.

It was unnatural to face down an opponent in his weaker form, but there were some advantages to it. Stealth was one of them. He was no nymph, of course, but he'd become a little bit more comfortable in the woods in the time he'd spent on Alashiya's land. In his smaller form, and especially at night when his skin darkened, he could blend into the trees much easier. If he stayed downwind, he'd be practically invisible.

Even if Sergei thought Taevas was hiding, he wouldn't expect him to be *stealthy*. Dragons didn't fight that way. Their surprise attacks came from the sky. The bulk of their fighting techniques relied on their brute strength more than anything else. It would be expected that he'd try to get the jump on them as quickly as possible, then attack.

He *would*, but first he had to even the playing field.

Taevas listened to his own breathing, his mind clear of anything besides razor-sharp focus. There was no breeze. Even the owl that hung out around the barn was still and watchful as it stood on a sagging beam, its golden eyes keen.

It wasn't a peaceful stillness that settled over the land. It was a malicious sort of quiet. The kind that waits.

A reedy figure bled out of the darkness across the grassy yard.

Taevas didn't tense. He didn't hold his breath. The rage he felt when the figure walked up to the front door and tried the knob like he *owned* it was muted. Locked away for a better time.

It wasn't too hard to guess that this was most likely Monty, the arrant who'd been to the property before.

The figure had the unmistakable shape of a rifle strapped to his back and despite the lack of sunlight, appeared to wear a baseball cap pulled low over his eyes. He moved with the slow, loping gait of someone used to sneaking up on the unsuspecting.

Taevas bit the inside of his cheek when Monty shoved his shoulder into the door. The old, crumbling door frame didn't stand a chance. He disappeared into the darkness of her home, violating the sanctuary she'd guarded for so long.

Watching as his Chosen's dwelling was breached was a nightmare. *Letting* it happen was worse.

What if she'd been in there alone?

The memory of watching someone break into her home so easily, so carelessly, would keep him up at night for years to come.

Alashiya's wards would've given her plenty of warning to run, but they weren't foolproof. The possibilities turned his stomach. Knowing that Monty was there in her sanctuary his finger inch toward the trigger of his ancient gun.

Taevas set his jaw. Acting now would be a death sentence. He had to wait. He *had* to.

His gaze swept across the yard to the treeline where Monty had emerged from. Alashiya had counted three men, Sergei, and Monty. There was always the chance that reinforcements were going to be called, but his gut told him that those men were on their own. An easy number to handle in his hardier form, certainly, but not impossible on two legs. He just had to get eyes on all of them. Especially Sergei.

Come on, you son of a bitch.

Another figure slipped from the trees, this time from a little farther away. Gun in hand, they circled the house before meeting up with Monty, who emerged from the side door. Another figure carrying a gun walked quickly to meet them at the door. They said nothing, but Monty made several clear gestures toward the trees.

One of the new men nodded once and backed toward the trees again, his gun raised. He wasn't gone long. Less than a minute later, Sergei followed him back out into the yard.

The moment the big dragon was free of the greenery, his wings sprang out to mantle around his shoulders. He stalked toward the house a lot less quietly than the humans had. Shrouded in darkness, he appeared less like Jaak and more...

The rattle of cuffs. A starchy pillow under his cheek. Sharp, searing pain in his wings. A huge shadow, blurred and dark, gesturing furiously in his direction.

He'd been sure before, but now there was no doubt in his mind.

Taevas watched the group move back toward Alashiya's house for a moment longer before he slipped deeper into the forest. He'd spent days learning the almost invisible trails his Chosen had so gently laid over her years walking the land. It turned out that even the featherlight footsteps of nymphs would eventually leave a path. He gratefully followed them around the back of the barn.

First, Sergei would want to confirm Taevas had been in the house, then they'd look in the barn — which meant that Taevas didn't have long to make it to the car.

Just as he thought, they'd left one man to guard the new, mud-flecked SUV. The man stood by the driver's door, his stance military-straight and gun at the ready. No doubt he was the get-away driver.

Taevas held still in the shadows a few yards away from the

guard and tested the air. Without much of a breeze it was difficult to get a good lock on his scent, but there was the faintest hint of ozone in the air.

Witch.

There was no time to wonder who he was or what Sergei was doing with one witch, or perhaps three. That would have to be worked out later.

He weighed his options. Fighting witches was tricky work. On one hand, they were small, weak, and could only protect themselves in one shape. On the other, it was almost impossible to tell what kind of abilities they were hiding by sight and scent alone.

For all Taevas knew, the witch might've been nearly powerless.

He could've also had the ability to stop Taevas's heart with a single touch, or rip open the fabric of the universe to drag him back into captivity before there was a chance to struggle.

As he'd learned in the war, there was no one-size-fits-all way to fight a witch, but the best bet would always be surprise. If this plan stood even half a chance of working, then he didn't have another choice, anyway.

Soundlessly propping the shotgun against a tree trunk, Taevas stooped low to pick up a dusty stone. Not knowing what his opponent was capable of, Taevas couldn't risk relying on Alashiya's wards to shield him from view, so he had to be careful to remain out of sight when he tossed the rock into the trees far to his left.

The guard's gun came up instantly. He swung to the side and peered into the trees from over the hood of the SUV.

Taevas leapt.

The gun was his first priority. His left hand went for the barrel of the bolt rifle at the same time that he kicked one knee out, sending the guard stumbling. Unable to completely dislodge the guard's grip, Taevas slammed butt of the rifle into his nose.

Blood splattered the side of the SUV. They grappled for the gun for too long.

A crackle of electricity built around the witch. The man's eyes, utterly devoid of feeling, went white with violent power. Dragons could take a lot, but the kind of voltage a powerful witch packed made even the most dangerous lightning storms look like child's play. He'd seen what could happen when the unwary tangled with a witch and had no interest in being cooked alive.

The witch reached for Taevas's bare shoulder and only just made contact as his head was slammed against the bloody side of the SUV. Bone crunched under Taevas's grip. When he went limp, he was tossed aside with a grunt.

Their scuffle lasted less than a minute, and the guard had only touched him for a second or two, but damage had been done. Taevas bit back a howl of pain as the skin on his shoulder bubbled. Ripping the gun away from the guard's hand, he stumbled back and shook his head hard.

There was no time for pain.

An examination of the guard proved mostly useless. He was dressed in basic hunting gear, but had nothing in his pockets. No tags, no tattoos. The only interesting things about him was that his hair was shaved close in a soldier's style and that he wore a plain gold chain around his neck.

A dragon who looks like Jaak and a handful of witches. Did he hire mercenaries?

Pulling some old, salvaged cord from his pocket, Taevas quickly bound the man's wrists to his ankles before dragging him into the bushes. He'd probably live, but Taevas wasn't particularly concerned one way or the other.

Slinging the rifle's strap over his shoulder, he ripped open the driver's door. The vehicle was brand new and obviously luxurious, with a spacious back seat, leather interior, and a navigation panel that came with autonomous capabilities. Taevas had been in enough cars like it to recognize the particular warp of the windows as being bolt-proof.

Aside from its defensive capabilities, it was a bizarre choice for a getaway vehicle, and even stranger for an abduction. Autonomous vehicles were flashy and easily traceable, whereas an older model wouldn't have been noticed on the road. Clearly, someone in this operation had more money than sense.

What the fuck is happening here?

Taevas's mind spun, but he still made sure to find the key fob skillfully hidden in the cup holder, of all places. Leaving it there, he popped the trunk and circled around the back.

Inside was everything he expected: dragon-ready restraints, a black bag, a rolled up tarp, a biometrically locked hatch holding what he could only assume was more weapons, and a small plastic case. Within the case, he found nearly a dozen capped syringes of what looked like two different medications. He recognized one as a powerful sedative, but the other was unlabeled.

Taevas's lips thinned. It didn't take a genius to guess that whatever was in those unlabeled syringes was the suppressant. His skin crawled just holding it.

As he aged, he'd learned that there was no true honor in war or fighting, but there was something truly vile about drugging an opponent.

His first impulse was to empty the case onto the dirt and slam his heel down on them, rendering them useless. But now wasn't the time for morals.

His Chosen had been threatened. Nothing, not even his honor, mattered more than that.

Shoving a handful of syringes into his pockets, he quietly shut the trunk. His gaze darted to the trees. Worry for Alashiya pulsed with every beat of his heart.

I could end this now, he thought, bracing a hand on the hood of the vehicle. *I could take this car, track her down, and we could run.*

He wanted to. By all the gods, he *wanted* to.

But if he left now, the car would almost certainly be tracked by Sergei from the air. If he picked up Alashiya without finishing things, he'd put her in even more danger. They could be chased. Run off the road. Hunted from above by a dragon who probably wouldn't hesitate to burn the vehicle and anyone in it.

Regret tasted like bile on his tongue. Taevas couldn't help but wonder if he'd made the wrong decisions. If he'd taken the risk of being surveilled and just *called* someone from the Thompsons' phone, would any of this have happened? What if he'd just left on his own with a promise to return for his Chosen?

He couldn't escape the feeling that he'd messed everything up. His people and his Chosen needed him to make the right decisions, but he couldn't. The great Isand, who'd united the clans and signed the Peace Charter — a failure at the one thing that truly mattered in life.

And now Alashiya was out there somewhere on her own, afraid and angry with him. If he never saw her again—

No. No. That wasn't an option.

Taevas shook himself and turned back toward the house. Following a different trail than the one he'd used before, he got back to the yard just in time to see Sergei gesturing harshly for his men to search the woods.

Gods, I hope Shiya got off the property.

All he wanted to do was slink into the trees and take out the guards one by one, making sure no one would be able to hunt her down, but he forced himself to trust her instincts. The only reason *he* had been able to find her when she hid was because he was intimately familiar with her scent. If those men were as human as they looked, witch or arrant, they wouldn't have that advantage.

She was a nymph. A queen. They could walk within a few inches of her and be none the wiser. He had to believe that.

Taevas watched the men stalk into the darkness between the trees. He held his breath as a shudder passed through the leafy canopies. Perhaps it was a breeze, but something felt different. While he'd always gotten the sense that the forest was alive and hostile, it didn't compare to the electric current of menace that pervaded the air.

The forest hadn't exactly been kind to him when he chased Alashiya down, but it hadn't felt like *this*. Perhaps it was because it'd known he didn't mean her any harm. Maybe it sensed the connection between them or that to some degree Taevas had been imbued with her essence and recognized him as belonging to her.

These men had no such claim.

CHAPTER FORTY-ONE

THE HAIR ROSE ON THE BACK OF HIS NECK. HE GLANCED to his left and found the many black eyes of an old, skinny birch tree staring back at him.

The forest around his Chosen's land had been soaked in nymph blood and magic for over a century. It hadn't protected her grove when the shifters attacked, when they were new to the land and its power, but he wondered what it was capable of doing *now* for the lone steward that had loved it for so long.

Mentally crossing his fingers that the forest was capable of doing more than causing a twisted ankle, Taevas crouched low and moved as quickly as he was able around the back of the barn. He circled around to the side that had taken the most damage when he arrived.

Half the roof had caved in on top of the old rusted pick-up truck Alashiya said belonged to her grandparents. He'd briefly considered attempting to repair it, but after moving some debris and peeking under the hood, he'd been forced to set the plan aside. Taevas was good with politics, computers, and wood. Not mechanics. Even if he had the parts, he didn't have the first idea where to start on an engine that hadn't been touched in over forty years.

That didn't mean the truck was useless, however.

Ducking under fallen beams and the half-crumbled wall, Taevas used it for cover as he slipped inside the barn. It went against his instincts, but he swung the bolt rifle over his shoulder, allowing him to move more easily amongst the rubble and a lifetime of discarded objects.

Putting himself into position, Taevas fished in his pocket for the suppressant. He kept his gaze on the cracked door of the barn, where he could just make out Sergei's broad shape, as he used his thumb claw to flick the cap off the syringe.

The itch to pull the rifle over his shoulder and aim...

I can't. He'd probably survive it, and then I'd lose every advantage I have.

Dragons didn't have the tough skin of elves or gargoyles, but they could take a hit. Unless he went for a head shot, instinct would see Sergei shift instantly, limiting the damage, and effectively destroying Taevas's entire plan.

So instead of taking the shot, he sucked in a deep breath and groped behind him for the ancient tool box he'd become so familiar with during his stay.

His fingers closed around a handful of screws. Like he did with the guard by the SUV, he tossed all but one of the screws into the darkness. They clattered against old, moth-eaten furniture and rusted farm equipment.

Taevas pressed the back of his head against a beam and prayed that he was out of sight and that Sergei wouldn't do the smart thing, which was to shift at the first sign of trouble.

It was impossible to tell at first. The sound of the door being pushed open could've come from talons or a tail. Taevas didn't dare lean out of his hiding spot to check. He was forced to wait and listen.

The sound of a boot scuffing against the dusty floor made him smile.

Sergei moved just out of sight, every heavy footfall telling his progress as he tried to hunt the source of the noise. Taevas's hiding place was in a far corner, where Alashiya's grandfather's workbench had been nearly swallowed by stacks of boxes, crates, and a couch propped up against a wall and a beam. The shadows were dark and the smells of dust and mold were overpowering. For Sergei to spot him there, he'd need to come close — which was exactly what Taevas wanted.

Taking yet another risk, he flicked the last of his screws a little bit ahead and to the right of his hiding spot. The noise it made was soft, but dragon ears were keen.

Sergei had barely taken a step past the dusty couch before Taevas moved. The needle of the syringe was just a silver flash as it sank into the meat of the blue dragon's bicep.

Slamming the plunger down, Taevas narrowly dodged a swipe at his head. He wasn't quite so lucky with the punch aimed at his ribs. Freshly healed, they cracked instantly.

"Fuck!" Sergei snarled, going in for another hit. "You are so much more trouble than you're worth!"

White spots floated in front of his eyes as they grappled in the tight space. Sergei had more weight on him, which was an advantage in the close quarters, but Taevas knew the barn. He wasn't sure how long it would take for the suppressants to kick in, so he had to keep them in a confined area that wouldn't allow Sergei to shift. Twisting to one side, he used Sergei's momentum to slam his side into the sturdy workbench.

From somewhere outside the barn, a man's scream broke the quiet of the night before it was cut off abruptly.

Taevas threw his entire weight behind a punch to Sergei's kidney. Speaking through gritted teeth, he demanded, "Who *are* you?"

"What? Don't recognize me?" Sergei kicked Taevas's thigh at a harsh angle, making him stagger back as he fought to keep his balance. Face twisted in a furious grimace, Sergei spat, "You really don't fucking know who I *am?*"

Taevas raised his arms, blocking a rain of heavy blows until there was enough of an opening to land a jab to Sergei's throat.

The bigger dragon choked, his eyes bulging, as Taevas whipped his elbow across his face to shatter his nose.

"You look like one of Jaak's boys," he grunted, shoving Sergei far enough away that he could bring the rifle back over his shoulder. Aiming it at his head, Taevas breathed through the pain in his ribs, face, and wings. "It's hard to say, though, since he had so many of them. What number was your mother, huh? Was she the fifth Chosen? The tenth? They never seemed to last long."

Sergei gripped the edge of the work bench. His face was a mask of horror — all blood and fangs and fury. His chest rose and fell with huge, labored breaths when he snarled, "Don't talk about my fucking mother!"

"No, you're right. That isn't fair. She wasn't actually his Chosen, was she? None of them were. He treated his women like he treated the rest of us — like they were disposable." Arching his brows, he asked, "You aren't here to get revenge for that son of a bitch, are you?"

Sergei swiped the space beneath his nose. Blood smeared across his night-darkened cheek in a grisly swipe. "You know, you've always talked too much. I found you a lot more tolerable when you were drugged."

Taevas flicked the safety off. The hum of the plasma cartridge coming online filled the dusty air. "Sorry, I'm just trying to get a read on the dragon stupid enough to kidnap me. What was the plan, Sergei?"

A blue glow lit the backs of Sergei's bloody teeth. Even in such a tight space, it was obvious he wanted to shift. His muscles bunched and Taevas's finger inched toward the trigger, but nothing happened.

A cruel sense of pleasure washed through him as he watched the realization flash in Sergei's eyes.

There would be no shifting. No more surprises. They were on equal ground now.

"I knew I should've just killed you," Sergei growled.

"Sounds like you really don't like me. Must be because I killed your daddy." A bitter taste flooded Taevas's mouth. "You know, I always wondered if any of his offspring would come after me. People told me I should keep an eye on all of you just in case, but I thought it just wasn't fair to judge all of you based on what your father did. I guess that was naive of me."

The strong tendons on either side of Sergei's neck stood out sharply when he snarled, "You think you were merciful? That you were *kind* to let us just disappear?"

"When the alternative was banishing innocent children from the 'Riik in the middle of a war? Yeah, I think I was right."

Sergei was silent for a beat. "Good gods, you really think that, don't you? That you did us a *favor.*"

Tamping down his rising impatience, Taevas held his aim directly between the bases of Sergei's shiny horns when he asked, "Seems you don't agree with me. I'd love to hear why."

"You took everything from me. Isn't that enough?" A smile twisted Sergei's bloody lips as he leaned forward, fearlessly putting him even closer to the business end of the rifle. "And now I'm going to take everything from you. Including that pretty nymph you've been nesting with."

A flash of icy fury passed over every inch of Taevas's body. Gripping the gun, he softly asked, "Is that so?"

"I thought I smelled something familiar on her, but I was distracted by everything else. How soft she is. How good she'll look in *my* nest. How it'll fucking *kill* you when she's carrying *my—*"

"Finish that sentence and I'll stop caring about the ethics of executing you right here, right now." Taevas had to work hard to keep his breathing under control. Everything in him wanted to strike out and eliminate the threat. "I saw how your father treated his *Chosens.* You want Alashiya? You'll have to kill me first."

Sergei hadn't exactly seemed calm and reasonable before, but something changed in his expression. It morphed into the kind of rage that men struggled to come back from.

Eyes wide and veins tracing paths across his temples, he hissed, "I am *not* my fucking father!"

Interesting.

Taevas took half a step back, his mind whirring. That didn't sound like someone who'd come for revenge on Jaak's behalf. It *sounded* an awful lot like someone who hated the old Isand almost as much as Taevas did.

Knowing it was probably only a matter of seconds before one or all of Sergei's backup came running to the barn, Taevas tossed out, "You got a problem with Jaak? Weird that you'd throw everything away to get revenge on his behalf."

"I'm not here for *him*," Sergei hissed. "I'm here for my mother."

"What on Burden's Earth did I do to—"

A cacophony outside the barn cut him off. It was the roar of an engine tearing through foliage, the screech of tires, and a man's furious shout. Before Taevas could even begin to wonder what had happened, Sergei lunged for the rifle.

They wrestled, stumbling and lurching toward the barn's entrance. Aware that if either of them got a shot off at this close range there was a fifty-fifty chance he'd be hit, Taevas desperately tried to put some space between them.

They burst out the rotting door and into the yard. Sergei barreled down on him, using his weight to force Taevas off balance and release his grip on the rifle. The glare of headlights illuminated the yard, casting the two bloody dragons in a spotlight as they fought for control over the weapon.

There was no time to wonder who was behind the wheel or if that shape on the ground was Monty, crumpled and missing his hat. Taevas's sole focus was on Sergei, until his opponent's tail swiped around to hook on the base of one of his wings.

One hard jerk was all it took. Agony unlike anything he'd felt before brought Taevas to his knees. His grip on the gun spasmed as Sergei ripped it from his hands.

The whine of the rifle going off wasn't as loud as a shotgun's blast, but it was no less devastating in its impact. He didn't feel the pain of the shot as he fell backward into the grass, however, he *did* feel something when he watched the SUV surge forward and slam full-force into Sergei.

Staring blankly at a dusty tire, Taevas could only listen to a door opening, the nearly silent tread of swift footsteps over grass, and the cocking of an old shotgun.

A high, trembling voice made him shudder with equal parts relief and fear. "If you killed my husband, I swear to every god listening that next time I find you, I'll shoot something you'll never be able to fix."

The crack of the shotgun rang in his ears, blocking out everything else. His vision darkened, but he forced himself to hold on and ignore the pain starting to lick across every nerve like dragonfire until he felt the cool touch of his Chosen's fingers on his cheek.

"Oh, gods, Taevas!" His name came out ragged but so, so sweet.

"Kill him?" he wheezed, trying to get his eyes to focus on her blurry outline.

Alashiya was close to him. So wonderfully close. Her hands were everywhere, probably looking for some way to help, but there was little to be done for a bolt shot.

"N-no," she gasped, "I only got him a little. I—"

Searching for her hand with fingers that were beginning to go numb, he slurred, "Left pocket. Sedatives."

"Sedatives? Why do— For Sergei?"

"Can't follow."

He must've lost consciousness for a minute, because he couldn't recall any questions or arguments before feeling her extracting one of the sedative syringes from his pocket. That was very unlike her. His queen always argued with him. It was one of his favorite things about her.

Time moved strangely as his body went into shock. It felt like little more than a moment but also a very long time before she came back to him, speaking quickly to assure him that she'd done it. There were tears in her voice. He absolutely loathed that.

"Shh, no crying," he murmured. "You can't drive if you're crying."

"Oh gods, you're right. I need to get you to the ranger's station or— or a..."

"No." Taevas found her wrist and held it fast. "You need to... we need to go to the 'Riik. Don't trust anyone. No one but clan or Wing."

"That's hours and hours away!" A note of raw hysteria had entered her voice. "Taevas, you could *die!*"

"Won't." At least, he was pretty sure. It wasn't like it was the first time he'd been shot, so he was fairly certain he would be able to tell if he was about to die. Probably.

Soft hands clutched his cheeks, holding tight. "How do you know? Tell me how you *know!*"

"Because," he breathed, "I just found you."

Chapter Forty-Two

She'd run out of tears two hundred and ten miles into the drive.

Her eyes burned with strain as the sun rose, casting an ugly, watered-down sort of light over the forested landscape. Every muscle in her body was tight. She had to keep her teeth clenched hard to stop them from rattling. Everytime the modern navigation system in the SUV chimed to let her know they'd be turning soon, or merging onto a road, or that she'd strayed slightly over the line, she had to swallow a scream.

She was a *terrible* driver.

It didn't seem to matter much, though. The stolen SUV came equipped with a semi-autonomous driving feature she'd accidentally activated when she clumsily tapped '*Dragon Roost, Drummond Island*' into the glossy screen. A pleasant voice had calmly instructed her to keep her hands on the wheel at all times in case of emergencies but that she could otherwise relax.

Like that was possible.

Alashiya couldn't stop herself from glancing over her shoulder and into the backseat every minute or so. She had to see for herself that Taevas's chest still rose and fell. That his eyelids still flickered. That his clawed fingers twitched.

She wanted to believe him when he said he wouldn't die but she couldn't. Not when she'd seen the ragged, cauterized hole in his shoulder — dangerously close to his chest and all the vital things it contained.

He'd already been weak from illness and whatever drugs he'd been pumped with. It was difficult to imagine his body, dragon-tough as it was, would be able to keep up with yet another horrible injury. Not to mention the swelling and cuts on his face and the bruises that banded his powerful rib cage.

She'd been tempted over and over and over to stop, to ask the SUV's computer to take them to a hospital. Alashiya had stared out into the bright cone of light projected by the vehicle's head-lights and thought, *He'll die because of me.*

But everytime she made the choice, she couldn't follow through with it.

This is my fault. I didn't listen to him before. I was selfish and scared. If I'd listened, we could've left days ago.

It didn't matter to her that disregarding his instructions had *also* saved him. If she'd listened that night, she wouldn't have snuck back toward the house, stolen the SUV, and used its shiny grille to stop Monty from storming into the barn, his gun raised. But that didn't mean much when the whole awful thing could've been completely avoided in the first place.

Alashiya hadn't stopped shaking since she managed to load Taevas into the backseat. The tremors had died down some, but they continued to run down her arms and torso in little rivers of terror. If she wasn't glancing over her shoulder to make sure Taevas hadn't died then she looked up through the tinted sun roof, her stomach curdled with the anticipation of seeing a winged shape against the stars.

Time didn't pass in minutes but in road signs, navigation alerts, and the little sounds of pain Taevas made whenever they hit a bump.

Alashiya had lived nights of horror and grief. She'd listened to the screams of her family as they were slaughtered until the forest took pity on her and dragged her into the darkness, where roots pierced her skin and breath was a memory. She'd discovered her grandmother slumped over the kitchen table, her paring knife clutched in the tight grip of rigor mortis. She'd watched the slow decline of her grandfather as he lost himself to grief and ill health, helpless to do little more than witness the creep of Grim's shadow.

She was no stranger to loss or pain, but *this*... Alashiya didn't think she'd survive it.

Taevas deserved better than a pitiful death in the back of a stolen car. He was kind and smart and wonderful. So wonderful, even when he was a huge pain in the ass. To live in a world where he didn't exist was utterly unthinkable.

Every leaf would lose its color. Every drop of water would sour. Every sunrise would turn pale and sickly.

Whatever happened between them didn't matter. Even if he opened his eyes and had no memory of her, she would be okay. He'd be *alive*.

So she locked her fingers around the wheel and didn't think of what she'd left behind or what she'd done. She didn't wonder if Monty was still alive or notice that she was smeared with blood. She drove and she drove and she prayed so loudly that it was a scream in her mind, a howl to be heard by the gods who'd never seen fit to listen to her before.

Alashiya barely registered it when she crossed the border into the Draakonriik. Even the thought of being so far away from home would've made her sick to her stomach before, but now she only felt the smallest spark of relief.

When the gray sky split open to release a torrent of summer rain, she didn't notice. The other cars on the road were blurs of muted color. The landscape was a smudge in the corner of her eye.

The navigation system assured her over and over again that they were on the fastest route to Drummond Island — and that it was a restricted space, which would require identification to enter

— but as the hours crawled by, Alashiya felt in her bones that they wouldn't make it.

The hook behind her breast bone tugged softly but insistently, and the whispers of her grove were loud. It was as if everyone was trying to speak at once, all of them with something vital to tell her, but she couldn't make sense of the din. Exhausted, terrified, and desperate to do as Taevas asked of her, she wished she could cover her ears until it all went away.

There were two hundred miles left when the whispers coalesced into one unified voice.

It pierced through the haze that had clouded her mind with a single word: *Stop.*

Alashiya jumped. Her aching fingers spasmed on the steering wheel, and before she knew what she was doing, she'd already disengaged the self-driving function and clumsily guided the vehicle off the road.

Her pulse throbbed in her ears as she sat for a moment, unable to process what she'd done or why.

Stop, the grove instructed her, clearer than they'd ever been. It sounded like her grandmother but also like her father, her aunties, her cousins, and everyone she'd never met but loved in the very foundation of her being.

It sounded like the First. The queen, Kubaba.

Her eyes burned with tears she could no longer make. "I stopped," she croaked, yanking on the wheel like tearing it off might fix everything. "What do I do? What do I *do?*"

Bring him in.

"Bring him— I'm *trying* to take him home."

Alashiya twisted around to look at Taevas. She'd lowered the back seat to make a big enough space and thrown Adon's robe over him in a desperate bid to keep him comfortable. With the way he was sprawled and the robe obscuring her view, it wasn't easy to see everything, but she knew instantly that he'd gotten worse.

Bring him in, the voices urged her. *Bring him home.*

A chill permeated every cell of her body. Her fingers fumbled with the latch of her seatbelt. "Taevas? Taevas, please— I'm trying—"

Her legs were numb when she threw herself out the driver's seat. Stumbling and immediately soaked to the bone, she could barely draw a breath in through the constriction of her throat as she tore open the passenger door.

Alashiya threw herself into the backseat and crawled on her hands and knees to be beside him. Cupping his ashen face with wet, shaking hands, she frantically searched for a pulse, for a breath, anything at all.

The tiniest flutter of his long lashes was all she got. The hook in her chest pulled hard enough to hurt.

Alashiya slumped against the siding. Bile churned in her empty stomach as she stroked the sweaty hair back from his cheeks and forehead. "I can feel you leaving me," she choked out. "You said you wouldn't. You promised you'd always chase me. You *promised.* You said you'd give me anything I wanted. You said you'd— you said I'd never be alone again. You can't break your promises, *argaman mlk.* You just can't."

She leaned down to press her lips to his cool forehead. A distant rumble of thunder rolled over them like the tolling of a funeral bell.

Whispering into his skin, she asked, "How can I argue with you if you're dead? How can you smother me in bed if you leave me now? How can you boss me around if you abandon me here?"

Bring him home.

Alashiya's shoulders shook with a sob. "I can't. He won't make it."

Shiya, the grove called, as sharp and immediate as a lightning bolt through her mind. Kubaba's voice was the crack of a sturdy branch in the wind. *Bring him to us.*

For a moment, all she heard was the drumming of rain on the SUV's roof and her own ragged breathing.

"We're the stuff of life," she whispered, repeating words

spoken over generations. "We carry Blight's gift. We guard it and give it to others."

Alashiya's gaze slid over to the floor of the backseat, where the bag Taevas had packed had been tossed haphazardly just before she figured out how to use the damn silly key fob to start the vehicle. The hook in her chest became an unbearable, tearing thing.

She'd seen the glint of her sewing shears in the depths of the bag when she pulled out the robe. A wild, awful sort of hope grew alongside the pain in her chest.

There was no telling that it'd work, and there was so very much wrong with what she planned to do, but Alashiya didn't have a choice. If the ghosts of her grove were wrong, then at least she'd know she tried everything.

Swiping her eyes with her sleeve, she put all thoughts except the need to save him out of her mind and leaned over to grab the bag. Her hand didn't shake when she closed her fingers around the cool metal of her shears. A heavy sort of calm settled over her.

As gently as she could, Alashiya rearranged his arm so his right hand lay against her thigh. It rested there, limp, his claw-tipped fingers half-curled like he reached for her even now.

"I'm sorry," she said, voice stronger than it was before. "I'm sorry that I'm taking this choice from you. I'm sorry if you wake up tomorrow and hate me. I'm sorry that I don't care. I can't let you die."

Taking the shears into her left hand, she spread the blades and pressed it into the center of her palm. Speaking loudly now, as if he might hear her better if she raised her voice, she vowed, "I swear to carry you. I swear to honor you. I swear to provide for you. I swear to warm you when the night is cold and find you when the days are dark. I swear to love you now and in the hyphae, long after Grim has returned what her father gave us."

She always thought she'd feel it, that she'd flinch beneath the shield of her veil as the cool blade sliced her skin. But she didn't. She felt nothing — no pain, no fear, no hesitation. Blood pooled in her hand and ran down her wrist to stain her cuffs as she placed the blade against Taevas's palm.

"I won't ask you to say the words back to me," she whispered. "Just live. That's all I need."

Cutting him was harder than cutting herself, but she did it. One quick, shallow cut across his palm. His skin was tougher than hers, and yet it gave way under the sharp blade of her shears.

Licking her dry lips, Alashiya sent up one last prayer before she sealed their hands together.

There was no witness to bind them tightly, ensuring their blood mixed, so she had to do it herself. Alashiya bound them with the gold-embroidered sash of his robe, clumsily and without ceremony, as she pressed down hard, pinning his limp hand against her thigh. There was no cheer from friends and family. There was no levity, no relief, no thrill over what the future held.

There was only stillness. The thump of her pulse in her ears and in her hand. The nearly inaudible rasp of Taevas's shallow, watery breaths.

A tear, pulled from somewhere deeper than the well of her grief, slid down her cheek. "Please. Please stay."

Thunder rolled overhead again. It was loud enough to shake the SUV. Wind howled through the open passenger door and whipped heavy raindrops inside. Alashiya caught the flash of lightning through her closed eyelids.

She held herself there for so long that she lost all sense of time. She'd never done this before, but she thought she'd know if it worked. He'd be there, his essence woven into the hyphae and twined with her own. But how long would that take? She'd always thought it was immediate. Was it different for someone who wasn't a nymph? Was he just too weak?

Did I do it wrong?

CHAPTER FORTY-THREE

AS THE MINUTES DRAGGED ON WITH NO CHANGE, despair began to seep into the fragile weave of her hope. She dared not let go, but she couldn't hold on forever. If her blood couldn't help him, then she had to keep going.

Choking back the wave of dry sobs that so desperately wanted out, Alashiya pressed one last kiss to his lips before she reluctantly pulled the knot of the sash apart and peeled her bloody hand away from his.

The grove was silent. The hook in her chest had disappeared. She was utterly alone as she climbed out of the backseat and stared at the desolate stretch of road. Rain pelted her from what felt like all sides. Above her, streaks of lightning danced through the dense clouds. Blood dripped from her fingertips to soak into the wet gravel beneath her boots.

Alashiya closed her eyes. *Please. Please. If anyone is listening, please save hi—*

A white light flashed through her eyelids, so bright and all-consuming it seemed to sear her all the way to the backs of her eye sockets. For a split second there was no sound — or perhaps it only seemed that way, as Alashiya's mind struggled to process the crack of lighting that struck the ground not six feet away from her.

She turned away instinctively. Hunching against the open door, it took her a moment to process that she hadn't been hit, and a few more to regain her hearing and sight.

Blinking hard to clear her eyes of the dancing lights, she almost missed the voice that called out to her. "Do you need help?"

Heart lurching, Alashiya turned to gape at the woman standing where the lightning struck. Naked as a jaybird, taller than Alashiya by at least a foot, and peering at her with eyes of pure black, she didn't seem to notice the rain — or that her bone-white hair drifted upward like a glowing, sparking banner of moonlight.

All of her glowed. Against the gloom of the rain-soaked road, the being who stood before Alashiya appeared otherworldly in the extreme.

Her lips parted, but no sound came out. She didn't know what to say. She didn't even know what kind of being she was talking to.

The woman's angular brows swept down over her inky eyes. "I saw you from above," she explained in a lilting, accented voice. "You parked terribly, which only bad drivers and people in trouble do. And you are bleeding. This isn't normal for you, yes?"

A bubble of hysterical laughter escaped Alashiya, which only made the woman's frown deepen.

Taking one fluid, almost floating step toward the SUV, she noted, "That... doesn't sound like a happy laugh. Do you—"

A jolt of alarm drew Alashiya's back up. Pressing herself into the gap between the partially opened door and the frame, she bellowed, "Don't come any closer!"

The woman stopped instantly. Her head tilted to one side. Alashiya couldn't tell where her gaze went when her eyes were so... different, but she was almost certain they crawled over the blacked out windows of the SUV.

"I won't hurt you," the woman explained, the words lilting up at the end so they almost sounded like a question. "I was just out looking for— This doesn't matter. I only want to help. Did you know you are bleeding a lot?"

A burn had set in to the slice in Alashiya's palm and crept upward into her arm. It didn't matter. Who cared if she got an infection or somehow bled out from it? Nothing mattered except Taevas.

No one but clan and Wing, he'd said. No one else could be trusted.

Alashiya swallowed hard and wished she hadn't left her shears in the car. "Don't come any closer, please."

"Why not?"

"Because I don't know you," she answered, gritting her teeth against the burn that had begun to permeate not just her lower arm, but her shoulder, too.

The woman eyed her for a heartbeat before nodding once. "This is wise. I didn't like speaking to strangers either, until I learned to do it well. Tell me your name so we aren't strangers anymore."

"I..." She lifted her uninjured hand to wipe rain out of her eyes. Despite being drenched in cool water, her head felt hot and her skin a little too tight. A pressure built in her chest — like some great thing was coiling, loop over loop, end over end, readying itself to spring.

"I'm Alashiya," she finally answered.

The pale woman blinked. Little sparks fizzed in the air every-time a raindrop touched her skin. "I haven't heard this name. Who gave it to you?"

Alashiya felt like she'd stepped from one nightmare to another, except this one didn't even have the decency to make sense. "Why does that matter?"

"My name was given to me by my *ema* and my *isa* and my cousin," the woman offered, like it was very important. Her expression was grave, and if Alashiya looked closely enough through the haze of rain, she thought she saw exhaustion there. "Now you tell me who gave you your name and we'll both know something about the other. We won't be strangers anymore."

Alashiya could only hear every other word. The impending sense that something was happening, that some great change was about to overcome her was a roar in her ears. Heart beginning to race, she answered, "I think my mother named me. She— she said I should have a queen's name."

A fleeting half-smile lit the woman's aquiline face. "It is a very good name. Mine is Hele. It is better."

Alashiya's bloody hand slid away from the door. From the stranger's lips, it sounded like *heh-lay*. Hele.

I know that name. I know Hele.

What had Taevas told her? She scrambled to recall details, but everything was so fuzzy, and the horror of the last several hours clung to her mind like a film. All she could remember was that Hele was adopted and a genius and an elemental. Alashiya had never seen one before, but she couldn't imagine a being made of pure magic *not* looking like the woman standing there.

Please, please, please. Please be her.

A hum replaced the heat in her skin — a rising pulse of magic as deep and ancient as the roots from which the first nymph sprang. And there, woven into that old magic was him. *Taevas.* As big and loud and beautiful as he was in life, so too was he in the hyphae.

A strong royal purple thread braided with hers, tying them together forever — and holding him to this side of Grim's riverbank. To life.

Alashiya stumbled away from the door to grab the woman's arm. Electricity rattled the nerves in her hand, but she held tight. Voice cracking, she begged, "Are you Hele? *The* Hele?"

The woman looked down at her with a deep frown. "I am Hele Aždaja, of clan Orlova and Piiritu. Chosen of Vael, cousin of the great Isand Taevas Aždaja, and daughter of Valerie and Constantin. Why?"

I know those names. They're clan. Oh gods, they're clan!

Alashiya's legs couldn't hold her any longer. She crumpled to the ground. Pressing her hands into the wet gravel, she bowed her head and begged, "Please, Hele— You have to save him!"

Hele crouched beside her. Tentatively running her hand over Alashiya's spine, she asked, "Save who, strange woman?"

Alashiya turned her face up. Rain slid down her cheeks, over her lips, and dripped from her chin when she gasped, *"Taevas."*

CHAPTER FORTY-FOUR

IT'D BEEN A VERY LONG TIME SINCE TAEVAS WOKE UP IN a hospital room, but it wasn't an experience one never forgot — or could mistake for anything else.

He knew where he was long before he put anything else together. The scent of sterile air, the starchiness of the sheets, the lethargy that came with mild pain medication... It was all familiar and awful in its mundanity.

Taevas lay in the bed, unmoving. His eyelids were too heavy to lift, and his limbs were even worse off. But for the first time in what felt like months, there was no pain. There was only the odd metallic aftertaste of medication on his tongue and a fuzziness in his mind, like dozens of people stood just outside, speaking in low voices.

That... was strange.

Taevas's brow furrowed. Working his dry tongue against the back of his fangs, he tried to focus on the distant murmur. He definitely wasn't alone. That should've bothered him. He hadn't been around anyone except his Alashiya in weeks. There was no way—

His claws curled into the crisp sheets. *Shiya. Where's my Shiya?*

She was near. He *knew* she was. Taevas could feel her presence with absolute certainty. She stood beside him, close enough to feel her body heat but not touching. The great, burning glow of her was *there*.

So why couldn't he smell her?

Something was wrong. An alarm bell began to toll in his mind, cutting through the pleasant haze of sleep and medication.

It took several tries, but he eventually managed to pry his eyes open enough to take in the blurry shapes of a modern hospital suite. Sunlight spilled in from a window to his left, casting the rest of the room in soft shadows. The hum of the air filtration system was low but constant, and the machines hooked up to him made their own gentle noises as they did their jobs.

Besides his own breathing and the hospital sounds, the room was completely silent. The crowd he'd heard was nowhere to be seen. He couldn't make out any conversation or even the tread of shoes in the hall.

Disoriented, Taevas forced his head to turn. He expected to find his Chosen in the chair next to the bed, but when his eyes finally focused, he discovered his uncle slumped there.

Constantin had his forearms braced on his knees and his head bowed. Taevas couldn't make out his face, but he didn't need to. The position of the older dragon's wings said enough.

I'm home, he realized, trying to work some moisture into his mouth so he could speak. *But where is my Shiya?*

The certainty that she was *right there* only confused him more. Taevas swore he could feel the beat of her heart, ever-so-slightly out of sync with his own, and the rhythm of her breathing. She was nearby and she was awake and she was well. All of that was exactly what he wanted, but he couldn't shake the feeling that something was wrong. Terribly, completely wrong.

They were clearly in the 'Riik, which was a relief, except he couldn't remember how they'd gotten there. His memories weren't patchy and disjointed like they'd been when he woke up in Alashiya's barn, and yet there was a huge gap that spanned the time between being shot and waking up in the hospital room.

A series of incredibly important things must've happened during that time, but he clearly hadn't been awake to witness them, which set his teeth on edge. Because if he'd been unconscious, that meant that his Chosen had done exactly as he asked and gotten him all the way to the Draakonriik on her own.

The need to see her, to know exactly what had happened while he was passed out, pressed down on him. A low alarm began to sound from the machine closest to his bed. A series of quick beeps made Constantin jerk upright.

"Vennapoeg," he croaked, rising from his chair to grip the rail on the side of Taevas's bed. "Thank the gods you're awake. How are you? Can you speak?"

His uncle's lined face seemed to have aged another couple decades since Taevas last saw him. Despite all his losses and hardships, Constantin looked good for his age. His laugh lines were deep and his eyes sparkled with good humor, just as Taevas's father's had.

But the levity that normally shined from him was dampened when he squeezed Taevas's hand and pressed a kiss to his knuckles. His eyes closed as he whispered a prayer of thanks to the gods.

"Onu," Taevas managed to rasp, "what happened?"

Gently lowering Taevas's hand back onto the bed, Constantin shook his head and let out a long, shuddering breath. "I need to ask you the same thing. I only have half the story."

"Tell me."

"You're not well, *vennapoeg.*" Constantin adjusted the blankets across Taevas's chest, his brow deeply furrowed and his lips pressed tight. "You should rest before we debrief. Gods know it will take a long time. A *very* long time."

Feeling more himself, and therefore more alarmed, with every passing second, Taevas arched his neck against the pillows and blinked hard.

Work, he commanded his mind and body. *We've been weak for too long. Wake up, get moving, find our Shiya.*

"Give me the brief version. Everything after I was taken. Tell me about the Wing." His voice sounded like soundpaper, but the words came out clear enough.

"You need water." Constantin hurried over to a little table, where a pitcher of water and a cup were waiting. He came back to the bed just as fast and carefully angled the soft silicone straw toward Taevas's lips.

When half the cup had been drained, he said, "I'll give you the short version and then I'll call the healers in to check on you."

Taevas swallowed. His voice sounded marginally better when he muttered, "Fine."

"First, no one in the Wing was injured when you were taken," his uncle informed him. "That stumped us for a while, and there was a very thorough investigation into whether we had a traitor, but there's no evidence of that."

Encouraging him to take another drink, Constantin continued, "There was an attack on the solstice. Not just you, but every leader in the UTA. There's a lot of evidence that it was coordinated by a militant faction of Glory's Temple — some new version of the Ardeo — but actually linking the attacks has been difficult. It looks like every hit was planned by them but carried out by separate groups either hired or with their own motives. It's been a fucking mess to untangle."

The Ardeo? Taevas frowned. The Ardeo had once been a spectacularly powerful military branch of Glory's Temple, but it'd been disbanded hundreds of years ago when the Collapse began. Since then, Glory's Temple had taken a much less active role in politics and state games, but since they were the largest religious organization in the world, they still held considerable power.

None of that explained why they'd coordinate hits on all the leaders of the UTA, or how in the world Sergei was involved.

Dread coiled in his belly when he asked, "Deaths?"

Constantin set the empty cup on the bedside table with a sigh. "One."

"Who?" Bile crawled up his throat. *Please don't say Teddy. He's just a boy, and he's freshly mated. Killing him... that's too fucking cruel.*

"Queen Sigrid," Constantin answered, his tone grave. "She was shot in her home. Lee was attacked but came out fine. Sophie Goode was in critical condition for a while. She was just released from the hospital."

"What about Teddy?"

Only his uncle's small smile stopped Taevas from snapping at him to talk faster. "Your *protege* is fine. He and Healer Goode were nearly shot at a solstice ceremony, but were saved by High Priestess Zaskodna and her mate, who broke open the whole mad plot."

Taevas felt a little bad for the amount of relief he experienced, but he'd never been particularly fond of the old war bat Queen Sigrid, so it couldn't be helped. He liked her daughter Astrid more anyway.

Relaxing a little, he said, "That explains a little bit of what happened to me. I was kidnapped, but something clearly went wrong. They weren't prepared to hold me for as long as they did."

The smile fell from Constantin's face. "Our understanding is that the new Ardeo were working in collaboration with other groups. If they'd planned to pass you off or something, that could've been disrupted when everything was exposed."

"I don't know who else they were working with, but I know who kidnapped *me.*"

Constantin's expression hardened. "Who?"

"One of Jaak's offspring. A man named Sergei." Taevas let out a long breath. "I don't think he's dead, so we'll need to hunt him down. Shouldn't be too hard. He's a big blue bastard with gilded horns. Hard to miss."

"One of *Jaak's* sons?" Constantin looked as confused as Taevas had been. "We knew there was a dragon involved, but we didn't even think it could be connected to one of them. They've been quiet for decades. Was this all for revenge?"

Taevas tried to shrug, but the bindings on his wings made it difficult. "I don't know. Things got a little messy when I tried to ask him about it."

"I'll let the investigators know. If he's anywhere in the UTA, we'll have him in custody within the week. If he's flying... That might be a bit harder."

Taevas allowed himself a grim smile. "He's not flying. I injected him with the same suppressant he gave me."

"That sure makes it easier." His uncle shook his head, his salt and pepper curls swaying around his horns. He clapped his hands. "We'll talk more, but for now we need to make sure you're healthy. The 'Riik is fine, our enemies are on the run, and we have our Isand back. Everything else can wait."

It very much did not *feel* like everything else could wait. Taevas had a thousand questions, but the one on the tip of his tongue wasn't about his territory or his people or the Ardeo, of all things. It was about Alashiya.

Before he could demand to know where she was, his uncle had already pressed a button on one of the many screens scattered around the large hospital bed. What felt like less than a second later, a small fleet of healers, nurses, and doctors swarmed the room.

Everything was a bit of a blur for a while after that as they asked him to wiggle his toes, take deep breaths, and stare into little pen lights. There was a lot of murmuring, and although everyone fawned over him and seemed palpably relieved he was awake, no one spoke to him about his injuries or recovery. Someone said something about getting him checked by a mind healer, and another made baffled noises about not being able to heal a scar on his right palm, but that was all he caught.

It was a storm of activity, little of which made any sense to him. They moved as a unit and, after assuring him that all was well, they left as one.

Exhausted and even more irritable than he'd been before, Taevas pressed the button to elevate his bed, which put him into a slightly more dignified sitting position.

It wasn't comfortable, necessarily, but he didn't feel the pain that came from having his wings wedged between his back and the mattress, so there had been many improvements since he was last awake. *"Onu,"* he began, quickly reaching the end of his rope, "where is my—"

A knock on the door interrupted him. Letting out a sharp breath, Taevas gestured for his uncle to open it.

He supposed he should've expected it, but it still came as a surprise when practically his entire clan burst into the room. Purple and red and white and green and tan faces gathered around him in a swirl of activity and tears. Even the far-flung members of his clan had come to see him.

Everyone spoke at once, and he lost track of the number of one-armed hugs he received. A toddler was carefully hovered over him so she could plant a series of messy kisses onto his cheeks, her little red wings flapping with delight.

Taevas gratefully stroked Emilia's dark hair out of her eyes and tried to summon a smile for her, but he couldn't quite manage it. Paloma, his cousin Artem's mate, gave him a worried look as she gently pulled her daughter away. While everyone else was overjoyed, only she seemed to notice that Taevas's gaze couldn't settle in one place for long, or that he grew more tense with every passing second.

Leaning close, she murmured, "Is this too much? I can get everyone out of here."

Taevas shook his head. "No, I..." *Where is she?*

His gaze roved over all the familiar faces until he found two standing just behind the small crowd — his radiant cousin Hele and Vael.

Vael wore his Wing uniform and appeared as though he hadn't slept in days. His dark green face was gaunt, his eyes shadowed. He had one arm tightly wrapped around Hele's slim waist like he *needed* to be touching her. Hele looked little better. She didn't require sleep, but the air of exhaustion and worry hung around her like a miasma.

Ask, something whispered in the back of his mind. Not his voice, but someone else's.

Before he could open his mouth, Constantin caught the direction of his gaze and cleared his throat. Gesturing for Hele and Vael to approach the bed, he explained, "You have our Hele to thank for finding you. She was chasing a lead near the border of the Packlands when she spotted the car."

Taevas's eyes narrowed. "You... found me?"

Hele patted her Chosen's arm, which fell from her waist reluctantly, before she stepped up to the bedside. Taking one of Taevas's hands, she explained in her blunt way, "I saw a car parked dangerously by the side of the road and went to check that everything was well. When I found you inside, I used the nav system to call Vael, who ordered an m-gate to the hospital."

The hair stood up on the back of his neck and arms. The way she said it, it sounded like she'd found Taevas abandoned by the side of the road. But that couldn't be right. Alashiya had been with him. He *knew* that. He also knew that she'd never leave him. Not willingly.

A cold feeling settled into his chest — the prelude to an explosion of instinctive panic. "Side of the..." Gaze bouncing between Hele and Vael's grim faces, he asked, "You found me in a car? *Alone?*"

A ripple of tension went around the room. Even Emilia, who'd been happily babbling a story to her grandmother about taking Taevas to visit a river, went quiet.

Vael braced one hand on the railing of the bed when he roughly explained, "No. Not alone. There was a woman with you."

Shiya.

Taevas tensed. The heart rate monitor beside his bed began to beep in earnest when he demanded, "Where is she?"

Hele and Vael shared a loaded look. Taevas knew them both well. Certainly well enough to see the aftermath of a blistering argument in that singular look. Hele was angry with her Chosen, but what that had to do with Alashiya was beyond him.

Speaking slowly, Vael said, "The nymph was found with a cache of weapons, sedatives, and black market shift-suppressants. She was also covered in your blood and had obviously been transporting you across territory lines."

Taevas understood what he was saying. He heard the words, picked up the implication. But it was so patently outrageous, and the consequences of the accusation so horrific, he simply *could not* process it.

His tone was flat when he asked again, "Where is she, Vael?"

Obviously trying to soothe him, Constantin answered, "Vael took her into custody for kidnapping and attempted murder of the Isand, Taevas. She's being held in—"

He didn't make the decision to rip out his IV, nor lurch upright to grab Vael by the scruff of his neck. It just happened. All he heard was that Alashiya had been taken into custody. In an instant, he knew exactly where they'd be holding her, what kind of questions they'd be asking her.

His Alashiya. Held for kidnapping and attempted murder. In *his* territory.

Somewhere in the back of his mind he knew that Vael had done the only sensible thing in the moment. Even if Alashiya told him the whole truth, the story was outrageous and the only evidence available pointed to her as the main suspect. He knew what was in that SUV, and all of it was damning.

But to think that his Chosen, as soft and kind and devoted as she was, could have all her efforts to save him rewarded with suspicion and imprisonment... Shame and outrage were a potent cocktail swirling with the pain medication in his veins.

He'd sworn to keep her safe. He'd told her again and again how wonderful the 'Riik would be, how she'd be treated with nothing but respect by his people. But the very first time she set foot in his territory, his own fucking clan turned on her.

Taevas's mind was blank with rage when he roared, "You threw her in *jail?*"

He was barely aware of Artem quickly ushering his mate and child out of the room, or of several people gently but firmly attempting to get him to release one of his oldest friends. Taevas's tail rattled with menace, and if his wings hadn't been firmly strapped in place, he would've mantled them in aggression.

Vael's dark green skin went chalky, but he didn't flinch. "Of course I did! Her story is insane! She was found wi—"

"*Minu tutar,* please stop talking. You are making things worse." A pale, glowing hand came between them and settled on Taevas's wrist. A jolt of electricity ran down his arm, forcing him to release his grip with a hiss.

"There," she murmured, pressing on Taevas's rigid shoulder. "Do not kill my Chosen, cousin. Explain why you are angry."

No matter how fast he breathed, he couldn't seem to get enough air. "That *nymph* is the reason I'm alive. She sheltered me, fed me, cleaned my wounds, and then drove me hundreds of miles to bring me home. And you put her in fucking *jail!*" Jerking his shoulders to dislodge Hele's hands, he braced himself to throw his legs over the edge. "Tell me where she is *now.*"

There was a flurry of activity and protest as several people attempted to keep him in bed at once, with only marginal success.

Vael, the biggest dragon standing, grappled with him even as he argued, "Damn it, Taevas! What were we supposed to think? She was covered in your blood! She had the same suppressants in your system! She had no alibi or witnesses! And you were in her fucking car, on Grim's door!"

"Because she was *saving* me!" he bellowed. "And what did she get for it? Thrown in fucking jail! Where she's probably terrified and confused and— If you don't get her here in the next ten minutes, I'm going to hunt her down myself!"

Using his greater weight to pin Taevas down, Vael grunted,

"Fine! We'll release her! Just stay in the fucking hospital, for fuck's—"

Hele's head popped between them, completely heedless of the possible danger of getting between two brawling dragons. Something keen shining in her inky black eyes, she asked, "Why do you want to see the strange woman so badly, cousin?"

Taevas cast her a wide-eyed look of outrage. "Because she's *mine.*" He looked around at the slack-jawed faces and, needing there to be absolutely no uncertainty going forward, he informed them, "She's an Aždaja! She's your Emand!"

Everything went very still. Even Vael, who'd been growling as he struggled to restrain his Isand, seemed to stop breathing. For several seconds, it was as if no one in the room dared move, let alone speak.

It was Taevas's thundering snarl that broke the spell.

Vael released him abruptly, his skin ashen as he took one long step away from the bed. He didn't blink or ask for clarification. He simply held Taevas's wild stare as he lifted a hand to his ear, activating his comm implant.

"Radek," he breathed, voice hoarse. "Bring the nymph to the hospital. Now." There was a slight pause, no doubt as Radek asked *why* and *how,* but Vael cut him off with the only explanation necessary: "She's Taevas's Chosen."

CHAPTER FORTY-FIVE

THINGS COULD'VE BEEN A LOT WORSE. SHE WASN'T sure how, exactly, but it had to be true.

Alashiya sat in the uncomfortable metal chair in the interrogation room, her wrists shackled to the shiny tabletop. She was slumped over, her forehead cushioned by her forearms, in an attempt to hide from the glaring overhead light.

She'd lost count of the hours she'd spent there.

So many dragons had come and gone that she'd lost track of them, too. Except for Inspector General Anneli Saar, of course. Vael had handed her over to the stern-faced dragon almost as soon as the m-gate opened on the side of the road. She'd been Alashiya's main interrogator, though many more dragons had made an appearance, demanding answers she didn't have or to just glare at her from the doorway.

She was fairly certain it was some sort of strategy to break her. It hardly seemed like it could be a coincidence that those glaring visitors came by like clockwork, always *just* after she managed to snatch a moment of sleep.

What they hoped to gain from keeping her delirious with sleep deprivation, she couldn't fathom.

Alashiya was past exhaustion. She was past hunger. She was

past the discomfort of the cold air piped directly onto her from above and below. She was past everything except the dull ache of worry for her husband, who'd been whisked away from her so fast, she hadn't even gotten the chance to say goodbye.

Her only comfort was that he was alive.

They hadn't told her so. In fact, they'd refused to answer any question at all. But the hyphae didn't lie. Taevas was alive somewhere not terribly far from her. That was all that mattered.

Alashiya desperately wanted to let sleep pull her under. It was a heavy drag on her mind, begging her to let go, but she'd been awoken so many times that it'd become muscle memory to jolt upright whenever she gave in. To keep herself from slipping, she curled and uncurled her right hand into a fist. The sharp burn of her scabbing marriage cut was a painful but invigorating stimulant.

With nothing else to do, she stared at her warped reflection in the shiny silver surface of the table, too tired to keep her head up but too paranoid to sleep. Her mind was a shifting landscape of abstract shapes and warped memories, but she still managed to pray that she'd done the right thing.

Her eyes closed.

It was no surprise to her when she jerked awake not a moment later. Skin prickling with awareness, she lifted her head just enough to see a huge, pale green dragon in black military gear closing the door with the heel of his boot.

Normally, she would've been afraid. Everything about him screamed of a threat. His face was all hard angles, his eyes narrowed, and his monstrously large fists clenched. A swirl of tattoos peeked above the collar of his tight black shirt, and when he took a step toward her, the whole tiny, sterile room seemed to quake.

But even as he advanced on her, tail thrashing behind him, she felt no fear. Only resignation.

Her fingers, half-frozen by the continuous blast of cold air, curled into tight fists against the tabletop. *Whatever happens now, I know I did everything in my power to do what was right.*

She wasn't entirely sure what she expected, but watching the dragon kneel beside her chair wasn't it. He said nothing as he immediately began to disengage the locks on the shackles holding her ankles to the chair legs, so she didn't dare let herself feel relief.

The best she could hope for, she supposed, was that she was finally being put in a cell. At least there was likely to be a bed there.

For as big and deadly as the dragon's hands were, he was shockingly gentle as he eased her ankles out of the metal restraints. That done, he stood up and, broad shoulders hunching, began to do the same for her wrists.

Blinking owlishly, Alashiya forced her head up just in time to catch the door opening behind him.

The inspector came rushing in, her orange face darkened with outrage. "Radek!" she barked, storming across the short distance to slam a hand down on the table. "You can't just waltz in here and take my suspect out of custody! She's the primary—"

Radek? Alashiya stared at him with renewed interest. Taevas had told her the names of everyone in his Wing. His name sounded very familiar, but she wasn't in any state to be certain of it.

Radek had been nothing but stoic since he entered the room, but the moment the inspector reached for Alashiya's wrist, a monster took his place. His face, already harsh, transformed into a visage of pure ferocity as he rounded on the inspector.

"Touch her again and I'll take your hand," he snarled.

Alashiya wasn't sure how the inspector managed it, but she somehow held her ground. Sounding only a little thready, she protested, "This nymph is a criminal held on suspicion of kidnapping and attempted murder of our *Isand.* I can't let you just walk out with her!"

Radek's fingers, each one as thick as two of hers put together, were exquisitely gentle as he eased her wrists out of the shackles and guided Alashiya to stand. When she stumbled, he tucked a hand under her elbow and held her weight until a little bit of her balance returned.

Turning his back on the inspector, the terrifying look on his face faded into a dark frown. He took in Alashiya with a long look. "He's gonna fucking kill us all," he muttered.

"Radek! I know you're out of your mind, but you can't just break the law!"

Alashiya's gaze darted to the inspector, who looked about two seconds away from pulling her hair out by the roots. Glancing back at Radek, she dared to ask, "What's going on?"

"You're safe now," he gruffly assured her. "I promise."

She eyed him warily. "I don't mean to be rude, but there's only one dragon I feel safe with, Mr. Radek. And you're not him."

A soft huff escaped his proud nose. "Good instincts."

Gently placing a hand on her elbow, Radek half-turned to give the inspector a narrow-eyed look. "Inspector, I'm relieving you of the custody of Alashiya Ardz. She's officially under the protection of the Isand's Wing. Any questions you have for her can be forwarded through me. Understood?"

The inspector was stunned into silence for all of a heartbeat before she sputtered, "Protection of the *Wing?* What in— Why?"

Radek's tail snapped behind him like an angry barn cat, but he didn't push Alashiya to walk faster as he guided her toward the door. His hand was steady and careful as he patiently matched her much shorter strides.

He only bothered to answer the inspector's question when they were nearly out of the room. "Because," he rumbled, giving the inspector a pitying look, "she's our new Emand."

Alashiya didn't know what that meant, and she didn't get any clues from the inspector. They didn't stick around to see her reaction.

A small fleet of grim-faced dragons waited outside the interrogation room and formed a tight column around them. Radek stuck close, his hand gently pushing her forward. The only time he spoke was when he snapped a command at one of the group. It was in a language she didn't know, but she figured out what he'd asked for when the dragon returned with a soft gray blanket.

She had no idea just how cold she was until Radek wrapped it around her shoulders in a tight swaddle before depositing her in the backseat of a bulky black vehicle with darkened windows. Her teeth chattered and a wave of nausea crashed through her as Radek put the car in drive and peeled away from the curb at what felt like breakneck speed.

Swallowing a mouthful of saliva, she croaked, "Where are you taking me?"

Radek didn't take his eyes off the road, but he did flip open the center console and pull out a water bottle. Passing it back to her, he commanded, "Drink."

A spark of irritation burst in her at his bossiness, but she didn't have the energy to complain. Only when she'd taken a long drink from the bottle did Radek answer her question. "I'm taking you to the hospital."

A shudder of uneasiness ran through her. She'd never been in one of those before. "Why?"

"To see the Isand."

In an instant, every bit of her exhaustion melted away. The water bottle crunched in her tight grip as she leaned forward. "You're taking me to— I'm going to see Taevas? Really?"

"Yes," he muttered, casting her a wary look in the rearview mirror. "And to have you checked out, too. Has anyone even looked at that cut on…"

Whatever the end of the sentence was, Alashiya didn't hear it. Her ears filled up with white noise as she processed the fact that she'd be seeing Taevas soon.

A part of her had been absolutely certain she'd never see him again, so the joy of knowing that wasn't true was indescribable.

Alashiya hardly blinked as the minutes passed. She didn't look out the window. She barely noted the security checkpoint. She didn't feel the fabric of the blanket over her shoulders or the bottle crumpled in her fist.

When they entered the hospital, the hallways were a smear of white and pale blue. The small group of dragons who'd escorted her out of the station reappeared, but she didn't notice them, either. Her attention was honed on the awareness that every step brought her closer to Taevas.

He's all right, she silently chanted. *He asked for me. That must mean that he's awake. That he's well. I'm going to see him.*

Her right hand flexed, making the cut on her palm burn. Her stomach bottomed out.

Oh gods, I'm going to see him.

Anticipation and joy crackled in her veins. So did a creeping dread.

She didn't regret anything she'd done to keep Taevas alive, but she hadn't exactly thought through the consequences, either.

Her stomach tied itself into a series of increasingly painful knots as worries began to bombard her from all sides. Would he be angry at her? Would he even understand what she'd done?

Before she could make herself sick with anxiety, the group of dragons peeled off to line the long, quiet stretch of hallway on the top floor of the hospital. They joined several others already stationed there.

She wasn't entirely sure what made them stand out, but she could immediately tell that the three dragons closest to the door were different from the others. The way they held themselves, their sheer size, and the look in their eyes made them seem... more. More *what*, she couldn't even begin to speculate about.

All she knew for certain was that every single pair of eyes was on her.

Alashiya tightened the blanket around her shoulders and ducked her head. The gods only knew what she looked like, with dried blood crusted over her arm and the rest of her painted with rain-streaked dirt. She could hardly blame them for staring.

No one said a word as Radek approached a door and rapped

his knuckles against it twice. Without another second of hesitation, he pushed open the door and steered her inside.

She'd been prepared to see Taevas in a hospital bed. What she wasn't prepared for was everyone else.

The room was practically bursting with dragons, and every last one of them stared at her like she'd just gotten off the first shuttle from Mars. For half a second, the room was blanketed in complete silence. Then, a voice she'd come to love so much barked, "Everyone standing in her way, *move.*"

A stricken look rippled over every brightly colored face in the room. Suddenly there was a whirl of activity as dragons stepped aside, allowing her to get a direct look at the bed.

The breath left her lungs in a great *whoosh.*

Taevas was there, sitting up, clean, free of bruises and blood. He had on a loose white shirt with an open back. It appeared his wings had been bound tightly with some sort of splint. His deep purple skin glowed with vitality in a way she hadn't seen before. Compared to how he'd looked when she last saw him, Taevas was the very picture of robust health.

And he looked *furious.*

"Shiya," Taevas choked out, "come here."

She wanted nothing more than that. The only problem was that she couldn't seem to move. There were so many eyes on her. The instinct to run and hide from all the dangerous strangers was a siren blaring in her mind. She didn't think she'd ever been around so many unknown people at once in... ever.

But there was nowhere to hide. There were no trees, no loamy forest floor, and no safe haven of her house. Everything around her was clean and modern and sterile, free of all of the things that made her feel safe. She stared at Taevas, helpless, her discomfort rippling through the hyphae with mindless panic.

A flash of understanding crossed Taevas's expression. Lifting his left arm, he gestured for her to come closer. In a gentler voice, he coaxed, "All is well, *metsalill.* They're clan. You're safe."

After the twenty-four hours she had, Alashiya really couldn't be sure of that, but she knew one thing for certain: *Taevas* was safe. Taevas was home.

Taevas was her grove.

The soft gray blanket fluttered to the ground as she hurried across the room. Her eyes stung fiercely, but her body seemed to have lost the ability to make tears. It was a blessing, really. She didn't think she could handle crying in front of so many strangers.

The moment she was close enough to the bed, Taevas lunged. He snatched her to his chest, his tail a tight coil around her waist, and pressed her face into the crook of his neck.

The relief was instant.

His scent, the thrum of his thundering pulse, the warmth and darkness that came with being sheltered by the fall of his hair... It was no forest or hiding place amongst the roots of her trees.

It was better.

Alashiya shuddered. Her fingers curled into the strange shirt he wore. She didn't feel the sting in her palm or her exhaustion. The hyphae hummed with joy in her, like his nearness struck a chord that sent music to even the most distant branches of the network.

My grove, she thought, breath hitching. *I have a grove.*

CHAPTER FORTY-SIX

A FIERCE KISS WAS PRESSED TO THE SIDE OF HER HEAD. "My Shiya," Taevas breathed. "What's happened to you?"

A bubble of laughter escaped her. Pulling back enough to get a good look at his face, she cupped his cheeks and breathed, "Nothing. Nothing happened to me. I'm fine. I'm so, so fine."

Taevas didn't share her elation. If anything, he looked even more alarmed than before. Gently peeling her right hand from his cheek, he took a long look at the scabbed wound and streaks of flaking blood on her arm. His gaze stayed there for a heartbeat before he took in the rest of her.

Without taking his eyes off her face, he snapped, "Call a healer. *Now.*"

Someone jumped into action immediately, sending a ripple of activity around the room, but Alashiya didn't bother looking to see what was going on. She didn't care about anyone else. She didn't even think about them. Reunited with her husband, her fear had withered into nothing.

"I'm really fine," she assured him, unable to stop smiling.

Taevas tenderly brushed matted curls away from her cheeks and forehead with the backs of his claws. "You're absolutely not, but you will be. When was the last time you had something to eat?"

Alashiya had to think hard. "When we had breakfast at the house, I think? I don't know how long ago that was."

A burst of hushed conversation happened behind her. Taevas glanced over her head and explained, "She's a nymph. They eat more than we do. Tell them to bring a vegetarian meal — and for fuck's sake, someone get her clean clothes."

Cringing a little, she dared to take a peek at the dragons as they all began talking over one another. One of them, a gorgeous purple woman with short dark hair and skin that glittered with flecks of gold, put up her hands. "All right, all right! I'll get the clothes," she announced.

Backing out of the room, she muttered, "Don't know why I'm the one being forced to miss the show. *I* didn't throw her in jail. Blame the big green idiot for that one."

An older woman with similar features followed her out. "I'll get her meal sorted and make sure Alex doesn't come back with something ridiculous." She shot a small, nervous smile Alashiya's way. "Don't worry about anything, okay? We'll take care of everything."

It was lucky that the older dragon didn't seem to expect a response. Alashiya had no idea what to say to her or any of them.

Taevas distracted her from the awkwardness by firmly rearranging their positions. He collapsed one side of the bed's railing with an impatient push, allowing him to pull her onto the bed.

"Ah! No, Taevas, I'm dirty," she protested, cringing at the thought of soiling the perfect whiteness of the hospital sheets. "I can stand until—"

Taevas clicked his tongue at her but otherwise didn't bother arguing. He simply grabbed her by the waist and put her exactly where he wanted her, which happened to be tucked under his arm and firmly nestled into his side.

A knock on the door stalled more protests, and before Alashiya could process what was happening, a healer in an elegant gray coat with an open hand emblazoned on the chest was checking her over.

Taevas watched with a deep frown. "Have you healed a nymph before?"

"No," the healer answered, calm in the face of the Isand's hawkish scrutiny. "But I'm familiar with their unique anatomy and the theory, sir."

"I want a specialist," Taevas insisted. "Tell my team to find one. I want a dedicated healer for her who understands her needs."

Embarrassed, Alashiya muttered, "I really don't need that. I'm sure he can do it just fine."

"Of course he can. And that works for now, but you deserve the best in the long term, *metsalill*. Not just fine."

The healer met her apologetic gaze with a smile and a small shake of his head.

It'd been a long time since she'd seen one, but Alashiya was immediately put at ease when he gently took her hand and began his inspection. His magic was warm and a little ticklish but not uncomfortable as he confirmed what she already knew — that she was over-tired and in need of some food but otherwise perfectly healthy.

"You need fluids, a good meal, and a lot of sleep," he explained, gently lifting her bloody hand between them. "I'll fix this cut right up and you'll be good to go."

Alashiya stiffened. She didn't dare look anywhere but at her lap, afraid that if she met the gazes of anyone in the room, they'd see the guilt in her eyes. There was nothing wrong with healing her marriage cut, but having everyone's attention on it reminded her of what she'd done.

Desperately hoping no one would ask how she'd gotten the cut before she got the chance to talk to Taevas privately, she ducked her head and waited for the healer to finish his work.

After what felt like a very long time, he made a soft sound. Taking several small, cool wipes, he began to clean the blood. "I'm sorry, I can't seem to get the scar to heal. The Isand may be right about you needing a specialist."

Taevas tensed. "Why? Is something wrong?"

Everyone in the room except for Alashiya and the healer seemed to hold their breath. Shaking his head, the healer calmly informed him, "It's fully healed, Isand. I just can't seem to get the cells to refresh on the skin's surface, which means there's a small scar. I think it's related to the symbiotic mycelium in her tissue, but I can't be sure without more research." Turning to Alashiya, he asked, "Is that normal for you?"

"Yes," she answered, trying very hard to sound normal. "Don't worry about it."

She couldn't explain that the scar wasn't a scar but a visible branch of the hyphae, which would soon link up with the others on her body, creating a dense network of silver lines up and down her right arm. It was how all nymphs would know she was married, and something she never thought she'd be privileged enough to have.

It was lucky that no one seemed to know anything about nymphs. Both the healer and Taevas took her response at face value, though the healer looked a tiny bit disgruntled that his work wasn't completed to his satisfaction.

After turning down the offer of an IV, Alashiya let out a quiet sigh of relief and leaned into Taevas. The room got very quiet as the healer excused himself. She wasn't an expert in dragon body language, but Alashiya got the feeling that no one really knew what to do with themselves.

The only person who seemed comfortable was Hele, who she spied standing in the corner of the room with Vael. His expression was something close to pain.

When Alashiya made eye contact with Hele, the elemental offered her a wide smile and a wave.

"Hello, strange woman," she chirped. "I knew I was right about you."

Taevas huffed. "In what way?"

Hele drifted closer. She'd been nude last time they saw each other, but now she wore a loose, flowy dress in dark green. For as different as she was, she seemed to be right at home amongst all the dragons. "I told my mate that the nymph was telling the truth. I said you'd be angry when you woke up, but everyone thought you were going to die, so they didn't listen to me."

"You didn't think I was going to die?"

"No," she answered immediately. "You're too stubborn."

Alashiya avoided Taevas's playful glare as she laughed into her hand, but all the humor in her faded quickly when Vael came forward. She wasn't afraid of him, exactly, but she wasn't comfortable with the man who'd accused her of hurting Taevas, either.

He'd been terrifying to her then. He was a little terrifying now, even when he looked at her with an apology grooved into every line of his face.

She continued to be afraid of him right up until he sank to his knees before her. The room went completely silent. His massive wings stretched out and flattened, the inner membrane facing the floor as he braced his claws on his knees and bowed his head.

She balked, overwhelmed by the sight of such a powerful figure knelt before her, apparently unbothered by the many solemn eyes that watched him.

"I apologize, Alashiya," Vael rasped. He didn't look her in the eye. Instead, he kept his gaze level with her shoulders, as if he didn't dare lift his eyes to meet hers. "I should've listened to you and to my mate. I didn't, and because of that, I mistreated the woman who saved my Isand's life. Please forgive me."

Alashiya leaned over to gently touch the powerful dragon's shoulder, nudging him to rise to his feet. He was her husband's best friend and his stalwart protector who'd spent several sleepless weeks scouring the UTA for him. She couldn't be angry at him no matter how she'd been treated.

"You were scared because you love him. I love him, too. I can't imagine what it's been like for all of you this whole time. So of course I forgive you, Vael."

Taevas nudged her cheek, urging her to look up at him. Speaking in a whispersoft voice, he asked, "You love me?"

A sharp pain struck her. *He doesn't remember my vow.*

Of course he didn't. Because their wedding was secret and necessary and when he was on the brink of death, totally oblivious to how she intended to tie them together.

Cupping his cheek with her scarred hand, she ignored all the curious people in the room to murmur, "Yes, *argaman mlk.* I love you. I'd do anything for you."

Taevas closed his eyes and let out a slow, measured breath. Grabbing her hand, he pressed a reverent kiss to her scar. "I know," he whispered into her skin. "I love you, my queen."

She sniffled, fingers curling against his jaw. *I hope you feel the same way after I tell you. Gods, I hope I didn't ruin this.*

Pulling her hand back just enough to frown at her scar, he asked, "Will you tell me what happened?"

She'd told the abridged story so many times now that it came out automatically. "After I got you in the car, you passed out. I drove as far as I could, but when it looked like you weren't breathing, I pulled over. That's when Hele found me. She called Vael, and then... then we all went through an m-gate and ended up here."

She did her best to tamp down the swell of panic that rose in her at the memory of how close she'd come to losing him. "Are you all right? You look better, but they wouldn't tell me anything. I was so worried that I'd messed up and you'd—"

Taevas pinched her chin between his forefinger and thumb. In his sternest, most *Isand* voice, he firmly informed her, "You did *nothing* wrong, my Shiya. You were brave. Braver than anyone I've ever met. If you hadn't ignored my orders, I'd be dead right now. I owe you my life. *Again.*"

Keeping his eyes on her but speaking to the room, he explained, "When I knew there would likely be an attack, I told her to hide in the woods. Instead of listening to me, she came back around, stole the attackers' SUV, and ran over two of them. Didn't you, my warrior queen?"

Warrior queen? Alashiya's ears got hot. "I ran over Monty. I only bumped Sergei. You were too close."

"Yes, that's right." Taevas's eyes gleamed with a vicious sort of pride. "You ran over Monty, but you got out and *shot* Sergei."

A murmur went around the room. She squirmed uncomfortably, taken off guard by the sudden shift to admiration. She didn't feel any pleasure in the violence she'd participated in. There was nothing inherently virtuous about it.

But she was proud that she'd protected her husband, if nothing else. And in a secret, shadowy part of her, she was maybe even a little glad that she'd finally gotten some payback on a bully.

An older dragon to her left cleared his throat. It took a moment for her tired mind to recognize him as Constantin, Taevas's uncle and the man who'd been in charge of the Draakonriik in his absence.

He offered her a small fanged smile. "I had no idea nymphs were warriors. You could teach our soldiers a thing or two about resourcefulness, *vennatütar.*"

"Ah, I'm really not," she protested. "I don't like violence."

"And you'll never be put in a situation like that again," Taevas assured her.

Lowering her voice, she asked him, "What happens now?"

"You'll eat and rest a little, then we'll go home."

She blinked. Surely he didn't mean Birchdale. "Home?"

"Our roost," he clarified.

Constantin made a sound of objection deep in his throat. "You nearly died, Taevas, and your wings need care. You should stay at least another night in the hospital. We can escort her to your roost, or she could stay with us until you're strong enough to be discharged."

Taevas shook his head. "No. I can recover just as well in my roost as I can here. I want to go home, and Shiya needs to be somewhere safe where she can decompress."

The thought of being separated from him made her feel sick all over again, but Alashiya wasn't about to put her fear over his recovery. "You should stay," she whispered. "You were so sick, and your wings have caused you so much pain. I don't want you to rush your recovery because of me."

She could feel the gazes of everyone in the room bouncing back and forth between her and Taevas. Nothing about their interaction seemed remarkable to her, but she got the sense that it was some great spectacle to the clan.

Taevas stroked her matted curls and clicked his tongue. "This isn't Birchdale, *metsalill*. Healers can come to our roost at a moment's notice. We'll both be more comfortable there."

Alashiya wanted to argue more, but she couldn't shake the discomfort of being observed. She didn't know how to act in front of his clan. It was one thing to argue with him when they were alone in her home, but here...

In the hospital room, in front of these people, in the Draakonriik — Taevas wasn't just Taevas. He was *Isand*.

Avoiding his gaze, she muttered, "If you're sure."

Taevas pressed his lips to the crown of her head. Speaking into her hair, he breathed, "About finally taking you home? Absolutely."

CHAPTER FORTY-SEVEN

OVER THE NEXT FEW HOURS, ALASHIYA LEARNED THAT when the Isand requested something, his people would move heaven and earth to give it to him as quickly as possible — even if they didn't necessarily think it was the wisest idea.

She was swept along in a tide of activity as the Aždaja clan and a fleet of hospital staff prepared Taevas to go home. At some point she was briefly hustled off to the suite's bathroom, where she changed into the loose dress Alex brought her. She didn't feel comfortable using the sparkling shower with an entire clan of strangers just outside the door, so she settled for a sink bath. She still felt grimy and her curls needed some serious help, but a wipe-down and fresh clothing helped enormously.

While healers and various doctors prepared Taevas, she was placed in a soft armchair by his bed and given a tray of food. She didn't register what it was or who gave it to her. Eating was a purely mechanical function. She'd only managed to get a bit of the food down before her overwrought body protested.

Although everyone smiled and rushed to make her comfort-able, no one seemed to know what to *do* with her, so she was largely left alone. Hushed conversation in a mix of languages hummed around her, occasionally punctuated by her husband's soothing baritone. She didn't remember closing her eyes or feeling when someone draped a blanket over her.

The next thing she knew, she was swaying gently as someone carried her out of the hospital room.

A jolt of unease nearly woke her completely when she realized it wasn't Taevas's shoulder under her cheek, but Radek's. She'd barely stiffened before a familiar touch feathered over her back.

"Easy, *metsalill*," her husband murmured. "Close your eyes. We'll be home soon."

She didn't remember much after that; just the impression of movement and the resonant hum of Taevas's voice. Time became malleable. It felt like she'd only just closed her eyes when her body sank into a cloud. Someone lightly jostled her legs as they removed her boots and socks before a thick duvet was pulled over her.

Taevas's scent was rich and soothing and *everywhere.*

She sighed and tugged the duvet up to her nose. Her eyelids were too heavy to lift, but a faint glow passed through them, allowing her to get the impression of movement as Taevas slowly bent to give her a kiss.

"Rest now, my Shiya. I'll join you in a little while," he whispered.

Words were slow and heavy in her mouth. "Don't go."

He made a soft, pained sound and brushed a curl behind her ear. "I have to speak to my uncle and my Wing, but I'll be close by. I won't be long. When you wake up, I'll be here with you."

Her eyes burned beneath her closed lids, and a watery sniffle betrayed the sudden wave of feeling that overwhelmed her. "D'you promise?"

"Oh, my Shiya." Taevas pressed several fierce kisses to the side of her head and cheek. Bringing one of her hands up to his heart, he said, "I'm so sorry that all of this happened to you. I'm sorry you were afraid."

"I don't care about that," she whispered. "I only care that you're okay. That you're not gonna just— just *disappear* again. You can't leave me. You promised."

"I will *never* willingly leave you." He kissed her palm before settling her hand back on the bed. In a softer voice, he commanded her, "Now sleep. The sooner you rest, the sooner tomorrow will come. And tomorrow everything will be better. I promise, my queen."

Tomorrow will come.

A stone lodged itself in her throat, making it impossible to respond. Alashiya could only nod and draw the duvet closer to her eyes, hoping it'd hide whatever telling expression she made.

Leaving his Chosen alone in their nest when she was so clearly in need of care was agony, but Taevas had no other option.

He limped down the long hallway that connected his sprawling living quarters with the rest of the tower. All of the floors were accessible via elevators and hidden staircases, but almost no one had permission to enter his private areas. He'd deliberately sectioned off a portion of the top floor for guests and entertainment, putting the atrium in the center as a barrier between the public and private spaces.

Even if a guest wandered into the atrium from the entertainment suite, they wouldn't have been able to open the doors to the private quarters. They were biometrically locked and warded. Dragons were intensely protective of their spaces on the best of days, but now that he had his mate in his nest...

Taevas padded across the shining marble floors of the atrium slowly, his body beginning to ache as the pain medication gradually began to lose its effectiveness. The sunset threw stunning reds and oranges and lavenders through the clear glass roof. The light drenched the carefully curated plastic plants and furniture that dotted the space.

He paused at the door to the entertainment suite, both to catch his breath and to look at the fronds of a large, fake tropical plant he'd never bothered to really look at before.

His lips pursed. Turning his head, he took a quick look around at the atrium, which he'd never spared more than a passing thought for. He'd had the tower built in the 1950s, and though it had been updated roughly every ten years, he'd largely kept the aesthetic. The simplicity of clean lines, bare walls, and natural light had always appealed to him.

When everything else in his life was a mess, he knew that his roost would be a place of calm. There was no clutter or visual noise. Just straight lines, polished floors, and quiet.

But now, observing the atrium that had always been something of a meditative space for him, he was unsettled. It felt... empty.

The potted plants looked oddly lonely in their clusters. The small table and chairs in the corner looked even more adrift. All the empty space that he'd once found so peaceful now felt... well, *empty*.

Taevas couldn't honestly say he missed much about Alashiya's home, but he now realized that it had an abundance of something his own lacked: *life*.

Every inch of it was marked by the people who'd lived there. The walls didn't just hum with magic but with the memories of Alashiya's grove. Everywhere he looked, there'd been a story, the smudged fingerprints of love and life.

What story did *his* roost tell? Taevas stared at the lone small table in the far corner, with its two seats — only one of which he'd ever used, because he never brought guests this far into his roost.

The urge to throw the table and chairs and lonely potted plants out burned under his skin. *This isn't right,* his instincts told him. *You can't have your Chosen here. She should have something better. I have to fix this.*

Taevas rubbed his temples. He'd heard people talk about the nesting urge, but he'd never thought he'd experience it. Dragons spent most of their adult lives padding their roosts, making everything *just right,* whether they wanted a mate or not.

But sometimes it happened that after a dragon found a mate,

they developed a marked distaste for all the work they'd done before. Everything they liked, everything they'd spent years collecting and carefully styling, might suddenly become completely intolerable.

"I don't have time for that right now," he muttered, forcing himself to turn away from the sad little table and chairs.

Redecorating would have to wait until after he'd stabilized his territory and gotten Sergei where he belonged — firmly behind bars.

Knowing that he was rapidly running out of energy, Taevas forced himself through the door and down the hall toward the main sitting area of the entertainment suite. The suite was huge. It had just about everything he could ever need for hosting not only his clan, but dignitaries and other territory leaders, should the need arise.

There was a private theatre, two dining rooms, an arcade, a pool, an office, and the main lounge, which was the main room, as the landing perch was connected to it via a wall of floor-to-ceiling windows. The lounge itself had just about everything he could need, including its own bar, kitchen, and sunken sitting area.

Most of his guests lingered around the bar or on the couches when he stepped inside. Half his Wing were busy fixing themselves drinks, and the other half were talking quietly by the windows. His aunt and uncle, Hele, Vael, and a few of his other relatives were scattered around the sitting area. Paloma and little Emilia were missing, as were Artem and Alex. His personal healers and two of his assistants were perched on bar stools, each one of them with a tablet or phone in hand.

Someone had acquired a ridiculous amount of takeout and scattered the boxes across the low table in the sunken sitting area and across the bar, but no one appeared to be eating. The low buzz of conversation came to an abrupt halt as everyone turned to look at him.

Trying not to show just how exhausted he was, Taevas drew

his shoulders back. He offered the room a crooked smile. "I know I'm handsome, but it's impolite to stare."

There were more watery eyes than he wanted, but his weak joke had done the job of breaking some of the thick tension in the air, so he couldn't complain too much. Clapping his hands together, he announced, "All right! I know there's a lot of shit to do and even more questions that need answering, so I'm going to cover the basics first and then work my way around to each of you."

A murmur of agreement went around the room. Taevas swept his gaze over everyone assembled, meeting their eyes for a beat before moving on to the next person. "Some, if not all of you, already know this, but to make everything clear — I was kidnapped by a man named Sergei, one of Isand Jaak Fersen's sons. I was held somewhere unknown for weeks. When they tried to move me, I was able to escape. That led me to Birchdale, where I was sheltered and nursed until Sergei found me again."

Ignoring the strong reactions that went around the room, he continued, "Now, most importantly... The reason I'm standing in front of you right now is because of the woman who took me in. Her name is Alashiya Ardz. She didn't know who I was and didn't expect a reward. She's a nymph who, at great risk to herself, put a roof over my head, fed me, tended my wounds, and saved my life."

He paused, letting that sink in. There could be no more confusion going forward. Alashiya would not, *could not,* be treated with anything less than the respect she'd earned. He didn't want that to hinge on the fact that he'd Chosen her, either.

He needed them to see her as she was — a remarkable woman deserving admiration all on her own.

Sucking in a deep, fortifying breath, he prepared to say the thing he never thought he would. Pride and no small amount of fear burned in his chest. "I've Chosen her. She's now a member of clan Aždaja and, as of today, your Emand. Unless otherwise specified by her, you will address her as such."

Half the room already knew who she was to him, but shock still washed over them all. The faces of his Wing were studiously blank, his assistants both looked ready to explode with questions, and his family shared a series of looks that ranged from disbelief to glee.

Feeling the questions about to bubble out of the group, Taevas cleared his throat. "Alashiya has lived a very, very sheltered life, and she's been through a lot in the past few days. She doesn't know much about dragons, so I ask you to be gentle with her while she gets used to things."

He turned to find the hulking dragon hovering by the glass-walled exit to the perch. "Radek, I'm assigning you as her personal guard until we can assemble her own Wing. Hele, your job is to help her acclimate." Turning to his head assistant, he ordered, "Katya, whatever you wrote for the statement announcing I'd been found, I want you to add that I was rescued by Alashiya."

Katya, a keen, normally unflappable dragon with dark blue skin and a willowy frame, gave him a wide-eyed look. "Ah... Should..." She cleared her throat and tried again. "Should I include that you've Chosen her, sir? Or would you prefer to wait—"

Taevas waved a hand. "I've waited for her my whole life. I'm not waiting a moment longer. Put it in."

Katya let out a slow breath. Her eyes were wide and her brows raised, but she nodded. "Yes, sir."

"Andrejs, while I catch up on everything I've missed, I need you to make a dossier on the state of nymphs in the UTA. I want population statistics, voting habits, territories, clan names — everything. When you're done, you'll deliver it directly to my Chosen."

His other assistant, Andrejs, was already making notes on his tablet, his claws flying over the screen. Without looking up, he asked, "Would you like me to contact their congressional representative, sir?"

Taevas rubbed the base of his horns. He knew that would

have to happen if Alashiya wanted to take any sort of active role in her people's future, but he wasn't about to spring that on her. Not now, anyway, when there was already so much to adjust to.

"Wait on that. She'll be overwhelmed as it is." Finally, he turned to Vael, who visibly braced himself. "What's the status on the hunt for Sergei?"

"An all-territory alert has gone out and a collaborative search between the Shifter Alliance and the 'Riik is happening as we speak. If he's injured and still dealing with the effects of the suppressant you gave him, then we're optimistic he'll be found."

"And what about the others? Did you sweep Shiya's land?"

Vael's lips quirked with an impressed smile. "We checked it as soon as we apprehended her — *after* we managed to get through her wards to see the place properly. Two men were found unconscious and injured in the woods not far from her home, and there's evidence of another who left the scene."

Taevas suppressed a growl. "That'll be Monty. I'm sorry to hear he might still be alive. He's the hunter Sergei hired to search the woods for me. I don't know who the others were. Are they in custody?"

It unsettled him, the way nearly everyone in the room shared long, knowing glances.

"What?" he asked, patience wearing thin. "What aren't you telling me?"

Constantin spoke up. "The other men who were working with Sergei... they're not speaking. They can't. That's actually how we know who they work for."

"What are you talking about?"

"According to the information the leaders have been able to put together since the attacks, it appears that whoever is behind this new version of the Ardeo has assembled a force built on mind control."

Constantin looked a little queasy as he said it. Even his rich skin tone, dark with its nighttime coloring, became chalky as he continued, "Whatever magic is responsible, it goes deep, making questioning them almost impossible. And there's failsafes. When others have tried to break through it, an aneurysm is triggered, killing them instantly. That's part of why we couldn't use them to confirm or deny what the Emand told us. The men can't answer questions one way or another."

A lot of the strange behavior of Sergei's men suddenly made sense. There hadn't been a lot of psychic control during the war, but it happened. Usually only when someone was desperate and needed canon fodder, though, because it was hideously impractical from a tactical perspective. A brainwashed soldier was little better than a toy to be used and discarded at will.

They couldn't think for themselves, couldn't make the snap decisions necessary to win a war. They acted on orders and that was it.

Wind, release, dispose.

Of course, the benefits were that they never questioned their superiors or hesitated, no matter the danger. It was a steep trade, but if you were going for maximum impact with no regard for longevity, then it could be effective.

Repugnant in the extreme, but effective.

Taevas's lips thinned. "I want a full report on what the fuck has been going on by tomorrow afternoon."

Constantin nodded. "Consider it done."

After making his rounds amongst his people, Radek caught him on his way back to his nest.

Figuring the man had a question about his new duties, Taevas braced himself for a delay in getting back to his mate. What he didn't expect was for a large plastic evidence bag to be shoved into his hands.

"This was found in the car with you. It looked important," Radek gruffly explained. "Everything else I should be able to get by tomorrow, but this felt... different, so I grabbed it."

Taevas looked down at the opaque plastic bag. The weight of it was familiar, but he couldn't be entirely sure what it was until he pulled the seal apart with the tips of his claws.

Neatly folded inside was a robe of unsurpassed beauty. It was made of burgundy velvet, embroidered with golden thread, and stained with unmistakable dark splotches of blood.

His throat burned as he delicately extracted the sash his mate had so lovingly embroidered for him. Everything in him went still as he held it draped over his palm.

The golden thread gleamed in the light — as pristine and beautiful as it was when he watched her work from the comfort of her floor nest. It appeared shockingly untainted by the blood that crusted the velvet all around it, as if the thread had sucked up whatever drops had fallen on it.

Something that sounded suspiciously like his Alashiya's voice whispered in the back of his mind as he thanked Radek and walked away, bloody sash in hand.

CHAPTER FORTY-EIGHT

His dreams were dark and winding and full of strangers.

He got the impression that he was in a vast room. It was so large he couldn't see the walls, let alone the exits. How he got there or why, he couldn't say. All he knew for certain was that he'd been there before.

And that he wasn't alone.

Alashiya stood beside him in the darkness. Her presence was utterly unmistakable. She spoke to him in that soft voice he loved so much, harmonizing with the whispers of so many others all around them. It felt a bit like he was in the middle of a clan meeting, but instead of being the leader, he was just another member tucked under the wing of a large, loving family.

Nothing they said made any sense to him. While their words were unintelligible, the tones and inflections were welcoming. He thought he might've been asked questions and perhaps he answered, but all he really knew for sure was that he was met with a palpable warmth and relief.

Warm hands touched his back and shoulders in the dark. Old and young lips skimmed his cheeks. Someone strong gripped his forearm in a warrior's handshake. A pair of lithe arms squeezed him in a welcoming embrace, and he got the sense that he'd just been accepted by a being that was not one person, but many hundreds — a consciousness that was new and unspeakably old.

Welcome, welcome, a woman's voice whispered in the fading shadows of early dawn. *Take care of our queen, argaman mlk.*

The whispers slipped away as wakefulness returned, smudging his memories of that warm, dark world until they were little more than a gut feeling. It was an exquisite relief to wake up in his nest. It was even better to wake up beside Alashiya.

The entire ordeal of the last few weeks seemed like little more than a fever dream as he lay ensconced in his bed, swathed in silk sheets and the scent of his mate. Her body was slack under the weight of his arm. The room was silent except for the soft sounds of their breathing.

He didn't open his eyes for a long time.

Alashiya's home hadn't been *loud,* exactly, but it wasn't quiet, either. Birdsong, crickets, the rush of wind through lush tree canopies — all of it bled through the thin walls of her dwelling. He didn't realize he'd grown used to it until he experienced the silence of his roost again, where only the howl of wind whipping off the lake could make it through the sturdy walls.

And yet... when he strained to listen, he swore he could hear the murmurs of far-off voices. The only clear one he could make out was his mate's.

The vaguest murmurs reached him. Snippets of phrases, soft sighs, and little hums filled his mind. If he focused hard enough, he thought he could make out the sound of Alashiya's voice more clearly, but none of what she said made any sense.

Taevas frowned. *Must be the pain meds.*

The healers had been vague about what damage had been done to his wings, saying they would discuss it more when he had a chance to rest and let his body recover. He'd been advised to take more pain meds before he went to sleep the night before, so he attributed his strange dreams and the echoes of far off voices to whatever potent cocktail they'd given him.

Soft fingers touched the downturned corner of his mouth. "Are you hurting?"

His eyes opened. Alashiya lay in front of him, her long curls fanned out across a plush pillow and her skin aglow in the warm light of dawn. Dark circles ringed her eyes and her cheeks looked too thin, but her eyes were bright as she watched him.

"I'm fine," he whispered, struck by a sense of deja vu.

"Are you sure?"

Taevas took her hand and kissed the pads of her fingers. "Yes. Yes, I'm sure."

"You look so much better." The relief in her voice and expression nearly broke his heart.

"Thanks to you." He hooked his hand around the back of her neck and drew her close enough to touch their foreheads together. Infusing his voice with every ounce of painful feeling in him, he rasped, "I'd be dead without you, my Shiya. I'm sorry for sending you away. I'm so, so sorry."

"I forgive you," she replied, voice thick with tears. "As long as you're okay, I'll always forgive you."

"I don't know that you should, but I'm grateful regardless." He exhaled slowly. Taevas wanted nothing more than to stay in bed with her forever, but that wasn't an option. The 'Riik waited for him — them.

But they had a little bit of time before the world came crashing down on them, and he intended to make the most of it.

"Will you let me care for you this morning?" he asked, delicately trailing his claws through curls in desperate need of detangling.

A small smile quirked Alashiya's lips. "Are you saying I need a shower?"

"I'm saying I have a marble bathtub big enough to fit the both of us," he replied. It was good to see her smile. Maybe even the best thing in the world.

"And you waited this long to tell me?" She rose slowly, clearly still exhausted from all that she'd been through, but he wasn't exactly speedy either.

Together they made their slow way over to the large en suite bathroom. The tiles were cool under his bare feet as he carefully stripped her of her clothing. Alashiya was oddly quiet when he took her hand and guided her down the steps into the steaming pool of the bath, but he supposed that was to be expected.

Everything, from the sparkling bathroom to the territory it sat in, was new to her.

Hoping to help her relax a bit, he settled into the bath behind her and wrapped his arms around her waist. They soaked in silence for a long time, comforted by each other's nearness and the sounds of their breathing. Only the occasional drip from the faucet interrupted the soothing rhythm.

Steam curled around their naked bodies, and the scent of fresh water filled his lungs as he rested his cheek on the crown of her head. *Finally*, he thought, immeasurably grateful. *Finally, we're home.*

But Alashiya didn't seem to feel the same peace. She was stiff against his chest. Her nails curled into his forearms like she was afraid he'd disappear. His chest rumbled with a soothing purr, but not even that seemed to relax her.

A tremor of something like instinct worked its way through him and settled behind his breastbone with a small tug. He *knew* Alashiya needed comfort. Not just because he knew her personality, but because some innate part of him was attuned to the very core of her.

"What's wrong?" he asked, rubbing her cheek against her curls. His chest tightened painfully. "Are you uncomfortable here?"

She sucked in a trembling breath. "No. I don't know. Maybe."

"What can I do?"

"I don't know," she answered again. "Taevas..."

Leaning around her to get a look at her troubled expression, he prodded, "You can tell me anything. Whatever you need to be comfortable here, it's yours. This is your home, Shiya."

Her gaze searched his. "Is it?"

"It may not feel like it yet, but it is," he promised her. "This is your roost. These are your people. This is your clan."

Her fingers tightened on his arm. "And what if they don't like me? What if I don't fit here?"

Taevas gently shifted her forward, until he could comfortably tip her back into the water. Holding her head between his hands and staring down at her, he swore, "Then I'll carve a new place for you to fit in, Alashiya."

Chapter Forty-Nine

Stepping into Taevas's tower was a bit like walking into another world. Everything, from the height of the building to the materials it was made of and the scent of the air was so foreign. She'd suspected from the start that it would be, but nothing could've prepared her for the reality of being immersed in his world.

Alashiya thought she'd be afraid. She wasn't.

There was no tangled knot of dread in her belly or anxiety squeezing the breath from her lungs as she stared out the floor-to-ceiling window across from their bed. There was only a steady sort of certainty in her that defied place or setting.

How could she be afraid when her grove was near?

There were much more serious reasons to worry, and after what she'd been through, it seemed silly to have been so very afraid of leaving her home. Yes, everything was different and strange, but what did that matter? She could adapt.

If he lets me stay.

Alashiya swallowed hard and cast a furtive look at her husband as he toweled himself off. He looked perfectly at home in the sprawling, modern bedroom with its strange sunken bed draped in a gauzy canopy that spilled from the ceiling in a water-fall of fabric.

Everything about it was the complete opposite of hers. There were no cozy rugs or moss on the windows. Every bit of furniture, from the side tables to the arm chairs in the corner, matched. Even the light fixtures, something she would've thought universal, were foreign to her because she couldn't actually *find* them. They were certainly there, but she couldn't for the life of her pinpoint where the soft glow emanated from. It just seemed to emerge from the tops of the walls and baseboards.

The room would've felt disturbingly clinical and devoid of life if it weren't for the signs of *her* littered throughout it.

Alashiya wandered toward the bed, one of Taevas's borrowed shirts swishing around her thighs. She had to kneel down to sit by the mound of pillows at the head. Her chest squeezed as her fingers skimmed the embroidery on the pillowcases. And when she turned her head, there was the gift she'd been bold enough to send him — a hoop of nearly transparent gossamer covered in pressed wildflowers she'd painstakingly stitched in place.

Her magic hummed against her fingertips, making every stitch feel alive.

Blood to blood. Hyphae to hyphae.

For years, she'd imagined what it would be like to see all her work in one place. Her throat tightened as she traced familiar designs and fabrics, the soft sounds of her husband preparing for the long day ahead a soothing song in the background.

"When you're ready, we'll go shopping for whatever you need to make our roost feel like home." Her husband's voice drew her gaze back to him.

He stood in front of a black glass door, one clawed hand on a barely visible door knob. He was as naked as a jaybird, his tail swinging lazily over his tight purple backside, but he didn't seem to notice or care.

Tucking her hands into her lap, she replied, "I don't need you to change anything. This is how you like things, right?"

Perhaps she could get used to the bare walls and the clean lines and the lack of greenery. She had her doubts, but she wasn't about to demand he change his entire house to suit her.

It became clear instantly that she'd made a misstep, however, when his eyes narrowed. "My Shiya, come here."

Wary, she rose from the bed to pad across the room. Even the stone floor beneath her feet felt somehow modern and cold, a bizarre contrast from all the rock and stone she'd ever felt before.

When she drew close to his side, Taevas flicked his wrist. The glass door slid open on a well-oiled runner, making hardly a sound as it revealed a massive dressing room lined with racks and built-in drawers. If she had to make a comparison, she would've put it closer to what she knew of museums rather than a closet. Everything, from sunglasses to silk ties to handkerchiefs had their own special display cases.

What struck her wasn't the strangeness or the luxury of it. Maybe to some it would be a gratuitous display of wealth, but to her it was a sign of overwhelming respect.

Her husband's closet was a *shrine*. Dedicated to her.

She thought that seeing her work on his pillows and blankets was moving. Seeing every carefully displayed jacket, vest, shirt, and handkerchief in their glass cases...

Strong arms circled her waist and drew her in close. The heat of Taevas's body warmed her spine as a sense of rightness zipped along the hyphae. His tail looped around her leg, holding her possessively. "Look at how you've already made your mark on me, my Shiya. You think I care if you change the color of our roost's walls? If you hate the couch or think my taste is shit? This has been your home for a decade. It's about time you really made it yours."

"I never imagined I'd get to see everything together," she whispered. "It really does feel like I've been here."

"You have been," he insisted.

Worry was like grit under her skin, making it impossible to really accept his assurance. Instead, she diverted his attention by padding around the space, her fingertips trailing over the glass cases and velvet-lined boxes with care. Her magic greeted her with a feeling a lot like relief when she touched a familiar crisp white shirt. It was the same one he wore in the photo she'd seen on Debbie's tablet, with all the painstaking white-on-white embroidery she'd experimented with.

Taevas moved around behind her, plucking underthings and a pair of pants from a drawer, as she fingered the mother of pearl buttons.

"What's the plan?" she asked.

"For today or more long term?"

Not sure she could face the idea of long term plans yet, she answered, "Today."

"I am going to meet with my Wing and my council to get up to speed on everything that happened while I was gone. *You* are going to rest. Eat. Be pampered for the first time in your life."

Alashiya turned around to fix him with a troubled look. He was tightening a black leather belt around his hips, his claws deftly handling the sleek gold buckle in a few graceful movements. He looked so whole and hale standing before her, but she couldn't banish the image of him in the back of that car, his powerful body ruined.

"What about the healers? You should still be in the hospital. You said you'd rest if you were home, but none of that sounded like rest."

"I'm sure they'll be hovering," he replied, running his claws through the long, wet strands of his hair. "But aside from my wings, I feel good. Better than I have in weeks."

"Did they tell you what's wrong with your wings?"

He looked away quickly. Reaching for the same white shirt that had drawn her attention, he wordlessly asked for her help in maneuvering around his bound wings. Only when she was behind him did he answer her. "No, they didn't. I think they're waiting to give me the bad news."

Alashiya's heart squeezed. Pressing her palm between the powerful joints of his wings, she whispered, "I don't believe that."

"Wings are delicate, my Shiya," he replied. Something in the matter-of-fact way he said it left her feeling like he was trying to cover up just how devastating an inability to use his wings would be. "It's possible they won't ever be fixed. Or they'll never be completely the same. I might never be able to fly again. Or... or embrace you as I should."

Wrapping her arms around his waist, she carefully avoided his wings as she pressed her forehead into the muscled gap between his shoulder blades. She didn't offer him platitudes or empty hopes. She knew what it was like to ache for something taken from her.

"I'll be here no matter what happens," she murmured, pressing her hands into the bare skin below his unbuttoned shirt.

Taevas bowed his head. Releasing a slow breath, he rumbled, "I know, my Shiya. That's why I want you to rest today. Let me take care of you for a change."

A wave of unease rolled through her. "You want me to stay here? By myself? I don't have anything to do."

He squeezed her hands. "That's the point. You've never had a true day of rest in your life. Let me take care of you and give you the chance to settle in — especially after what you went through at the hands of our own people. You earned some pampering, Shiya."

Her throat constricted hard. "Taevas, I just..."

Perhaps hearing something in her voice, he grabbed her forearms and used them to guide her back around to his front.

"Something's bothering you," he murmured. "Tell me what it is, Shiya. What's *really* bothering you?"

She didn't want to. She didn't even know if she could. Alashiya didn't regret what she'd done to keep him alive, but that didn't mean it was right. But she also couldn't keep it in any longer. As she'd come to realize, putting off the hard things didn't make them any easier to deal with. If anything, it made it a whole lot harder.

I'm not a coward, she reminded herself. *I'm brave. I can do this. I can tell him.*

His arms tightened around her. "Tell me what?"

Alashiya jumped. "What? I didn't say anything."

"Yes, you did." A puzzled frown deepened the corners of his mouth when he slowly repeated, "You said, *I can do this. I can tell him.* Just now."

"No, I didn't." Goosebumps lifted the fine hairs on her arms.

"You did," he insisted. Taevas lifted a hand to rub his forehead. "I heard you. I *keep* hearing you. When I was in the hospital, I could've sworn... I woke up and I could've *sworn* you were right next to me. I could feel you."

Her stomach curdled. Alashiya's toes curled reflexively against the cool stone as she wrapped her arms around her middle. Bile crept up the back of her throat.

I thought I had a little more time.

She'd hardly had a moment to really sit with what she'd done, let alone how long it would take for the hyphae to present itself to him. Of course she could feel him in it, but she'd always been told that it could take days, even weeks for spouses to integrate into the network. Some, like a handful of her relatives, were never truly able to access it.

The idea that Taevas would be so quickly accepted by the hyphae and able to hear her hadn't even occurred to her.

A wild, reckless sort of joy lodged itself behind her breastbone. It burned like a flame in her chest, hot enough to sear away the fear that threatened to seal her lips shut. What a gift it was to know her family had accepted him.

To deny it, to pretend it didn't exist, would be a rejection of that honor.

Bracing herself for his reaction, Alashiya forced the words through the constriction of her throat. "Taevas, I... There's something I didn't tell you about what happened when we were driving here."

Unable to look at him, she reached for his right hand. The one with the scar the healer couldn't fix. The one that she bound to her in that stolen car. The one that made him hers.

Holding their hands side by side and palm up, she aligned the silvery lines. Hers had already begun to branch into fine roots — a visible extension of the vast network that permeated her body. His was shallow and thin, a testament to how unwilling she was to hurt him.

Her eyes stung as she stroked his scar with the tip of her finger. "I thought you were going to die. I felt you just— just slipping away and there was nothing I could do. We were too far away from help. I didn't know how to save you."

Taevas stroked her damp hair back from her cheek with his free hand. In a soft voice, he asked, "What happened, my queen?"

Turning her hand over, she pressed their palms together. Their scars aligned, hyphae to hyphae, blood to blood. She didn't want to cry. She wanted to own what she'd done and why she'd done it. But the tears came anyway. They were a violent release of grief and the shadow of a loss that would've buckled her.

A tear streaked down to drip from her chin when she confessed, "I didn't know how to save you but I couldn't let you go. I'm sorry. I'm so sorry."

His fingers curled around the back of her neck. Tilting her head up so she was forced to look him in the eye, Taevas growled, "Whatever you did, you have *nothing* to be sorry for. You saved me, Shiya. You saved me again and again and again. I promise you, whatever you did, you're forgiven."

"You don't know that."

"I do know that." He squeezed the nape of her neck. Pressing their foreheads together, he insisted, "Because I know you. Whatever you did, you did it because you had to."

"That's not true. A part of me just wanted to," she admitted, breathing hitching. "A big part of me was too selfish to let you go. Even if you hated me— I didn't care."

He huffed. "I could never hate you."

Alashiya squeezed her eyes shut. "I married you, Taevas."

There was a long pause. She couldn't look at him. Instead, she reminded herself that he was alive. That she'd brought him back to his clan and his people. That she'd been selfish, yes, but she couldn't regret it when it saved his life.

"You... what?"

"I married you," she repeated, voice hoarse. Squeezing his scarred hand, she explained, "I cut your hand and I cut mine and I — I married us. I brought you into the hyphae because I thought it could stabilize you or— or give you some strength or—"

"Shiya, *Shiya*. Stop. Open your eyes." The strangled note in his voice made her flinch away, but her eyes opened.

Taevas stared at her with a fervent, incredulous expression. His eyes were wide, the skin pulled tight over his cheekbones, and his mouth pressed into a rigid line. She had no doubt that his wings would've mantled if they hadn't been strapped to his back. The hyphae buzzed with activity in the back of her mind, whipped to a frenzy by whatever intense feeling he was experiencing.

She knew she could tap into it if she wanted to. She might even be able to speak to him if he could already hear snippets of her thoughts. But she didn't dare. She'd violated his trust enough.

"I'm sorry," she choked out. "I understand that you're angry. You should be. Just— please don't send me away."

To be hated was one thing, but to be physically separated from her husband would be a misery beyond comparison. They were bound in the hyphae now. Prolonged separation would diminish them both, physically and mentally.

Maybe she deserved that misery, but he didn't.

"Of course I'm angry," Taevas hissed. He grabbed her hand and held it between them, palm up to show her scar. "Are you telling me that I missed our *wedding?*"

Alashiya stared at him, unsure how to react. "You were dying. I didn't know what else to do."

"Can we do it again?" he demanded through clenched teeth.

She blinked. "I... Huh?"

"Can we do it again, Alashiya." It wasn't a question this time.

"No," she answered, "it can only be done once. Why?"

"Because I can't have missed our fucking wedding, Shiya!" he exclaimed, voice raw.

She sniffed hard, too overwhelmed to feel any relief. "You're not mad that I took the choice from you? That I brought you into the hyphae?"

Taevas let out an incredulous laugh. "Are you mad that I Chose you? I didn't ask either, Shiya."

"You..." Her shoulders shook, making it hard to speak. "You *Chose* me?

He cupped her cheeks and pressed a quick series of fervent kisses to her trembling lips. "I love you, *naine*. I've loved you for a decade. If I'm angry, it's only because I wish I could remember the moment when you claimed me, too."

Alashiya stroked her hands down his naked chest, feeling the heat of his skin and the thundering beat of his heart. Her voice was thick with a different type of tears when she explained, "I cut us with my sewing shears and bound our hands together with the sash from your robe. It wasn't a very pretty ceremony."

Taevas jolted with surprise. "The sash? Gods, no wonder it was bloody."

"Yes," she answered, miming the way she'd wrapped their hands together. "I said my vows and wrapped our hands together. I had to be sure you got enough of my blood, so I tried to do it as tight as I could."

He tilted his head back and blinked at the ceiling, apparently struggling to wrap his head around what she told him. "But... but you told me how much a wedding meant to your grove," he protested.

"I can wear my veil and my jewelry when I'm dead. I don't need anything other than you."

"No, Shiya," he growled. "No, it *matters*. You deserve that. You deserve to have the wedding you dreamed of."

Alashiya stroked the hard line of his jaw, a great, expanding warmth filling her chest. "You ridiculous, bossy dragon. I don't care about any of that. If you'd died, I never would've gotten the chance to wear my veil anyway."

"You would've found someone else," he whispered. "You're too perfect to be alone, Shiya. You deserve more than that. More than me."

She rose up onto her tiptoes to press a soft kiss to his lips. "I made my choice when I turned my ass around and came back for you. Whatever happens next, we do it together, okay?"

Taevas rubbed his lips back and forth against hers, sharing breath and warmth and reassurance with her in a way that made every cell of her body hum.

The hyphae bloomed under the glow of their connection, the energy of it reaching deep into the very root of her soul. The strong purple thread of him wound its way through her, strengthening the parts of the network that had grown weak and withered with disuse.

Alashiya held him close, tears stinging behind her eyelids as she took what felt like her first deep breath since the death of her grove.

Like the slowly decaying warren of her home, the hyphae had gradually begun to shrivel and close off its branches. But life had been breathed back into it — *her*. That was worth more than any perfect wedding or fairytale romance could ever be.

Taevas rubbed the tip of his nose against hers. They didn't open their eyes as they breathed together, their hands roaming slowly over each other's bodies like they needed to memorize every dip, curve, and bone. In a voice that was hardly more than a breath, he said, "I can feel you. I can hear you. Thank the gods that's not just the pain meds talking."

A soft laugh tumbled out of her. "You're part of the hyphae now. We'll always be with each other, even when we're not."

"You Chose me," he said, delight beginning to shine through. "You *Chose* me."

"I did," she replied, cheeks cramping with the force of her grin. "With the blessing of my family, by the way."

Taevas pulled back. Looking like he was putting some pieces together, he shook his head. "Is that who I've been hearing?"

Alashiya patted his chest. "They're chatty."

Huffing, he muttered, "Well, at least I'm used to dealing with a clan."

"They seem... interesting."

"That's a word for it." Gently smoothing her damp curls back behind her ears, he visibly gathered himself before telling her, "They're going to smother you, I'm afraid."

Not knowing how else to release her suddenly nervous energy, she began to button his shirt for him. It was such a mundane, domestic task — one she'd dreamed of doing a thousand times for her Adon. Her husband.

He Chose me. The thrill of that buzzed from the top of her head to her toes.

"What if I'm not good with them?" she asked, neck bent as she focused on her task.

"You will be." He pulled his shoulders back and allowed her to do her work. The warmth of his pleasure glowed in the hyphae with every brush of her fingers. "My cousins Hele and Alex are coming to spend time with you today. You can tell them if you're comfortable with Vael coming by, but Radek is non-negotiable. He's the head of your Wing now."

Alashiya conjured the image of that massive, angry-looking dragon who'd rescued her from the interrogation room and blanched. "*My* Wing?"

"Your Wing," he reiterated, tilting his chin up to allow her to finish buttoning his shirt. He flashed her a dazzlingly white smile full of fang and his particular brand of charm. "You're my *wife* now, remember? That makes you Emand."

Her fingers paused their work. "I... don't know what that means."

"It means you aren't just queen of nymphs anymore," he explained. Gently pulling her hands away from his collar, he held her gaze when he continued, "You're my mate. My wife. My Emand. You rule the Draakonriik beside me now, my Shiya."

If her eyes got any wider, there was a real fear that they'd simply pop out of her skull and land at his strange taloned feet.

"No, I'm not," she sputtered.

Taevas chucked her under the chin. "Yes, you are. So you might as well rest while you can, my queen, because you and I have a lot of work to catch up on."

Alashiya was pretty sure she forgot what it was like to breathe. She was so shocked that she barely registered when he dropped a kiss onto her forehead and moved to exit the closet, his tail swishing with an unmistakably smug rhythm.

Only when he paused and cleared his throat at the doorway did she turn woodenly to face him. "And *naine,*" he growled, "we'll continue our conversation about our wedding when I return."

Taevas left her in what she could only describe as some sort of lounge, with the surly-looking Radek standing guard by the door. She'd been bundled into one of his robes and left there with vague instructions to "use the MET to order anything she needed" and "watch some TV" while she waited for his cousins.

Alashiya had no idea how to do either of those things, so she curled up in the strange, sunken sitting area and stared out the windows in silence. Outside, a glorious expanse of water ringed by green called to her. White-capped waves licked at a rocky shore, reminding her of stitches appearing and disappearing on an expanse of blue fabric.

It was a lot easier to stare out at the majesty of nature in awe than it was to think about the revelation Taevas had left her with — a fair turn, considering what she'd revealed to him, but over-whelming nonetheless.

Emand.

She'd never even heard the word before, but it landed with all the weight of an anvil in her mind. She could *feel* what it meant to Taevas. She just had no idea how to process what it meant to *her* yet.

Alashiya had no idea what the responsibilities of an Emand were. What she'd need to do as his wife. What it even meant to exist out in the world beyond Birchdale.

It was too overwhelming for just about anyone to think about all at once, let alone the morning after her surprise release from interrogation. So Alashiya laid down on her side, curled up with one of the many decadently soft blue blankets folded over the back of the couches, and watched the waves from a dizzying height.

Free to reach for Taevas in the hyphae, she luxuriated in the feeling of closeness, the echo of his heartbeat and rhythm of his breath. He wasn't there with her, but he was *there*.

She didn't mean to sleep, but it was inevitable after the days she'd had. Alashiya slipped into a doze beneath the weight of the blanket, her cheek cushioned by a plush throw pillow. The deep bass of his voice rumbled through her mind, unintelligible but comforting, and drifted through gentle dreams.

When she woke some undetermined time later, it took her a long moment to remember where she was — and to realize that it wasn't her husband's fingers stroking her hair.

A long-fingered, glowing hand patted her cheek. "Good morning, strange woman."

Alashiya jolted awake. Bewildered, she sat up on her elbow and peered at the elemental. "Hele?"

Fathomless black eyes crinkled with a smile. She sat beside Alashiya on the couch, her willowy body draped in a frothy forest green summer dress. A glittery hair clip in the shape of a heart held back the bone white hair by her ear, but it did nothing for the rest of the mass, which floated in a glowing ribbon over and behind the black leather couch.

"You've been asleep for a while," Hele told her. "Have you had breakfast yet? I hope not. My sister said she's bringing a feast."

Sitting up properly now, Alashiya rubbed the grit from her eyes. "I... no. I haven't eaten." Without thinking, she added, "I didn't know how to use the talking thing Taevas told me to use."

Hele tilted her head. "The MET?"

Cheeks warming, Alashiya quickly looked away. *Oh gods, now she's going to think I'm some country yokel.*

"I've never used one before," she quickly explained, hoping it wouldn't make her sound even more unsophisticated.

Hele didn't appear to judge her for her ignorance. Instead, she nodded sagely. "I didn't know anything until my clan taught me. It's a good thing you've joined ours. Now *I* can teach you."

"Um... thank you?" Alashiya self-consciously tucked the lapels of her borrowed robe tighter against her chest. She looked around at the massive television mounted on the wall and all the other foreign bits of technology scattered around the lounge with trepidation.

Taking a deep breath, she haltingly explained, "I haven't used much technology. I only ever had access to the computers at the library in town. I don't know how to use anything here."

Hele patted her knee. "Don't worry about looking silly for not knowing. My *ema* says the only way to do that is to not ask for help when you need it."

"Your... *ema* sounds smart."

The rustle of paper announced the presence of someone else a second before a new voice sing-songed, "Are we talking about our mama? Because if so, you're damn right."

Alashiya twisted to look at the doorway, where a purple dragon stood. Her arms, shimmering with gold flecks, were laden with bags and her short black hair curled stylishly around her horns. Alashiya vaguely recalled her face from the hospital but her name escaped her.

As if she could read her mind, the dragon lifted her chin and offered, "Alex."

Clearing her throat, she replied, "Hi, Alex."

"She hasn't eaten breakfast," Hele announced. "Did you bring a feast?"

Alex grinned a huge, toothy grin and lifted the bags. Sauntering across the room, she nearly gave Alashiya a heart attack when she vaulted over the low back of the couch to land in the sunken pit. "I did," she crowed. Turning to present the heavy bags to Alashiya with a flourish — one that utilized both tail *and* wings — she declared, "A feast for our new Emand, long may she reign!"

"Oh," Alashiya breathed, shrinking back against the cushions. *Oh no.*

CHAPTER FIFTY

IT'D BEEN A VERY, VERY LONG TIME SINCE ALASHIYA hung out with... well, anyone besides Taevas. And she'd never known people like Hele or Alex.

It was one thing to hear about them from her husband's stories, but it was something else entirely to sit with them and be treated like she'd been part of the clan for forever rather than a handful of days. Alex's dry humor and sharp tongue were a perfect contrast to Hele's brusque sweetness. Neither of them expected her to talk much, but they never treated her like she wasn't there, either.

She wasn't sure when or how it happened, exactly, but at some point after half a dozen decadent pastries had been consumed, Alex cajoled Alashiya into slathering something cool and jelly-like onto her face while Hele meticulously buffed her nails. She'd been instructed not to panic when it dried to a hard, rubbery mask. A show of some sort had been put on the television, but neither of the women appeared to pay any attention to what was happening on the screen, so Alashiya didn't either. It took all her focus to keep up with the two of them, anyway.

Trying to keep her head back so the mask didn't tug uncomfortably on her face, she asked, "What exactly is this supposed to do?"

"It's got collagen and seaweed extract," Alex explained. "What dress size are you?"

Alashiya tried to look out of the corner of her eye at the dragon, but all she could make out was pale green goo. "Why?"

"Taevas gave me his cards and told me to help you get anything you wanted. I'm getting a headstart." She shrugged. "I already did, actually. Some basics have been delivered if you want to change out of that robe and put on some skivvies."

Alashiya pictured the sash and trendy, high-waisted short-shorts Alex seemed to favor. She'd done a fine job getting her something to wear in the hospital, but she wasn't entirely sure she trusted Alex to fill out her entire wardrobe. Having new clothes was a big enough change. She didn't think she could handle trying to figure out how to strap her much heavier chest into one of those barely-there tops Alex wore so well.

Might be worth a try, though, she thought. What was a little more change on top of everything else, anyway?

"I don't know my size," she admitted. "I make all my own clothes. I can give you my measurements, if that helps?"

The feeling of something cool being brushed on her nails preceded Hele asking, "You make your own clothing?"

"I do. I'm a professional embroiderer, actually."

"That's lucky," Alex said, her claws tapping on the glass face of her tablet. "I don't know anyone who likes embroidery more than my cousin. Have you *seen* his wardrobe? The man's obsessed."

Warmth filled her chest. Feeling a little shy, Alashiya admitted, "I've seen it, yes. I... I'm actually the one who did most of the work."

Alex popped into her line of sight. "What? You're kidding, right?"

"Um, no," she answered.

Alashiya had expected a lot of questions about what

happened with Taevas, but up until then, both women had carefully avoided anything related to what had brought her there. She got the impression that they had come to some sort of agreement prior to arriving to act as normal as possible, which she appreciated. There really wasn't any way to avoid it forever, though, so she took a deep breath before telling the story.

A trimmed down version that didn't include her fixation on Adon, anyway.

"Good gods," Alex muttered. "What are the odds of that?"

"Not very high." Hele blew on Alashiya's nails. "Thank you for saving our cousin, Emand. I didn't think he was dead, but we were all starting to worry. And sorry again for my mate's mistake. He's hard-headed."

Trying not to squirm with discomfort, Alashiya replied, "Ah, please don't call me that."

"Why not? It's what you are."

Alex hummed in agreement as she began to gently peel up the edges of Alashiya's mask. "You're the big man's Chosen, which means you're the Emand to his Isand. And not to scare you or anything, but as of eight AM this morning, *everyone* is required to call you that."

"What?" She winced as the mask gave way, along with some of her eyebrows. Wiggling her nose to chase off the ticklish feeling, "What are you talking about?"

Alex dropped the rubbery mask onto the coffee table with a flick of her manicured claws. It landed with a wet smack, the mouth hole spread in a comically wide smile. "The announcement went out this morning that Taevas is back — all thanks to *you,* our new Emand, Alashiya Ardz, who's also an embroiderer of some renown, apparently. It's been splashed across all the news feeds pretty much non-stop."

Alashiya, who'd just taken a sip of coffee, choked. "He *what?*"

"Look." Hele replaced the cap on her nail polish before snagging a glossy black device from the cluttered coffee table. A few taps of her glowing finger changed the show on the television to what she recognized from glimpses of Debbie's tablet as a popular news program.

She stared, gobsmacked, as two attractive people spoke to the camera with Alashiya's government ID photo superimposed between them. A rapidly scrolling reel of information ran across the bottom of the screen, displaying truncated details about Taevas's return and her mysterious role in it.

A wave of nausea rolled up from her gullet to burn her throat as she listened to the newscasters relate what few details about her were available to the public, like her age, her hometown, and her family.

"Why... why does anyone care about who I am?" she breathed.

Hele shrugged. "You're a hero."

Alashiya didn't feel particularly heroic. She never had. Staring in bewilderment at the screen, she said, "I didn't do it to be a hero. I didn't want anything to do with Taevas at first. And then after— I just wanted to save my husband. That's not heroism. That's just... loving someone."

Alex slung an arm around her shoulders and gave her an affectionate squeeze. "Don't worry about all this attention, okay? We'll protect you and make sure you feel safe here."

Eyes stinging, she swung her head around to give Alex a panicked look. "I— I don't know how to do any of this. I don't know how to be an Emand. I barely know how to be a queen of a grove. What if I fail? What if I embarrass everyone? What if—"

Hele switched off the television. "Alex, hand me a blanket, please."

"Good call." The dragon passed the soft gray blanket to her sister, who immediately wrapped it tightly around Alashiya's shoulders.

The squeeze, as well as both women's arms wrapping around her, brought an instant comfort. It was a bit like being held by her husband and also hiding in the deep greenery of her forest, except it came with the added benefit of the easy acceptance of two remarkable women.

Hele held Alashiya's waist and pressed her cheek to her blanket-covered shoulder while Alex tucked her head beneath her purple chin.

"This world is very overwhelming," Hele whispered in a soft, knowing voice. "But clan makes it better. You have nothing to fear, Emand. We're here to help you and explain when things are confusing or scary."

"Taevas told me all about you," she whispered, breath hitching. "I hoped I'd get to meet you. So... please just call me Shiya, okay? That way we can be friends. I think I'm going to need those."

"We're not friends," Hele announced, matter-of-fact. "We're clan. This is better."

Alex and Alashiya shared a small burst of laughter.

Pulling back a little, Alex offered, "Hele's taken the clan thing pretty far. Did my cousin tell you she's been running around the continent adopting elementals?"

Alashiya wiped her eyes. "Yes, he did. It sounds amazing. I wish we had someone like you."

Hele tilted her head curiously. "We?"

"Nymphs," she answered. "We used to be connected kind of like one big clan, but we've been cut off from each other for a very long time."

"Why?"

"Because we drifted apart. And no one has had the resources to bring us back together, I guess." Alashiya tightened the blanket around her shoulders. It seemed like a lifetime ago that she and Taevas discussed her "terms" but it had only been a few days. She'd barely had time to even consider what she could do with what he offered her.

But sitting there, surrounded by the warmth of a family that was now her own, she couldn't help but wonder what it might be like to weave those old threads together again.

Alex and Hele shared a look. Speaking slowly, the dragon

replied, "Well, you know who has a lot of resources? The Emand of the Draakonriik."

A polite knock on the door cut off Alashiya's reply. Their heads swiveled to find the hulking form of Radek standing in the doorway. As gruff as the day before, he announced, "Emand, you and the Isand have visitors. You should probably put some clothes on."

Alex stood up and propped her hands on her hips. "What? Is it clan? If not, tell them to fuck off. She just got let out of *jail*. Can't a hero nymph friggin' relax around here, big bad Rad?"

Alashiya hadn't met so many new people in her entire life, and she wasn't exactly eager to meet more, so she was grateful for Alex's sudden fierceness. She wasn't sure she even knew how to relax in the way Taevas expected her to — especially after what she'd just heard — but she wanted to try.

The stony look on Radek's harsh face made her hope on that score wither.

"If the Emand doesn't want to meet the sovereigns of the Elvish Protectorate, that's her choice," he replied, completely unbothered by Alex's snark.

"There are elves here?" Alashiya gasped. The blanket fell from her shoulders as she gripped the back of the couch.

Radek blinked slowly. "Yes, ma'am. Theodore Solbourne and Margot Goode will be arriving shortly."

She looked askance at Hele and Alex. "Isn't Theodore Taevas's protege?"

Alex grinned. "Okay, I changed my mind. You should *definitely* put some clothes on."

CHAPTER FIFTY-ONE

TWENTY MINUTES LATER, ALASHIYA FOUND HERSELF fidgeting nervously beside Radek. She'd changed into a silky, ankle-length pleated skirt and a white linen blouse — two things she couldn't imagine Alex wearing, but she had apparently read Alashiya's needs better than she initially gave her credit for.

Her old boots clicked on the marble floor as she let Radek lead her down sunlit corridors. She tried not to stare at everything, but it was hard not to gawk. The roost was beautiful, but it was strangely empty. All high, vaulted ceilings and seamless windows and white walls. It hardly seemed like a home to her, but she tried not to be too judgemental.

She thought she was doing pretty good until they reached the atrium.

The first couple times she walked through it, she'd barely noticed it. Now, as Radek guided her across the empty expanse of it, she couldn't help but look around with confusion, her nose wrinkled.

"Something wrong?" the dragon grunted.

"No." She paused, rethought her answer, and then said, "Actually, yes. Why is this room empty?"

He shot her a glance. "There's a table and some chairs."

"One table and two chairs in a room the size of my house." She gestured to the glass ceiling, which let in a stunning amount of pure, glittering sunlight. "With all this light— Do you have any idea how many plants you could grow here?"

Radek stopped at one of the many doors that ringed the atrium. Opening it for her, he rumbled, "No, I don't. That's something you should take up with your Chosen, Emand."

"Oh." She frowned. "I don't want him to think I don't like his house. It's just very different from mine."

It couldn't have been *more* different, really. Taevas's reaction to her home made a lot more sense to her now. Not because his roost was *better*, but because she couldn't imagine two more opposite dwellings if she tried.

She'd only seen *one* plant so far, and she'd been horrified to discover it was fake. How he justified that, she couldn't even begin to fathom.

Radek gave her a strange look. "A dragon's roost is his pride," he explained, like it should be obvious, "but it doesn't mean fuck-all if his Chosen doesn't like it. Trust me, ma'am. He'll want you to change things."

Taevas had said as much, so she supposed she ought to take it seriously. Still, it felt a little rude. Shaking her head, she asked, "Do you have a spouse, Radek?"

He turned his gaze forward. A subtle tightening of his mouth was the only sign that perhaps all wasn't well when he answered, "Yes. I have a Chosen. Her name is Vivian."

Fearing she'd stepped in it but not knowing how to back out of the conversation now that she'd started it, Alashiya floundered. "Does... did she make changes to your roost, too?"

"Not yet," he answered.

Something about the way he said those two words felt like a definitive end to the conversation. Alashiya blew out a breath and nodded. She wasn't offended by Radek's taciturn attitude. If anything, it was comforting in its familiarity. Most of the men in Birchdale hadn't exactly been warm and fuzzy, either.

They continued their journey in silence until they reached another large doorway. Radek put his hand on the knob, but he didn't open it for her right away. Hesitating, he rumbled, "Ma'am... thank you. For saving Taevas."

Her chest squeezed. Laying a hand on his massive bicep, she told him, "Call me Shiya."

Radek gave her a curt nod and opened the door. Peering around him, she spied a much larger lounge area than the one she'd been holed up in with Alex and Hele. A glossy bar spanned one side and a huge sunken seating area the other. Across from the entrance was a wall of windows that opened up into what she could only describe as some sort of rooftop patio.

Her eyes were instantly drawn to Taevas, who appeared to be holding court from the comfort of the couch. She recognized a few of the dragons gathered around him, but there were two healers dressed in their elegant gray coats she didn't know as well.

Her husband's head whipped in her direction. A luminous grin spread across his gorgeous, perfect face. "My Shiya," he called, slinging an arm over the back of the couch. "Come here!"

Despite automatically rolling her eyes, she couldn't suppress a smile when she complained, "Always so bossy."

The gazes of the people gathered around him bounced between them. Eyebrows lifted when Taevas wiggled his claws at her and teased, "We both know who the boss is here, *metsalill*, and it's not me."

Trying to ignore the scrutiny, Alashiya crossed the floor to step down into the sitting area, drawn to Taevas like a sapling to light. They reached for each other at the same time, their fingers linking as Taevas drew her down to sit beside him. He certainly didn't seem to care about their audience when he swooped down on her and delivered a quick but passionate kiss.

Flushing to the roots of her hair, she muttered, "Was that really necessary?"

"Very," he replied, sneaking in another kiss. Chuckling at her obvious embarrassment, he sat back and gestured at the hovering healers. "You're just in time for my check-up — which will hopefully be quick, because we've got sovereigns incoming."

"We'll do our best, sir," one of the healers dryly replied.

The dragons began to talk amongst themselves as the healers leaned over to lay their hands on Taevas's forearms, which were revealed by his rolled up shirtsleeves. Whispering in his ear, Alashiya asked, "Can you remind me of everyone's names?"

He tilted his chin toward the men, some of whom she recognized from the hospital. Radek had joined them, but he didn't appear any friendlier with them than he had with her. If anything, he looked even more sour when one of them, a deep blue dragon with a broken horn, clapped him on the shoulder. "This is my Wing. The one next to Radek is Pasha."

Jerking his chin toward another clump of intimidatingly large dragons engaged in rapid, hushed debate, he told her, "The green one you know. The pale guy is Roman, and the red one with the patterns is Aivar."

Alashiya tried not to stare at them, but it was hard. Each member of the Wing seemed more intimidating than the last. Vael and Radek were known entities, at least, but Pasha, Roman, and Aivar were different.

Pasha's broken horn and ear piercings gave him a roguish quality only enhanced by his wild eyes and wide, sharp-toothed grin. Roman was a ghostly white, with deep-set black eyes and high cheekbones. Pale blue tattoos crawled up his neck to cover nearly half of his face and the shaved part of his head, which must have been extremely painful to have done. And then there was Aivar, who would've seemed fairly normal if he didn't appear to be caught between shifting from his day to night color. Velvety black coloring swirled with luminous crimson, giving him a striking marbled effect that made her fingers itch for her needle and thread.

Despite their obvious exhaustion, all the Wing members seemed keyed up and excited, their deep voices rumbling as they debated something in their language. It was good to finally be able to put names to faces, but Alashiya still shied away when they glanced at her, their curiosity obvious.

"So what's the verdict?"

Her attention was pulled back to Taevas, whose smile had fallen as he addressed the healers. The one apparently in charge, a mature-looking man with dark skin and pretty, cinnamon-brown eyes, let out a slow breath. "It's hard to say, in all honesty. I believe your ability to shift has been stabilized, which is the good news. We were able to flush the last of the suppressant out of you when you were in the hospital, but it did considerable damage to your nervous system. If we don't figure out how to fix it, your ability to shift will continue to be unreliable and..."

Taevas's jaw worked for a moment before he prompted, "And?"

"And your wings won't recover." The healer rubbed the back of his neck, a deeply troubled look on his face. Alashiya reached for her husband's hand and held it tightly when he continued, "There was some intentional damage done to the bases of both wings — electrical, it looks like — which would've been easy enough to repair if not for the additional injury caused by the suppressant. I'm not saying there's no hope, but it's going to be a long road. I suggest we find a specialist to begin the process immediately."

A wave of feeling washed through the hyphae. Alashiya's breath hitched as she brought his hand up to her lips. She pressed a kiss to his knuckles and reached through the hyphae to soothe him there, too. The steady beat of his heart thumped alongside her own when she sought out the gorgeous purple strand and followed it back to the source.

Easy, argaman mlk, she whispered to him. *All is well. We're with you.*

His rigid expression softened. Taking a deep breath, he said in a measured voice, "All right. I'm alive. I can live without my wings for a while longer."

"I'm also concerned about what looks like an aggressive

fungal infection," the other healer, a younger woman with short brown hair and a gold nose ring, interjected. "I'd like to prescribe you some medication that should hopefully take care of it before it settles in and does more damage."

"Ah—" Alashiya shrunk back a little when the healers turned their shrewd gazes on her. It was her husband's turn to give her hand a reassuring squeeze.

Clearing her throat, she said, "Forgive me if I'm wrong, but I don't think it's an infection like you're thinking. It doesn't need to be cured."

Both healers' eyebrows raised. The one with the nose ring, clearly trying to be respectful while still skeptical, asked, "And why do you think that?"

"Because he's my husband," she answered, casting a glance at Taevas. "I'm a nymph. When we married, I... Well, he's in the hyphae."

The younger healer didn't appear to understand what she was trying to say, but after a long moment, the older of the pair made a thoughtful sound. Snapping his fingers, he said, "Arbuscular mycorrhizal nymphalia. I've never seen it myself, but I remember reading about it in my apprenticeship. Do you mind if I confirm it's the same infection?"

He held out one smooth hand. Shrugging, she put her hand in his. There was that ticklish warmth again, but it only lasted a moment before he let her go. Giving his partner a nod, the healer said, "Identical. And *fascinating.*" He paused, his mind clearly working fast behind those red-brown eyes. "I am *very* interested in the way it interacts with your nervous system, Emand — and what that might mean for the Isand."

Alashiya blinked. "Well, I don't really—"

"Sovereigns on approach," Vael announced, the tips of his fingers pressed to the space above one ear.

Instantly, all members of the Wing lost their casual postures. Every dragon rose up as one. Vael vaulted over the couch to stand at attention directly behind Taevas. Radek joined him to take up his post behind her. The other dragons assembled by the glass wall, where they stood at attention, their backs perfectly straight and chins up.

The faintest sound of whirring wind began to filter through the glass as a shadow passed over the rooftop patio.

Sniffing, Taevas rose from the couch. Offering her his hand, he told the healers, "We'll continue this conversation after my meeting with the sovereigns."

The healers made their polite goodbyes and rushed off toward the door, where a beautiful dragon in a pencil skirt had manifested out of thin air. Gesturing for the healers to pass through the door with her tablet, she called out, "Isand, Lee Seymour is requesting a call."

Taevas narrowed his eyes. "Oh, I've got some things to say to Lee. Katya, tell him I'll call him tonight."

"Yes, sir. And when the Emand is ready, she has several messages as well."

Alashiya started. "I do?"

"Yes, ma'am," Katya replied. "The nymph representative from the United Congress has called several times, and a few others have left messages as well."

Nymphs want to talk to me? Alashiya paled.

"Don't worry about any of that right now. You're the Emand. Everyone can and will wait until you're ready," Taevas muttered.

"What if I never am?" she whispered, wiping her sweaty palms on her pretty silk skirt.

"My brave queen? Impossible." Taevas shook his head. Stroking her back, he crisply informed Katya, "Hold all calls for her until she says she's ready."

"Understood." Katya nodded and turned on her white stiletto heel to follow the healers out.

"Deep breath, *metsalill*," he murmured as he guided her out of the sitting area and toward the wall of windows. "Remember, elves only bite if you insult their mothers. And witches... well, best to get on their good side early."

"Ha-ha," she deadpanned, jabbing her elbow into his side.

Nerves tightened her stomach as she watched a small white aircraft with a golden sun and thistle crest on its tail land across the rooftop. The whooshing sound cut off abruptly, and not a moment later a door opened on the craft's side. A short silver staircase extended. Several helmeted, black-clad soldiers jogged smoothly down the steps and fanned out around it, making two columns.

A massive figure in a sharp black suit appeared at the top of the steps. A much smaller person stood beside him, their hands linked. Her red hair whipped in the wind as he guided her down to the roof. Only when they passed under the awning attached to the glass wall did she notice the man was pale blue.

Taevas nodded toward Pasha, who tapped what looked like a small screen on the wall. One of the massive panels of glass slid aside. Wind whistled inside immediately, rustling her hastily braided hair. Alashiya braced herself as the sovereigns stepped inside, their clothing flapping.

She'd never seen an elf in person before, but she'd read about them. Jewel-toned, towering, almost indestructible, and secretive, they kept themselves apart from every other group in the world. Stand-offish was the nicest way she'd seen them described.

It came as a bit of a surprise, then, when the blue elf paused, gently released his wife's hand, grabbed a fistful of Taevas's shirt, and dragged him in for a rough embrace.

"You son of a bitch," the elf hissed.

Even Taevas, her outgoing and affectionate husband, seemed taken aback. It took him a second to catch up before he wrapped his arms around the elf with a hearty slap to his back. "Hey, kid," he rumbled, pleasure warming his voice.

"You picked a shitty time to take a vacation, old man."

"This is the thanks I get for giving you time to shine?" Taevas pulled back to grip his shoulders. Peering closely at the elf's handsome blue face, he asked, "You okay?"

"We're okay," the elf answered. Clearing his throat, he

gestured toward the woman who'd come with him. "Lost a decade off my life, probably, but other than that..."

Taevas released him and offered the small redhead, clearly the witch of the pair, a smile. "I know how that feels." He half-turned and extended his hand to Alashiya, who took it tentatively. Reeling her into his side, he announced, "I'd like you to meet my Chosen, Alashiya Ardz. She saved my life and brought me back to the 'Riik. Shiya, this is my protege, Theodore Solbourne, and his much more talented wife Margot Goode. They run the Elvish Protectorate."

Margot, a keen-eyed young woman with fox-like features, came forward to take her free hand. "Hi, Alashiya. It's a pleasure to meet you. I can't tell you how relieved everyone is that you brought your mate back to us."

Trying not to shy away from their scrutiny, she shook Margot's hand and gave them both quick smiles. "I'm happy he's back with his people, too," she replied, still uneasy about everyone knowing her before she knew them.

"I'm *not* his protege," Theodore brusquely informed her. Despite that, he took Alashiya's hand from his wife and gave it a long, grateful squeeze. "Thank you. He's annoying, but I'm fond of him. And I really wasn't looking forward to all the meetings I'd have to take if he was replaced. I *cannot* wait to hear exactly how all of this played out. I'm extremely curious about how he managed to go from kidnapped to mated to a hero like yourself."

It was bizarre in the extreme to be the focus of so much warmth and admiration from people who were so important. She'd gotten used to Taevas, but she also hadn't really believed him when he told her who he was. Now it was all very, very real, and that meant she had to act like it didn't feel like a fever dream to have the leaders of a territory treat her like she was important.

Somehow it felt more natural when it was just the dragons doing it. When the sovereigns looked at her like that, Alashiya had to fight the urge to squirm. Only Taevas's steadying hand on her back stopped her from blurting out that she really wasn't anyone of note, that she'd just done what felt right, and that there was never any choice when it came to her husband.

Instead, she took a deep breath, straightened her spine, and replied, "Welcome to our home. I'm... I'm very happy I finally get to meet you."

Her husband's lips twisted in a rueful smile. "You're going to love the part where I crashed through the roof of her barn."

She gave the elf's hand a shake before sidling a bit closer to Taevas. Theodore seemed lovely, but it was true that all elves carried with them a predatory aura. Just standing near him made ancient instincts bristle.

Probably because a few in her line had been eaten by elves, back when they could get away with that sort of thing.

Wrapping her arm around his waist, she fell back onto the manners ingrained into her DNA. "Have you two eaten? I haven't found the kitchen yet, but I'm sure I can make us something if Taevas points me in the right direction."

The reaction from the pair was instant. Theodore waved one massive hand, dismissing her offer, and Margot protested, "No, absolutely not. I can only imagine what you've been through in the last few days. There is no way you're cooking for us. Besides, my husband only eats raw meat. I don't know much about nymphs, but I'm pretty sure you're vegetarian, aren't you?"

Alashiya balked. "Ah, yes. I... I don't know if I can do that."

Theodore laughed. Running his claws through his wavy black hair, he teased, "You and my wife have that in common. It'd be an honor to be served a meal made by the new Emand, but I wouldn't do that to you. That's not why we came, anyway."

Suddenly serious, Taevas asked, "You didn't just come to see us, did you?"

Theodore clapped a hand on Taevas's shoulder. "No," he answered, a peculiar note in his voice. "We didn't."

He turned toward the windows and gestured for one of the masked guards that had followed them inside to open the door.

Alashiya and Taevas shared a glance as the elf lifted two fingers, his dark gaze fixed on the white aircraft across the roof.

From within the darkness of the open hatch door, a hulking figure emerged. Light glinted off metal-capped horns as a bloody and shackled Sergei was escorted down the steps by his own small fleet of guards.

Sounding grimly pleased, Theodore announced, "We brought you a present."

CHAPTER FIFTY-TWO

It went against every instinct he possessed to allow Sergei into his roost or anywhere near his mate, so after the initial uproar over his arrival died down, he was promptly moved to the Wing barracks. Situated at the base of Taveas's tower, it was still far too close for his liking, but it would have to do for now.

"We caught him trying to cross the border," Theodore explained, his arms crossed over his chest and his glare locked on the filthy dragon slumped over the table in the makeshift interrogation room. They stood shoulder to shoulder looking in through the small square window in the door. "Patrol didn't know who they had until your people put out the alert this morning. They almost let him go."

The muscles of Taevas's jaw worked as he ground his teeth. "Has he said anything?"

"No," Theodore replied.

"Did a mind healer check him?"

"Yup. No sign of any tampering." Theodore sniffed. "You know this prick?"

"Not before this, no," he answered, "but he's one of Jaak's sons."

"Ah. That explains it, I guess."

Taevas made a noncommittal sound in the back of his throat. He wasn't so sure. The things Sergei said hadn't made any sense. Revenge for his father's death seemed the most logical reason for all of this, but he'd been adamant that Jaak's death wasn't the reason behind his kidnapping. Of course, there was always the chance that he was lying, but something in Taevas's gut made him question that easy answer.

Theodore turned slightly. Giving Taevas a long look, he asked, "What's going on with your wings?"

A spasm of feeling wracked his chest.

He didn't want to talk about it. He didn't want to think about it. He didn't want to remember how Healer Cutner's tone changed when he said his wings might never be the same.

To not be able to fly was one thing, but to not be able to embrace his Chosen...

He'd hardly had the chance to process his joy over being *married* to his Alashiya, but knowing they had that bond helped soothe some small measure of his rage and grief over his injury. It didn't make it bearable, necessarily, but whenever he looked at that new, silvery scar on his palm, he was reminded that she'd claimed him in a way that could never be undone — all without the expectation of ever being wrapped in his wings.

He was determined to get his wings back, but if he didn't, he'd survive it. Because he had her.

Sucking in a deep breath, he said, "I was pumped full of black market suppressants and had my wings electrified to stop me from escaping. The nerves are shot."

Theodore's dark brows drew together with concern. "What did your healers say?"

Not wanting to get into the gritty details, he answered, "They're concerned but cautiously optimistic."

"You need to talk to my wife," Theodore insisted.

"She has enough on her plate." Taevas cast the elf a look. "Didn't her grandmother get shot? And I heard her cousin is still missing."

Theodore pursed his lips. "Sophie's fine. Physically, anyway. And right now, Sergei is the only real lead we have on Ruby. If you can get him to talk, there's nothing she wouldn't do for you." He paused. The scent of ozone and copper filled the air as his eyes went distant. After a handful of seconds, the elf added with a rueful twist of his lips, "My wife would like me to inform you that she considers it her duty to heal you whether or not you help us find Ruby."

Taevas tried not to show his surprise. There were rumors that the pair shared a telepathic bond, and after spending time with them he'd been nearly certain, but Theodore had never confirmed it. What was shared between mates was sacred and private. To hear him so casually share it now was a show of trust Taevas didn't expect and never would've asked for.

Touched, he looked away from the young elf and cleared his throat. "I'll do what I can regardless. But if... if you could, I would appreciate it if you encouraged Margot to keep in contact with my Shiya. She'll need a friend who understands what it's like to live the lives we do."

"Of course." Theodore nodded toward the window. His chin lifted. "Now go get our answers."

Clapping Theodore's shoulder, Taevas stepped back and opened the door.

Sergei didn't look up as he entered the room. He didn't appear to notice or care when the door shut behind Taevas. The dragon sat with his hands cuffed behind his back, his wide shoulders slumped and wings held rigidly. His ankles were shackled too, but he didn't appear particularly threatening with or without them.

The cocky dragon who'd thought to kidnap an Isand and claim *his* Alashiya was no more. Left in his place was a dirty, injured man in chains.

Their fight had certainly done a number on Sergei, but as Taevas sat down in the metal chair opposite him, he couldn't help but think that Alashiya was responsible for his worst injuries. On top of his bruises and slashes from Taevas's claws, it was obvious where the grille of the SUV had split his cheek and cracked a horn — which was probably only a hint of the extent of the damage done to the rest of him.

The shotgun blast had hit the other side of him. Alashiya clearly hadn't aimed for him directly, but it caught his upper shoulder, arm, and the corner of his jaw. A large swath of small, painful wounds had crusted over, clearly untreated.

It'd obviously been a rough couple days for the guy.

Taevas sat back in his chair. His tail swung in deceptively lazy circles to his left, the tip curling and uncurling reflexively. He couldn't say he felt particularly sympathetic.

"It was damn stupid to try and cross into the EVP. You're lucky the elves didn't kill you."

Sergei snorted. Still glaring at the tabletop, he rasped, "Like you aren't?"

Thinking of his wings, his weeks of delirious captivity, and the grief and pain his people had gone through, Taevas replied, "I haven't decided yet."

Sergei rolled his injured shoulders but said nothing for a long time. When he did speak, his tone hardened. "What happened to the nymph?"

"Don't talk about her," Taevas snapped, tail rattling.

"I just want to know if she's all right."

Keeping his cool wasn't normally an issue, but when Sergei spoke about Alashiya, his calm disintegrated. "You don't get to know that. She's not yours. You led Monty to her fucking *nest*, you piece of shit."

Sergei shook his head. Scowl grooving lines on his bruised face, he protested, "He knew her land. I needed his help to find you. Once I had you, I was going to take care of him. I told her I would. I don't tolerate men who bully women."

"And you think she would've willingly gone with you after you invaded her land and kidnapped me?" Taevas scoffed. "I didn't think you were particularly smart, Sergei, but that is really fucking stupid."

"*All* of this was really fucking stupid," Sergei snapped. Finally looking up from the table, he fixed a bloodshot glare on Taevas and curled his upper lip over his fangs. "None of this was my idea! None of this was what *I* wanted! But I thought, *why not?* Why not take the one good thing I could get out of it? I could take her out of that shit hole and protect her and be a good mate. I *could.*"

The heat of territorial rage burned in his chest, but Taevas was the one Alashiya Chose. He was the one who'd been welcomed into her ancient family. *He* was the one with the queen in his nest.

Sergei was just the big prick in handcuffs.

Speaking in a carefully measured voice, he asked, "Whose idea was it if not yours?"

A dry, humorless laugh escaped Sergei's throat. "Why would I tell you that?"

"Because if you tell me everything you know, I might be more inclined to let you live." Taevas bared his teeth in something that could only generously be called a smile. "You broke my wings. You drugged me and held me captive for weeks. And worst of all, you threatened my Chosen. Suffice it to say that I'm not feeling merciful."

Whatever he expected, it wasn't for a look of disgust to cross Sergei's beaten face.

Sitting back as best he could with his hands cuffed behind his back, he hissed, "All I did was get the soldiers access to you. I didn't touch your wings. I didn't drug you. And I sure as fuck never threatened the nymph. I don't hurt women. I wanted to protect her."

"I remember you being where I was held," Taevas shot back. He mockingly flicked his claws at his horns. "You're a hard man to forget, Sergei. Even when drugged."

Sergei grimaced and appeared to immediately regret it. Wincing, he dabbed at his split lip with his tongue. "I was called in when shit hit the fan. When I got there, you were already fucked up because the soldiers had no idea how to handle you. My only job was to move you."

Whether Taevas believed him or not wasn't important. They were on the right track.

"Who gave you that job?"

Sergei's expression shut down. "I can't tell you that."

"Why not?"

"Because I *can't.*"

Trying to rein in his temper, Taevas calmly informed him, "You understand that this is bigger than either of us, right? You didn't just kidnap the Isand. You are also the only known, uncompromised informant to what looks like an attempt to kill *every leader* of the UTA — including the elf standing outside this door. If you don't start talking, I'm not the only one you'll answer to."

Sergei said nothing.

Taevas scrubbed his palm across his mouth. He didn't want to be there talking to Sergei. He wanted to be back with his Chosen, beginning their lives together. He wanted to hear more about their wedding and fuck her in the nest *properly* this time.

He wanted Alashiya, plain and simple.

The smooth skin of his scar tickled his lips as he tried to get a hold on his impatience. Closing his eyes, he sucked in a deep breath.

Why would he do this?

He wracked his mind, looking for a reason someone like Sergei would do something as extreme and risky as helping kidnap *him.* If it wasn't his idea, then it really wasn't for revenge. And if it wasn't for revenge, then what else was there?

His gut told him that if he found that reason, he'd be able to crack Sergei and get the information they all so desperately wanted.

The echo of Alashiya's heart was a soothing beat in his chest as he glanced at his palm. The silver line stared up at him, foreign and familiar and perfect. She stood there beside him, her hand on his shoulder, even when she was high in the sky above him, having tea with Margot Goode. Safe. Content. His.

What could motivate a man like him to do something so... desperate?

His fingers curled into a fist.

Meeting Sergei's impenetrable gaze, he asked, "It's your family, isn't it? Not Jaak. Your *real* family."

The color drained out of the dragon's face, leaving it a chalky blue. He didn't reply, but there was a nearly visible crack in his composure as he held Taevas's stare.

Scenting blood, Taevas stretched his memory back, searching for anything that might be relevant, any shred of a clue that might help them unwind the mystery Sergei seemed determined to die protecting.

A distant memory, so vague he wasn't entirely certain he hadn't made it up, tickled the back of his mind.

"You know," he began, speaking slowly, "I used to get reports every year on Jaak's offspring and former partners. My uncle thought it was best to keep track of you, just in case you ever decided to act out. I'll be honest — I skimmed them for the last couple decades. But I remember one of them. There was a rumor that Enel Luik took a religious path and joined a temple."

He stared hard at Sergei's frozen face as he continued in a soft, sure voice. "I only noted it because I thought it was interesting. A dragon in Glory's Temple? You don't see that every day, do you?"

Sergei's expression didn't change, but his breathing picked up. Air whistled through his broken nose with every deep pull.

"I never thought of her again," Taevas continued, ruthless. "I figured a woman who went into religious life had found peace and should be left alone, especially after what she'd been through. I had no idea she had a son."

Color returned to Sergei's cheeks with a vengeance. His blue skin darkened to nearly purple as he tried to maintain his composure.

Taevas dug into his memories of a time he did his best to

forget. Jaak's many mates hadn't been something he was interested in when he was fighting the war. They were victims, just as the entire Draakonriik was a victim. The rumors of how he treated them had only added fuel to the fire of his rage.

But he remembered a story about an Enel, a young dragon from an ancient noble family who'd been bartered and sold to Jaak in exchange for a position in his shambling, cannibalistic government. Whether it was the same woman who joined Glory's Temple, he couldn't yet confirm — but when he glanced at the shiny, dented metal capping Sergei's horns, he suspected he was on the right path.

Taevas clasped his hands together and braced his forearms on the table. "I loved my mother," he confessed. "I admired her. She taught me how to be a protector, and how to stand up for what I believe in. But sometimes I hate her, too, for the decisions she made. I wonder why she couldn't have just done something different. Why she didn't just choose her family over her morals. Why *I* had to suffer for her choices."

Sergei's throat bobbed. The chair creaked under his bulk as he shifted his weight. Still, he said nothing — even as a tear streaked down his bloody cheek.

Taking a breath, Taevas looked down at the table. "I would still do anything for her, if she were alive. If she needed me, I'd be there." Lowering his voice, he asked, "Did your mother need you, Sergei?"

CHAPTER FIFTY-THREE

THE SUN HAD ALREADY SET BY THE TIME HE FINALLY
made it back to the nest. Once he finally got him talking, Sergei's
interrogation had taken hours. Debriefing with Theodore and his
Wing had taken another interminable stretch of time.

His mind buzzed with everything he'd learned, but his recov-
ering body screamed for rest.

Returning to his nest after a long day had always been a relief,
but there was nothing like stepping through the door to find
Alashiya sitting cross-legged on the bed. Her curls had been piled
on top of her head and she'd put on one of his comfortable
workout shirts. She didn't seem to mind the slits in the back as she
hunched over a tablet. Her fingers tapped clumsily against the
glass. Going by the hard set of her mouth and brows, she
appeared determined to learn how to use the device.

When she glanced up at him, little squares of light reflected in
her eyes. "Oh!" She set the tablet aside and crawled to the edge of
the bed. "You're back!"

"I'm sorry that took so long," he sighed, closing the door
behind him. Drawn to her as inexorably as he'd always been, he
crossed the room and sank onto the bed beside her. He didn't

hesitate to snag her around the waist and pull her into his lap. Her shapely legs stretched out, bare and beautiful, as she looped her arms around his neck.

His tension instantly released when she looked up at him with those soft eyes. "What happened with Sergei?"

Taevas let out a long breath. "I had to make a few promises, but I got him to talk."

"Why did he do it?"

Still conflicted even hours after hearing the story, he answered, "His mother asked him to."

Alashiya blinked. "His *mother?*"

Tucking her close to his chest, Taevas told her what Sergei had reluctantly revealed — only after securing immunity for himself and his mother in exchange.

After years of instability following Jaak's death and the subsequent fall of her own family's standing, Enel had indeed joined Glory's Temple. It was the only thing that brought her joy, Sergei told him. He'd been primarily raised by his grandparents, but his love for his mother was clear. Even when he explained her descent into darker fixations and the desire for revenge against Taevas for ruining her family, he did his best to support her.

His only hesitation came when his mother entangled herself with a shadowy group he couldn't seem to trace. Suddenly she wasn't just devout. She was *determined.* And the deeper she went, the more desperate she became. Then came the day she begged for his help, saying she would be in danger if she couldn't deliver. Sergei claimed he had no idea what he was getting into until he saw the reports that Taevas had been kidnapped, then was called in to help the Ardeo soldiers with his transport.

By then, his fear that his mother had gotten into bed with people who wouldn't hesitate to hurt her if he didn't comply had crystalized.

"My father terrorized her," Sergei had explained, haltingly and with palpable bitterness. *"The world threw her away and told her*

to survive on her own. Even my grandparents didn't care what happened to her. I'm the only person who cares. I'm the only person who'll protect her. So I did what I had to do."

Taevas didn't want to feel any sympathy for Sergei, but he did. He understood what it was like to feel that driving need to protect, even at great cost to himself. It didn't mean he forgave the man for the part he'd played, but it did mean he wouldn't kill him.

"He doesn't know much," he explained to Alashiya, "but he was able to give us more than anyone else. He said that he was instructed to bring me to the border between the Orclind and the EVP. He thinks that whoever has orchestrated this whole thing is in the desert."

"Why were you the only one kidnapped?" She nodded toward her discarded tablet. "After Margot and I had dinner, I wanted to read about what happened. Everyone else was attacked, but you were *taken*. Why?"

"He didn't have an answer for that," Taevas replied, shaking his head. "Or much else, for that matter. From what we can tell, it seems like he was used for his ability to get the soldiers through the 'Riik's security. When the assassinations went sideways, he was brought back to assist a change in plans. The best he could offer was speculation."

"Does any of it sound plausible?"

Taevas weighed the benefits and drawbacks of telling her what he suspected. He didn't want to scare her when they'd only just gotten some stability, but she was his partner. His equal. Keeping things from her was an insult to her.

So he swallowed his impulse to protect her and said, "I think there's real credence to the theory that they intended to tamper with my mind."

Alashiya stiffened. Fingers curling into his shoulders, she rasped, "Why would they brainwash you but kill everyone else?"

"I don't know for sure, but if the goal was to destabilize the alliance, it would be smart to keep one of the original signers alive and biddable. Compared to Sophie, Sigrid, or Lee, I'm the most personable. Maybe I was the easy choice. That way the public would have a familiar face to trust as they took over." Feeling the way she'd gone stiff in his arms, he smoothed his hands down her spine in a soothing stroke. "But it's just a theory. We won't know anything for certain until we uproot the source of all this violence."

A pervading sense of worry bled through that strange new sense he possessed, the one that was attuned to his Chosen. He could feel her even when they were apart, but when they touched... It was like she existed inside him. All around him. That vital glow that he'd so admired enclosed him, blocking out the dullness of the outside world.

And when he caught whispers of her thoughts, he understood better than ever why Theodore would jealously guard his connection with Margot. There was no gift more precious than the ability to connect with his mate mind to mind.

"Don't worry," he whispered, touching their foreheads together. "Whatever the plan was, it failed. We're safe. We're surrounded by friends and allies. That's all that matters."

Alashiya stroked the cords of his neck, her touch delicate. "We're safe with our grove."

His lips quirked. "Our grove. Our clan. As long as we're together, we'll be all right. It's you and me forever, my queen."

Giving him a narrow-eyed look, Alashiya said, "You know, we never did finish our negotiations."

"We didn't, did we?" Sitting back a bit so he could look into her eyes, he commanded, "Go on. What does my queen demand?"

"I want to help nymphs," she told him. "I want to do something like what Hele's done with the elementals. I don't know how, and I'm pretty sure I'm unfit for the job, but..."

Frowning, Taevas pinched her chin between his thumb and forefinger, forcing her to meet his gaze. "You are *not* unfit. You are the perfect person for that job, my Shiya."

"I don't know if that's true. I've been hiding my whole life. My people deserve someone who's outgoing and brave and ambitious. That's not me." She pressed her hand to the space above his heart. It beat in time with her own when she continued, "But I'm here. I care. I have you and I have your— *our* clan. That means the job is mine, whether I'm the best fit for it or not."

Taevas let out an amazed breath. "I felt the same way when I became Isand. I was scared shitless. Suddenly everyone was looking at me like I knew what to do and how to help them. What did I know? I was just a pissed off kid with too much blood on his hands. I felt like the biggest fraud in the world."

"But look at how well you've done," she whispered. "Look at how much your people love you. They were willing to go against the entire UTA because they refused to believe you were dead. You're so, so loved, Taevas."

"I am. And you will be, too." He tilted her chin up to press a soft kiss to her lips. She tasted like sweet wine and wild things and *home*. "Because you're kind. You're brave. You know what's right. And you have so much love to give this world, my Shiya."

"I never really thought about loving the rest of the world. I only ever wanted to love you."

His chest squeezed tight. It was the strangest thing to feel such joy and regret bundled together. Voice raw, he pleaded, "I want another wedding. That's my condition. I'll give you whatever you need to reunite the nymphs. In return I want a wedding I'll actually remember. I know we can't do the full ceremony again, but I can't have missed being Chosen by you. I can't stand it, *metsalill.*"

Of course, he would give her what she needed regardless, but if he had to negotiate, then he was going to demand the only thing he really wanted: her.

"But your people don't do weddings," she said, brows pinching.

"Our people will do whatever you ask them to. And so I am asking you, my queen, to marry me one more time. In front of our clan. In front of the world. I want everyone to know what a lucky son of a bitch I am."

A whisper-soft laugh, a sound of pure joy, escaped her plush lips. Cupping his jaw, she teased, "Didn't you announce that to the world this morning? I saw the news, you know. It scared the shit out of me."

He winced. "I probably should've warned you."

"Yes, you should've."

"But I didn't want the rumor mill to start working and have to reintroduce you to the people on the backfoot. I wanted them to know exactly who you are and what you've done." Holding her gaze, he added, "I meant what I said, Shiya. You don't have to do anything until you're ready. Being Emand is a big job you didn't exactly sign up for. Everyone will understand if you need a while to adjust."

Twisting to lay her back onto the bed, he hovered over her. Their lips brushed with every word he spoke. "And selfishly, I *want* you to take your time. I'm used to having you all to myself, *metsalill*. I don't want to share your attention with the world."

Alashiya threaded her fingers into his hair as her soft thighs cradled his hips. "What should I do in the meantime? I've never had nothing to do. I need to work."

"Trust me, my Shiya, there will be enough work for two lifetimes. There's no reason to rush into it." Running his hands down her sides, he began to slowly bunch up the large shirt. "Your Isand commands you to rest, pamper yourself, get acclimated, and do whatever you need to in order to feel like this is your home."

Swallowing hard, she asked, "Are we never going back to Birchdale?"

Pausing his exploratory touches to brace his elbows near her shoulders, he shook his head. His long hair, braided tight by his ears, swung over his shoulders to tickle her cheeks when she dropped her hands to his chest. "I would never take your home from you, my Shiya. I know what your family sacrificed to give you that land, and I know how deep your bond is with it. But...

we can't live there. Not if we want to be the leaders of the Draakonriik."

Alashiya looked away. Her expression was hard to read, but he could feel her distress and longing like it was his own. The murmur of her thoughts bubbled up like a spring of fresh water in the back of his mind — a melodious trickle of cool, sweet vitality.

...live anywhere else. Away from the trees, the roots, the earth... But my husband... my grove is worth everything.

Throat seizing, Taevas croaked, "Look at me."

When her eyes flicked back in his direction, so glossy and warm and lost, he told her, "Alashiya, I meant what I said back in Birchdale. I'll leave all of this for you. If you can't do this, then I can't do it either."

"Taevas—"

"No, listen," he pleaded. "I mean it. None of this means anything without you. You're my Chosen, Shiya. My only. My *world.* I've been Isand for a very, very long time. I could transition out of power and hand over the mantle to another dragon. It would take some time, but I can and will do it for you."

He could see she wanted to argue, to immediately protest, but his mate held her knee-jerk reaction back. Instead, she took a deep breath and really considered what he offered her.

"Thank you," she murmured. "Thank you."

He touched their noses together. "I made the mistake of not following you once, *metsalill.* Never again. I go where my queen goes. If that's away from here, then so be it."

Alashiya peppered gentle kisses to his cheeks, his lips, his nose, and his jaw. Her fingers moved down his chest to slowly begin unbuttoning his shirt. "My Adon. My *argaman mlk.* I love you. But I'm not the only one. Your people and your clan... All I've seen today is people who love you. This is your grove. I can't take you from them."

"But can you be *happy* here?" he breathed into her lips.

"I think I can," his brave mate answered, only a slight hesitation in her voice. "But I have conditions."

"Name them."

"We spend time in Birchdale every year. I want to connect with my forest. And when we have children, I want them to be able to run in the wilderness like I did."

His heart rate picked up. Exhilaration buzzing through him, he replied, "Done. It'll be our vacation home — ah, once we make some renovations. The Wing can come with us, and so can the clan, if we want them to."

He'd never taken a vacation before, but he was a mated man now. Soon enough he'd be a father. No one could dare blame him for taking time off. And if Lee had a problem with him staying in his territory for a couple weeks a year, Taevas would happily remind him that he could shove it up his ass.

"And I want to make changes here," she continued, untucking his shirt from his pants. Her deft fingers moved to the buckle of his belt. "I need plants. I need soil. I need *color.*"

If her touches didn't do it, hearing her talk about making their roost *hers* would've made him hard instantly. His breathing deepened. Tail coiling around one of her calves, he balanced his weight on one arm and used the other to ruck up her sleep shirt. Silky golden skin, heavy breasts, and the divine cradle of her cunt greeted him.

Pressing a hot, wet kiss to the thrumming pulse at the base of her neck, he promised, "Anything."

Her breath hitched as she dipped her fingers past the waistband of his slacks. "I want to visit Stalton's Atelier."

"Oh," he muttered darkly into her skin, "that I am more than happy to do, *naine.*"

Gently extracting the rigid bar of his cock, she gave it a slow, agonizing stroke. "And one more thing."

"Tell me," he gasped. "Tell me, my queen, and it's yours."

Using her free hand, she grasped his jaw and forced his head up until he met her heavy-lidded gaze. "Your queen needs you to make love to her in this nest."

Gods, he thought, *this is more than I could've dreamed of.*

After years of stroking his cock to the scent of her in this very nest, it was the most exquisite sort of triumph to spread her perfect thighs and feast on her slick cunt at last.

Alashiya wrapped her fingers around his horns, guiding him where she needed him, as praise spilled from her lips. And after she came on his fingers and tongue, he turned her onto her stomach, gently guided her onto her knees, and fulfilled another dream of his — sinking into her perfect cunt from behind.

Taevas draped his much larger body over her back as he slowly rocked his hips, savoring every gentle stroke. It was only her second time, so he restrained himself from rutting into her like a beast. They'd have to work up to that.

What a pleasure that'll be.

He cupped her jaw and nuzzled her cheek as he whispered, *"Minu metsalill,* I intend to be here forever. In this nest. Inside you. This is all I've ever dreamed of."

Alashiya gripped the pillows she'd so lovingly embroidered, her cunt rippling round his cock in a way that made him hiss with pleasure. "That's it, *argaman mlk.* That's perfect," she moaned.

Their first time was a revelation, but now that they were married, he didn't just get to bask in the fire of the divine he sensed in her. He got to *feel* it.

Alashiya's heartbeat and panting breaths synced with his. Her needs bled into his own. Her thoughts were an endless stream of love and potent desire.

When she needed him to move faster, he didn't have to be told. When she wanted him deeper, until he sheathed himself to the hilt with every forceful stroke, he answered her wordless call.

And when she demanded he finish, he was helpless to refuse her. Taevas emptied himself inside her with a low cry. Alashiya clenched hard as his release painted the hot walls of her cunt.

"So," she said, breathless and unmistakably sated, "do we have a deal, Isand?"

Taevas pumped shallowly, luxuriating in the wet glide. Scraping his teeth against her jaw, he reached down to stroke her with greedy fingers. She shuddered beneath him.

Not even close to done with her, he growled, "Not so fast, Emand. We might have to negotiate all night. I hope you're prepared to take me again. And again."

Alashiya reached back to fist a hand in his hair. "I'm queen of this grove. I can take anything you give me."

CHAPTER FIFTY-FOUR

CONSTRUCTION BEGAN ON THE ATRIUM THE SAME DAY
nymphs began to show up at the gates of Drummond Island.

At first, no one quite knew what to do with them. A single
envoy was one thing, but as the weeks since their return to the
Draakonriik passed, word had spread through the fine, distant
networks of groves that existed in the UTA. It wasn't just the
nymph congressional representative who showed up looking for
an audience with the new Emand. It was the queens of groves
great and small, sprawling and singular.

They traveled at great effort and expense, sometimes on foot
and sometimes in vans, luxury vehicles, or even on bicycles.
Nymphs from all walks of life showed up. The dragons greeted
them warmly but with bewilderment, unsure about what would
draw so many of the historically shy people to the heart of their
territory.

Alashiya herself didn't quite know what to make of it. She'd
barely begun to settle into the 'Riik, which was so foreign to her it
might as well have been another planet. To suddenly have an
influx of nymphs at her proverbial door, looking to her for favors,
guidance, or just out of pure curiosity made her vaguely nauseous.

But they were there, and she couldn't send them away.

A temporary hub was set up on the mainland to house and meet with the visitors. Alex, who'd recently gotten a promotion in the government's PR office, was assigned to take over the project. Alashiya had no idea what she'd do without her. While she took meeting after meeting, hearing from nymphs of all walks of life and parts of the continent, Alex managed their lodgings, complaints, and other needs. She also put out memos and ran interference when it just became too much for Alashiya.

It often did.

She had no idea how much power being the Emand gave her until the nymphs came, each one of them expecting her to fix their problems. It wasn't all land disputes and complaints about taxes. It was pleas for help finding lost grove members, requests to join hers, and the worn-in sort of desperation that cloaked the lost. Sometimes she felt like they came to her more for a listening ear than for a solution.

It quickly became apparent to her why Taevas wanted to ease her into life as the Emand. Alashiya could draw on the hyphae for lessons on how to be a leader, how to be a good queen, but managing a modern territory was a different beast entirely. It took fleets of skilled people to get anything done, and even then, she was amazed at what they were capable of doing.

When she jokingly pitched her idea for what to do with that empty atrium, she didn't think it would actually be *possible*. Perhaps, after everything, she should've known better.

Within a week, Taevas found contractors, engineers, and specialist gardeners to help achieve her dream. The floor was torn out, an extensive irrigation system that mimicked natural conditions installed, and several tons of soil, rock, and plantlife moved in. An artificial creek carved a winding path through the thicket of undergrowth, subtly following the main branch of the paths to the various doors that ringed the room.

Over the months that followed, Alashiya took her meetings with the queens there, tucked beneath the boughs of young birch trees carefully transplanted from her land. It didn't feel like home right away. Nothing could. Not when her constant companion had been the forest and its ancient heartbeat.

But roots grow in healthy soil, and so did her connection with the 'Riik.

As her own little forest began to flourish, she did, too. The atrium filled out with verdant ferns, prickly berry bushes, and wildflowers. A beehive was brought in, and so were rescued birds who couldn't be rereleased into the wild. Whenever life in the 'Riik became too strange and overwhelming, Alashiya followed the burbling creek, her bare feet cushioned by the forest floor, and came home again.

Taevas called the atrium her sanctuary, but it was one she was happy to share with everyone. While Hele and Alex were frequent and beloved visitors who brought joy, laughter, and often something new for her to experience, it was Radek who joined her most often. She'd heard whispers and less-than-kind jokes about him in passing, but to her he was a kindred spirit. They both found peace in the little forest, and although they didn't talk much, they shared what was important: the understanding of impossible loss.

After a lifetime of loneliness, she didn't take any bit of companionship for granted — even if she still enjoyed her alone time. When she really needed that, she retreated to her sewing room, which connected to Taevas's woodworking shop. Everyone knew to leave her alone when she had her needle in hand.

She spoke to her ghosts while she worked, just as she always had, but now she pulled silken thread wound with gold through fine fabrics for the pure joy of it rather than the grinding need to survive. Sometimes Taevas joined her after a long day of meetings, but he knew her well enough to sit in companionable silence until she set her needle aside.

Then they'd retire to their suite for the evening, where they'd cook dinner together — something she insisted on when he had the audacity to suggest they continue to use his chef — and discuss the events of the day. In the most important ways, nothing had changed from how they spent their time in Birchdale. Her fears that she wouldn't fit in his life were unfounded when the only thing that mattered was how well they fit together.

It was while they sat at their kitchen island, sharing a meal and a glass of wine, that she brought up the idea of the Nymph Network.

"I don't want to rule anyone. Or *more* people than the 'Riik, I guess," she explained, sharing a worry she'd been mulling over for weeks. "Not in the way my ancestors used to, anyway. I want to be the... the connection between my people."

Taevas nodded and took a sip of his wine. He'd always been in favor of her reviving the defunct title of her line, but they'd debated it enough that he didn't appear surprised by her decision. "What's the best way to do that, d'you think?"

"I... think I'm going to take their oaths," she answered, "but not as their queen. I want to take it as their equal."

Setting down his glass, he asked, "What does that entail?"

"It's a bit like a marriage ceremony. If the queens of other branches of the hyphae make a blood oath to me, it will reestablish the link between us, with *our* grove at the center. That's how Vasileia explained it to me, at any rate."

Alashiya shrugged. She pushed a spoonful of golden rice and steaming, sauteed vegetables around her plate. "She knows the old stories in a way I don't. Some things get lost even in the hyphae, and my grandma passed away when I was so young... If she knew it, she never got the chance to tell me."

Vasileia, the ancient nymph who represented their people in the UTA congress, was full of stories even the hyphae couldn't tell Alashiya. She had vague details of a ceremony and ancient gifts given, but it had been at least two thousand years since the last oath had been taken. Time could bury even the most important memories, it seemed.

But elders often carried knowledge that would otherwise be lost, and Vasileia had given hers as a gift. It was another form of *tēq*. Another essential form of love.

If the old woman wasn't constantly complaining about the fact that Alashiya should've taken her grandson as her husband instead of "that swaggering dragon" she would've said it was a bit like having her beloved grandmother back. Seeing as Vasileia *did* complain at every available opportunity, Alashiya viewed her as something like a cross between a meddling aunt and a shrewd mentor.

"It won't fix everything, but it will help bring us together again. Make us feel like we aren't all just floating islands being slowly swallowed by the sea." Alashiya set her spoon down and took a deep breath. Reaching for her mate's night-darkened hand, she traced the silver scar bisecting his palm with the reverence it deserved. "I'd like to do it at our wedding."

Taevas's grin stretched from ear to ear. "You want all the nymphs at our wedding?"

"I do," she answered, bringing his knuckles to her lips for a kiss. "But only if that's okay with you."

A rumble of pure delight emanated from deep within his chest. Tail coiling around her bare ankle, he said, "As far as I'm concerned, the more people there to witness you claiming me, the better."

Alashiya still felt queasy at the thought of standing up in front of so many people, but she knew how important it was to Taevas. So when the entire Aždaja clan showed up in Birchdale alongside the nymph queens, several alphas from the Shifter Alliance, *and* the sovereigns of the EVP, she couldn't exactly say she was surprised.

Despite all the preparation that had gone into the affair — as well as the renovations that had been done to the house and barn — Birchdale wasn't prepared for the onslaught. Their wedding took over the tiny town. Every rental property was booked, a fleet of caterers had been assembled, and the wards around her land had been heavily modified to make it easier to find.

The hardest part of the entire process had been convincing the forest to allow so many strange visitors through. In the end, there was nothing to be done for it other than to coax, cajole, and lay out clear signage for all visitors to stay on the designated path.

The night of their wedding, everyone assembled in the lush garden she'd so relied on all her life. Candles hung from glass globes strung in the branches of her fruit trees and fireflies danced along the path to the firepit. Taevas's blue flame roared within it, ice cold and deadly. Its pale glow limned the man himself as he stood proudly at the end of the path.

When Alashiya emerged from the flower-decked doorway Taevas had once nearly destroyed, her gaze immediately found his through the gauzy film of her veil. She thought she'd be afraid or nervous — and she had been, listening to all the voices outside as the women of her clan and Debbie, to a smaller degree, helped her get ready — but as soon as she looked past the crowd and found him...

There was no fear. There was no reason to hide.

I love you, she whispered through the hyphae as she stepped out onto the green path. Her bare feet sank into wild grass and wildflowers. Her golden anklets tinkled as she drifted toward him, drawn to his towering form wreathed in dragonfire.

Her veil, long enough to brush the backs of her calves, whispered around her. It carried all the memories of those she loved, but it carried the hopes of her future, too. A great purple dragon, wings spread, filled out the once empty space in the back. A curl of blue flame erupted from his mouth and a tangle of vines curled around his tail, symbolizing all that they were and would be. Securing it to her curls was a wreath of laurel leaves — the only crown she allowed Taevas to give her.

Beneath her veil, she wore a dress of air-light, violet silk and her ancient gold arm bands. Every inch of her carried the love and memory of her people, present and long since passed. Behind her, Hele and Alex, dressed in their own purple gowns, carried the sash of Adon's robe, one hand on each tasseled end. Traditionally, one of her chosen bridal entourage would carry the ritual knife, but since it wasn't necessary in this case, they'd made a compromise.

When she passed the assembled nymphs, they brushed her shoulders with their fingertips, offering love and luck as her own grove might. It was only a few dozen steps to reach him, but it felt like an eternity before she joined her husband by the fire. He looked regal and almost too striking in his burgundy robe embroidered with gold, his raven hair pulled back in a tight braid. Gold rings glittered on his fingers as he reached for her hands.

Pulling them out from beneath her veil, she slid her palms against his to grip his sturdy wrists.

"I love you," he rumbled, dipping to touch their foreheads together. Her lashes fluttered as the world shrank to fit the space between them. "I love you so very much, *minu metsalill.*"

There was no officiant. No speeches or formality. There was only their love and their vows. Alashiya breathed deeply, soaking in the strength he offered her, before she nodded toward her bridal entourage.

Hele moved to one side and Alex the other, until they were facing each other with Taevas and Alashiya between them. Together, they wrapped the sash — already bloody from their first marriage ceremony — around their hands. Their job done, they stepped to the side.

Knowing how much this meant to him, Alashiya shoved down her nerves and summoned the words that had come so easy to her once before.

"Taevas, I swear to carry you. I swear to honor you. I swear to provide for you. I swear to warm you when the night is cold and find you when the days are dark. I swear to love you now and in the hyphae, long after Grim has returned what her father gave us." Her throat tightened, making it nearly impossible to speak. She had to clear it before she could continue, but even then, her voice was thick with emotion.

"I knew you first as Adon, then as the monster in my barn, and then the bossy dragon sick in bed. I've had the privilege of seeing you at your lowest, *argaman mlk,* and even though I know you'd rather I only knew you at your strongest, I wouldn't change it for anything. Because even when you were stripped of everything, you were still kind, patient, compassionate, and so very dear to me. I am proud to claim you, Taevas Aždaja, and to never let you go."

Taevas's pleasure was a fierce note in the hyphae, a plucked chord that vibrated through the entire web of her being. A tear streaked down his darkened cheek and glittered in the light of his flame.

"My Alashiya. My *metsalill*. My beloved Chosen," he rasped, voice almost guttural with emotion, "I swear to carry you. I swear to honor you. I swear to provide for you. I swear to warm you when the night is cold and find you when the days are dark. I swear to love you now and in the hyphae, long after Grim has returned what her father gave us."

His fingers tightened around her wrists, holding tight as his violet eyes gleamed. To her, to both of them, they were entirely alone as they pledged themselves to each other. "You are the bravest person I know. When you had no reason to and every reason not to, you took this strange, beaten dragon into your home. You nursed me. You eased my pain. You were kind even when I didn't deserve it. It is the greatest miracle of my life to have been tied to you through happenstance, and it's one I will never, *ever* take for granted. I am proud to be claimed by you, my Shiya. I'll follow you wherever you lead and love you until my last breath."

It was a good thing the only makeup she wore was Alex's golden body shimmer. If she'd dared to wear anything more, as Debbie suggested, it would've run down her face in rivulets.

Since there was no need to cut their hands, they'd decided that they would steal from other ceremonies to seal their union. Vows done, Alex delicately lifted the front of Alashiya's veil and draped it over her crown of laurels before stepping back once more.

"I Choose you," Taevas announced, his grin wild and triumphant.

Laughing with that same reckless feeling, she answered, "I Choose you."

She expected to be swooped down on with a passionate kiss as they'd agreed, but her husband had one last surprise in store for her.

His massive wings, which had been through countless rounds of painful physical therapy and healing sessions with Margot, mantled high and wide around his shoulders. Before she could begin to process *that,* they snapped forward. The world became muted and dark as they closed around her. The pale light from the fire and the glow of the candles filtered in through the thin, delicate membrane of his wings, making them glow. His tail snaked around her waist, and his big, clawed hands cupped her jaw as his mouth descended on hers — all fierce, hungry lips and seeking tongue.

Somewhere outside the safety of his closed wings, a cheer erupted. She didn't hear it. Alashiya slung her arms around his neck and allowed him to lift her off her feet. "Your wings," she sobbed between kisses. "Taevas, your *wings!*"

"Flying is a ways off," he breathed, "but I refused to go another day without embracing my wife."

She'd noticed he removed his splints, but she assumed it was for the ceremony. Taevas hated them. She couldn't blame him, but they were necessary to wear outside of healing sessions and physical therapy to avoid severe bouts of nerve pain. Sometimes she wondered if he'd wear them at all if she didn't insist on it — as if muscling through agony would somehow make it better. But that was her stubborn, hard-headed dragon, who'd put his discomfort aside at every opportunity if it meant serving his people and his clan.

He'd given her no indication at all that he'd made so much progress with his recovery. Relief, happiness, and a little exasperation bubbled in her veins as she pressed kiss after kiss to his lips within the safety of his wings.

It was a long while before he reluctantly retracted them. The guests erupted into knowing laughter as he cast them a look of playful annoyance, as if it was *their* fault he was forced to release her. Laughing, Hele and Alex unbound their hands and took the sash away. It would be tucked safely in Alashiya's cedar chest.

The matching robe, however, would return to its place: hung on the wall above their nest in place of the tapestry depicting their courtship, which was traditional to her husband's people. Taevas had insisted it was better than anything that could be made by another artisan, so why replace it?

Alashiya's face heated as several dragons, mainly members of the Wing, whooped and hollered. A child's gleeful scream preceded a violet blur erupting out of the crowd. She stooped just in time to catch Emilia, who'd escaped from her parents at great speed. Propping the little girl on her hip, Alashiya asked, "Did you want a kiss, too?"

Emilia looked up at her with big, candy apple red eyes — a gift from her father, Artem. Being the only Aždaja child at the moment, and a deeply precocious one to boot, Emilia had learned the fine art of getting exactly what she wanted whenever she wanted it.

It was lucky for all of them that she generally only wanted as much love from her clan as possible.

Little claws, surprisingly gentle, stroked Alashiya's veil when she answered, "Yes!"

The crowd laughed as the couple squeezed the little girl between them, each delivering a smacking kiss to her grinning cheeks. Taevas plucked her from Alashiya's arms to throw her high in the air, eliciting another scream as her little wings flapped.

"If no one else wants a kiss, it's time we feast!" he announced, swinging Emilia around in a wide circle.

Putting the giggling toddler under one arm and slinging the other around Alashiya's waist, he tossed his horned head back toward the barn. A grand array of tables, fairy lights, candles, flowers, a band, and a truly astonishing amount of food had been set up inside and outside the renovated barn.

When they led the guests down the slope, Alashiya's eyes stung at the sight. Once, entering the barn had been exercised in grief and the echo of dashed hopes. But now the hyphae sang with joy as she stepped up to her new cedar throne, carved by her husband to match his own, behind their overflowing table. Music and laughter filled the air with life. Little Emilia's clawed feet clicked on the new concrete floor as she scampered off to find her parents — and sweets — fulfilling a dream her grove had so earnestly believed in.

Her land, her forest, had been renewed. Its heartbeat was fierce and joyful as a new sort of grove danced, ate, and celebrated together. It was perhaps not exactly the kind of grove her grandparents had in mind when they set their sights on it, but she didn't feel any complaints in the hyphae. Only a deep relief.

And when the other queens approached the table to exchange a single drop of blood with her, that feeling bloomed into something infinitely larger and more complex. It no longer belonged to just her own family, but to all of them. Their networks, too long apart, reunited.

It wasn't the same as everyone existing in one hyphae, which would get rather loud and crowded, but more like building a bridge over a stretch of water. At any time, they could cross it and know that they weren't alone.

Not that being alone wasn't nice *sometimes*. Like when Taevas dragged her onto the dancefloor, something she'd been dreading since he brought up the idea of having one in the first place, only to snap his wings around her once again.

They swayed to a slow song, her cheek resting on his powerful heart, within the privacy of his wings.

"This is a good place to hide," she whispered, bare feet hardly touching the floor as he swept her gently around.

A deep rumble tickled her cheek. Pressing her closer, he promised, "We can hide here together, *metsalill*, for the rest of our lives."

Epilogue

Alashiya didn't like New York. Taevas hadn't exactly thought she would. He couldn't blame her. He was used to the constant movement, the vast swaths of concrete and towering buildings that seemed to cling together in strange clumps. People living on top of each other, everyone moving in step and yet to their own rhythm, was simply another part of life.

But to his mate, it was almost incomprehensible.

The air smelled wrong, she said. The lack of greenery appalled her. Even the feeling of the sidewalk under her feet made her uncomfortable, like a cat walking on plastic wrap.

The first time he took her to their other roost in Manhattan, she refused to leave it except for one very important excursion: the visit to Stalton's Atelier.

Alashiya, dressed in a long green coat, new faux leather boots, and the minimum of what he considered the respectable amount of jewelry for his mate to wear, stood beside him. She turned her face up to look at the old storefront. Snowflakes stuck to her luscious curls and the tips of her eyelashes. As usual, her gloved hand was tucked into the crook of his elbow. Everytime she breathed, a puff of steam drifted in the frigid air.

She quirked a brow. "Well, I can honestly say that I'm under-whelmed. I always pictured it to be... bigger. And newer."

"It's been in this spot for two hundred years. Shops weren't big back then, and they haven't really changed much since they opened," he explained, pointing to the faded gold sign in the window. The building was old and charming in its own way, but it was definitely showing its age. The antique veneer gave the shop an air of sophistication and legacy, though, which helped it stay in business.

What *also* helped, of course, was taking the vast majority of the profit from selling *his* mate's labor. Amongst other unsavory business practices he'd discovered.

Grinning, Taevas grasped the tarnished brass knob and pulled the door open. Ushering Alashiya in ahead of him, his gaze swept across the familiar shop. The scents of dust, fabric, glass cleaner, and an old man's cologne washed over him as he stepped inside.

There was no one behind the long glass counter, but that wasn't a surprise. He'd made sure that it was Stalton Sr. working that day, and the old man tended to take long lunches. He could afford to, after all.

Peeling off his gloves a finger at a time, Taevas watched Alashiya move around the small shop. If he didn't know what went on behind closed doors — and in their account books — he would say the place was charming in an old world sort of way. The shelves were cluttered, the glass cases full, and the racks draped with handmade garments made of the finest fabrics. Milk glass lamps cast the shop in a soft glow that sparkled off of brass fixtures.

It was the kind of place that boxed its magically enhanced garments and tied them with fabric ribbons. It was also the kind of place that stole from his mate. And *him*.

The loss of her gifts and the criminally low pay were bad enough. But what really pissed him off was the stolen time.

Bending over a glass display case, Alashiya whispered, "Is this where you first saw my work?"

Taevas sidled up behind her. Flattening his hand on the small of her back, he pointed to a spot to her left. "Right there, where the ties are now. I wandered in after a meeting went too long and needed a break. I saw it and just... had to have it."

"The one with the sparrows, right?" she recalled, drawing on her vast internal inventory of his wardrobe. Alashiya took it as her duty to go through everything he owned at least once a month, searching for tears, holes, and loose buttons. Infusing his clothing with more of her magic, more of her blood, was a sacred act of care for her. It wasn't an exaggeration to say that she was more familiar with his wardrobe than he was.

"Exactly." He rested his chin on top of her head. "I should wear it more, but it's so hard to choose when I have so many wonderful pieces of art to pick from every day."

"Welcome, welcome!" an old man's voice came from the darkened doorway behind the counter. The sound of shuffling feet preceded the appearance of the old, weathered dragon. His teal skin was lined with deep wrinkles, his shorn hair was white, and his wool waistcoat was accessorized with a gleaming gold watch chain.

Stalton Sr. hadn't changed a bit since Taevas saw him last, and neither had the old man's reactions.

His eyes widened comically as he finally spied who exactly stood on the other side of the display case.

Straightening his spine, he squawked, "Isand! Oh! Oh! It's so good to see you again!"

"Stalton," he greeted, his smile full of fang.

Completely ignoring Alashiya, the old man rushed up to the case. Words left his mouth at a rapid pace, hardly leaving room for a breath, let alone a thought. "Oh, the news was just so terrible. I was worried about you — well, weren't we all! Gods bless you, Isand. I couldn't tell you how happy we all were when we saw you'd come back to us. Though I never had a doubt you would. Never, never."

"I'm certainly glad to be back," Taevas replied, cutting off the torrent. Pulling Alashiya into his side, he waited for some recognition to light the man's eyes, but it never came. "This is my Chosen, the Emand Alashiya Ardz."

At last, some understanding lit Stalton Sr.'s face. He rushed to shake her hand, his arms pumping enthusiastically. "Ah, the new Emand! Welcome! I'm so glad to welcome you to my family's atelier."

Alashiya's smile was thin-lipped and anticipatory. "Thank you. I've been looking forward to seeing it for a *very* long time."

The fact that Stalton Sr. appeared to have no idea that he was talking to the same woman he'd been stealing from for decades made the seething rage burn that much hotter in his gut. Did he not even know her *name?* It wasn't exactly common.

To think his Chosen meant so little to this man that her name didn't even ring a bell...

Taevas tried to quell the rattling of his tail as he gently steered Alashiya back by her shoulders. He didn't want her in the crossfire when he did what he came here for.

Glancing between them, Stalton Sr. asked, "Was there something specific you were looking for?"

"There is, actually." Taevas planted his palms on the glass display case. "What did you do with all my gifts, Stalton?"

"Gifts?"

"Everything you were supposed to forward to the artisan whose work I've bought at every opportunity. You know, the one *you* claimed didn't want to have any contact with me. The one you *lied* about." His smile fell. Fire licked up his throat to tickle the backs of his teeth when he snarled, "The *artisan* who happens to be my *Chosen,* the nymph standing *right fucking here."*

The color drained from Stalton Sr.'s aged face. His wide eyes flicked back and forth between Taevas and Alashiya, who stood patiently to one side, her arms crossed and expression unbothered.

She didn't have much of a stomach for revenge, but she appreciated justice. That was why she made a cake when Monty was sentenced to jail for aiding an attempt on the Isand's life and trespassing on her land. It was also why she didn't protest when he said he wanted to get back everything she was owed.

It was a matter of honor. This man had made himself an obstacle between a dragon and his Chosen — a very, very unwise decision.

"Is that... Are you really one of my artisans?" he sputtered, eyeing her with renewed interest.

Alashiya gave him a pitying look. "I am. Do you remember when I asked for ITA's name? You said it was none of my business. And you told *him* that I had no interest in talking to him when he asked for me."

Taevas drummed his claws on the glass case. "For *years*. I asked to speak to her for *years*. And when I sent gifts for her, you told me you'd send them along. But I've been to my Chosen's dwelling, Stalton. There are no gifts. No silk. No art. No custom desk or platinum watch or European chocolate or books on wildflowers. Nothing."

Putting up his hands, Stalton Sr. let out a nervous chuckle. "That's not... Things get lost in the mail so often. Isand, I— I don't know what you're talking about."

"You do," Taevas replied. He rose to his full height and tilted his head toward the door behind the counter. "And you are going to return everything I sent to my Chosen *today* or I'm going to officially recommend your case to the 'Riik's auditors. I'm sure they'd love to see what my investigators have found in your books."

Stalton's lined face went white. "But—"

Taevas held up a hand. Turning his head to look at his mate, he said, "You know what, *metsalill?* I've changed my mind."

Alashiya let out a huff, no doubt sensing some theatrics were to come. "About what?"

"I'm going to report him to the auditors regardless."

"Oh?"

"Yes," he announced, swinging his head back around to bare his teeth at the old man. "Because you don't get a reward, Stalton.

You don't get an out. You're going to give my Chosen what she's owed, and then you're going to suffer the consequences of your actions — all of them, including the smuggling you and your sons have been doing."

"Smuggling, huh?" Alashiya wasn't good at pretending to be surprised, but that was okay. He loved the bland amusement in her voice.

Holding Stalton's panicked gaze, he confirmed, "Smuggling banned m-enhanced artifacts and antiques. Incomplete reporting to the tax board. Stealing from the Isand himself. Quite the list of infractions you've racked up, Stalton."

The old man looked like he was having a hard time catching up. His mouth opened and closed several times while sweat beaded on his forehead and upper lip.

Taevas clapped his hands. Stepping back toward his mate, he commanded, "Apologize to your Emand, Stalton."

The poor man still looked too stunned to really understand what he was apologizing for, let alone mean it, but he choked out, "I'm— If I did anything to you, I apologize. I had no idea— I wouldn't—"

"Yes, I'm sure you wouldn't have if you knew, but that's not the point, is it? You should've treated her with respect before. You didn't, and that was a mistake." Taevas laid his hand on Alashiya's back and guided her toward the door. "I'll be collecting my Chosen's gifts today, Stalton."

Alashiya glanced over her shoulder as he ushered her out the door. "Good luck."

Taevas held the door open for the first officer who slipped inside. Three more followed after him. An entire small fleet of officers waited on the street outside, accompanied by both the Isand and the Emand's Wings. Taevas passed them with a nod and a smile, entirely satisfied.

Wrapping her arm around his waist, Alashiya asked, "Happy now?"

"Oh, very. Do you want to get some dinner?"

Looking up at him with a soft smile, she offered, "How about we just go home? I miss our nest."

"Ah, my queen," he sighed, coiling his tail possessively around her wrist. "Home it is."

THE END

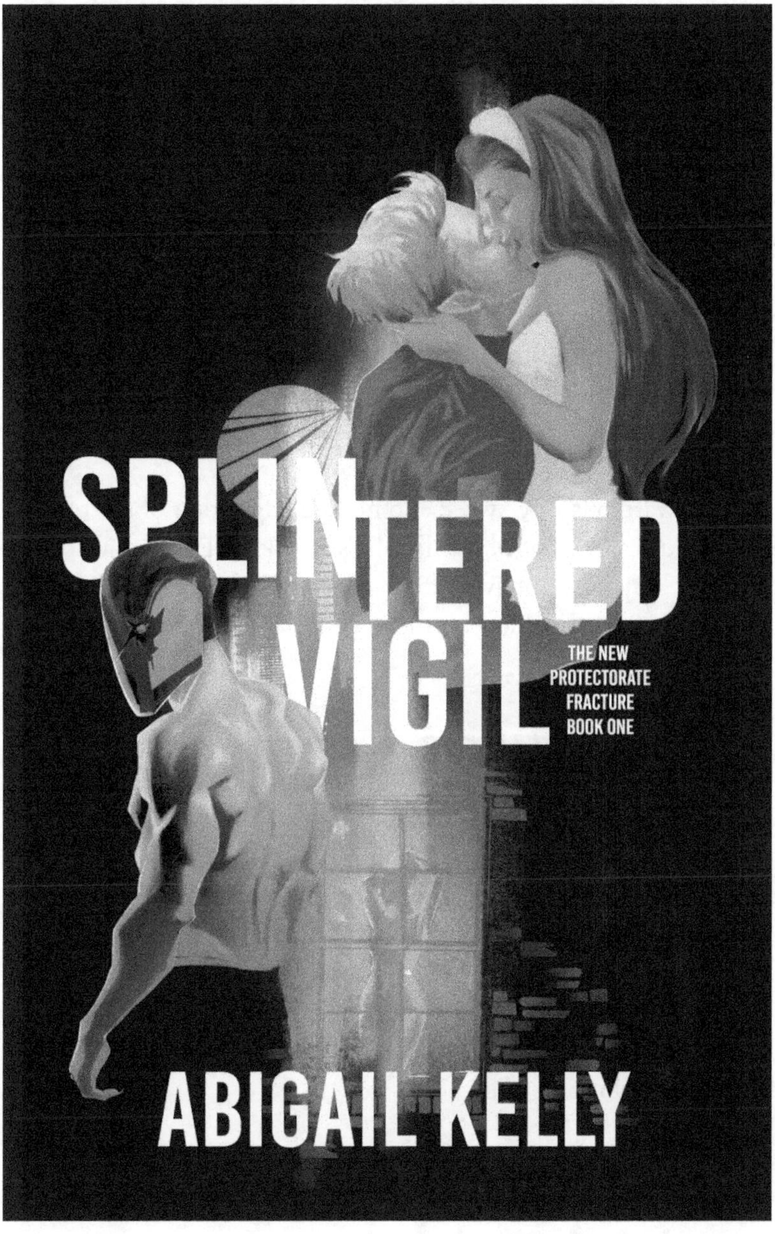

SPLINTERED VIGIL

THE NEW
PROTECTORATE
FRACTURE
BOOK ONE

ABIGAIL KELLY

SPLINTERED VIGIL: THE NEW PROTECTORATE
FRACTURE: BOOK ONE

Finders keepers.

Sloane knows he shouldn't watch her. A predator trained from childhood to do what no one else will, his specialties are murder, mayhem, and torture. He's a danger to just about everyone, including the soft human woman he stalks day and night.

Losers get a bolt in the head.

Cecilia Warren is soft, sweet, and blessedly ignorant of the bloodshed he deals in — until the day she's attacked. The plan is to save her, not keep her. But everything goes awry when he finally gets her in his claws. Instincts blur loyalty. Desire makes letting her go impossible.

If they want to take her, they'll have to kill him first.

The mission objective shifts when he goes from protector to captor, secreting her away and going AWOL from the terrifying shadow unit known as Fracture. They have orders to hunt him down and free Cecilia against her wishes. Sloane won't give her up and he won't back down, even if that means destroying himself to protect the only good thing he's ever known.

Pre-order Splintered Vigil now!

Also by Abigail Kelly

Find all new releases, short fiction, comics, bonus chapters, and exclusive content on the Works by Abigail Patreon!

Grim's Delight: The New Protectorate Syndicate: Book One

A bloody war nears its end.

Felix Amauri is the rightful heir to the most powerful vampire crime family on the continent. After years of taking out challengers to his claim, everything he's fought for is finally within reach — until one sloppy assassination threatens to ruin everything.

To be human is to be prey.

For years, the worst thing Dahlia McKnight could picture was becoming a vampire's toy. She never imagined that she'd witness a brutal assassination, let alone that she'd be turned in the process. One day she's a waitress, the next she's the sole heir to a vicious crime family embroiled in a war of succession and the target of an icy vampire prepared to do anything to take what he's owed.

He needs her for more than just her blood.

Learning to be a vampire is hard enough, but when it's discovered that she can carry another vampire's offspring, nothing will stop Felix from claiming her. If she wants to be more than just his plaything, it'll mean becoming the predator she was born to be.

Available in Kindle Unlimited, ebook, and paperback!

GLOSSARY

A full character directory and map can be found at Abigailkkelly.com

PLACES

United Territories and Allies: What we would consider the continental USA. A loose federation of sovereign states established after the Great War. The UTA capital is United Washington, in the Neutral Zone.

The Elvish Protectorate: Also known as the EVP. Stretches from Oregon to New Mexico. Capital city is San Francisco. Led by the elvish sovereign Theodore Thaddeus Solbourne and Margot Goode.

The Coven Collective: Also known as the Collective. Encompasses Washington state. Capital city is Seattle. Led by a large coalition of witch covens, with Sophie Goode acting as their leader.

The Orclind: Encompasses much of the Midwest. Led by the Iron

Chain, a close-knit government made up of orcish clans and Queen Sigrid Seagrim. Capital city is Boulder.

Shifter Alliance: Takes up a section of the midwest and all of the south. (Unfortunately includes Florida.) Run by a very, very loose alliance of shifter packs from three capital cities — Minneapolis, Oklahoma City, and Atlanta. Unofficial leader is Lee Seymour.

The Draakonriik: Also known as the 'Riik. The second smallest territory, it takes up all of the Great Lakes region and stretches to New York. Led by Taevas Aždaja, the *Isand* (ee-zand) of the dragon clans. Pronounced: *dra-kon-reek*

The Neutral Zone: Also known as the New Zone. Technically it is held by a coalition government consisting of representatives from the UTA, but in reality it is run by a syndicate of feuding vampire families. It is a small strip of land squeezed between the Draakonriik and the Shifter Alliance.

GODS

Light & Darkness: The primordial gods who created all the others. Also known as The Lovers and First Union. Both are generally represented as female.

Loft: God of the sky and creator of flying beings. Twin sibling to Tempest. They know no gender. Also known as the Boundless One.

Tempest: God of the ocean and creator of all water beings. Also known as the Hungry God and the god of love.

Burden: God of the Earth, creator of all beings who live within it — most notably the orcs. Husband of Glory.

Glory: Goddess of sunlight, magic, and creator of elves. Worshipped by witches for giving the gift of magic to humanity.

Blight: God of forested places and disease. He works in partnership with his daughter Grim and shares her dominion over demons and all reviled creatures.

Grim: Goddess of death. Known as the Merciful One and the Brilliant Lady. She is widely beloved.

Craft: God of change, newness, and messengers. Creator of humanity and viewed warily by non-worshippers as the Chaos Maker. They change their gender frequently, but generally is referred to using he/him pronouns.

TERMS

Alpha: a broad term used by many communities generally associated with a leader — either of a small family group, a pack, or even a territory.

Anchor: a vampire's mate. Anchors are carefully chosen and usually longterm-to-permanent arrangements, as they take considerable energy to make/become. A vampire must inject their venom into a host many times before their blood chemistry adjusts such that they become unsuitable for consumption by another vampire and their sleep cycle switches to a nocturnal pattern. At this point, they can can also produce/carry to term a vampiric child. Temporary anchors do exist, although they are relatively rare due to the intense withdrawal symptoms associated with ending the regular venom intake.

Arrant: someone born without m-paths, or the ability to channel and use magic.

Burnout: the colloquial name for the degenerative medical condition caused by excessive magic in humans. Over time magic can damage nerves and brain tissue, which will inevitably result in death if not treated with with development of a witchbond.

Change: an elvish term for a sudden shift into adulthood. This is marked by 5-14 days of "madness", usually triggered by some stressful event around the age of 16-18. The elvish body is flushed with hormones to the point where sudden growth, overwhelming hunger, and aggression take over. Viewed as an incredibly vulnerable time, only immediate kin are charged with the care of their loved ones — which includes isolating them, preventing harm to themselves/others, and feeding them. The change marks the second phase of an elf's life, when they are no longer coddled children but young adults who can accept challenges and family responsibilities. Formal adulthood is attained at 30.

Changeling: a term first used to refer to fey children fostered out to non-fey homes, now more widely used to mean any person raised by people who are not the same beings. *Ex:* A dragon couple raising a human child.

Chosen: the formal term for a dragon's mate. The act of finding a mate is called *Choosing,* and is considered sacred.

Consort: an elvish mate. A term used exclusively by elves to refer to someone they are biologically compelled to pair up with. This usually involves intense sexual attraction, but can vary from person to person.

Demon: a being with horns or antlers, pointed ears, and symbiotic shadows. They are generally considered to be some of, if not *the* toughest beings in the world, as their shadows can make them almost indestructible. They are also naturally extremely strong and durable. Demon clans tend to be extremely close-knit, partially due to the fact that the world at large is not wholly accepting of them and their mythological connection to the god Blight. Identifying mating features are utter devotion, heightened protectiveness, and the sharing of shadows. This is when a mate is "given" a piece of the demon's symbiotic shadow, which will then live on that person for the rest of their life.

Dragon: a person with a dual form. In their bipedal form, they have claw-tipped wings, horns, and a tail. In their quadrupedal form, they are roughly the size of a standard SUV and can fly at extremely high altitudes for weeks at a time. They come in a variety of extremely saturated colors that shift with the time of day (light to dark). They breathe cold blue fire and can see the Earth's magnetic field. Identifying mating feature is marked change in behavior, including the overwhelming urge to nest.

Elemental: a being created by a spontaneous magical eruption. They often take on the attributes of whatever weather they happen to be born into, *i.e.* a lightning storm might produce a lightning elemental, or a blizzard might make a snow elemental.

Empath: a person with the ability to feel and manipulate the emotions of others.

Elf: someone born with jewel-toned skin, claws, pointed ears, and four fangs. Very secretive and considered apex predators who require a strict hierarchy to function. Average height of 6-7ft. Identifying mating feature is the retraction of claws.

Fever: shifter mating imperative triggered by the "animal's" choosing of a mate. Marked by a perpetual near-shift — elevated body temperature, increased aggression, build-up of magic, and the compulsion to mark. A shifter displays their readiness to find a mate by creating a den.

Fey: a person with nearly vestigial, insect-like wings, small fangs, and claws. Usually live in large groups. Identifying mating feature is bioluminescence.

Foresight: the ability to see multiple possible futures. The average number is between 2-4, with the likelihood mental instability increasing with each subsequent possible future.

Great War: a conflict between the territories of the North American continent that began in 1817 and ended in 1917 with the signing of the Peace Charter, which established the United Territories and Allies of modern times.

Halfling: the elvish term for an elf with mixed heritage.

Healer: a person who possesses the ability to see into and heal bodies through touch.

Isand: the title of the leader of the Draakonriik. Pronounced *ee-zah-nd*

M- : *M-* is frequently used as shorthand to denote when something is infused or otherwise combined with a magical element.

Marriage Sigil: a custom symbol branded into the foreheads of spouses (pairs or multiples). Each one is unique and infused with a small amount of magic as a reminder of the power love holds. They are typically sought out by worshippers of Glory — mainly witches and arrants. Elves, though worshippers, don't usually take a marriage sigil when they find their consorts or form a unions with other elves.

Mate: a catchall term for a significant other. Used by many cultures, it has varying degrees of weight. To shifters, orcs, and demons, the word mate is synonymous with family, monogamy, and dependence. It is much more loosely used within arrant society, as well as amongst elves, who generally prefer the term *consort.*

Merfolk: a catch-all term referring to sentient beings who live in the ocean, lakes, or rivers. Due to the nature of the ocean and its inhabitants, classifying all beings individually is almost impossible, so a much broader term is used to refer to both mammalian and non-mammalian beings than would be used for those on land.

Met: acronym for *magically enhanced tech.* A branded home assistant that can do everything your Alexa can, as well as small, low-level magic to help around the house.

Metallurgic Inoculation: a vaccine given to all elves within hours of birth to make them immune to iron poisoning.

M-siphon: a containment device used to imprison a magical being and siphon off their magic. Highly illegal.

M-lev: a play on *maglev,* meaning a high speed train that levitates using magnets. In this case, magnets *and* magic.

M-weather: magic weather. Very common, but can result in "clusters" or storms that wreak havoc if not properly contained. In rare circumstances, it can also produce a sapient being known as an *elemental.*

Nymph: a person who possesses a symbiotic mycelium that allows them to communicate with plants, hibernate beneath soil, and access the collective memories and experiences of those in their family line. Every nymph is part of a network known as a *hyphae,* and all hyphae are connected to the original.

Orc: a person with green, gray, russet, or blue skin, two fangs, and claws. Widely renowned for their strength and beautiful voices. Identifying mating feature is "the kohl", or altered, dark pigmentation of the hands and feet developed after meeting their mate.

Pixie: a small, winged creature with compound eyes with about the same level of intelligence as a rat. In the wild they live in trees and in burrows, but have adapted to living in walls, pipes, mailboxes, etc.

Pull: elvish mating imperative. A sudden hormonal shift caused by exposure to a compatible partner's pheromones, marked by the retraction of claws and volatile mood shifts. The pull is only "satisfied" when hormone binding occurs — the term for long term exposure to a mate, resulting in permanent biological dependence on their pheromones. This process increases fertility and often results in the conception of multiples. Lack of exposure to a mate can cause severe physical reactions (lack of appetite, muscle pain, headaches, insomnia) as well as the deterioration of mental stability.

R-siphon: also known as *reverse siphon.* New technology that redistributes magic away from the siphon instead of into it.

Shifter: a person who can shift into an animal form. They can partially shift (changing only parts of their bodies at will) and often take on characteristics of their other half. Famous for their strength and tenacity, as well as their dual-voiced "shifter purr" which many people find deeply attractive. Usually found in packs.

Sigil: a symbol used to channel magic. Western countries use the alchemical alphabet formally codified in the 1800's, though many, many variations are used all over the world.

Sovereign: the title of the ruler of the Elvish Protectorate. It is capitalized when used in place of a name.

Turbo Virgin (c): Theodore Thaddeus Solbourne, Sovereign of the Elvish Protectorate and Head of the Solbourne Family.

Union: an elvish marriage. Usually done for financial, political, or procreational benefit. The parties involved are not fated or biologically compelled to be with one another, and might have many lovers or even a consort outside of their union.

Vampire: a person who drinks blood to survive and cannot go out in sunlight. Vampirism can only be "caught" with the exchange of fresh blood, and as of 2045 is much more widely spread through procreation. Vampires can only breed with their *anchors.* Identifying mating feature is marked change in behavior, including overwhelming desire and need for total isolation.

Ward: a magical barrier with varying levels of protection. A ward can be something as simple as a proximity alert — "someone walked into my garden" — or as complex as full on defense — "someone crossed the threshold and has now burst into flames". The severity of the ward depends on the complexity of the sigils used to create them, and wards can have many layers, each one with a unique purpose. Personal wards can also be used, such as in clothing or embedded into jewelry, though they tend to be expensive and difficult to foolproof.

Were: a person infected with the were virus, a much mutated strain of the vampirism virus, resulting in altered physiology and magical ability. They can be identified by their heterochromia, or different colored eyes. They are the newest magical race and viewed warily by the general public for a variety of earned and unearned reasons. Identifying mating feature is marked change in behavior, including highly increased territorial instinct and the urge to nest. Pronounced *ware.*

Witch: Humans with the ability to use magic, which is passed down genetically. A person needs to be born with m-paths (a unique nervous system) to use it, however, humans were not initially adapted to use magic safely. Geneticists believe they acquired the ability through interbreeding with other beings. This interbreeding resulted in many unique qualities, such as the massive variety of abilities, power levels, and unique skills known to select families. However, it is also responsible for "burnout", which is the degenerative neurological condition a witch with mid-to-high level power will experience if they do not share their magical load with another being via witchbond. Witches are classified from least to most powerful — brightling, brilliant, and gloriana.

Witchbond: a magical bond formed between a witch and another being. Due to the nature of magic and humanity's much more recent adaptation to it, witches of *brilliant* and *gloriana* power must form a bond with another being usually beginning around 150-200 years old. This bond filters magic through the other being, neutralizing its damaging effects and reducing the chances of burnout to almost none. This bond also gives a power boost to the partner. A witchbond is permanent and can only be severed if one of the partners dies, at which point the surviving partner can form a new bond. Though commonly associated with a romantic partner, a witchbond is not inherently romantic and can be shared with a friend, sibling, or (ill-advised) an enemy.

Wraith: sentient shadow beings not dissimilar to elementals. They can affect the world around them in small ways, but can only speak to a very small number of demons. They lack physical forms but those that fully develop have complete sentience, personalities, and desires.

ABOUT THE AUTHOR

 Abigail Kelly is a writer and illustrator of alternate histories, love stories, and women with drive. Her work is heavily influenced by both her modest family roots and her passion for history. Her favorite authors are Shirley Jackson, V. E. Schwab, Ursula K. Le Guin, Kresley Cole, Nalini Singh, and just about anyone who writes about the weird and wonderful.

She lives in San Francisco with her dog, Babs, who remains stubbornly illiterate.

CONTENT WARNINGS

Experiences of war, PTSD, loss of family, elder care (past), murder, kidnapping, medical care, blood, needles, suggestions of agoraphobia, isolation, implied sexual harassment, virginity, and explicit sexual content.